MARGARET SANGER

Bust of Margaret Sanger by Barbara Phillips Perle
(on display at The Community Church of New York)

MARGARET SANGER

A BIOGRAPHY
OF THE CHAMPION OF BIRTH CONTROL

MADELINE GRAY

RICHARD MAREK PUBLISHERS
NEW YORK

Library of Congress Cataloging in Publication Data

Gray, Madeline.
  Margaret Sanger: a biography of the champion of birth control.

  Includes index.
  1. Sanger, Margaret, 1879-1966. 2. Birth
control—United States—History.
HQ764.S3G7   613.9'4'0924   [B]   78-13000
ISBN 0-399-90019-5

TO GEORGE FRIEDMAN
Great teacher, doctor, friend

CONTENTS

PREFACE

Margaret Sanger had the habit of slipping handwritten, undated notes into odd places in her files. One such note reads: "My biography will be harder to write than that of Havelock Ellis, because I am not consistent and I have seldom revealed what I really feel or believe."

It has been my fascinating task to search out what Margaret Sanger did feel and believe. The search took me to Mexico, Montana, California, Virginia, England, and many other places, as I sought out every person alive who had known her. At Smith College in Northampton, Massachusetts, I read the 200 boxes of letters, diaries, and campaign records she had given the college after it awarded her an honorary degree. I read, as well, over 190 boxes of similar material in the Library of Congress in Washington, D.C., where her letters are preserved as a record of a great social movement.

Since I knew nothing about her when I began, except that in twenty years she had won a stunning victory in a field where others had tried and failed for centuries, I began my personal interviewing with the most obvious source, her eldest son, Dr. Stuart Sanger. I spent a week in Mazatlán, Mexico, with Dr. Sanger and his wife, Barbara, not only collecting anecdotes, but coming away with permission to read, copy, and quote all his mother's formerly restricted letters and diaries. This privilege unlocked secrets of her private life, which included the story of her last tragic years, during which she was addicted to Demerol, a drug in its own way as powerful as morphine.

Most of the people who could verify her addiction lived in Tucson, Arizona, so it was there that I went next. I talked to Drs. Roland Murphy and Jackson Pyre, who had tried to wean her from Demerol; to Dorothy MacNamee, Grace Sternberg, "Cricket" Bloom, Robert O'Connor, and Ted Steele, who had been her friends; to Arthur Brown, the architect who had designed her fan-shaped house; and to Jack Spieden, who had sponsored Tucson's first dinner in her honor, a dinner she was too old and ill to attend.

In Los Angeles I saw Anna Lifschiz and Florence Rose, her former secretaries, each of whom vied with the other in telling me how much they had adored her, even though she treated them ruthlessly at times. They introduced me to a paradox that would be confirmed over and over again: people either worshipped Margaret Sanger or couldn't bear her.

The writer Robert Allerton Parker told me he disliked Margaret intensely, both because of her tremendous ego and the lies she told. When I remonstrated: "But look at the admiring letters you wrote her," he answered. "You had to write to Margaret Sanger that way."

After that, I went catch-as-catch-can. By good luck Joan Sanger Hoppe, daughter of Bill Sanger by his second wife, was living near Northampton, Massachusetts, at the time. We had two days of intensive talks before she passed me on to her mother Vidia in Ridgewood, New Jersey. And so it went. Everyone revealed something new about this extraordinary woman and sent me on to someone else. I was told to go to Santa Barbara to find Elizabeth Grew Bacon, an English suffragette who had become an ardent worker for birth control, as well as Lisa Voronoff, who had been Margaret's maid for ten years.

Next there were Dr. Robert Hepburn, son of Mrs. Thomas Hepburn, who had been Margaret's National Legislative Chairman, and Dr. Gloria Aitken, daughter of Hannah and Abraham Stone. A most unexpected bounty was finding Mrs. Edward Griswold, a ninety-year-old woman who was a neighbor of the Sangers in Hastings-on-the-Hudson. She was still there, full of memories and tales.

I alternated travel with reading in the archives. And the more I read, the more I realized how valid Margaret's penciled note had been. The letters in the files, especially those to and from Bill Sanger and J. Noah Slee, her husbands, showed a woman who had hidden her private life because it was quite different from her public life—hidden it because, what with society, the Catholic Church, and even the medical profession against her, she would almost surely have failed in her crusade. The letters and diaries also revealed an egocentric woman who had drawn a tight circle around herself into which no rival was allowed to step. And they also revealed her lifelong guilt feelings over her lost daughter Peggy, feelings she could not bring herself to admit to those around her.

In England I received an exclusive picture of H. G. Wells from his sons and had delightful visits with Helen Child, widow of Harold Child, one of Margaret's lovers. I also met Michael Balkwill, son-in-law of Hugh de Selincourt, another lover, and lunched in Oxford with Mrs. Rotha Pears, Hugh's niece.

A great find was Amy MacDonald, wife of Angus Snead MacDonald. Angus was one person about whom the Sanger family knew next to nothing. I had read so many love letters to him, merely addressed as "Dear Angus" or from him signed simply "Your Angus," that for a long time, until I came upon a telegram to him, I did not even know his last name. Then, when I got his name, I had no idea where he could be found. His wife was discovered, after much detective work, in Orange, Virginia, and several weekends with her were a delight. An equally great find was Alexander Sanger, son of Dr. Grant Sanger, Margaret's second son. Alexander had written a long thesis about his grandmother in order to win honors in history at Princeton, a thesis that revealed much of her hidden years as an active member of the far left anarchist group, the Industrial Workers of the World. Best of all, Alexander had photocopied all the issues of Margaret's revolutionary magazine *The Woman Rebel* before they mysteriously disappeared from the New York Public Library. These he graciously recopied for me. In Cambridge, Massachusetts, I met Loraine Campbell, who had traveled with Margaret on the tour that included the sensational Holyoke incident.

Most generous of all were Olive Byrne Richard, the daughter of Margaret's sister Ethel, and Margaret Sanger Marston, Stuart Sanger's daughter. These two women sat with me for uncounted afternoons in my Washington hotel room.

In the end, I found much of what I had been seeking—the as-close-as-possible truth about the woman who did much to solve one of the most vital problems of our century—how to put into women's hands the power to decide when and if they wanted to bear a child.

Finding this truth made me understand why, though she built up so many false images in public, she shattered them in private. She put so much material that was against her own interest in the files, it was as if her Catholic conscience had kept prodding her to say: "I can't possibly reveal my personal story while I am alive. But here is that story now, biographer. You tell it for me after I've gone."

This is what I hope I have done.

Amherst, Massachusetts, 1978

Note: The misspellings and confused dates in Margaret Sanger's letters and diaries are her own.

A DISTURBING CHILDHOOD

Maggie Higgins was a small Irish redhead who, as Margaret Sanger, was to be called everything from a saint to a spitfire to a woman who did more for other women than anyone who ever lived.

She was born on September 14, 1879, though she would never admit her birth date; indeed, she would become enraged when asked her age. On her various passports she never gave the same date twice; she even altered her record in the family Bible, changing her birth year from 1879, as her mother had written it, to 1883. But as time went on, her ink faded and her mother's showed through. It is quite clearly, 1879.

What made her equally angry was to be called a renegade Catholic. Though, like her mother, she was baptized and confirmed a Catholic, she left the faith early and never returned.

She left it primarily because of her father, Michael Hennessey Higgins. Michael Higgins was a powerfully built man with a shock of red hair that turned white early, a small powerful body, and bright blue eyes. He lived up to his middle name by spending much time drinking in the local pub, where he held forth on his favorite topics of socialism and free thought.

As a boy he had been left behind in Ireland to complete an apprenticeship to a stone mason, then followed his mother to a farm in Canada at the age of fifteen.

But life on a farm held little appeal for him. So in 1864 he left for

13

New York, where he hoped to enlist as a soldier in the Civil War. Because he was under sixteen, the best he could do was become a drummer boy; still, he was delighted to be in uniform, and forever after he boasted that he had personally led the march with Sherman to the sea.

At nineteen, Michael proposed to Anne Purcell, a rather nondescript girl from a strict Catholic family. Her parents objected to the union because Michael was a freethinker, but he was so handsome and persuasive he whittled down their objections, and the marriage soon took place.

After some wandering, the couple settled in Corning, New York, which they never left. Babies started to arrive regularly. Also, Anne was showing signs of tuberculosis and Michael had heard that Corning was noted for its "good country air." It was an up-and-coming place with its thriving glass works, and Michael hoped he could find steady work there carving headstones for cemeteries.

At first he prospered. He was even commissioned to renovate St. Mary's Catholic Church, though normally he wouldn't be seen in any church. "Where were you yesterday, you heathen?" Father Bustin would ask him on Mondays. "At home with my family where I belong," Michael would answer. "Not in God's house, where you belong," Father Bustin would shoot back. "The Lord will catch up with you some day!"

This was partly Irish banter, but it didn't seem like banter when two disasters struck. First, Michael's partner ran off with all the profits. Next, his shop burned down. Frequently he offended people with his loud speeches on his favorite topic, free thought. The local pub or shoe store served as his forums for these speeches. When he couldn't be found at either place, he was apt to be out hunting with his large pack of dogs or wandering about testing his belief in phrenology.

Michael's commissions disappeared rapidly when he offended the local Catholic hierarchy by supporting Henry George, a prominent social reformer who advocated a single tax on land only—a measure the poor strongly supported since few of them owned any land. Several popes had asserted the traditional Church doctrine that private property was a sacred right, and as the Church owned a great deal of land, this was considered an especially important pronouncement. In fact, when a Corning priest, the Reverend Edward McGlyn, endorsed George, he was quickly excommunicated.

The pro-Georgian group in Corning fought back, calling the Archbishop who had ordered the excommunication a public enemy, and Michael Higgins joined the battle. When George came to town to lecture, Higgins gave a grand dinner in his honor, mainly to shock the clergy. Then he named his next child Henry George Higgins, an act that was sure to keep the controversy alive.

The next battle was over Bob Ingersoll, another famous man of his time, known particularly as a foe of orthodox religion. When Ingersoll came to Corning to speak, and Higgins rented a hall owned by the church for the lecture, another storm broke out. Even though the hall had been booked and paid for in advance, the pastor of St. Mary's discovered at the last moment what the topic was to be, and got the Mayor to padlock the door before Ingersoll arrived. Higgins grabbed Maggie, who was standing at the edge of the small crowd that had gathered in front of the door, and invited them all to follow him to a clearing in the woods behind his house. He hoisted Ingersoll onto the top of a tree stump and had him lecture from there.

Defiant activities like these cost Higgins many commissions; he was soon living in poverty, a poverty all the harder to bear because by now his family was growing at the rate of almost one new baby a year. As a devout Catholic, Anne Higgins would not in any case have practiced birth control, and Michael either knew nothing about it or considered it unmanly. The result was that Anne, by now an active tubercular, became pregnant eighteen times. Out of these eighteen pregnancies, she suffered seven miscarriages and delivered eleven children, four red-headed girls and seven boys. Each pregnancy made Anne's tuberculosis worse; soon she was too sick to do more than barely speak to her children, except for Ethel, her youngest daughter and pet. Anne would while away the time curling and recurling Ethel's beautiful hair as she lay on the parlor sofa wracked with coughs, while Maggie looked on with jealous eyes.

Michael tried moving away from the center of smoke-filled Corning to the outskirts, where he hoped the fresher air might benefit his wife. Nevertheless, he considered it unmanly not to have sexual relations at least every Saturday night. As a result, she stayed pregnant almost constantly until she reached the menopause, by which time she was so ill she had to be carried up and down the stairs. Yet once when Michael got a really good commission, and Anne expected him to bring home some much-needed groceries, he bought a big hand of expensive bananas instead and handed them out with a grandiose gesture to all the passersby.

With such a sick mother and an improvident father, most of the work of running the crowded household fell to the girls. Mary, the eldest, a gentle girl whom Maggie always referred to as "a veritable saint," took on the hardest jobs. As a rule, women of the time gave birth at home with the help of a midwife, but Michael Higgins felt competent enough to do anything anyone else could do, so at first he delivered the children himself, plying his wife with his favorite remedy for everything, good Irish whiskey. When Mary became a teenager, she became his midwife-helper, and soon was so competent she delivered the neighbors' calves, too.

Mary had to leave home at sixteen in order to earn much-needed money. She was lucky enough to get a job as a companion to the Abbotts, one of the richest families in town. This meant being a nurse and baby sitter to the young, reader and general attendant to the old, and lady's maid to the middle-aged.

Maggie often visited Mary at the Abbott home, and what struck her most was its cleanliness and air of leisure. The adults were clean, the house was clean, the children were clean, while at her home there were dirty dishes, dirty beds, dirty clothes, dirty hands and feet that constantly cried out to be washed. And as to leisure, Mrs. Abbott and her daughters seemed to have endless time to play croquet on the lawn or to stroll in pretty dresses about the town. Maggie decided the reason for the difference was that the rich had only two or three children, while the poor had half a dozen or more. How the rich managed to do this she hadn't the slightest idea, but she swore she'd find out some day.

The second oldest Higgins sister was Nan. Nan was not at all a saint. She was sharp-tongued and snooty, and sassed her father regularly. Nan left Corning as soon as she could, heading for New York, determined to take on any job during the day that would earn her enough to pay for secretarial school at night. This left Maggie at fifteen to manage the home.

All her life Maggie Higgins spoke of her Corning childhood as joyless and filled with drudgery and fear. The drudgery came from the endless work in the tumbledown houses which were all the family could afford, houses not only on the wrong side of the tracks, but often right next to them. Yet if they somehow got hold of a better place for a while, they were either threatened with eviction for nonpayment of rent, or the house, like her father's shop, burned down. The fear of fire thus became for Maggie particularly strong.

But her worst dread was the flames of hell. When her father wasn't around, she used to sneak off to church on Sundays, stealing money to buy flowers to lay at the Virgin's feet. In church she heard all about hellfire, especially the kind that lay in wait for lukewarm Catholics. "An ardent Catholic will be saved," the priest would preach, "sometimes even a cold Catholic. But a lukewarm Catholic will be vomited out of the Lord's mouth straight down into hell." Her mother lukewarm? Yes. But only because she was too ill to go to church. Indeed, a priest once came to their house to ask sternly what was keeping Anne away, and she could only reply that she wasn't up to the long walk. She didn't dare tell him that her husband would probably have blocked her if she tried to come to church, or add how, when she began to say grace at table, he would interrupt with: "Let's all just pray to stay strong and well and get rich fast." One day when Maggie was on her knees saying the Lord's Prayer, she came to the line, "Give us this day our daily bread," and her father cut in: "Why are you asking God for bread? Is God a baker?" True, when he noticed the startled look on her face, he had continued in a kindlier tone: "Always think things through for yourself, lass. Don't take anything for granted, even things that have been repeated for centuries. You'll only grow up when you begin to think for yourself."

One day Maggie was openly disgraced in church. She was about six years old and was standing in line to get one of the free Christmas gifts that were being handed out to the youngsters. When the priest caught sight of her, he said sharply, "Get out of line, you child of the devil." The other children giggled and snickered, and Maggie ran off in shame.

Finally, on March 23, 1893, Maggie was baptized in St. Mary's though it had to be kept secret, as her father would have been furious. Again with much trepidation, she was secretly confirmed a year later, on July 8, 1894. The baptism and confirmation were probably her last desperate efforts to join the Catholic community, but even after these events, she was not invited to become a member of the Children's Society of St. Mary's or the Purgatorial Society (which met every day in November to pray for lost souls). Realizing that she was an outsider, and an outsider she would remain, she gave up soon afterward and left the Church.

In later years she lumped together her childhood frustrations under the general heading of "Corningitis," saying that whenever she was on a train that merely rode through the town, she got a sharp pain in the pit of her stomach.

Olive Byrne Richard, her niece, who also had been brought up as a

Catholic in Corning, put the blame on their Irish heritage. She wrote
in a later letter:

> I also was afflicted at one time with Corningitis, an affliction I
> shared with you until I found out that poor old Corning was not to
> blame, except that what we felt was first experienced there. Actu-
> ally, it was Irish fear. All the Irish feel it inherently and they
> seem to embrace any religion or way of life that nourishes it, be-
> cause fear is thrilling to them. They are afraid to live; afraid to
> die. They laugh a lot because they are afraid they will cry. They
> usually die of a fearsome illness and go to a fearful place. I still
> find it hard at times to be reasonable about it.
>
> But all the Higgins girls did something about it. Mary to soothe
> the fearsome path of the people she loved; Nan eventually to say,
> "I will be bigger than it is" and help others to be so; Ethel to run
> away from it; and you to say, "What is the biggest fear there is? I
> will fight it!" In your experience, your mother's fear of pregnancy
> was the biggest. You found it possible to project your fear into the
> world that it might be united with a common fear and form a
> Goliath worth slaying. Actually, when you now travel through
> Corning, you should wake up laughing and with thumb at nose.

Olive Byrne's explanation is probably as good as any, for Maggie's
childhood was not as terrible as she made it out to be. If she was full of
fear, she at least acquired the weapons to counter it—courage, the love
of beauty and art.

She learned courage at her father's side, particularly during one
strange trip to the cemetery. At that time, her mother had lost a child,
a boy of four who died of croup. Because she had no picture to remember him by, she mourned him keenly. Michael, who knew how to make
death masks, stole into the cemetery at midnight, dug up the freshly
made grave, opened the casket, and made a plaster cast of the boy's
face—a cast he could then reverse and carve into a bust. Maggie was
chosen to go along with him and hold the lantern while he worked, and
she did so without a whimper. But then, she was familiar with cemeteries. Michael had often taken her there to point out the various
schools of art illustrated on the tombstones—those of the Italian
school, the English school, the Spanish school. With no other museum
in town, it was his way of teaching her art as best he could.

She also learned how to fight. There is always a certain amount of bickering in large families. But in the Higgins family, the bickering was constant, and Maggie, a middle child, jockeyed hard for position.

When she was about seventeen, her fighting spirit showed itself dramatically. She had been given a rare gift, a pair of warm gloves—a great luxury during the cold Corning winters. She was so proud of these gloves she kept them on in school and sat openly admiring them. When her teacher saw her, she exclaimed sarcastically: "Miss Higgins, you are so busy admiring your gloves you seem to be above a little thing like paying attention to the lesson like the rest of the class is doing."

The other pupils giggled. That did it. She ran out of the room and straight home, where she burst in and announced: "I am never going back to that school again! Never!" Mary, who usually could calm her, was sent for; she couldn't budge her. Back to that high school—the only one in Corning—Maggie would not go.

But Mary too was stubborn. "You must get an education somehow. You must," she argued. "You'll never get anywhere without it. You'll never even get out of this town."

Maggie was unmoved.

Then Mary said something she'd been saying all her life: "All right, I'll think of something else. I'll work something out." She immediately got a list of all the boarding schools in New York state and sent away for their brochures. When they came, she read them carefully. One in particular appealed to her. It had the grand name of Claverack College or the Hudson River Institute. Three miles from the town of Hudson, it boasted of being one of the oldest and least-expensive co-educational institutions in the state, as well as one of the most moral, since it taught the elements of a "pure and noble womanhood." Also, it would let Maggie wait on tables and wash dishes to pay part of her way.

Maggie capitulated. In Corning she was not only an ostracized child, but a lonesome one; her family had of necessity moved so frequently she seldom had had a chance to make girl friends. At Claverack there would be lots of girls and, hopefully, boys.

Like many a man who is loudly liberal in public, Michael Higgins was a patriarch at home. He regularly thrashed his sons "to make men of them." And as soon as his daughters reached adolescence, dates with boys were forbidden. When on the rare occasions he did permit callers in the parlor, he sat in the next room with the door open, pretending to read. At 9:55 he would stand up and give the coals in the fireplace an audible shake. At 9:58 he would cough loudly, and at 9:59 he would shout, "Good night!"

Indeed the hour of ten o'clock was so firmly fixed as a bedtime deadline that once when Maggie and Ethel were allowed the privilege of going unescorted to an evening concert, they ran all the way home, yet still didn't make it by ten. They found their father waiting at the door. Ethel he yanked inside, but on Maggie, he slammed the door, announcing sternly: "You're older and need a lesson." He let her sit on the porch cold and shivering for an hour before he relented and let her in.

When Higgins had been drinking he was more unpredictable than usual. Whiskey made him either more light-hearted or more pugnacious, and it was hard to predict which it would be. When he was gay and fairly reasonable, he would tell Maggie: "Make sure you leave the world better than you found it, lass." When he was pugnacious, he was so fierce it made Maggie's own temper flare up. Soon the feuding between them had grown so intense that when Maggie proposed leaving for Claverack, both father and daughter were glad to be quit of each other for a while.

CLAVERACK AND ROMANTIC DREAMS

Maggie and Michael, driving a rented horse and buggy, arrived in Claverack on a fine autumn day. They drove straight to the school, an imposing wooden building set among twenty acres of lawn, trees, and playing fields.

Maggie bid her father a hasty goodbye and dashed out to explore. She discovered to her delight that every floor had a sink with running water; at home water had had to be carried in from a well. Better yet, there was a library right in the building, whereas Corning didn't have one in the whole town. Best of all, the reception rooms were furnished in elegant red and green plush; at home there was nothing so fine.

She quickly changed her name on the register from Maggie to the more dignified Margaret, then chose courses which struck her as romantic: elocution, painting, and belle lettres. She also applied for membership in a literary society where, according to the catalogue: "The young ladies and gentlemen are improved in Declamation, Composition, and Extemporaneous Speaking."

Next she chose a church to attend. Though, like most private schools of the time, Claverack had been founded by a minister, this one, the Reverend Flack, a Methodist, was tolerant in religious matters. Daily morning and Sunday evening services in the school chapel were compulsory, but on Sunday mornings the students could attend any of the three churches in the town. For reasons she never divulged, Maggie chose the Episcopal.

At this time she also formed her first adolescent crush. A Claverack memoir tells the story:

> I immediately fell in love with Esther, a girl whose beauty, form and loveliness was to be compared only to the statue of the Virgin Mary. I started down the hall early one morning and beheld the loveliest creature I ever saw in my life. She was getting water from the sink in a coffee-pot. Her hair had fallen over her shoulders, she was slender as a lily and seemed so unreal that I fled past her in fright. But I could not go far away. Esther held me fascinated for the entire year. I cried at night because I felt her loveliness to be something I could not reach . . . She, and all that she was, represented an entirely new world to me. She was the queen of this new world, the heroine of every book I had read come to life.

After Esther, Margaret formed a friendship with Amelia:

> Amelia Stuart was unattractive as Esther was beautiful. She was shorter and younger than I, but her wit and keen sense of appreciation fired my Irish imagination. Her loyalty and praise and admiration fed all the hungry spaces in my being . . .
>
> Some of the older girls carried on a whispering campaign about the affection and devotion Amelia showered on me. It did not worry us. We continued our friendship through the years. I gave my first son her family name . . .

By eighteen, Margaret's sexual urge was fully developed. She had not reached puberty until sixteen, and from thirteen on had been frantic with worry lest menstruation and all it implied might never arrive. When it did come, her interest in sex was greatly intensified.

Margaret places first sexual awakening at about age nine. In her autobiography she ascribes this awakening to her father and speaks of male sexuality as "blind, imperious and driving." She tells how she came to fear her father as a man who exemplified this:

> The only memory I have of any sex awakening . . . was when I was ill with typhoid fever . . . I remember nothing beyond go-

ing upstairs to a cold room and a colder bed. . . . It was pitch dark. I felt about me and knew I was in Mother's bed. . . . Then I heard heavy breathing beside me. It was Father. I was terrified. I wanted to scream out to Mother to beg her to come and take him away. I could not move, I dared not move, fearing he might awaken and move toward me. I lived through agonies of fear in the few minutes. Then Father's breathing changed—he was about to awaken. I was petrified; but he only turned over on his other side with his back toward me. . . . I was cold; I began to shiver; blackness and lights flickered in my brain; then I felt I was falling—and knew no more.

This fear and distrust of men is quite different from her attitude in later life. Probably these feelings were heightened because as a child she considered herself the plainest of the four Higgins sisters. The others were quite lovely. Ethel, the loveliest of all, had the reddest, curliest hair and the clearest and most delicate skin, while Margaret, shown in a family picture wearing a drab dress while the others sparkled in white, appears straight-haired and dull.

But puberty brought a sudden blooming to Margaret. She had a slender figure, burnished hair, and wide sparkling eyes that looked sometimes hazel and sometimes violet blue. At eighteen she was charming.

Unchaperoned dates were forbidden at Claverack, just as they had been at home, but that didn't deter her. There were twenty acres of lawn and trees and in the nearby cemetery there was an old horse shed, the back of which faced the road, making the front dark, private, and sweet smelling. What better place for Margaret to meet boys and exchange kisses, especially since it had the extra allure of being "off limits"?

Her first boyfriend, a student named Corey Alberson, came from a well-to-do family and wanted to marry her. Margaret described him as "fine, clean and honest," and they became secretly engaged, planning to marry when she graduated.

Margaret probably didn't wait for sex until marriage, however. Years later, she told of her "trial marriage" with Corey; indeed, for several summers she went on vacations alone with him.

But Corey, Esther, and Amelia did not use up all of her energy at Claverack. She plunged into writing, memorizing, and declaiming essays.

* * *

In declamation class I recited an essay on woman's suffrage and the facts of woman's history. I sent long letters to father for more information and got oh! what letters in reply. All about Helen of Troy, the battle of Nebedenazzar, Ruth, Cleopatra, Poppaea, Queens, Women Authors, Poets and Mothers. It was a great essay. I stole away first to the cemetery and stood on the monuments over the graves and said every word aloud. Again and again, each day I recited in the quiet of the dead.

It made no difference that when she later recited her essay in class, the boys guffawed and drew pictures of her on the blackboard in mannish trousers, smoking a long black cigar. She sniffed disdainfully, erased the board, and went her way.

After suffrage, I took up the silver question of Mr. Jennings Bryan. No one else knew anything about it. They were all for gold, so I took the other side and studied and worked on a debate. I gradually became known to have advanced ideas; only serious boys paid attention to me, and the girls came to me in all their sorrows and woes. In recitation and acting I excelled.

Soon she was playing the lead in a school play, and when her teacher complimented her and told her she'd make a good actress, she immediately agreed.

I went home one vacation and announced I was going on the stage. Shocks and disapproval were evident. Father pooh-poohed the idea, but my sister Mary, the most saint-like woman who walked the earth, agreed with me as to my ability and said I should go to Dramatic School as soon as I finished Claverack; that she would apply at once to Charles Frohman and I should try as an understudy to Maude Adams. Great hopes! Splendid aspirations! A wise sister!

Mary raised enough money to have Margaret photographed in various dramatic poses, and they sent an application to the renowned producer. A reply came with a form letter asking her age, height, color of eyes, hair, and skin. Margaret eagerly started on the form, but when she came to the size of her legs, ankle, knee, calf and thigh, she stopped cold.

Enthusiasm for the stage vanished. It was not that I did not know the size of my own legs. I did. But to see that personal and intimate information go coldly down on paper and be sent off to strange men, was like cutting yourself into parts. I could not see what legs had to do with being a great actress . . . I did not fill in the printed form, nor send the photographs. I just put them all away and turned my desires to more serious studies where brains, not legs, were to count.

But soon her Claverack days came to a sudden end. Her father ordered her home because her mother, who was ravaged not only by tuberculosis but also by cancer of the cervix, was dying. Maggie unexpectedly found her in the care of the Sisters of Mercy; indeed Michael Higgins had relented so far as to let the nuns send for a priest. "Surely," he had said, "get her one if it will make her feel closer to the Lord." So on March 31, 1899, a priest had come and given Anne the last rites, as she murmured, "My Heaven begins this morning."

At the actual moment of death, Margaret stood cold and dry-eyed, refusing to kneel. She had never been close to her mother; she couldn't pretend to be now. But her father felt the loss keenly; he became sad and disoriented. He neglected his work more than ever. Most of his time was spent either sounding off in the pub or roaming the woods with his dogs, while Margaret endlessly cleaned, washed, and cooked.

Infuriated, she now fought with him constantly: "Dammit, you killed my mother. She was only forty-nine when she died. But those eighteen pregnancies didn't hurt you a bit. You—you'll live forever!"

She let their run-down house deteriorate even more. Realizing she could never get enough money to return to Claverack to graduate, she decided to leave Corning for good. When Amelia invited her to visit her at White Plains, she packed her clothes, borrowed the fare from Mary, caught the first train, and vowed never to return.

WILLIAM LAD

The turn of the century was a turning point in Margaret's life. She was twenty, and while she luxuriated in being a guest of Amelia, she knew she couldn't stay forever; she had to find a job.

In 1900, only three kinds of jobs were open to women—teaching, nursing, and typing. Two years of high school or their equivalent were considered enough preparation for teaching, so Margaret got a job at a kindergarten in New Jersey. Assigned to a class made up mainly of the children of new immigrants, she found that her pupils didn't seem to understand a word she said. At the end of each day she was so tired she dragged herself back to her boardinghouse, threw herself down on the bed, and woke up a few hours later only to undress and go back to sleep. Two terms of this were enough.

She would try nursing. As a child she had dreamt of becoming a doctor, hoping to fulfill her father's desire that she "leave the world better than she found it." But with so little education, nursing seemed the most she could hope for in the medical field. She went back to Amelia's and learned that a small hospital in White Plains was looking for nurse-probationers, which meant women who would serve a trial period before the authorities decided whether or not they were fit to enter nursing school. Margaret was delighted to be accepted as a probationer.

The hospital was a large old mansion with five pleasant rooms for patients and several for the staff. There were, however, no conveniences of any kind; water had to be brought in pitcher by pitcher from a well and bedpans were emptied in an outhouse. Still, it was a haven for Maggie, as it offered room, board, and a small salary.

But hospital work proved even more exhausting than teaching. "The girls say I am very thin and have lost my red cheeks," Margaret wrote Mary on December 29, 1900. "But at least there's only a short time to go until we get a New Year's vacation."

The regular hospital routine interested her very little; she was intrigued only by midwifery. In her textbook the chapter on birth is the only one underlined. However, even midwifery, she found, had its problems. She complained to Mary that "just keeping myself in comfortable shoes takes most of my salary." Worse, she seemed to have caught the dread tuberculosis from her mother and ran a fever of 100 degrees almost every day. The hospital doctors thought the infection was centered in the glands on one side of her neck, and in June 1901, she underwent neck surgery. Afterward, she felt much better; still she was told she would always be more or less troubled, unless she gave up living near New York where tuberculosis was rife. Mary got another letter:

> So you see I am having a fight. If I can only get through the three years of nursing school (if I am accepted), I can go out and nurse in the West . . . Colorado for instance. . . . The supervisor does not want me to give up the profession for anything, and lets me go out for a walk in the fresh air for three or four hours every afternoon, though this makes the other girls furious, since they have only one hour off at most.

During the summer vacation she planned to spend a few weeks with Corey in Buffalo and to stop on the way back for a brief visit in Corning. But at the last minute she told Corey he couldn't come along to Corning to meet her father as he had asked. She didn't say, of course, that her reason was that she was ashamed of her home. He got so angry that soon afterward he stopped seeing her altogether. This was especially hard on Margaret, because Ethel, the favored younger sister had, at seventeen, eloped after a wild drinking party with a handsome local boy, Jack Byrne.

At a party for the hospital staff, Margaret was introduced to the architect William Sanger, a tall dark-haired man with burning black eyes and a thin set mouth turned down like an eagle's; he had drawn up plans for a new home for one of the doctors and had come up from New York to White Plains to get them approved.

Margaret thought Sanger mildly attractive; with him it was another story. A bachelor of twenty-nine, he had seldom gone out with girls because he had been too busy studying and working to support himself, his widowed mother, and his sister. He studied nights at the Art Students League of New York or the Architectural School of Cooper Union. Days, he worked for a glassmaker who designed stained-glass windows. Now he had his first job as a draftsman with the famous New York architectural firm of McKim, Mead and White; he was working on the plans for Grand Central Station and the Woolworth building. The job did not pay much, but it was an excellent start.

The slim young redhaired girl grabbed at his heart. When he discovered that she had to go back on duty right after the party, he went to the hospital waiting room and sat there waiting for an opportunity to talk with her again. When Margaret appeared he begged her for a date on the next morning. She agreed. Dazed and content, William sat down again and waited until her duty was over and she appeared.

On that first date, he seemed bewitched, giving in to her every whim, lunching and dining at restaurants far too expensive for his slim purse. Before he left he made a date for the following Sunday. In the weeks that followed he sent flowers every day, enclosing with them long ardent notes urging her to marry him as soon as he was financially secure.

Margaret would promise nothing. She was delighted by his wooing, but she was torn between marriage and nursing school. Bill was undaunted. Every Sunday he continued to hurry to White Plains with flowers, candy, and small gifts of jewelry. On their walks together, he told her romantic stories about his English-born father, Edward, who had run off to sea at an early age, worked on an Australian sheep farm, and fallen in love with William's mother on a trip to Germany. Edward Sanger had made a great deal of money, then lost it in several unsuccessful schemes. When he died, he left almost nothing. William, only twelve, had had to give up his dream of becoming a violinist and take the first job he could find. Now, for the first time in his life, he wanted to break away, marry, and have a place of his own.

All of this impressed Margaret greatly. Here, obviously, was a man who was poor but responsible. This time she took him home, realizing that now she did not have to be ashamed of her background. She also hinted that he might soon consider himself engaged.

Higgins and Sanger got along famously, as Higgins was delighted to find that Sanger held radical views like his own. In fact, Sanger went even further. Not only was he against all organized religion, he was an active member of both the Socialist Party and an anarchist group. He was also painting pictures on weekends, hoping to give up architecture and become his "own man." The two men talked eagerly into the small hours.

Still, Margaret hesitated about marriage. Back at the hospital she wrote Mary telling her how "the William lad" wrote her every day, telephoned her often, took her out regularly, and promised her both a diamond and a gold watch. Yet, she was not prepared to marry now:

> If I could get two or three good (private maternity) cases it would start me off nicely, and then too I must get some clothing made. I hate long engagements myself but I would rather finish training, and when I think of all the hard work, the bitter tears I shed night after night for the training, the lonesome nights I passed waiting for some old tramp to die, then when it is finished without a laurel to get married—then I want to stop it all. I would love one year of private nursing and get some money, and then if anyone wants me, all right. But the Lad does not care about waiting longer than six months.

Then, flirting with marriage again:

> There is so much to think of . . . bridesmaids, the time, the place, the dress, the trip and everything. I suppose it had better take place at home. Have we a *house* or a *barn*? I am dying to meet his people. I wonder if this excitement will pass.

Margaret also sent Mary one of William's love letters:

> I don't know how you can stand on your feet all night, dearest. I don't see how you can stand it, you are truly heroic. You are giving up the best time of your life in your present professional vocation and I thank God that I came; that our souls met and that you

will give up this strenuous life in very short order if it is in my power to do so. . . . I'm laying tracks for a lot of work—for a home with you as Presiding Queen dearest, a real home with love the necessary household utensil to shed its light upon our life. We shall have it, of course we shall.

Yet she was as torn as ever. In June 1902, still a probationer, she wrote Mary wondering if she'd be admitted to nurses' training school. A few weeks later she was wondering no more: "I have been accepted for the three-year course and no doubt shall be such an angel at the end of that time I shall fly heavenward." When William heard this, he was downcast until he hit on a new tack. He would ask Mary to persuade Margaret to give up the thought of nursing once and for all and marry him immediately.

At the last minute, he didn't wait for Mary's answer. He decided to take the bull by the horns. On his next Sunday date with Margaret, he hired a horse and buggy from a New York livery stable, got a marriage license, arranged for a minister and two witnesses, and drove to White Plains where Margaret was waiting on the hospital porch. But the horse proved unmanageable and would not stop. He had to keep driving around and around until he managed to toss a note to her explaining the situation. Then keep driving until she was able to toss a note back saying she couldn't have gone out with him anyway; an emergency had arisen and she would have to take her time off the following day instead.

He had no choice but to drive back to the stable and order a better horse for Monday.

On Monday the horse behaved, and Margaret cheerfully got in beside him. But when he told her about the license in his pocket and the waiting minister, she became livid; she would marry him, yes, but in her own good time. William didn't listen; he literally carried her off. On August 18, 1902, with a Reverend Norris performing the ceremony in his parlor, Margaret Higgins and William Sanger were married, with the bride getting as hearty a kiss as one ever got.

But outside again, she insisted he drive her back to the hospital immediately, and there, she ran up the steps and slammed the door, leaving him nonplussed. Immediately, she wrote Mary:

That beast of a man William took me out for a drive last Monday and drove me to a minister's residence and married me. I wept with anger and would not look at him for it was so unexpected. I had an old blue dress on, and I looked horrid. Now the only thing is to make the best of it. No one can know of it—only our family—but he wants to furnish an apartment and live here in the city until he can build a home for us in the country. He is the loveliest of men but I am mad at him. He is collecting (plaster) casts, furniture, old rugs, silver, etc. for our home and is happy to think he outdid Corey and two doctors. . . . Good night dear Mary. I am very sorry to have had this thing occur but yet I am very, very happy.

She also wrote Nan:

Here I am no longer a Higgins. That man of mine simply carried me off. I vow I will not live with such a beast of a man.

Then, wavering:

He is so happy and so am I . . . He sends me flowers—flowers—books—and now jewelry—a marquis ring today (turquoise) and yet I won't go out. He stands waiting on the corner every day after three o'clock . . .

I am sure I could not have a better husband—he is my ideal in many ways but I wanted to wait.

Soon William was writing Mary. . . :

It was a tremendously serious affair to get married at the time we did, without the knowledge of the authorities at home, but to be candid, to me it was a question of getting married then or never.

As for the hospital arrangement I can say that when we were married I did not think the diploma question would loom up in such prodigious proportions. But since then I have persuaded Margaret to change her mind and she will send in her resignation in the next few days. . . .

We shall be located in the city for the present, but eventually intend to settle down permanently in New Rochelle, one of New

York's most delightful suburban towns. Now my dear Mary the deed is done, and it can be jotted down in the family Bible that we are happy, Margaret and I—and will remain so.

Michael Higgins was not told about the wedding until the couple went up to Corning for Labor Day, after Margaret had relented and gone to live with Sanger several weeks before. Whatever her reservations, he promised her devotion, leisure, and a beautiful home; and these were among her most cherished dreams.

4

THE RESTLESS HOUSEWIFE

The Sangers first settled into an apartment on 119th Street in Manhattan where rents were cheap, and Margaret busied herself collecting pots, pans, and dishes. But no amount of pots and pans and dishes could turn Margaret into a housekeeper. After years of drudgery in Corning, cleaning, cooking, and washing dishes bored her to distraction. Also, maids were easily hired in 1902. Room and board plus five or ten dollars a month was usually enough to attract a new immigrant girl.

She soon became pregnant with a much-wanted child. Although she certainly didn't plan on having eleven children like her mother, she did want two or three. Yet as soon as she became pregnant her tuberculosis flared up, this time in her lungs as well as her neck, and Bill quickly arranged to send her off to Trudeau in the Adirondacks, one of the best private sanitariums in the country.

The treatment at Trudeau was the only one known at the time—fresh air, good food, and enforced rest. But this regimen bored her even more than housekeeping. Margaret, as Bill quickly learned, had two strongly opposing drives. On the one hand, she enjoyed lolling about in the soft, pretty clothes he delighted in giving her. On the other, she was bursting with intellectual and physical energy, eager to be out in the world. Now she yearned for the excitements of New York, of which she had had barely a taste; she ran back from Saranac without asking permission, and Bill, unable to deny her anything, opened his arms wide and welcomed her back.

During the last months of her pregnancy, he also took over as many of the household chores as he could. On the maid's day off he hurried home after a ten-hour stint at the office, cooked dinner, served it, and washed up, content to have his Peg lolling on a sofa nearby. The baby was born on November 18, 1903—a rosy, smiling, nine-pounder, blue-eyed like Michael Higgins. She named the baby Stuart, after her friend Amelia, though Bill dubbed him "Sunny Jim." Despite Bill's misgivings, Margaret had him baptized an Episcopalian.

With such a large baby and such a small mother, labor had been long and difficult; her TB flared up even more strongly from the strain. Bill sent her back to Saranac, and this time, she went willingly, taking Stuart with her and staying a full year, since she was now terrified of dying of tuberculosis. But Bill kept reassuring her: "I won't let you die, sweetheart, I won't let you die," and vowed he would get her out of New York and into the suburbs as fast as he could. He also vowed he would not let her get pregnant again soon.

Shortly after Margaret and Stuart returned from Saranac in June of 1905, Bill bought a half-acre plot in the charming suburb of Hastings-on-the-Hudson. He began to design his own house and to save the money to build it. Later he said that the happiest days of his life were when he was saving for a home even though they had to live in a rented place that was little more than a shack in the meantime. Within a year his house on Edgar Lane had been started. It was an imposing three-story structure of hollow tile, covered in Italian-style pale pink stucco with large rooms and many bathrooms. The house had a Juliet balcony for Peg to sun herself on, open fireplaces everywhere, bay windows that looked out on the sweep of river, a nursery for the children, and a painting studio for Bill. He summed it up as "full of tranquil space."

It was far too expensive a house for Bill's pocketbook, and he was often hard pressed to pay the contractors. Yet he was as romantic and impractical as Margaret and a tireless worker. He was also a perfectionist who kept changing his mind, especially about the relative size of the nursery and studio. Margaret wanted a small studio and a large nursery; Bill wanted a small nursery and a large studio. They had a terrible fight over this, and as usual, Margaret had her way.

One thing they did agree on was a stained-glass rose window. Since Bill had so much experience with stained glass, he trusted this to no workman. Margaret, he found, had a fine sense of beauty, so they worked together on it, placing bits of glass in place piece by piece, and moving and removing them, until a beautiful rose window was completed.

In February 1908, when the house was finally finished, they drank a bottle of wine to celebrate and moved in. It was a blustery night, and Bill helped the maid stoke the coal furnace particularly high to protect Margaret from the cold. They were hardly under the bedcovers when the maid called out "Fire! Madam, fire!" Flames escaped from the overheated furnace and spread to the main floor.

By the time the fire was out, the heavy supporting beams in the cellar were badly scorched and the rose window ruined. Because Bill's funds were by now very low, he repaired most of the damage himself, reinforcing the damaged beams, but a new stained-glass window was out of the question. One of plain glass had to be substituted instead.

Margaret's Irish mysticism led her to believe that the fire was a bad omen, and she could not be comforted over the loss of the rose window. She also complained that the smell from the scorched beams continued to pervade the house.

The truth was that suburban living did not suit her. She had envied the idle life of the rich women in Corning; now she realized this life was not what she wanted.

Even though she bore another much-wanted son in July 1908, she ran away from Hastings every day she could, either to visit Amelia in White Plains or to roam the exciting streets of New York. Dark-eyed Grant looked like his father, and on the whim of his mother, was baptized a Presbyterian, again over the objections of his father. A neighbor, Mrs. Edward Griswold, remembers going over to the Sanger house one day and finding Grant crying in his crib, his throat sore with the painful ailment thrush, his bottle on the floor, while an Irish maid sat complacently looking on.

For want of something to do, Margaret started a women's reading circle, but this proved too tame to hold her interest. She switched to a series of lectures on reproduction and sex, which she gave at home to neighborhood children, accompanied by their mothers. While the children were barely old enough to understand her, their mothers were impressed with Margaret's months as a nurse-probationer, and their eager questions made her realize how much they wanted information. It was a significant first step toward her lifelong career.

But even these talks began to pale. A third baby, especially if it were a girl, would fill her need. Though her doctor had warned her against having more children, less than three years after Grant was born, in May 1911, she gave birth to a beautiful baby girl whom she named Peggy, after herself. This time, the child was not baptized. Bill, who had twice before given in to his "Peg's" vague religious leanings, held firm in his anarchist conviction that religious ceremony was hollow.

Though the blonde, blue-eyed infant seemed a good omen, Margaret found caring for her as boring as caring for the boys. As Peggy grew, her clothes were often held together by safety pins; once a button fell off, it stayed off. "I just never will learn how to sew," she explained. Yet she would run cheerfully to massage a neighbor's sprained ankle, because nursing she enjoyed. She loved to hug and kiss her children, but taking responsibility for them was something else.

Bill kissed and hugged them often, too. Indeed, Margaret's niece Olive remembered that he was the first man she had ever seen who kissed his wife and children good night. No man she knew in Corning had ever done that.

Still, Margaret couldn't find enough to interest her in Hastings. After living in her new house only a few years, she urged Bill to sell it and move back to town. He was appalled. Everything he had worked and hoped for since he met her was centered in that house—his family, his painting studio, his architect's vision of tranquil space. But Margaret persisted until he offered to sell it, at the low price of twelve thousand dollars, almost exactly what it had cost him for the materials alone. He sold it to a local furniture dealer named Fishel, accepting a small down payment and a long-term mortgage. He signed the deed of sale with a trembling hand.

Forty years later, in a letter to Grant, Bill still regretted the sale. "I've asked myself so many times whatever possessed me to sell my house. I realize I was as blind as a bat to have ever consented to part with it. It's all over the dam a long time now, but it broke my back to have been renting living space ever since."

It broke his heart too, because he had put into that house all he knew of design and construction and all he knew of love. Once when he was an old man, he went to Hastings and stood in the road, looking at the house intently for a long time, then turned and walked slowly away.

HIDDEN YEARS

In her autobiography, Margaret was not always completely honest about her life. Though she leads the reader to believe that her commitment to birth control followed immediately upon her years in Hastings, this was not the case. In between there were long stretches of time spent in socialist and anarchist activities, years in which she learned the propaganda techniques that were later to stand her in such good stead.

This period of radical activism began when she moved back to New York early in 1911. Bill, who had long been interested in radical politics, originally attended political meetings regularly. Because he was tremendously energetic, he soon became part of the inner circle of the Socialist Party. Once, he even ran for alderman on the Socialist ticket, making an unexpectedly good showing, though he lost the election.

During his sojourn in Hastings, however, he was not involved in politics, since he was eager to catch the commuter train and get home to his family. With their return to New York, he began to go to Socialist meetings again. Because his mother lived with them in the apartment on West 135th Street, she was able to care for the children.

Margaret occasionally got a well-paying job taking care of a newborn baby, but when she was free, he took her along because he couldn't bear to be away from her, even for a minute. To his delight, he found that she reveled in politics. During their courtship he had seen

37

her through Mary's eyes as a "conservative Irish girl"; now he found
she was more her father's daughter. When the group got into such
heated discussions that they drowned out her low voice Bill would
shout: "Listen to my Peggy! Listen to her! She has something to say!"
Rather to everyone's surprise, she did.

At home they would continue the discussions, discovering that they
both were torn between anarchist left-wingers who believed in "direct
action" or quick violent strikes to right the workers' wrongs, and followers of comparatively conservative labor leaders, like Eugene Debs
and Morris Hillquit, who believed in the slower "political action" or
legislation, instead.

Indeed, when William Haywood, the extreme left-wing leader of the
Industrial Workers of the World came to town, it was Bill Sanger who
invited him to speak at the Socialist local, over Debs' and Hillquit's objections.

Bill and Margaret found themselves attending so many meetings
that Grant, now a shy and nervous boy of three, asked them one night:

> Are you going to a meeting again?
> Yes.
> A soshist meeting?
> Yes.
> I hate soshism!

They also started having get-togethers at home. The first person to
be invited was William Haywood, whom Margaret described as "an uncouth, stumbling, one-eyed giant with an enormous head." He had lost
one eye in a mine explosion and was almost universally referred to as
"Big Bill." Melvin Dubofsky, author of a history of the I.W.W., describes him:

> Big Bill looked like a bull about to plunge into an arena. He
> seemed always glancing warily this way and that with his one
> eye, head tilted slightly as though to get a better view of you. His
> great voice boomed; his speech was crude and so were his man-
> ners; his philosophy was that of the mining camps where he had
> spent his life. But I soon found out that for gentleness and sympa-
> thy he had not his equal.

*   *   *

Others came to the Sangers' house, too; among them Jessie Ashley, Big Bill's lover. Dubofsky describes them:

> Jessie and Bill were the oddest combination in the world—old Bill with his one eye, stubby roughened fingernails, uncreased trousers and shoddy clothes for which he refused to pay more than a minimum; Jessie with her Boston accent and hornrimmed glasses, a compromise between spectacles and lorgnette from which dangled a black ribbon, the ultimate word in eccentric decoration.
>
> Jessie was one of the most conspicuous of the many men and women of long pedigree who were revolting against family tradition. She was the daughter of the president of the New York School of Law . . . and one of the first women lawyers in New York. . . . A Socialist in practice as well as in theory, she spent large portions of her income getting radicals out of jail. . . Nevertheless, her appearance at strike meetings were [sic] slightly uncomfortable; class tension rose up in waves.

Emma Goldman and her lover Alexander Berkman also came. Emma, a fiery anarchist, was a short, strong, stocky woman who believed that violent deeds would make people noble and good. So did Emma's lover, Alexander Berkman, who had tried to assassinate Henry Clay Frick, the head of the Carnegie Steel Company, during the unsuccessful Homestead Strike of 1892. Berkman served fourteen years in jail for the attempt, emerging from prison a hero-martyr.

Indeed, Berkman was such a hero that Emma became jealous, though her jealousy didn't stop her from defending him. Just before a lecture given after he came out of jail, she heard that a fellow radical was going to criticize him. She strode into the lecture hall in a wide coat underneath which a bull whip was tied securely about her powerful body. At a crucial moment she leapt onto the platform and horsewhipped the speaker while the audience cheered.

Berkman's martyrdom greatly impressed Margaret. She spent long evenings talking with him in the little Russian restaurants that dotted Second Avenue, smoking endless cigarettes and sipping tea.

She also spent long evenings discussing the emancipation of women at Emma's home on East Thirteenth Street. Emma, a highly educated woman, made her living by writing and selling an anarchist magazine called *Mother Earth,* as well as by lecturing on Shakespeare, Russian literature, free love, and the problems of women. *Mother Earth* might be filled with typical epithets about "capitalist monsters" and "exploited wage-slaves," but Emma's lectures, especially those on women's problems, could be extremely sound.

Like Margaret, she had been a nurse working particularly among the poor, so she knew firsthand the need for birth control. She had also attended one of the first international conferences on birth control—the Paris Neo-Malthusian Conference in 1900—and regularly distributed leaflets on contraception at her lectures.

Margaret undoubtedly received her first concrete ideas on the subject from Emma, who distributed her leaflets without interference from the police because, as she boasted, "They just didn't expect me to be bothering with such things." Emma, too, was the first person to direct Margaret to the writings of Havelock Ellis, the great English pioneer of sexual reform, though Margaret always pretended she had stumbled on Ellis herself.

Margaret met many of the other leading radicals of the day through Bill Sanger. Among these were Leonard Abbott, a formerly conservative New Englander, who was founder of the Free Speech League; Gilbert Roe, a lawyer and one-time partner of Robert La Follette, Progressive Senator from Wisconsin; Lincoln Steffens, the muck-raking journalist; Clarence Darrow, the most famous liberal lawyer of his time.

This group founded the Modern School, an anarchist school in which the historian Will Durant, a Catholic turned anarchist, was a teacher. When Stuart was enrolled there at eleven, he was in school for the first time in his life. According to him: "Since it was an anarchist place they let us do anything we liked, so I did nothing. I just fiddled around or played ball all day." One morning, however, he woke up: "I don't want to be a dumbbell. That means I'll have to learn to read and write." He insisted on being transferred to the Wood School in Long Island, a Christian Science school where Mrs. Wood herself took him in hand. In a year he was steeping himself in Frank Merriwell and the other boys' books he had missed.

Characteristically, Margaret barely noticed what was happening to her children. She declared she was seized with a mysterious "nervous malady" whenever she had to take care of them, and clutched at the first outside interest that came along.

A fine opportunity arose when she met Anita Block. Anita, a Barnard graduate and ardent Socialist, was editor of "Woman's Sphere," a section of the Socialist newspaper, the *Call*. She telephoned Margaret one night to say that a speaker scheduled for a labor meeting was unable to come. Would Margaret take her place? Margaret had never made a public speech and was terrified. Quaking, she faced the audience of ten. She started to speak on labor relations but found she just didn't know enough, so she switched to her favorite topic, sex and reproduction. The audience was delighted and asked for more, with the result that at the next meeting seventy-five people came, and Anita asked Margaret to do a series of articles on similar subjects to enliven her page.

Though the pay was small, Margaret took the rather simplistic material about frogs, birds, and bees she had used in her Hastings talks, expanded it, and plunged. On October 29, 1911, she started a Sunday series called "How Six Little Children Learned the Truth," branching out from there into the need for contraception with typical socialist invective about "the deprived childhoods of children whose mothers are forced to abandon them to earn money" and carrying on with, "Why should these countless fathers and mothers surrender to these few monster exploiters—to this Capitalistic system which bases its existence on the fiendish exploitation, and ultimate murder, of these children?"

In another article, called "Impressions of the East Side," she bewailed the fact that the only way that poor women knew how to limit their families was to line up on Saturday nights at five-dollar-quack abortionists, often as many as forty waiting their turn.

The *Call* series led to a better financial offer. She formally joined the Socialist Party, and the Womens' Committee unanimously elected her "organizer" or chairman at the dazzling salary of fifteen dollars a week. For this fifteen dollars she was to run around to other locals and urge them to give up their rooms once a week to women, to arrange street-corner meetings, supervise press releases, and start naturalization classes for immigrants.

Her noontime street-corner meetings proved particularly successful. Working men and women often stopped to hear her out of mere curiosity, expecting a shrill termagant like Emmaline Pankhurst or Carrie Nation. Instead, they saw a petite redhead with wide violet eyes who spoke in a rather frightened, gentle voice as she distributed Socialist leaflets.

But her most important contribution was teaching naturalization classes. From 1881 to 1925, over two and a half million Jewish immigrants alone fled countries where they had been impoverished and tormented, to become victims of one of the most cunning sales spiels in history—spiels that told them freedom and gold were waiting for them in America, when actually the idea was to make money for ship owners by filling the steerages of their ships. The immigrants made their way across Europe by wagon, train, or foot, their samovars and featherbeds strapped to their backs, honestly believing that all they had to do when they got to the States was to stoop down and pick up the gold.

The peak year for such immigration was 1906. It was just after the Russian pogroms of 1903 and 1905 in which hundreds had been slaughtered, imprisoned, or raped, for merely marching to Moscow holding up a picture of the "Little Father," their Czar, as they tried to present a limited-suffrage petition to him.

These immigrants arrived in New York at an inspection station romantically named Castle Garden, speaking no English, and with hardly a cent in their pockets. (It is estimated that the average amount of money they had was eight dollars.) Often they stayed at Castle Garden for weeks, half-starved, awaiting clearance. The majority became Socialists as a matter of course, for while they might not know exactly what socialism or "political action" meant (since they had had no political rights at all back home), at least it seemed to promise escape from the endless grinding work which was all they could find, once they settled on New York's lower East Side.

In 1897, while Margaret was still at Claverack, a Yiddish daily paper called the *Forward* had been founded in New York. Most of the new immigrants had never seen a newspaper, but the women had learned to read a little Yiddish from the "Ladies Bible," and when they recognized a few familiar words, they painfully worked through the rest; they in turn often taught their men.

One of the most popular features of the *Forward* was the "Bintel Brief" or bundle of letters into which they could pour out their hearts and receive in return advice from "worthy editor" Abraham Cahan.

Many of their early letters show their passionate concern with socialism:

I am a Socialist and my boss is a fine man. I know he's a Capitalist but I like him. Am I doing something wrong?

I am a Socialist and I am going with an American girl. She

wants to go to dances and balls and affairs and I would like to know if you think it's alright for me to go too.

My son is already twenty-six years old and doesn't want to get married. He says he is a Socialist and he is too busy. Socialism is Socialism but getting married is important too.

Then there were letters from skilled men and women, carpenters or dressmakers, who endlessly tramped the streets looking for work only to be confronted with signs saying curtly: "No foreigners need apply," just as a generation earlier the Irish had been confronted with "No Irish need apply." It was for these people that the naturalization classes Margaret gave twice a month were so vital. It was a proud day when these immigrants could speak enough English to get their "citzen papers" and prove they were foreigners no more.

Meanwhile, Margaret kept up her articles for the *Call*. She soon grew bold enough to venture more explicitly into the field of human reproduction, talking about eggs and ovaries and sperms. For girls like those who wrote to the "Bintel Brief": "Is it a sin to use face powder?" "Shouldn't a girl look beautiful?" this was heady stuff indeed. The series was called *What Every Girl Should Know* and drew many letters of praise and gratitude. But when Margaret announced that her next articles would be on venereal disease, she ran into trouble.

The *Call* was notified by the post office that, if it ran such articles, the entire issue would be suppressed for violating the Comstock Law. So where her column was to have appeared, the paper left a large blank space that said only:

WHAT EVERY GIRL SHOULD KNOW.
BY ORDER OF THE POST OFFICE—NOTHING.

Margaret had never heard of the Comstock Law and was furious when her material did not appear. She flounced into the office and called Mrs. Block cowardly and spineless. Mrs. Block told her to look up the law for herself. She did and found it had very sharp teeth— teeth that would some day bite her hard.

The Comstock Law was passed by Congress in 1873. Its main purpose was to close the mails to "obscene, lewd and lascivious" material, particularly the erotic postcards from abroad which, during the confused post-Civil War period, were flooding the country. Anthony Comstock, its sponsor, made his point by putting on an exhibition of erotic postcards in the senate building, something sure to draw large, curious crowds. But at the last minute he added a rider, branding all information relating to contraception as lewd and lascivious and making anybody giving out such information, even a doctor, subject to a heavy fine plus one to ten years in jail. The bill was pushed through the House and Senate on the last day of a lame-duck Congress, along with 260 other bills that many Congressmen later admitted they hadn't even read.

Comstock was a man obsessed. Born on a Pennsylvania farm of a pious Fundamentalist family where everyone, including the hired hands, had to attend a daily prayer session, as well as drive twenty miles each way in open wagons to attend four Sunday services, he saw everything connected with sex as sinful. His favorite Bible quotation was: "Whosoever looks on a woman to lust after her has already committed adultery in his heart," and he yearned to save souls by keeping them from all temptation.

Once his harsh law was passed, he got the courts to convict owners of dress shops who left naked wax dummies in their windows before redressing them, on the premise that "bare dummies can cause lustful thoughts." He ran an uncompromising campaign against the painting called "September Morn," which showed a chastely posed nude rising from the waves.

He reserved a special fury for doctors who gave contraceptive information. No one could stop them from doing this in their offices, but let a doctor be caught sending a letter through the mail and Comstock was ready to pounce. For this purpose he frankly used decoys. He would write a suspect a letter signed with a woman's name—a letter that told a story of disease, poverty, and despair. If the doctor replied compassionately with a few simple birth-control suggestions, Comstock had his evidence and used it without mercy. He obtained five-year sentences plus large fines for several such doctors.

Comstock was so wily,·not only had he gotten his harsh law passed, but he had gotten himself appointed as a special agent of the post office, with the power to see that it was strictly enforced. Still better, he had fixed things so that, instead of taking a salary, he kept a substantial portion of the fines for himself.

One doctor fought back. Comstock was a big man but this doctor was bigger. When Comstock arrived personally to arrest him, the doctor grabbed him by the scruff of his neck and threw him down the stairs. Comstock bided his time. Many years later he dragged this tired man into court, having trapped him through a decoy letter. By then, the doctor was old and ill. Comstock saw to it that he got ten years in prison at hard labor.

When this outrageous case was reported in the papers, people decided things had gone too far. In 1902 a petition with seventy thousand signatures was presented to President Grover Cleveland, asking him to use his influence to repeal or at least modify the law. Cleveland was ready to try, until his Methodist wife dissuaded him. The law stood firm.

After Margaret read all this, she understood the *Call* position. Besides, the post office later withdrew its objections to her article on venereal disease; and not only was it printed, it eventually became a pamphlet given to the soldiers of the First World War.

Margaret's enthusiasm for Socialism and the *Call* soon faded. In 1912 the New York laundry workers went on strike. When she spoke at a meeting asking them to support a "political action" measure to try to improve their wages and working conditions through legislation rather than through repeated strikes, she was heckled by a woman who stood up angrily and said, "Oh! that legislative stuff! Don't you know we women might be dead and buried if we waited for politicians to right our wrongs?" Always a nervous speaker, this rebuff hurt her so much she complained that her meetings were not well-attended and asked to resign as organizer. The party agreed and figured out a way for her to do this. She would ask for a five-dollar raise, the party would refuse, and she could use the excuse to get out of her job, though she could still retain her party membership.

Because she was in one of her restless stages and couldn't sit still, she decided to switch her allegiance to the I.W.W., if only because she felt more of a kinship with its members who were the outcasts of the working class—the unskilled loggers of the Northwest, the men without skills, or those with only the minimum needed to pick fruit, dig a ditch, or tend a machine in a factory or mill. In a sense, Margaret felt she was an outcast, too. She had never forgotten the priest who had ordered her out of line, or the children who had ostracized her even after she had been confirmed in the Church. She was shocked when she learned how, in one Tennessee mine explosion, 207 unorganized workers died because safety devices were lacking and there wasn't a thing the rest could do about it. When the men protested, the company simply fired them or hired company police to beat them down, while the mass of the public called them "revolutionaries who should be happy to have any jobs at all." Public conscience hadn't been stirred until the infamous Triangle Waist Company fire of March 1911.

The Triangle Waist Company was a factory housed in the top floor of a dilapidated ten-story loft at 22 Washington Place, New York. The company made ladies' shirtwaists, and even on a Saturday, the factory was going full blast. In mid-afternoon over three hundred workers, mostly women, were working at their machines, the floor around them littered with oily rags and odd pieces of material from the cut patterns. Suddenly, the oily rags and floor litter caught fire, and the fire became a raging blaze that spread through the top floors. The panicked women tried to escape by the stairs, but the employers had locked the heavy stair doors to limit the times workers could go to the washrooms. The women, their flimsy clothing now in flames, began to jump out of the windows instead.

Firemen were summoned but were slow in arriving; the safety nets they spread to catch the hysterical women were either too small or too few. More than two hundred women, some of them girls of thirteen or less, burned to death or died as they crashed from the high windows to the pavement below. They were buried in a mass grave. Thousands followed the cortege, yet legal technicalities enabled the owners of the factory to go scot free.

Only a short time before, when some of the Triangle workers had tried to join the International Ladies Garment Workers' Union, they had been fired. The owners used "poor business conditions" as an excuse, though they quickly filled the place of these employees. When the other workers attempted to go on strike as a result, the strike was squelched by hired thugs who beat up the male pickets. Prostitutes, hired to mingle with the female pickets, shouted obscenities, which were labeled "disturbances of the peace," and used as a pretext to arrest some of the pickets. Even then, public sympathy and the courts sided with the owners. The presiding magistrate, in sentencing one picket, cried out, "You are on strike against God!" Only after some wealthy women, with the support of the clergy, bombarded the newspapers with letters that could not be ignored did public conscience become aroused.

It was in the excited after-the-fire atmosphere that the I.W.W. was born.

I.W.W. stood for Industrial Workers of the World. "Big Bill" Haywood, who composed their constitution, believed that only a world organization could be successful against capitalists. He called the deaths of the Tennessee miners and the Triangle shirtwaist-makers "murder with the connivance or deliberate negligence of the capitalist class." He went on to say that the way to fight back was with "any militant direct action they had the power to enforce," including wrecking machines or tearing up railroad tracks so factory deliveries could not be made. He reasoned that direct action was necessary because unskilled or migratory workers who had no financial reserves could not follow the same slow procedure the skilled craft unions used. With bankruptcy a constant threat, they would have to resort to quick direct force whenever possible.

But fighting capitalists through an international union was not the only goal of the I.W.W.; they were also ready to fight the Church and the U.S. flag. The Church, Haywood explained, was an institution designed to offer "pie in the sky" as a substitute for food on earth; one of his slogans was "Pie in the sky—it's a lie." As for the flag, a red one was substituted for the Stars and Stripes with the poetic slogan: "Live and die beneath the scarlet standard high."

All of this had a strong appeal both to Margaret and to the homeless derelicts who often slept on the floors of the I.W.W. halls, making them feel comparatively confident and unafraid for the first time in their lives.

Margaret probably joined the I.W.W. in 1912, but she did not start to work for them immediately. Bill, always fearful for her health, rented a little summer cottage in the Cape Cod seaport town of Provincetown, Massachusetts, a favorite inexpensive gathering place for artists and intellectuals. There Margaret basked in the sun for hours each day, while the children swam or played in the sands.

While their five-year age difference kept Grant and Stuart apart, Grant made up for it by his closeness to Peggy, to whom he clung as to a life-raft. They played and thought together to such an extent that they usually started their sentences with "we." This closeness was especially comforting because Margaret was usually off somewhere, leaving them in charge of neighbors or anyone she could find.

Her favorite "somewhere" was a cottage where she could find her friends, Bill Haywood, Emma Goldman, and Alexander Berkman. In this circle Berkman was known as Sasha, the Russian pet name for Alexander. The group met at Emma and Sasha's place where the discussions centered on marriage versus free love.

Emma held out strongly for free love. She called marriage "a vicious institution which made women into sex-slaves just as capitalism made men into wage-slaves." She thought marriage "institutionalized" women and made them "kitchen-minded" instead of "world-minded." Emma admitted that she had once been foolish enough to get married, but that was before she knew better. She had quickly gotten out of it and decided to have lovers only. She told Margaret that if she also was to become emancipated, she must repudiate marriage and go her own way.

These diatribes upset Bill so much that when he came up weekends he frequently refused even to go near Emma's house. Certainly he was an anarchist, but only to a point. On free love he drew the line. He wanted no one but his Peg.

Bill also opposed Emma's insistence on the morality of assassination. She defended it on the grounds that it was moral as long as the person assassinated was a tyrant who oppressed the working people or was in a *position* to oppress the working people. She boasted how the half-crazed Pole, Czolgosz, who had shot President McKinley in 1901, testified he had done so after hearing a lecture on assassination by Emma Goldman.

Margaret drank this all in uncritically. Freedom for her was an irresistible word. It called up pictures of Isadora Duncan and her "free dance," Amy Lowell and her "free verse," Edna Millay and her "free life" that burnt the candle at both ends. If freedom was making each of these her own woman, it would make Margaret her own woman, too. All it would do, Bill Sanger argued, was make him sick.

Yet theirs was a marriage of tempestuous quarrels and tempestuous reconciliations. They both knew that Margaret was miserable staying home, though what could she do? She was not qualified to work as a trained or registered nurse in a hospital, and without connections, well-paid private duty was hard to come by. When Bill Haywood and the I.W.W. came along, it was only natural for her to grasp at them eagerly, as they offered her a sympathetic cause, excitement, and maybe some money besides, as Fishel's mortgage payments were slow in coming, and sometimes didn't come at all.

The I.W.W. excitement came sooner than expected, in the form of the Lawrence, Massachusetts, textile mill strike.

The Lawrence strike was one of the first of its kind. It started on January 11, 1912, a gray, raw New England day. January 11 was Friday, a payday, the first payday since the Massachusetts legislature had passed a law reducing the working hours for women and children from 56 to 54 hours a week. As the majority of Lawrence's thirty-five thousand workers were women and children, the mill couldn't operate without them, so this meant reducing the hours for the men, too.

Not long before this, the hours had been reduced from 58 to 56 a week, but the owners had continued to pay the same wage. This time, when the employees were told of the law calling for a second reduction, they asked the owners if they would hold the wages steady, but the owners refused to answer. Now without warning the workers found their paychecks lowered in proportion to the two hours less work.

Accurate figures do not exist, but the best estimates place the average weekly wage at Lawrence in 1912 at eight dollars and seventy-six cents a week for men and six dollars for women and children. At this rate, at least two members of a family had to work in order to maintain themselves at the lowest level of decency. This usually meant the father and mother or the father and any child over the age of fourteen. "At the age of 14," wrote Melvin Dubofsky, "Lawrence's typical immigrant child would leave school no matter what his grade or academic standing, and substitute a 6:45 a.m. to 5:30 p.m. mill-day for his 9:00 to 3:00 school-day."

As for housing in Lawrence, all the houses belonged to the mill-owners, and the contractors who built the wooden tenements had jammed them so close together that vermin ran back and forth from one to the other. The rooms were so small that the men built shelves outside the kitchen windows from one house to another so that their wives could store extra food on the outside shelves. This way the women could open the windows and simply reach out and take the food in.

Tuberculosis and pneumonia were rife. In fact, chest infections eventually killed almost seventy percent of the Massachusetts mill-hands, while during the same years, they killed only four percent of the Massachusetts farmers. A reformer who visited Lawrence said: "I have rarely seen in any American city so many shivering men without overcoats as I have seen in that cloth-producing town."

The wage reduction for the two hours of less work each week

amounted only to about twenty-five cents, but under such conditions it
was crucial. Bread was selling at a nickel a loaf, so twenty-five cents
meant five less loaves.

Then, too, the Lawrence workers were mostly newly arrived Poles,
Germans, Italians, and Russians, who, like the New York Jews, spoke
almost no English. Some of them had come off the boats with the words
"Lawrence, Massachusetts" printed on paper bands around their fore-
heads so that the authorities could direct them. But they did know an
envelope containing twenty-five cents less when they saw one. On January 11 a Polish woman was the first to receive one of these thinner envelopes, and she called out angrily, "Short pay!" When the others received their envelopes, they took up the cry. "Short pay! Short pay!"
echoed through the corridors as they walked off the job. Within a few
days twenty thousand workers joined them. They had no plan; they
merely stood around talking and shivering, resolved not to go back until the cut was restored.

There were two obstacles to a strike. First, the various ethnic groups
were divided by language barriers. Second, they had no cash reserves.
At this point, Bill Haywood and other I.W.W. leaders volunteered to
take over. They immediately organized each group separately and sent
out a call to their fellow-nationals throughout the country for funds;
with this money they set up soup kitchens. Then they used their radical connections to solicit funds from all the other labor organizations,
including Socialist groups; they spent these on shoes, fuel, medical as-
sistance, and at least part of the rent. (Mill-owners didn't dare start
wholesale evictions even when no rent was paid, for fear that many of
the workers might leave town. Then when the mills started up again,
they would be left with hardly any workers.) Yet the mill-owners, who
had never before been confronted with this kind of thing, refused to sit
down at the bargaining table since they were sure the workers would
soon have to give in.

Haywood was an excellent newsmaker. He saw to it that the owners'
refusal to bargain was well-publicized, causing more funds to pour in.
When in desperation the owners arrested two Italian labor leaders on a
trumped-up charge of murdering a fellow striker, thousands of dollars
arrived.

Still, funds dropped sharply as week after weary week dragged on. It
was then, on February 6, 1912, that some Italian Socialists in New
York came up with a plan they were sure would get both new publicity

and help fill the treasury. It was a scheme that had succeeded in France, Italy, and Belgium, but had never been tried in America. The idea was to send some of the strikers' children to friendly families outside of Lawrence where they would be fed and cared for until the crisis had passed. The scheme took on at once. The *Call* in particular ran a stirring article asking for volunteer families, and within two days hundreds of letters came in.

Margaret was excited at the idea of helping with what she romantically thought of as a Children's Crusade. Representing herself to the strike committee as a trained nurse, she offered, for a reasonable fee, to help investigate health conditions in the homes of the volunteering New York families, choose the best ones, and then go to Lawrence with three other I.W.W.'s to select the most needy children and escort them down. In Lawrence she looked over the 119 children who had been selected for a trial and gave them the simple medical examination she was qualified to give. On February 11, all was in order.

The plan was to ride by morning train from Lawrence to Boston, march singing through Boston while they made the necessary change from one station to another, then continue their ride down. In New York, they would march from Grand Central Station to Union Square, New York's soapbox center, where speeches would be made for the benefit of the press by Bill Haywood and Elizabeth Gurley Flynn, a fiery orator called the Rebel Girl. Then the children would march a third time to a point from which they would be distributed to the waiting families.

But the walk through snowy Boston took much more time than had been expected; they missed the New York train and had to wait several hours for another. They were due at Grand Central Station at 3 o'clock. When that time came and no children had arrived, the crowd of almost five thousand radicals gathered to greet them were sure the owners had used their company police to stop them from leaving. As other trains arrived without children, the crowd became frightened. It was a bitterly cold day with temperatures close to zero. A brass band played and the crowd waved red flags to keep themselves warm. Finally, at almost seven o'clock, the train chugged in; Margaret and the children stepped out beaming while the cameras rolled.

The crusade was a great success and got a great deal of newspaper coverage. In fact, it got too much. When another exodus was announced, the owners of the mills decided to stop it, come what may. On

February 17, 1912, they posted an order saying that no children could leave Lawrence without their parents' written consent. Then on February 22, when consents had been received, they had the city marshal forbid their departure under any circumstances.

This proved the mill-owners' undoing. For the plan this time was to send the children to Philadelphia as well as to New York, and when a group of Philadelphia Socialists came to Lawrence to fetch them and were told they could not go, a real brawl occurred at the railroad station. The local police closed in on the women and children, clubbed them, and dragged them from the trains. The owners got such a bad press that public-spirited women such as Mrs. Amos Pinchot, wife of the Governor of Pennsylvania, and Mrs. Howard Taft, wife of the President of the United States, became actively interested. In fact, when a congressional committee was created to investigate the mistreatment of the children, Margaret was called to testify; Mrs. Taft was in the audience. Margaret told how emaciated the children were, how the examining doctor found almost all had enlarged tonsils and adenoids, and how she had taken notes on their clothing. In the bitter New England winter only 4 out of 119 had underwear, only 20 were wearing coats, and none had on woolen things of any kind.

This testimony, plus the lack of violence on the part of the strikers, turned the tide in their favor. A week later the owners gave in on the extra twenty-five cents, and all went back to the mill.

Margaret wrote some articles for the *Call* about the strike, saying: "Scratch beneath the skin of the patriot and you find the blood of the exploiter." But then, just as suddenly as she had resigned as a Socialist organizer, she resigned as secretary of the I.W.W. strike committee, saying that she had to find a way of earning more money.

That way came through her sister Ethel, whom she had convinced to leave Corning and come to New York. Ethel's marriage to Jack Byrne had become a shambles. Byrne, Ethel found, could hold neither his liquor nor a job; with their two children, the couple had to live as nonpaying guests in the home of Jack's parents, a home in which the strictest kind of Catholicism was practiced and where they forgave their son everything and his wife nothing. Ethel had stuck it out for a few years, even though Margaret kept writing her quoting Emma Goldman's philosophy: "It is only individuals that count, not families."

Finally, Ethel had left her children with their grandparents and come to New York where she had been accepted at the nurses-training school of New York's prestigious Mt. Sinai Hospital and emerged with the diploma Margaret had coveted so much.

Now Ethel, remaining at Mt. Sinai as a staff nurse, was able to make important connections. She often heard through her patients about wealthy women who still preferred to give birth at home and were prepared to pay well for someone to serve as a midwife, then stay on for a month or so as baby nurse. As often as she could, she got Margaret the double job.

Working as a midwife again, Margaret found she enjoyed it as much as ever; in no time she was working for the Visiting Nurses Association of the lower East Side as well.

The Visiting Nurses Association was a group of public nurses sent out by the Henry Street Settlement to take care of poverty-stricken women. They went into the homes of women too ill to look after themselves, rubbed their backs, changed their beds, cooked simple meals, and quieted the children. But their main task was to see their patients through the ordeal of childbirth in tenements where conditions were, if possible, more horrible than in Lawrence.

In one teeming district made up of the few blocks between Fourteenth Street and East Broadway, five hundred thousand people were living in buildings designed for one hundred; they crowded in seven or eight to a room, sleeping on wooden doors unscrewed from hinges each night and stretched across chairs, or horizontally on beds, or on the bare floors. With no knowledge of birth control, a fertile woman could get pregnant practically every year, increasing the floor and door sleepers at an alarming rate. As a result, when a woman didn't have the price of an abortionist, she would try to abort herself, using a steel knitting needle, an umbrella tip, or a soda bottle cap—any instrument sharp enough to bring on the terrible cramps and severe bleeding that emptied her womb.

On a hot summer afternoon in 1912, Margaret was hastily summoned to the fetid room of a woman named Sadie Sachs. Sadie, twenty-seven and pregnant again, had tried to abort herself and was hemorrhaging badly; Margaret could do nothing except run to fetch a doctor. After hours of work he was able to stop the flow. Margaret tells in her autobiography how, as the doctor was leaving, Sadie called to him despairingly: "Another thing like this will finish me, I suppose?" The doctor did not answer, but continued walking away. "Then tell me how to prevent it," Sadie pleaded. "Tell me the secret, please!" The doctor turned on his heel and answered brusquely: "Oh, so you want to have your cake and eat it too, do you? The secret is, tell Jake to sleep on the roof."

Sadie now pleaded with Margaret. "You tell me the secret then. Oh, please, PLEASE." But Margaret knew few "secrets." She knew about condoms, but that meant persuading a husband to wear one, a difficult task in a neighborhood where buying condoms would mean admitting to having frequent relations with his wife, a subject simply not talked about. Besides, condoms cost money; desire was immediate, and to a husband, nine months was very far away. Margaret also knew about douching, but how could a wife douche when no "nice woman" could possibly be seen sneaking through the halls to the only toilet, douche bag in hand? The oldest method of all, withdrawal, was popularly supposed to be bad for the health, and a woman had troubles enough without asking for *that*.

Evidently Jake chose neither to sleep on the roof, nor use a condom, nor withdraw. One night a few months later Margaret was called back to the same room. Sadie Sachs, pregnant again, had once more tried to abort herself. This time she was hemorrhaging so badly Margaret did not have time to fetch a doctor. She died within minutes, and as Margaret folded Sadie's thin hands across her breast and drew the sheet over her pale face, Jake walked up and down the room pulling at his hair like an insane man, crying: "Oh my God! Oh my God!"

As Margaret tells the story in her autobiography:

I left him pacing desperately back and forth, and for hours myself walked and walked and walked through the hushed streets. When I finally arrived home and let myself quietly in, all the household was sleeping. I looked out my window and down upon the dimly lighted city. Its pains and griefs crowded in upon me, a moving picture rolled before my eyes with photographic clearness: women writhing in travail to bring forth little babies; the babies themselves naked and hungry, wrapped in newspapers to keep them from the cold; six-year-old children with pinched, pale, wrinkled faces, old in concentrated wretchedness, pushed into gray and fetid cellars, crouching on stone floors, their small scrawny hands scuttling through rags, making lamp shades, artificial flowers; white coffins, black coffins, coffins, coffins interminably passing in never-ending succession. The scenes piled one upon another on another. I could bear it no longer.

As I stood there the darkness faded. The sun came up and threw its reflection over the house tops. It was the dawn of a new day in my life also. The doubt and questioning, the experimenting and trying, were now to be put behind me. I knew I could not go back merely to keeping people alive.

I went to bed, knowing that no matter what it might cost, I was finished with palliatives and superficial cures; I was resolved to seek out the root of evil, to do something to change the destiny of mothers whose miseries were vast as the sky.

The trouble with Margaret's story, which ends with a description of her stripping off her nurse's uniform, throwing her nurse's bag across the room, and deciding to devote herself immediately to the cause of birth control, is that it didn't happen quite that way. Almost four years were to pass before she dedicated herself entirely to birth control— four very busy years in which she was to write more articles for the *Call*, march in picket lines, start a newspaper of her own, escape to Europe as a fugitive from justice, and see her beloved daughter Peggy die.

During these four years, she learned more about newsmaking techniques. She started in the spring of 1913 by marching in the picket lines of the Paterson, New Jersey, silk strike.

On February 12, 1913, fifteen hundred men and women of the Duplan Silk Company of Hazelton, Pennsylvania, marched out and called for I.W.W. help. By February 23 the strike had spread to the much larger silk mills of Paterson. By now over eleven thousand workers were involved, and Bill Haywood sent Jessie Ashley and Margaret Sanger down to Hazelton to organize the picket lines. Each took turns marching at the head.

On the morning of April 7, Margaret and some other pickets were arrested. Margaret complained loudly to the magistrate about her unlawful arrest, for the benefit of attending reporters, and was fined five dollars. She refused to pay. Sentenced to five days in jail instead, she declared she would be happy to go to jail and was furious when a sympathizer stepped forward and paid her fine; going to jail, she figured, would make far better news.

Three days later she was arrested for picketing again. As the arresting officer led her off, a bystander made what the newspaper accounts called a "wisecrack" at her. She demanded that the officer also arrest the wisecracker, but he refused. Margaret jeered to the officer, "Then I'll slap your face instead," and proceeded to move toward him but he caught her arm and held her back as she swung.

In court she called her swing "direct action," insisting that: "There is no law or court today where 'political action' rules." She was released, this time without a fine, but she got bad publicity from her attempted slap. Haywood regretfully concluded that her usefulness at Hazelton had ended. He transferred her to Paterson instead.

In Paterson the strike was being mercilessly put down by the militia of the state and city governments. Margaret marched up and down the picket lines lecturing on birth control to the strikers, then helped bring a group of Paterson children to New York to be distributed to waiting families as she had done during the Lawrence strike. But bringing the children did not generate the same public appeal as it had before. Things began to look hopeless. The public was apathetic, the mill-owners were strong, and I.W.W. funds were running extremely low.

At this point John Reed, a writer and arrested picketer, came up with an idea which he was sure would raise a lot of money. He would write a pageant of the strike and stage it at Madison Square Garden with real strikers as the actors. The date was set for June 7, 1913. The Garden was rented with money supplied by Mabel Dodge, a wealthy friend of Reed's, and fifteen hundred strikers were brought in from Paterson. They first paraded by daylight from the railroad station to Washington Square and next by torchlight up Fifth Avenue to the Garden, while a brass band played the "Marseillaise." Then they reenacted the strike. The *Call* described it as a moving and powerful spectacle, but the benches of the vast Garden were empty. When it was over they found they had lost two thousand dollars.

Broke and dispirited, the workers had no choice but to go back to the mills with none of their demands met. Despondent, too, Margaret gave up working for the I.W.W. and gladly went off to Provincetown when Bill sent her there to rest.

MARRIAGE RIFT

Back from Provincetown, Margaret soon found a new interest. She started attending the "Evenings" given by Mabel Dodge in her Greenwich Village salon.

Mabel Dodge was a wealthy divorcée recently returned from Europe where she had spent most of her married life. France and Italy were places of glamour and romance to her, but at the insistence of her family she had come home to have her son educated in America. She sent the boy off to school and leased two floors of a brownstone on the corner of Fifth Avenue and Ninth Street, which she decorated all in white—white velvet chairs, white draperies, white woodwork and walls—quite unusual for the times. There she started a salon modeled on those in Paris, declaring that she was "empty" and had to be filled with other people's ideas. Her series of Evenings included intellectuals, radicals, and creative people of every kind as her guests. Each Evening centered around a particular theme; there were political evenings, poetry evenings, drama evenings, art evenings. At each, Mrs. Dodge, in flowing white chiffon, sat regally in an armchair until the moment of midnight, when a sumptuous supper was served.

Since most of her guests were accustomed to a late supper of little more than coffee and cake, and her tables were heaped with the finest meats, poultry, and French pastries, her invitations were rarely turned down. Her parties became a Village institution. Edgar Lee

Masters, who had recently published the *Spoon River Anthology,* was glad to lead a poetry evening; Gordon Craig, the stage designer, hastened downtown to conduct a drama evening. Mrs. Dodge soon declared she felt empty no more.

Several of the very best Evenings were when Margaret held forth on the subject of sex. Although free love had been practiced quietly for years by many intellectuals in the Village, it was being openly, even flagrantly pursued. Eugene O'Neill, after a marriage so casual he hardly bothered to mention it, took on one mistress after another, boasting about them at his favorite hangout, The Hell Hole. Edna St. Vincent Millay hopped gaily from bed to bed and wrote about it in her poems. Floyd Dell and Max Eastman championed it in their magazine *The Masses.* And, long ahead of her time, Mabel Dodge was looking for the "perfect orgasm." When she found it with an American Indian named Tony Luhan, she retired contentedly with him to his reservation, though they had hardly anything to say to each other. Good sex was enough.

But few championed sexual freedom as ardently as Margaret Sanger. She had absorbed many of her ideas from Emma Goldman and Sasha Berkman who taught special classes on the subject at the Ferrer School. There they spoke intoxicatingly of the "dignity of the human personality and the need for unfettered self-expression," enthusiastically endorsing the Swedish feminist, Ellen Key, who claimed that "the most sacred thing in life is individual desire, with special emphasis on sex-desire." Margaret devoured their words. "I love being ravaged by romances," she wrote in her 1914 journal. To her, emotion was a higher force than reason. "Emotion is that which urges from within, without consciousness of fear or of consequences."

Mabel Dodge listened avidly when Margaret spoke. She wrote in her memoirs:

> Margaret Sanger was a Madonna type of woman, with soft brown hair parted over a quiet brow, and crystal-clear brown eyes. . . . It was she who introduced us all to the idea of Birth Control and it, along with other related ideas about sex, became her passion. It was as if she had been more or less arbitrarily chosen by the powers that be to voice a new gospel of not only sex-knowledge in regard to conception, but sex-knowledge about copulation and its intrinsic importance.

She was the first person I ever knew who was openly an ardent propagandist for the joys of the flesh. This in those days was radical indeed when the sense of [sin was still so indubitably mixed with the sense of] pleasure. . . . Margaret Sanger personally set out to rehabilitate sex. . . . She was one of its first conscious promulgators.

Mrs. Dodge particularly remembered a night when she had given a small dinner party just for Margaret and another friend, and the three of them sat for hours talking about the possibilities of the body.

As she sat there, serene and quiet, and unfolded the mysteries and mightinesses of physical love, it seemed to us we had never [known it before as a sacred and at the same time a scientific reality.

Love I had] known, and pleasures of the flesh, but usually there had been a certain hidden, forbidden something in my feeling about it that made it seem stolen from life, instead of a means to the growth of the soul.

Margaret Sanger made it appear as the first duty of men and women. Not just anyhow, anywhere, not any man and any woman, but the conscious careful selection of a lover that is the mate, if only for an hour, or for a lifetime maybe.

The Evenings on which Margaret spoke publicly of these things delighted everyone except Bill Sanger. He would sit in a corner trembling with apprehension. He had kept her from going to Provincetown the summer before in order to keep her away from Goldman and her crowd, because he was sick of hearing Emma hammer away at the idea that marriage and fidelity were among the chief curses of mankind. Now he wrote: "Do you know how this last year has impressed me? That the so-called Labor Revolutionary Movement is not noble but an excuse for a Saturnalia of sex."

One unexpected benefit did come to Bill from the Dodge Evenings, however. He made his decision to go to Paris to realize his dream of becoming a modern painter.

Before 1913 there had been practically no modern art movement in America. The one man who had tried to break away from the academic conventions was Alfred Stieglitz, the noted photographer. In 1913 he arranged an exhibit of work by himself, his wife, the painter Georgia O'Keeffe, and a few other moderns. "People came and gaped," Stieglitz told Mrs. Dodge. "But hardly a single picture was sold."

It was then that a free-lance publicity man, James Gregg, came up with a bright idea. He would promote a really big modern art show. First he interested Arthur Davies, an artist who painted "strange poetic figures wandering in allegorical scenes," as Mrs. Dodge described them. Next he approached John Marin, the well-known watercolorist, and soon was in excited correspondence with Leo Stein, brother of Gertrude Stein, in Paris. Stein lined up works by Picasso and Matisse, and Stieglitz persuaded Mrs. Dodge, who viewed it all as "an escapade, an adventure," to underwrite the show. The result was the famous Armory Show of 1913, the talk for months of the American art world.

Bill Sanger visited the Armory Show again and again, becoming more convinced each time that he could paint as well as the artists on display. If only he could get the chance to work at it full time!

The main rub as usual was money. Bill always managed somehow to send Margaret and the children away during the summer months to escape the city heat, but with a mother to support as well, he was hard pressed for funds. If he was ever to get to Paris to study and work, even for a few months, he would have some tall figuring to do.

Meanwhile another summer arrived, and this time Margaret insisted on going back to Provincetown to join Emma. She took her sister Ethel along to help look after the children, explaining that taking Ethel would give her time to go to the libraries in Boston and New York and start reading up on contraception to enhance what little she knew.

Ethel was happy to have a vacation at the seashore, and Margaret soon started running to libraries. (The Comstock law stopped information only from going through the mails; it did not include articles in medical journals or medical books, nor did it remove anything already on library shelves.) Never trained in research, Margaret seemed to have missed much of the available material. It didn't matter too much, anyway. As for recent material in medical books and articles, she knew as much as they did. As for the old material, she knew more. But the very fact that the material was resting quietly on library shelves meant that the mass of uneducated people, who needed it most, didn't see it. It would take someone like herself to bring the whole subject of sex and birth control into the open, where she felt it belonged.

It is almost certain, too, that during the summer of 1913 she began to put her sex theories into practice by taking a lover. Later, musing on her life, she told a confidante about "an affair in Provincetown in 1913 that really set me free."

It is difficult to determine who Margaret's 1913 lover was because the Provincetown group almost always referred to each other by initials. There are, however, several letters in the files from a journalist, Walter Roberts, who wrote Margaret saying how surprisingly wonderful it was to wake up in the morning and find her lying close beside him.

In any event, Bill was furious when he came up to Provincetown weekends and almost never found Margaret at home. A delightful picture shows six-year-old Grant and four-year-old Peggy dressed in Greek costume for a local pageant. But Bill had dressed them, and Bill had taken the picture because, as Grant said: "Mother was seldom around. She just left us with anybody handy, and ran off we didn't know where." Margaret was not around even when Peggy caught polio in Provincetown, leaving her with a permanently damaged ankle and a shrunken leg.

Bill and Margaret quarreled violently over her taking a lover and her neglect of her sick child. They decided to make up on a second honeymoon in Paris, with the children going along.

The trip, they hoped, would accomplish many things. First, Bill, who knew nothing about medicine, thought the sea voyage would restore Peggy to perfect health. Second, Paris was the artist's mecca; if he could paint anywhere, it was there. Third, Margaret could learn more about contraception. Bill Haywood had told her many times, "If you want to know about contraception, go to Paris. The French have known things for years that we don't." So Bill Sanger began planning how to get the cash for the trip.

His problem was solved, when Fishel, the man who had bought their Hastings home and who had been extremely irregular in mortgage payments, came across with a large sum in August. Bill received it in Boston where he was working on a drafting project for his firm, a job he hoped would be finished in October, when they planned to sail.

It is probably just as well they had to wait until October, because Bill's mother died in September. He came to New York from Boston, alone, for the funeral. While there had never been any tension be-

tween his wife and his mother, Margaret was, as usual, off somewhere
else. Back in Boston, even while mourning his mother's death, Bill
wrote Margaret almost every day.

I just love to have you near me. Loved one, you are a real woman. I wish we could see all the lovely and the beautiful together.
. . . Sidestep New York and the radicals for awhile, and get a
healthy point of view not mixed up with sexuality under cover of
Revolution. . . . If you will get out of the quagmire of mysticism,
you will cast your sunshine again.

A week later he was despondent because Margaret had not answered
him.

The Sangers sailed to Europe at the end of October, going by way of
Liverpool instead of straight to Paris, because at the last moment the
Call had commissioned Margaret to do some articles on Glasgow, a city
then experimenting with socialism in the form of municipal low-cost
housing for the poor. But Margaret found that the new development
contained very small apartments; large families were not accepted.
And since the majority of the poor in Glasgow had large families, the
housing was not available to them. Margaret was more sure then ever
that without contraception no socialist scheme had a chance for success.

The Sangers left Glasgow in mid-November, traveling by third-class
train to Dover, then, after a miserable Channel crossing, went on to
Paris. Exhausted, they stayed at a Left Bank hotel until Bill could find
a cheap studio. Margaret, who had always hated and feared the cold
since her early TB flareups, found Paris almost as cold as Glasgow. But
she felt better when she and Bill began to meet important painters like
Monet, Matisse, and Modigliani. She felt even better when she heard
that Bill Haywood and Jessie Ashley were in Paris, eager to introduce
her to old-time radicals like Victor Davé. Through Victor Dave she met
doctors, midwives, and druggists who were willing to talk to her about
contraception. From them she learned that French women had long
known about certain simple chemicals which slowed the passage of the
sperm after it entered the vagina. Many Paris druggists were making
and selling glycerin suppositories containing these chemicals, while
women in rural districts were making their own, handing down the instructions to daughters just before their wedding day. Margaret also

learned about diaphragms, the rubber contraceptives that fitted over the neck of the uterus. Though these had originated in Holland, they had been used in France for over forty years. She got hold of some diaphragms and experimented with flattening them and hiding them under her girdle. This way, she believed, she could smuggle them past the U.S. customs.

Though they had been in Paris only a month, she told Bill she wanted to return to the States immediately to spread this exciting new information. In fact, she had already booked passage for herself and the children. Bill had counted on their staying away six months at least. They had another violent quarrel over this change of plans, and each stood firm. Bill refused to go home; Margaret refused to remain.

Though it meant spending the Christmas and New Year holidays on board ship instead of with her husband, Margaret sailed for home on December 23, 1913. Bill waved them goodbye as cheerfully as he could, though with deep foreboding and a heavy heart.

7

THE WOMAN REBEL

As usual, Bill was the peacemaker. On December 28, 1913, he wrote Margaret a letter explaining his decision to stay in Paris.

> I feel I will come through somehow. I want my work to count so that you will have the leisure to do your work without economic consideration, and be relieved of the direct care of the kiddies. Loved one, I don't want you to waste your life on anyone. I just want to have the privilege of helping you to be *yourself*.

On January 2, 1914, he wrote again. He had talked to Victor Dave about an English publisher for *What Every Girl Should Know*. Dave had also told him that there was an English group in Paris supporting not only woman's suffrage but sexual equality as well. He would look into these matters, too.

Again, he returned to the subject of their poverty and of his deep love for her. "It seems ages since you left. It's no joke to land in cold New York with a family and no money. Well, you are a brave dear woman."

He was painting straight through from 8 A.M. to 4 P.M. in order to catch the light. He asked her to write telling him her real thoughts. Had any one else seriously come into her life to make her leave so hastily? Maybe he could have kept Stuart with him and sent him to school in Paris. "It would have been a connecting link."

64

Bill received an answer from Margaret on January 11. It was written from an apartment at 4 Perry Street in Greenwich Village and was full of complaints. Now that she had full care of the children, her nervous malady had returned; she needed to be alone during the day for the sake of her intellectual development, but she would probably have to go back to nursing to earn money.

Two weeks later Bill wrote again about their marriage. Everyone in Paris seemed to know about their quarrel of the summer before; there was much gossip about their future relationship. He was worried that the radicals were associating her with a "J.K." and gossip had convinced him she had taken a lover. As to her suggestion that he even things up by taking a French mistress, he was aghast.

> I will let my name be associated with no other woman. . . . I would be amiss to all the fine emotion that surges within me if I fell from grace. . . . It cannot be, that's all. I still hold that intercourse is not to be classed with a square meal, to be partaken of at will, irrespective of the consequences. No other woman has interested me in the past or now, and until a woman comes across my life who means *more* to me than you do I stand on the old ground.

He went on to ponder the anarchist philosophy of sex, which was very different from his own.

> Personalities are crowding around you, and if you follow the anarchist teaching, it would mean you must *know these personalities in all relations*. Well, I have not yet adapted myself to this.
>
> Sometime I wonder whether I am not too constant and appear to narrow your life to knowing completely only one personality. But this I shall express again and again—that to be *alone* linked with your life is the jewel of my inspiration. You speak, dear love, that in our life together you have given me the best and deepest love—yes, and I have felt it—that you were the only woman who ever cared to understand me.
>
> But you have advanced sexually—you once said that you need to be in different relations (with men) as a service for the women of your time. To all this I have no answer.

Though Bill eventually burned most of Margaret's letters, their contents are usually clear from her diaries, or from his replies. In February 1914 she said she had not written him lately because she had been depressed to the point of toying with suicide. Bill's answer recalled that she had had a similar bout of depression in Provincetown after Peggy's illness. "It was awful. I hope you may never have one like it again."

Margaret replied with another complaining letter. Her present upset stemmed from the fact that, though she was at last getting along with her plans to publish a paper of her own, she was unsure of just what kind of paper it would be. Her primary goal was to make women, especially working women, more rebellious—rebellious about having to work such long hours in factories, rebellious about having to bear so many children, rebellious about having to be subservient to men. Still, she wasn't sure; she would have to feel her way.

Emma Goldman was making a living from her angry, defiant paper *Mother Earth.* Max Eastman was also doing well with his quiet, fun-poking paper *The Masses.* (*The Masses* had recently poked fun at Comstock with a cartoon of a policeman dragging a naked woman into court. "This woman," the caption read, "has just given birth to a naked baby.")

Margaret was beginning to favor the angry approach, because it seemed easier to do. But any kind of paper took money to start, and she was hard pressed. She would have to move from the exciting Village to the dull Bronx, which she hated. But the Bronx was cheaper, and her only sources of money were loans from her sisters or occasional nursing jobs.

At the end of February, Margaret told Bill she had found a dingy flat for herself and the children. She had brightened up the place with yellow draperies, further beautified it by hanging the pictures John Sloan and John Marin had presented to Bill after the Armory Show, and altogether made the place as cheerful as she could.

Now she was looking for a printer, which was difficult. Most of the printers she talked to refused to have anything to do with her project, but her radical friends had finally found a party member who had promised secretly to help her. Equally important, her radical friends had agreed to publicize her paper at their meetings and get her some advance subscriptions at a dollar a year for twelve issues, or fifty cents for six. Happily, almost a thousand women were sending in money, mainly to get the contraceptive advice they had been led to expect it would give.

With a nest egg of several hundred dollars from these subscriptions, plus loans from Jessie Ashley and Mabel Dodge, she was almost ready to start. But first she had to get Stuart out of the house; he and Grant fought almost constantly. Stuart was athletic and outgoing, Grant shy and nervous. As a result, they never seemed able to agree. She soon sent Stuart off to school, which at least kept him separated from Grant during the day.

Now Margaret was free to sketch out her first issue, then send out announcements to the press saying it would be an eight-page sheet called *The Woman Rebel,* with the slogan of "No Gods! No Masters!" taken from the I.W.W. slogan "No God! No Master!" Underneath the main slogan she was adding "a paper of militant thought, written, edited and published by Margaret H. Sanger of 34 Post Avenue, Bronx, New York."

The Woman Rebel, obviously not sure of what it wanted to accomplish, made its bow in March 1914. On page one there was a long rambling editorial written by Margaret, called "The Aim."

This paper will not be the champion of any "ism." All rebel women are invited to contribute to its columns.

The majority of papers usually adjust themselves to ideas of their readers but *The Woman Rebel* will obstinately refuse to be adjusted.

The aim of this paper will be to stimulate working women to think for themselves and to build up a conscious fighting character.

An early feature will be a series of articles written by the editor for girls from fourteen to eighteen years of age. In this present chaos of sex atmosphere it is difficult for the girl of this uncertain age to know just what to do or really what constitutes clean living without prudishness. If it were possible to get the truth from girls who work in prostitution to-day, I believe most of them would tell you that the first sex experience was with a sweetheart or through the desire for a sweetheart or something impelling within themselves, the nature of which they knew not, neither could they control.

It is these and kindred facts upon which *The Woman Rebel* will dwell and from which it is hoped the young girl will derive some knowledge of her nature.

It will also be the aim of *The Woman Rebel* to advocate the prevention of conception and to impart such knowledge. Other subjects, including the slavery through motherhood, through things, the home, public opinion and so forth, will be dealt with. And at all times *The Woman Rebel* will strenuously advocate economic emancipation.

Margaret was, therefore, taking on not only contraception, sex, and socialism, but marriage as well. An article by Emma Goldman—the only piece by her great rival that Margaret ever printed—denounced marriage as a "degenerate institution."

Margaret's next piece was followed by one taken directly from I.W.W. material. It ended with the plea: "One big strike for the eight-hour day!"

In the next issue she ran an article called "The Prevention of Conception." Beginning with the question: "Is there any reason why women should not receive clean, harmless, scientific knowledge on how to prevent conception?" she went on to tell her readers to demand this knowledge. Prevention of conception, she said, would not only free women from unwanted pregnancies, but would reduce the number of workers, and frighten the capitalist class. Equally important, it would defy the Comstock law. "No plagues, famines, or wars could ever frighten the capitalist class so much as the universal practice of the prevention of conception. . . . A law exists forbidding the imparting of information on this subject, the penalty being several years imprisonment. Is it not time to defy this law?"

Though no advice on contraceptives was included, its very mention and the reference to the law against it was what Comstock had been waiting for. He had been watching *The Woman Rebel* from the beginning, and quickly ran to the Postmaster General, S. Marshall Snowden, to bar the paper from the mails. Though his grounds were extremely flimsy, the Postmaster General went along anyway. When Margaret demanded his reasons, Snowden answered evasively . . . merely characterizing the whole paper as "indecent, lewd, lascivious and obscene."

Margaret countered by becoming more defiant. In the April issue she ran a special boxed statement in capital letters headed *The Post Office Ban*:

THE WOMAN REBEL FEELS PROUD THAT THE POST OFFICE AUTHORITIES DID NOT APPROVE OF HER. SHE SHALL BLUSH WITH SHAME IF EVER SHE BE APPROVED OF BY OFFICIALISM OR "COMSTOCKISM."

Another special box was called "A Woman's Duty"; it too was run in all capitals:

A WOMAN'S DUTY: TO BREED LARGE FAMILIES IN ACCORDANCE WITH SECTION 211 OF THE CRIMINAL CODE AS AMENDED BY THE ACT OF MARCH 14, 1911.

The rest of the April issue consisted mostly of articles supporting socialism and condemning capitalism. Since she avoided the subject of contraception, the Postmaster General let the issue go through.

But Margaret was eager to fight; she was, after all, her father's daughter. In the May issue she featured a high-pitched article called "Cannibals":

Compared with the diseased, perverted, hypocritical ghouls of American "civilization," cannibals strike you as simple healthy people. If they feed and fatten upon the charred flesh of human beings, cannibals at least do not hide behind the sickening smirk of the Church and the Y.W.C.A. They are open, frank and straight-forward in their search for food. They eat their victims outright . . .

Their tastes are not so fastidious, so refined, so Christian, as those of our great American coal operators, those leering, bloody hyenas of the human race who smear themselves with the stinking money of Charity to attract those foul flies of religion who spread pollution throughout the land.

Workingwomen! Keep away from the Y.W.C.A. as you would from a pesthouse.

Remember Ludlow! Remember the men and women and chil-

dren who were sacrificed in order that John D. Rockefeller, Jr.,
might continue his noble career of charity and philanthropy as a
supporter of the Christian faith.

Steer clear of those brothels of the Spirit and morgues of Freedom!

Two articles in the same issue mentioned contraception indirectly.
One was called "Are Preventive Means Injurious?" and assured her
readers that, contrary to popular belief, they were not. The other was
headed "Can You Afford a Large Family?" and said that few could.
Both articles were written in a manner that could hardly be called
"vile and indecent" by anyone but a Comstock. But then she added fuel
to her argument by adding in "A Woman's Duty":

A WOMAN'S DUTY: TO LOOK THE WHOLE WORLD IN
THE FACE WITH A GO-TO-HELL LOOK IN THE EYES, TO
HAVE AN IDEAL, TO SPEAK AND ACT IN DEFIANCE OF
CONVENTION.

As if this wasn't enough, it was followed by an article that spoke
about the dangers of abortion, especially a self-induced abortion,
which could kill a woman. The words about abortion stirred Comstock
to action. Once more he ran to the Postmaster General. Once more the
Postmaster General obliged. The May issue was called "lewd, vile,
filthy and indecent," and was suppressed.

A few copies of this issue were slipped through the mails by Margaret and her friends, who ran all over town depositing bundles of them
in so many mailboxes that it was impossible to catch them all. But the
bulk was seized.

Margaret was now boiling. She wrote to Postmaster Snowden demanding to know which articles had caused the magazine to be seized,
only to receive another evasive reply. At a loss as to what to do next,
she rushed a copy of the May issue to Bill in Paris. He liked it because
his Peg had produced it. But he was worried. Being a rebel was one
thing; breaking a law which might land her in jail for many years was
another. He begged her to tone down her material and be more careful.
Meanwhile he said he would like to do some cartoons for *The Woman
Rebel* so that he might become a part of it. In fact, he had already done
one cartoon showing a woman holding two children by the hand, look-

ing confidently toward the future. He enclosed it, hoping Margaret
would like it well enough to use it.

Margaret emphatically did not like it. She wrote him saying that the
only kind of cartoon she wanted was one of a woman lying prone on the
ground with a brute standing above her, trampling on her. Bill answered that, deeply hurt, he was abandoning the whole cartoon idea;
drawings of women being trampled on by men were not in his line.

What hurt him even more were new rumors he had heard about
Margaret's personal life. Her name was being linked, first, with a well-
known radical writer, then with a Greek anarchist, then with a "notorious free lover." He sent her one of his long, worried letters, closing
with talk of coming home if the rumors didn't stop.

But Margaret was in no mood either to tone down *The Woman Rebel*
or to discard her present lover. At the age of thirty-seven when she was
too tired or disturbed to sleep, only one thing seemed to relax her, and
that was sexual intercourse. If Bill wanted to stay celibate for a while,
let him. She knew what she wanted and would do as she pleased.

But with two out of three issues of her paper suppressed, she was in
deep trouble. Almost half of her subscribers were demanding their
money back, as most of them had received only a single copy. They also
felt defrauded because they hadn't gotten any of the expected contraceptive information, which, by now, Margaret was undoubtedly
afraid to give. The socialist and anarchist material was nothing new;
they weren't paying for *that.*

Even her staunchest friends began to waver. Jessie Ashley and Mabel Dodge refused to lend her any more money. Max Eastman, formerly an ardent supporter, became less enthusiastic, too. After reading
her diatribes against marriage, the Y.W.C.A., and John D. Rockefeller
all jumbled together, he ran an editorial in *The Masses* calling her
writing "over-excited and over-intolerant . . . the blare of rebellion
for rebellion's sake." At the end he tried to soften his editorial by concluding: "We will still hail the virtue of the fight and call it a bargain
at the price." But his point had been made.

Desperate and depressed, Margaret sent out a general press release
that included copies of all the issues of *The Woman Rebel,* asking if
suppression of some of them hadn't been unfair. Counting on the traditional backing of free speech by the press, she hoped in this way to rally new supporters to her cause. The results were the opposite. The
United Press Association called damning attention to her credo: "Look

the whole world in the face with a go-to-hell look in your eyes." The *New York Journal American* hit at another credo: "Rebel women claim the following Rights: The Right to be Lazy. The Right to be an Unmarried Mother. The Right to Destroy. The Right to Create. The Right to Live and the Right to Love." The right to be lazy, they said, was nonsense, and no one had the right to destroy. The *Pittsburgh Sun* ran an editorial calling her paper "a mass of dirty slush," ending with the sweeping sentence, "The whole thing is nauseating!"

Instead of achieving the image of savior, she was achieving that of a vulgar scold.

Clearly, unless she got a new slant for her paper, or better publicity for herself, her whole project was doomed.

She called a council of war. Several men had been helping her with *The Woman Rebel.* Among them were Otto Bobsein, an old-time Socialist who was doing book reviews for her; Robert Allerton Parker, a professional journalist who had come East from San Francisco to try to become a playwright like his friend, Eugene O'Neill, but hadn't made it; and Ed Mylius, a nephew of Henry James, who had published an anarchist paper in Paris which so cruelly lampooned King Edward V of England that the king decided to sue him for libel, making him a hero for his daring after he had fled to America.

Margaret invited these men to her apartment for an emergency conference. They decided that the first thing she needed was a catchier name for contraception than the delicate "preventive means." They considered "conscious generation," "Neo-Malthusianism," and several others. Robert Parker offered the final suggestion. He was a polio victim who was studying Yoga, in which control is an essential feature, hoping that control might help him with his partly paralyzed hand. It occurred to him that control might apply to birth as well. "Birth control," he mused. "Birth Control . . . I think I like it." They all liked it. As they put on their hats and left, they agreed that birth control was the best name for the movement.

When she became famous, Margaret would usually manage to mention when interviewed that she had invented the term. Robert Parker was gallant however: "I may have coined the words, but Margaret passed them around the world. Without her, birth control would never have become household words."

Yet a new name was only the beginning. Most of all, though she was still doing occasional nursing, Margaret needed money. She wrote to Bill asking for some, but he answered that he was even poorer than she was.

Luckily at this point Fishel, the man who had bought their Hastings house, came through with a mortgage payment that temporarily eased the situation for both. Bill was able to buy himself a cheap suit he badly needed, and Margaret was able to pay her rent, settle some pressing printer's bills, and get out another issue.

This issue contained more attacks on marriage, plus a diatribe maligning the Postmaster for banning the last issue. She urged her readers not to be disheartened; she would get future papers to them somehow; she would "under no circumstances promise to be good."

When this issue was allowed to go through the mails, Margaret's spirits went up. Bill Sanger's did not. Although he was writing regularly, she was hardly bothering to answer, except to tell him that she really would be happier if he did not write so often, as she preferred to be left alone "to develop myself intellectually." His replies were a mixture of anger and concern.

> You speak of being alone and wanting to be alone and to be left alone. All I can say, sweetheart, I wish by all that's good and holy that you *are* left alone. Indeed, I shall be glad when you finally inform me that you are finally left with yourself. Since you landed on American soil the opposite has been the case.

When she did not answer this letter at all, and he heard stories of her going around with still another anarchist whom he identified only with initials, he sent her a fiery letter:

> I want you to pull away from the whole anarchist crew—I mean *every one*. Propagate an idea no matter how revolutionary, I would not care what the world might think. But unless a relationship is based on real love, a love that is real and lasting I deny its right to exist in your life. The incident with ETH simply unnerves me. I would not have a finger pointed at you. The hour has come when you must make a clean sweep of the whole crew.

She shot off a short note reminding him again, almost cruelly, that he could even things up by getting himself a French mistress. He was aghast. "I am an anarchist, true, but I also am a monogamist. And if that makes me a conservative, then I am a conservative!"

By now the six months in Paris that Bill had allowed himself were almost over, yet he couldn't make up his mind whether to stay or come home. Theoretically, he felt he should return: "I don't feel my art is as important as one would imply. Yours is the grand fine spirit. How can you run a paper, nurse, and start a birth control league all at once . . . I want to return, to relieve you of the care of the children since this is the crucial time for you."

Still, he lingered on, though things were coming to a climax for Margaret. When the Postmaster General kept refusing to tell her which articles had led to his barring of her paper from the mails, she lost her head. She decided to run some articles in the August issue so obviously unacceptable that he would *have* to tell her what he objected to.

The first of these was signed by an Alice Groff and called "The Marriage Bed."

The marriage bed is the most degenerating influence of the social order, as to life in all of its forms—biological, psychological, sociological—for man, woman and child.

In order to attain the highest development of the sex-nature, the woman should not have the good of a master. Such good destroys her native spontaneity . . . or it arouses bitter antagonism and rebellion—as it prevents the development of her sex-nature to higher psychological issues.

Thus we see that scientifically considered as to physical, psychological, sociological hygiene—poetically considered, as to love . . . spiritually considered as to the flowering of the soul—the marriage bed is a decadent institution . . . an institution that arrays itself against the great fundamental principle of life— self-preservation.

Let this institution, then, be anathema to all thinking minds.

This was as close to gobbledegook as one could get, but in its virtual invasion of that sacred place, the marriage bed, she was sure it would make Comstock wild.

Another article had more point. It was from a radical magazine *The Menace*, which in turn quoted a Catholic magazine, *The Western*

Watchman. Its sarcastic heading in *The Woman Rebel* was "The Menace's Advice."

> *The Western Watchman* (Catholic) says, according to *The Menace:* "We say, a young girl's business is to get a husband. Having got a husband, it is her business to beget children. Under ordinary conditions of health a young wife ought to have a child in her arms or on her bosom all the time. When she is not nursing a child she should be carrying one. This will give her plenty to do, and she will have no time for political meetings or movements."
>
> How do the women like that program for a life vocation? According to this authority a woman is to look upon herself merely as a vehicle for the breeding of children. . . . This editor would not even give her the protection that is bestowed upon cattle (when he says) "when she is not nursing a child she should be carrying one." The home of such a couple, instead of being a place of comfort and refinement with food for the mind and the amenities of social life, is to be a rabbit warren, a sty filled with anemic, underdeveloped children, . . . and so continue until she drops into the grave the victim of man's distorted and perverted sense of duty. Out upon such a theory! For the protection of the female sex, let her be taught how to defend herself against such teachings as these.

But there were two really incendiary articles in this issue. The first was a front-page editorial, undoubtedly written by Margaret herself (other articles had been written by friends under assumed names). In this one she defended three anarchists who had been experimenting with making homemade bombs in a house on Lexington Avenue and ended by blowing up both the house and themselves.

The second was even more startling. Written by a Herbert A. Thorpe, it was called "In Defense of Assassination." This was an article that Emma Goldman herself had never dared print, but Margaret did so with calculation. "If this issue doesn't succeed in smoking out Comstock and the Postmaster General and making them tell me which articles caused the suppression," she wrote the well-known radical Upton Sinclair, "I'll follow it up with an article in defense of arson."

The assassination article did succeed in smoking out the Postmaster General, but not quite as Margaret expected.

On August 25, 1914, she received two visitors from the federal government, one of whom formally handed her a subpoena indicting her on three counts—two for publication of lewd and indecent articles and one for incitement to murder and riot. She was now faced, not only with the possibility of a defunct magazine, but of a long jail term. It is characteristic of Margaret that she claimed to have handled this confrontation with great aplomb. She wrote in her autobiography that she invited her visitors to sit down and proceeded to give them such a detailed lecture on the need for birth control among the poor that they wept, after which her father emerged from the next room and wept still louder. Putting his arms around her, Michael Higgins, she said, moaned in his best Irish brogue: "If only I had known then what I know now, your po-or mother would still be alive."

This story does not ring true. It is hard to believe that the subpoena servers had the time or inclination to linger and listen—or that Michael Higgins would agree to practice birth control under any circumstances.

In any event, as soon as the process servers left, Margaret sat down and did some hard thinking. She decided in the best radical tradition to make a dramatic gesture—appear in court alone, without a lawyer on the day the subpoena specified. Meantime, she wrote to the Postmaster General again, insisting that he disclose exactly which articles had caused *The Woman Rebel* to be barred from the mails.

He named seven. Oddly, he declared that the most offensive was "Are Preventive Means Injurious?" But he must have been nudged hard by Comstock, for in this article she had called Comstock and Comstockery stupid. That was something Comstock could not tolerate, for he, at last, was losing status. Many judges, tired of his arrogant manner and often silly complaints, had recently implied that he was getting out of hand. But Margaret had gone further; she had denounced him publicly. He was determined to stop her; he had her arrested and brought to quick trial.

In court, however, Margaret was so charming and demure that when she asked for a postponement in order to prepare her defense, the judge readily consented. The case was held over until the fall term, giving her six weeks of grace.

Elated, she plunged into activity. First, she got off a combined September-October issue of *The Woman Rebel,* using practically all of it to discuss her indictment. She stated that she would probably be tried in

October, and that if found guilty, she might be sentenced to as much as twelve years. She went on to say that "while practically every thinker of the civilized world is now accepting birth control, the arch-hypocritical government of the United States is not." Then, unexpectedly, she turned on her readers, berating them for not helping her enough. In a front-page editorial she declared:

The so-called radical press finds nothing significant or worthy of support in the attempt of the federal government to kill the propaganda for birth control. Solve the industrial problem, they solemnly declare, and all will be well. Do they realize that the "industrial problem" is never going to be solved until working men and WORKING WOMEN use every weapon and every method in their power to *master* the situation in which they find themselves, instead of remaining slaves in everything except the use of verbose and hackneyed plans that have a thousand times proved impotent and ineffective?

This off her chest, she sneaked as many copies as possible of this combined issue through the mails. In need of publicity, she next sent out a press release, concerning her indictment, to all the major wire services, and sat back to await the reporters she hoped would come. When they did, she repeated her praise of the anarchists who had blown up a house and themselves. She also asserted that her use of the article "In Defense of Assassination" was derived mainly from the thoughts of the great American philosopher, Wendell Phillips. But her great moment came when she repeated her credo of Women's Rights: "The Right to be Lazy. The Right to be an Unmarried Mother. The Right to Create. The Right to Destroy. The Right to Love and the Right to Live." The contrast between this credo, her charming manner, and what one newspaper described as her "unexpected beauty," made startling news.

She spent the remainder of her six weeks doing at last what she had been afraid to do before. She wrote a pamphlet giving specific birth-control advice and signed her name to it. (Oddly, however, she called this pamphlet and others that followed it *Family Limitation,* instead of using the far better name of birth control.) Still, in her pamphlet she told about various douches, described the condoms which were easily obtainable, and the diaphragms which were not. There were few diaphragms available in America in 1914, because those that were had been brought in illegally from France and cost about seven dollars, a price far beyond the means of a working man who earned three or four dollars a week. She also gave some rather curious advice: "Any nurse or doctor will teach one how to adjust a diaphragm, and women can then teach each other." Now, "any nurse or doctor" could not or would not do this kind of teaching, either because they didn't know how to do it, or were afraid of the law. As for women teaching each other, this was almost unthinkable in 1914 when women, as a rule, had been taught by their mothers not to touch their own genitals, much less those of their friends.

Nevertheless, writing such a pamphlet at all was a courageous and daring thing to do.

Finding a man to print it also took great persistence. Twenty printers flatly refused, one answering in horror, "That's a Sing Sing job!" But finally an I.W.W. member, Bill Shatoff, agreed to stay in his shop after hours, lock the door, and run off one hundred thousand copies immediately, plus more when needed. As soon as she got her hundred thousand pamphlets, she sent them off, divided in bundles, to friendly I.W.W. and Socialist locals around the country, instructing that they be held until she gave a signal for their release and sale.

All of this took so much of her time and energy that suddenly she realized the six weeks' grace given her by the court was almost over, yet she had done nothing to prepare her case. Leonard Abbott and Theodore Schroeder, both able lawyers for the Free Speech League—a group formed primarily to fight for freedom of speech as guaranteed by the Constitution—offered to help her, but she spurned their offers, saying that she didn't have the time to sit down and talk with them, that she still had the none-too-easy job of raising the money to pay the printer's bill for her unreleased pamphlets. She used the same excuse to avoid writing in detail about what was happening to Bill, merely telling him she wanted "to be left alone to think and dream and regret."

The new word "regret" struck an ominous chord. A letter from him, undoubtedly sent during the summer of 1914, reflects his growing despair. "I just wonder if I can go on. I feel my life has been taken away from me. Write me—sweetheart dear. I want you dear. I love you— with all my soul and spirit. Let me serve you!!"

She didn't reply. Nevertheless, he was the one who sent her the money to pay her bills. When he heard of her arrest and indictment, he at once shipped her the recent pictures he had painted, pictures which he meant to hold for a fall exhibit in Paris. When she got only one hundred dollars apiece for them, instead of the four hundred dollars he had hoped, he told her also to go ahead and sell the Marin and Sloan pictures which he had left in her keeping. These of course fetched excellent prices.

Yet Bill himself, whose own financial situation had become desperate, did not return. He had worked so long toward becoming a good artist that he hated the idea of returning to "wage slavery" as an architect. As passionately as he loved Margaret, he could not give up his goal. Besides, he had just been invited to exhibit in a London show the following winter. So, having sent her all his finished pictures, he hurriedly painted more. If he shipped these home, too, he asked her, would she help him choose which to exhibit and then return them? He favored one portrait in particular; it was of Peggy. "Peggy is a beauty. Ah me! She seems to have captured all the beauty of the family."

But France was mobilizing for war in 1914, and by late summer Bill was wavering. He remained in Paris until September, painting steadily, but by the end of the month, like most Americans, he had little choice but to return home. On October 1, with money borrowed from fellow radicals, he bought steerage passage for New York.

While Bill was at sea, Margaret got an unexpected jolt. On October 5 a police officer phoned to ask why she had failed to appear in court that morning when her case had been called. She answered that she had forgotten, appeared the next day instead, and asked for still another extension. Her autobiography states that she was granted only one more day; actually she got eight.

At this point she panicked and decided to look for a lawyer after all. Continuing to avoid Abbott and Schroeder, she sought out Samuel Untermyer, one of the best lawyers of his day. Untermyer refused to take her case, advising her to plead guilty and throw herself on the mercy of the court. He didn't see how she could do otherwise, as her most serious indictment was that of incitement to murder and riot. By pleading guilty, she might get a suspended sentence as a first offender, but he wouldn't take a case he couldn't possibly win.

Realizing at last that she was in a bad predicament, Margaret rushed home and reread the Comstock law. It provided a maximum of five years in jail for each offense. Frightened and confused, she wasn't sure whether she had published seven or nine offending articles in *The Woman Rebel*. If nine, she reasoned, she could be sentenced to forty-five years in jail. In truth, even if found guilty on nine counts, she probably would have been sentenced to serve them concurrently, remaining in jail only five years. But Margaret knew nothing about courts, and at this point was too distraught to learn. She decided to ask for another long extension to prepare a case and, if she didn't get it, to run away to a foreign country under an assumed name.

Now she did hurry to Abbott's office, but he was no more encouraging than Untermyer. He told her frankly that she had made a legal muddle of the whole *Woman Rebel* venture. She had said she was starting a paper mainly to test her right to give birth-control information to women who needed it, but she had done nothing of the kind. She had jeered at marriage, the Church, and the state. As she had finally written a pamphlet giving contraceptive advice, she could still have made a test case on the freedom-of-speech issue by openly mailing it, and notifying the authorities that she had done so. But she had not done this, and now that she was under the totally different indictment of incentive to murder and riot, the legal waters had been thoroughly muddied. He was afraid she was truly in a bad way. Though he would still go to court with her and do what he could if she wished him to.

On October 13, 1914, declining Abbott's offer to accompany her, she walked into court alone and asked for another long extension. She was denied it, but granted another eight days with a small amount of bail.

In her autobiography, Margaret again claims to have received only a one-day extension. She vividly describes how she spent that one day in a hotel room, her watch ticking off the minutes while she decided whether to stay or run.

She says she chose to jump the bail her friends had raised, and to run. Having done this, she claims, she phoned Grand Central Station and found that a train was leaving for Canada within the hour; she tells how she hastily packed a bag and dashed for the Canadian train, planning from there to catch a boat for England. More, she tells how she boarded the train without a passport, thought up the name Bertha Watson as she rode along, and later, on the boat to Europe, by chance met some "highly placed officials" whom she talked into getting her into England without a passport, even though it was wartime.

This is not the way it happened.

A handwritten note signed with her initials is in the Smith College

Archives. It clearly reads: "Bertha Watson was the assumed name I adopted on my flight to England while waiting for a passport and Comstock's attack." In other words, with the help of her anarchist friends, who were experts at subterfuge, a forged "Bertha Watson" passport was waiting for her in Canada. Canada had probably been chosen because a false Canadian passport was easier to get than an American one.

Also, since she had not one, but eight days grace before she had to run, she was able to make arrangements with two women friends in the Village, Helen Marot and Caroline Pratt, to take care of her children while she was gone. In addition she dropped a note to Bill Sanger, who had just landed in New York, telling him she was off to England and how to reach her there, got letters of introduction to radicals in Europe, and packed several large boxes containing copies of *The Woman Rebel* and *Family Limitation* to sell abroad.

From the train to Canada, she also made another of her defiant gestures. She wrote letters to both Judge Hazel, the man who had been the presiding justice on her case, and Harold Content, the prosecuting attorney, informing them that she was leaving the country under an assumed name and would return in a few months when she was better prepared. Then in each letter, she enclosed a copy of *Family Limitation* as a special thumb-to-the-nose.

In Canada she spent a few weeks visiting anarchist friends, saw Bill Sanger briefly after he begged to be allowed to come up and say goodbye, then sailed on November 3, 1914, for Liverpool. From the ship she sent coded cables to various locals that were holding the bulk of her *Family Limitation* pamphlets, ordering that they be released and sold for twenty-five cents apiece and the money sent to her under the name Bertha Watson, in care of American Express, London.

She would be away a full year instead of the few months she had promised and return a quite different woman from the one who left.

YEAR OF DISCOVERY

Aboardship, Margaret settled down to enjoy herself. She had letters of introduction to people in England and felt she was off on an adventure, no matter how it had come about.

The first day out she started a diary:

> The trip reminds me of the trip a year ago when we left from Boston for Glasgow. Dear Peggy how my love goes out to you—I could weep from loneliness for you—just to touch your soft chubby hands. But work is to be done dear—work to help, to make your path easier—and those who come after you.

She did not speak of missing Bill, Grant, or Stuart—only Peggy. She went on to justify her flight, using *Woman Rebel* rhetoric.

> United States—what stupidity controls thy destiny—to drive from your shores those who can contribute to the happiness of its down trodden people. Who can enlighten the ignorant—and help to raise the standards of knowledge.

The second day out she told of upsetting letters from home, received at Quebec, where the boat stopped as it steamed up the St. Lawrence River. We can only guess whom the letters were from:

* * *

The letters last night gave me a shock. How innocently we can say one thing and mean it, yet for other ears to hear it or other eyes to see it than those it was intended for it has an entirely different meaning. I presume that's why there are judges, juries etc. to keep us ever cold and calculating in our ideas and in our thoughts. I refuse to be so. I love being swayed by emotions, by romances—yet ever returning to the ideal. This is not what men have wanted in us. They have wanted a post, not a living tree. Let them.

She went on to talk about her resentment of the Catholic Church and of domineering men, claiming they had joined together to crush all freedom of thought, speech, and action. She was particularly bitter about men who wanted ignorant, servile wives whom they thought "charming and womanly." She would never be one of those!

Landing in Liverpool after a wet, cold voyage, she finds it cold and wet, too. She is suddenly depressed as she settles into a dingy boardinghouse, but she must stay in Liverpool to await more letters from home.

Soon however her mood changes. She has visited the Clarion Café, a place where Bill Haywood told her she would find radicals like herself. She has found one radical in particular, a Spanish anarchist, Lorenzo Portet, for whom she has "gone in a big way."

She has also applied for an American passport for "Bertha Watson," claiming her original one was lost. This time she has given her birthdate as 1881, her profession as journalist, and Mrs. A. E. Higgins (her unmarried sister Nan) as the person to be notified in case of death or accident. A new passport has been issued her, though it is good for a short time only.

By November 20 she is cheerfully writing her sister Mary:

You will be surprised to hear that I am in England but here I am and all well & happy. I am waiting to visit Edward Carpenter (an advocate of sexual freedom) before I go on to London . . . I am trying to get the interest of the Neo-Malthusian League to help me in my fight against the post-office authorities, and if the war were not taking all the attention of the English people I certainly should be able to make an international case of it, & make

U.S. puritanical ideas a laughing stock for the world. So if I do lose out in my case & am sent to the federal prison I shall have something to think of & have at least done something for the cause.

In December she left Liverpool for London and took a room at 67 Torrington Square near the British Museum. There she records an upsetting experience in her diary:

A picture fell from the wall and the glass smashed into thousands of pieces—a voice that father had died was heard or rather not heard, but seemed to be an inner voice within myself. Queer thing this—the first time it ever occurred to me and I am anxious to know what has happened.

Her spirits rise after she attends a lecture on Nietzsche, "the most splendid and understandable rendering of Neitzsche I ever heard." They rise still further when she goes to tea at the home of Dr. and Mrs. C. R. Drysdale, the outstanding English champions of birth control, who "hugged me and took me to their hearts."

On December 13, she made two momentous notes in her diary. The first was the receipt of an invitation through the Drysdales to meet Havelock Ellis, the man whose *Studies in the Psychology of Sex* had made him a world authority on the subject. The second entry concerned her decision to leave Bill Sanger. "Today I have cast the die. I have written Bill a letter ending a relationship of over 12 years."

Clearly, Bill's continued adoration was by now thoroughly boring. As she had recently said, she wanted new sensations, new romances. As for her children, they'd manage, somehow. She was off on an adventure into a new world, and she was determined to be free to enjoy it. Bill was in the way; he must go.

When Bill received her letter telling him of a final break between them, he was not completely surprised. In the few minutes he had seen her in Canada before she sailed, he had told her friends, he had felt "like a chilly intruder." When he got back to New York, he had taken a cheap place for himself on the top floor of a tenement at 103 East Fifteenth Street, the nearest thing to a studio he could find. Alone again, he settled down to working as a draftsman by day and painting at night, his only break being his visit to his children on his way home.

While Margaret's letter to him was on its way, he sent her a long impassioned letter in which he tried so hard to figure out what had happened to their marriage that in places it is almost incoherent:

I can see you pale with cold, wan and fatigued. Whatever the conflicting feeling there might be surging thru me now, I would want to be near you *now*—yes I do—to extend you that personal note in which I have found more joy than you have. I don't want to disguise under the cover of bitterness that I could just fly to you now and serve you and administer to your every need and desire. . . . For you I lay down my brush any time if it meant that for your comfort it was necessary.

The night I saw you first & gazed in those wide beautiful soulful eyes—I felt that soul-stir which was new to me—something just came in that by its very intensity gave me a feeling that I never felt before. And when I left you that night—I felt I left one whom I knew before. Your spirit filled me with the purest longing I ever experienced. . . . If I did not impress you so well the next day it was because I tried too hard to please you. Why did I not assert those very things that we two are craving for now—individual expression? You wanted all the personal love that it was within my power to give you—how many times you remarked that my personal love for you waned when I painted! You were afraid of my art!

When we planned the house—well you wanted it. And if I messed it up by building one beyond our means, I take all blame. . . . Love is blind. I lived in a period of desire to please you. When I finally designed that little palace I watched your every expression to see if you would understand. You did. You always understand. That is why my cup of bitterness is so full now. You have written to me in Paris that I should seek the women who might "enrich my life"—its veiled sarcasm did not move me to reply. . . . But if no other woman has come into my life it's because I feel your spirit so overwhelming in its beauty and its power. I had no trial marriages or experiences to decide like you did when you did not "feel sure" of yourself. I cannot weigh my life against yours. Yours is changeable, adolescent, uncertain.

When I work for wages I know that my services can be replaced by most any competent draughtsman, but when I paint I know no one can do it just like I do it. I become an artist and so do also with love.

You say that my personality is over-bearing; just the opposite—I have submerged it all that I might serve you. Few have taken me for my own sake, few like me, and you could well live without me—I know—bitter as it is. . . . You write me that you would not make a home for me had you known I meant a home in the sense that you would be a kitchen serf or be compelled to curtail one bit of your creative urge. . . . Now if you are a free woman this is as it should be.

Do you remember the letter you wrote me last spring to Paris—when you asked me to release you physically and spiritually from my life? You will never know the utter despair when I read that letter. You know the letter you received in reply in which I released you from every tie—and then you praised me to the skies for it. That was last March. That was, I knew, to live with R. How I felt you will never know! Just when I was finishing the "Penseur" I needed the inspiration of your life. . . . But you admit now you were willing to live with R if you could make a home with him and the children. They would in time be acclimated. If I had popped off it would have simplified matters greatly!! You said "If tomorrow I should care for R or any one else I shall do so" . . . (and) I released you, Peg, did I not?

My Lord! Oh, that night when I wrote that letter I drenched that letter in my tears that I could not shed for the utter anguish & despair & yet I loved you! I wrote that I was willing to go on to further adapt my life with you & help you. There was no reply to this . . .

But to my surprise you again wrote me. . . . You must have experienced a change of heart . . . & you recalled me in your life—yes you did. I sent you the photo of the "Penseur" inscribed with that note on the back. I sent it without a letter—I expected nothing—absolutely nothing—from you but perhaps that you received it. I saw the crew gathered around it—I knew what they would think. I did not care. So came your letter which was a milestone in my life—yes it was. It was the first real thing I ever experienced as regards my work. Every fibre of my being just pulsated with new life & joy. I felt I was made again. Oh it was beautiful.

You recalled me in your life—you said for the children's

sake. . . . You gave me the distinction few men can claim & coming from you it certainly meant something for you are a *good*
judge of men, that I was "thè hero of your dreams," that you were
"glad that the father of your children was an idealist."

So when I came back (to New York) I rightly felt that the matter of R and you was a closed book & that is why I never questioned your financial transactions or relations with him until the
outburst that night against me brought the matter to the front.

Now I feel you are holding nothing out to me. All is really lost.

Now the time has come to revalue the narrow family relation,
and its narrow personal love. Perhaps you call it narrow, I don't. I
realize now that this personal love with you no longer suffices &
you need the bigger love which will help you in your life's work.
You are to take that love from whomsoever offers it, you say.
Your personality belongs to the world. So I realize that the bigger
lover is the love that can give you the best of life and I take life to
be in your case the help you need to (do) the utmost in the propa-
gation of your creative urge. Who can do that better than I? Who
can give you spiritual, intellectual & economic help? This is the
man you want to find. I hold out to you the love which is as big
and broad as the very scope of your life's work . . .

Bill's letter ends here, either because the rest was lost or because he
simply ran out of steam. The situation had become hopeless anyway.
Margaret didn't answer him in any event, but made a short entry in
her diary instead: "It seems almost good to be alone—there is time to
get acquainted with ones self, to reflect, to meditate, to dream. There is
so little time these days for memories it's a luxury to have time for
anything but work."

Yet Margaret didn't stay alone long. A few days later she received
the eagerly awaited invitation from Havelock Ellis inviting her to tea
on December 22 at his London flat.

On December 22 she went to Brixton, a shabby section near the British Museum, climbed several flights of rickety stairs, and knocked tim-
idly at the door. Although she was about to meet the one man in the
world she wanted to meet most, she was afraid he might be intellectually beyond her reach. But as soon as he opened the door she felt better.
The man who stood before her looked so gentle she lost her fear. He
was also strikingly handsome, resembling, as she later said, a "tall an-

gel." His white beard was long and full, his white hair fell in a thick, deep wave over his forehead, his nose was straight and fine, and his eyes were cornflower blue. Her only disappointment came when he spoke; his voice was high and thin.

She followed him into a small, sparsely furnished room overflowing with books. Books were piled high on the wooden chairs. Books covered the wooden table. Books spilled from shelves onto the floor. He motioned her to a comfortable stool in front of a fire, and while he prepared tea she looked about. A fine Matisse and a glowing Pieter de Hooch above the mantel soon made her feel completely relaxed.

Their conversation started haltingly since, as usual, Ellis was overcome with shyness. But Margaret put him at ease so quickly that soon he was telling her about the trouble he had had after the publication of the first volume of his sex studies. His publisher had been arrested and convicted of indecency, making Ellis resolve never again to publish his work in England, but rather, to find an American medical publisher for the remaining volumes.

Margaret in turn spoke of her troubles with *The Woman Rebel*. She filled in Ellis' sudden silences with stories of her nursing experience in the slums, telling him of Sadie Sachs' death and her resolve to do something to end this kind of tragedy. Ellis was greatly interested in birth control, and soon he was describing methods she had not known before. There was an old Hindu method, for instance, called Karezza. With Karezza intercourse could be prolonged indefinitely; the man withheld his climax completely, and no ejaculation occurred. Its supposed advantage for the man was that the withheld spermatic fluid was reabsorbed into his system, becoming a part of his élan vital or life-giving force; for the woman it increased the possibility of having several orgasms during the prolonged sex act. "Ellis thinks the method splendid if the man is able to do it," Margaret noted later in her diary.

> He spoke openly and freely on the subject . . . which was a great relief. (He has) the shyness and reticence of the student, and the simplicity of a great soul and mind. I count this a glorious day to have conversed with the one man who has done more than anyone in this Century toward giving women and men a clean and sane understanding of their sex lives and of all life.

To Ellis, too, it was a glorious day; for the first time in his life he found himself immediately at ease with a woman. Indeed, they spoke from afternoon until midnight.

Henry Havelock Ellis' shyness dated from early childhood. His father was a sea-captain who was often away from home on long voyages. An only son with four sisters, this left Havelock almost exclusively in female company, with a mother who adored and coddled him, calling him her "Handsome Harry." Also, he loved books and was bored by sports, so at school he was practically an outcast. He had become afraid of boys and retreated further into his family and himself.

When Havelock was around ten, his father decided to take him on a long voyage, hoping it might make more of a man of him. But Captain Ellis showed no favoritism. Havelock (who soon dropped the Henry) was made to sleep below deck with the crew like an ordinary seaman, and soon the rough sailors, attracted to the handsome boy, began not only to openly display their genitals before him, but to coax him into handling them. A typical Victorian boy, who knew nothing about sex, Havelock was at first fascinated, then repelled. He drew back further into his shell, returning home more bookish than ever.

When Havelock was sixteen, Captain Ellis decided to take him along on another voyage. But this time the ship was on its way to Calcutta, and the ship's doctor thought the extreme heat there would be bad for Havelock's delicate health, so he was dropped off in Australia where a friend of his father found him a job as a teacher.

He stayed in Australia for two years, but he was such a miserable disciplinarian that he had to switch teaching jobs frequently. One job was at Sparkes Creek, a tiny outpost, where he taught a handful of pupils in one room of a two-room schoolhouse and ate and slept in the other. Here he wrestled alone with the adolescent problems of religion, social acceptance, and sex. He decided he was not particularly likeable, since he could get none of his pupils to obey him. Perhaps, he thought, he should try his hand at medicine, though it would be difficult to get money for the necessary training.

Fortunately, when he returned home, an older woman-friend provided him with a small loan. With this help, he managed to stay at a university long enough to get a degree of Bachelor of Medicine, a lesser degree than that of Doctor of Medicine, but one that would let him practice to a limited extent. A single session in the London slums, mainly delivering babies, proved too much for him, however. He settled down to the secluded life of a writer, working at home and seldom going out. After editing a series of Restoration plays, he wrote *The Dance of Life* and *Studies in the Psychology of Sex*, which eventually brought him notice.

When Havelock was in his late twenties, books like these drew him to the attention of Olive Schreiner, the author of *The Story of an African Farm,* an extraordinary novel which was making her a London celebrity. A staunch feminist, she nonetheless had to sign this book "Ralph Iron," because writing for publication was not considered modest in a Victorian woman. Now over thirty, she had had a series of intense but disastrous love affairs that left her eagerly desiring marriage. Having read Ellis' books, she started corresponding with him. Soon she was inviting him to tea, because his letters led her to hope he would be the congenial, marriageable man she was looking for. But when he arrived at her boardinghouse, she realized immediately that he was far too shy to meet her needs; he was so shy he was practically tongue-tied, and when she went upstairs to get her hat she cried from sheer despair.

After some weeks, however, Ellis got up the courage to invite her to spend a weekend with him in the country; the weekend only confirmed her fears. Ellis enjoyed kissing her and caressing her nude body, but he suffered from premature ejaculation; caressing a woman's genitals with his hand and mouth started and finished the sex act for him—all the more so when he was as strongly attracted to a woman as he was to Olive. He offered marriage but she refused. Yet because she so much enjoyed his companionship and fine mind, she became and remained his firm friend. All his life, whenever he was in doubt, he would seek advice from Olive.

Soon afterward, Ellis got up the courage to join a club of young people called "The Fellowship of the New Life," whose members were as out-of-step with Victorian society as he was. They took long walks in the country in the days when only tradesmen or peasants walked; they thought for themselves when few young people did. A member of this unorthodox group was Edith Lees, a small, lively woman of twenty-eight, who reminded him of Olive because she talked freely about sex though she had no personal experience of it. She fell in love with him and was delighted when he asked her to go off to Cornwall with him for a few days. Neither of them ever told exactly what happened there, but it was enough to convince her that she wanted to marry him, and she took the initiative by proposing at once. He hesitated. He was attracted by her intelligence and vivacity, but he needed strict privacy for his work and had very little money besides. She promised to honor his privacy and to contribute half the household expenses. They drew up an agreement stating that, not only would each pay half their expenses, but any extra contribution would be considered as a loan to their joint fund. Edith claimed that this arrangement started right from the beginning; she paid for half of her wedding ring.

They set off for a honeymoon in Paris, where Edith was surprised and chagrined to find that Havelock did not attempt to have any kind of sexual relationship with her, not even the kind he had had with Olive. Yet, she too found him such a delightful companion that she decided to stay, even though it meant giving up the normal life and children she craved. Her liveliness and sociability so well complemented his shyness that the marriage, while hardly a conventional one, worked well for a while. As Ellis' biographer, Arthur Calder-Marshall wrote: "He was her opium and she was his champagne."

As the years went by, however, Edith began to want more; she satisfied her sexual craving by taking on a series of woman lovers. Far from being upset by her lesbian liaisons, Havelock encouraged them. They assured him he would never be burdened with children he did not want; they also gave him case histories to describe in his studies of sexual inversion. He in turn gradually became involved with other women who admired him tremendously, took what little he had to offer sexually, and were grateful for that. There was one young girl in particular, the daughter of a friend whom he identified in his autobiography as "Amy," with whom he developed an intimate relationship that lasted for years. Acting on his principle of frankness he told Edith about Amy, explaining that she was mainly a "featherbed of a woman" who gave him the restfulness Edith couldn't provide. He also said that, because his relationship with Amy was only physical, it in no way interfered with his fuller and more spiritual relationship with Edith. To his surprise, Edith, who loved her husband in some ways like a child and called him "Havelock Boy," reacted violently to his revelation about Amy. She sarcastically spoke of her as Havelock's "femininity" and was so rude to her that Havelock let her visit him only when Edith was away with one of her own lovers.

Meanwhile, Ellis devoted himself more and more to his sex studies, trying to uncover truths that had been buried for so long under a mass of prudery. But he disclosed what he found in such delicate language, calling homosexual relations, for instance, "beautiful anomalies," and switching to Latin when he wrote about the more explicit aspects of all sex, that he was not widely read. Only a few people bothered to wade through his seven volumes, though those who did revered him. The few who sought him out personally, like Margaret, spoke of him as "The King."

When Margaret came into his life, Ellis was fifty-seven and suffering from a crisis of confidence. Since the people who revered him for his sex studies were in the main without great public influence, and Edith persistently dismissed those studies as "unimportant" compared to his more philosophical books like *The New Spirit* and *Little Essays of Love and Virtue*, he wasn't at all sure that his work had been, or ever would be, worthwhile. In addition, as he grew older, he grew even more afraid of meeting people, fearing that the secret of his sexual inadequacy would somehow be revealed. Moreover, his father had recently died, making him the head of a family with four unmarried sisters to support and little to support them on.

On top of all this, his marriage to Edith had also reached a crisis stage. Instead of remaining cheerfully vivacious, she was now swinging sharply from high to low in a way that today would be recognized as manic-depressive. When she was high she would dash off mediocre novels and plays, or rent unsuitable country places that she would attempt to sublet advertising them as "one outside privy, with four-room cottage attached." When she was low she would mourn her dead women lovers, sitting for hours in utter dejection beside their graves. At the moment she was earning some money through a hectic American lecture tour, speaking as Mrs. Havelock Ellis on some of her husband's theories of life and love. But the tour was not proving successful; her health was breaking down under the strain, and her letters were so gloomy that Ellis was almost considering suicide. His meeting with Margaret, twenty years younger than he and at the height of her beauty and charm, came precisely when he needed someone to bolster his ego.

Indeed, his attraction to Margaret was so strong that, as soon as she left after their first visit, he made a midnight entry in his diary: "Seldom have I found so congenial a companion, or found one so fast." Early the next morning he hurried out and bought her a single flower, taking it to her boardinghouse with instructions to send it up with her breakfast tray. If she hadn't been overjoyed the night before, she was now. "That flower was *something,*" she jotted in her diary.

Soon Ellis followed his morning flower with a note. His invitation to tea was addressed, "My dear Mrs. Sanger," and signed, "Havelock Ellis." Now he addressed her as "Dear Rebel," and spoke of the "lovely evening which I owe to you," adding, "only it was too short, and I cannot believe that seven hours should pass so soon." He went on to arrange a meeting with her at the British Museum, signing himself merely "H.E."

A few days later, Ellis was lamenting in another note that, although he had met her at the Museum and showed her how to apply for a special reader's card, he had looked for her again and missed her. He had wanted to tell her about a book he thought she should read and also talked to her about her own *What Every Girl Should Know,* which he would like to see published in England "but possibly a little re-written here and there." He would keep looking for her at the Museum the next time he went, which would probably be the next day, as he kept to a regular schedule of going three times a week.

So they began a series of morning meetings followed by long lunches at cheap Italian Soho restaurants, after which Margaret went back to the Museum, if only to keep warm.

Her evenings were spent with Portet, the anarchist who had recently come to London and by now was almost surely her lover. However, Portet was in a hurry to get back to his Paris publishing house and couldn't stay in London long, though he asked her to join him in Paris as soon as possible. With two new exciting men in her life, she was elated. Toward the end of the year she happily wondered: "What will the new year bring? I am sure it will be things unheard of."

THINGS UNHEARD OF

The year 1915 did bring Margaret "things unheard of." The first was that Ellis developed into her full-scale teacher. He became even more. He became her guru and possibly her lover, in his limited sense. In any event she developed for him an almost mystical reverence. Whenever in doubt she turned to him for advice, just as he turned to Olive Schreiner. He met her every other morning at the British Museum, getting there first and reserving two seats, as well as readying books and pamphlets on birth control for her to read.

Now for the first time in her life Margaret read selectively; Ellis told her the same thing Leonard Abbott had told her—that she must stop scattering her energies and concentrate on one cause. That cause, Ellis insisted, should be neither anarchy nor socialism; it should be birth control, a cause she was far more likely to win. It was also a cause in which she could become the Queen Bee because, as far as he knew, no one in America was promoting it vigorously at the time. But this could happen only after she had studied it in a far more scientific way than she had before and had learned to speak in a more moderate tone.

So she read only as he directed, studying hard for most of each day. She was surprised to learn that every group of people since the world began had in some way tried to control their fertility. A papyrus written as far back as 1800 B.C. described how Egyptian women would put crocodile dung or other gumlike substances into their vaginas, hoping that these would trap some of the sperm. Luckily, dried dung has no odor. The Egyptians also used lint tampons dipped in honey to slow the sperm, while Chinese women used wet tea leaves or thin pieces of oiled paper derived from bamboo.

And even the Jewish Talmud had a suggestion: Place a small piece of sponge around the cervix or tip of the womb; if slightly hollowed out, it would be held in place by suction.

But the most common method in every country was coitus interruptus or withdrawal of the man's penis before ejaculation. And along with these quite rational methods, there were irrational ones. Women told each other that sneezing hard immediately after intercourse would expel the semen. So, some said, would a sharp exhalation of the breath, spitting three times into a frog's mouth, or making magical passes over the bed.

During the sixteenth century came the first reliable method—a good male sheath. Crude sheaths made of strips of thin bark or mats of woven leaves had been used for centuries to protect the wearer in combat or to guard against tropical diseases. Then Gabriello Fallopius, the Italian who discovered and named the Fallopian tubes, came up with a male sheath of fine linen which was held in place by drawing the foreskin over the tip. He invented it, he said, to protect the wearer from venereal disease, which spread through Europe in epidemic proportions at the time. Fallopius claimed that he had tested his sheath on a thousand men, and that it had the further advantage that it could be carried inconspicuously in a trouser pocket and quickly slipped on just before intercourse took place.

But Fallopius was thinking only of protecting men. He didn't give a thought to protecting women from either disease or pregnancy. It took another century before a Dr. Condom introduced a sheath made of sheep's gut into the court of Charles II of England, a sheath he hoped would protect both men and women. Fine sheaths of this kind were made smooth by stretching them over oiled moulds and made pleasant by scenting them with perfume.

Still, such condoms were bought mainly by men who wanted to "take trips into Merryland" or consort with prostitutes, and so were also colored as gaily as possible, with green or scarlet ribbons threaded through the top end. A poem published in 1728 reads:

*   *   *

Happy the man who in his pocket keeps
Whether with Green or Scarlet Ribband bound,
A well-made C——— He nor dreads the ills
Of Shankers or Cordees or Buboes dire.

(In the late sixteen hundreds a Frenchman rummaging through a
prostitute's room reported finding, among other things, a box of alum,
useful in contracting the mouth of the womb; three flasks of weak nitric acid, an anti-spermicide whose action is similar to vinegar; a small
syringe; a sponge; and a little bag of mercury powder, a potent, if more
dangerous, chemical than weak nitric acid.)

Oddly enough, it was the eighteenth century lover Casanova who
spread knowledge of the condoms. In his autobiography he calls them
"English overcoats, little preventative bags invented to save the fair
sex from anxiety against an accident which might lead to frightful re-
pentance." Such concern for women in general was unusual for a man
of his time.

In France during the eighteenth century, women, too, began to protect themselves. Mothers gave instructions like this to their daughters:
"Wet a sponge in water mixed with a few drops of brandy as an anti-
spermicide, and insert it exactly over the neck of the womb. Even if the
pervasive semen goes through the spores of the sponge, the extraneous
liquid (from the vagina), mingling with it, may destroy its power."
They added that a light silk cord sewn into the sponge would provide a
means by which it may be drawn out.

Having absorbed this much, Margaret decided she needed a rest, and
started spending a good deal more time with Ellis. New Year's Eve of
1915 was a special occasion. As Big Ben began to toll the hour of midnight, Margaret impulsively leaned over and kissed him on the cheek.
He noted in his diary that the kiss had taken him "by utter and sweet
surprise."

In New York Bill Sanger was in no such high spirits. It was on that
very New Year's Eve that he found Margaret's goodbye letter when he
got home. After reading it over and over, he charged out of the house
and headed for the Hudson River docks. For hours he wandered in a
daze among the gloomy docks, sat for a while, wandered again, then
headed back to his studio where he threw himself on his cot and fell
into the deep sleep of utter despair.

It wasn't until January 10 that he was able to answer her in another agonizing letter.

Peg, after receiving your letter, I vowed I would not write you again—the letter excommunicating me from your life was cold & calculating—brutal almost and without compassion. Yes, you timed your letter right—it landed on New Years; that night for the first time in my life I felt to go on would be useless and as I wandered down towards the docks alone—I thought of poor (name unreadable). He went that way no doubt—why not I? . . . I live or exist now because I was too cowardly to die. I touched rock bottom on all the illusions one has in life. . . .

Your letter just indicated to me that at a time when this new personality came in you seized the opportunity.

Tonight I could not love anything, not even the finest woman that lives. I want to destroy within you now once and for all any illusion you might have that I am the legalized marriage type. I never was. If you were married and had ten children I would have taken you because I could not live without you and that's the secret of my life.

Now I care for nothing. I revelled in serving you. But your letter indicates that I am a hindrance in your life, so now I shall retrace my steps and seek seclusion in *my work* and *my thoughts* and *my children*. I shall not see you now. I brought thee roses on New Year's Day and you!—you—gave me a stone.

Margaret, as usual, didn't answer Bill's letter. She continued to read in the Museum daytimes and visit Ellis evenings, talking eagerly with him about what she had learned.

These relaxed evenings were soon interrupted, however, for Ellis began to tell Edith about Margaret. Shortly after the New Year, he sent Edith a series of letters in which he spoke of his "new friend" in enthusiastic terms. He said she combined the best traits of the American and the Irish, being quick, daring, impulsive, and utterly charming.

Several such letters reached Edith in Chicago on February 3, the day before a major lecture she was to give in Orchestra Hall. Exhausted from the struggle of an unsuccessful tour, as well as from rapidly developing asthma and diabetes, she was shattered. Unable to sleep, she got up at dawn on the day of her great lecture and wrote her husband a

six-page letter; she used a word to describe Margaret which was so bitter that Havelock, quoting the letter in his autobiography, used only a
blank space in its place. Her letter, in part, read:

MY DARLING BOY,
 Here on the great day of my public life I awake at five and write
my English letters . . . Of course I got a fearful jump when I
realized there is another —— in your life. . . . If it makes you
happy I am glad, but somehow it is a kind of strange realization
which makes it easier for me to die. I *want* to die, and yet I am at
my Zenith, and if I can only live two or more months I shall not
die in debt. . . . Thank God someone has put life and joy in your
sad face . . . (But) be careful, for I realize here how much hero-
worshipping is like drugtaking . . . I am terrified of tonight. But
my voice carries, even in a whisper, all over the big hall . . . I
wonder how you spent your birthday, Dear one. Which of the ——
came, or did they come in relays?

                                                    YOUR WIFIE,
 P. S. I drank to you and your new —— in a cocktail last night.

Edith continued her tour as best she could, though after all her expenses were paid she found she had cleared very little. Her health
grew steadily worse, too, and her letters once more carried the same re-
frain: She probably would never return to England; she longed for
death; she was a waif and an alien who should never have been
allowed to grow up. Finally, she urged Havelock to come to the States
and comfort her, but he replied that it was impossible. He had never
traveled that far; he was sure she could manage without him.
 At this point her health became so bad she collapsed. Ulcers in her
throat burst, she had a bad attack of angina, and her handwriting became almost illegible.
 Eventually, she got a passage home, though the journey was sheer
hell, made even worse when a fellow traveler told her she had heard
Havelock was planning to meet her in Liverpool "to break the news,"
possibly with Margaret at his side.
 In her fevered state of mind the first question she asked Havelock
when she saw him on the Liverpool wharf was "Are you alone?" It had
never occurred to him not to be, and he tried to reassure her that everything was all right by agreeing to stay overnight with her at a good ho-

tel before they took the train to London. He went so far as to sleep in the same bed with her, something he almost never did now, to put his arms around her and comfort her; she said it was the best rest she had had in weeks.

But when she pleaded with him to stay on a few more days, he said the hotel was too expensive; she could rest just as well in their flat in London where he could get on with his work. To Edith this was another test of love he failed to pass. He had refused to come to America to get her; now he was refusing to stay alone with her for even a few more days.

By the time they got to London Edith was close to a breakdown. Havelock put her to bed, but when he left her alone for a few minutes he returned to find her looking very strange.

"Is there anything wrong?" he asked.

"I've swallowed the whole bottle of morphia tablets," she replied.

He glanced at the empty bottle near her bedside, quickly mixed an emetic for her, and the tablets were thrown up. "I think she was rather pleased at the concern I showed," he later said.

When they went to Cornwall together soon after, she rallied enough to try to work on a book she had started. But it was too late. She sank again into a deep depression, made a second, unsuccessful suicide attempt, and was diagnosed by the country doctor as having what was then called "circular insanity"—a form of madness which comes and goes. She had had a spell of this before her marriage; the doctor thought she was having one again. Havelock refused to believe it and for a time kept her home and nursed her himself, waiting on her as tenderly as he could. But the nursing wearied him, and he accepted the doctor's suggestion that she be sent to the Convent Nursing Home, a place run by nuns. Remembering the convent school she had gone to as a girl and the gentleness of the nuns there, she agreed to go.

Havelock visited her almost daily and she seemed enormously comforted by his presence. But when he left she would call out "Havelock! Havelock!" so fearfully that the nuns had to run in and silence her.

The Convent Nursing Home had no experience in treating mental patients, and when Edith regularly began to have night screams, in addition to those she had during the day when Havelock left her, they asked that she be removed as soon as possible.

Hearing this, Edith made a third suicide attempt by throwing herself out of a window. As her room was on the first floor and she fell on soft earth she didn't hurt herself, but after that the Convent Home insisted she leave immediately.

Her doctor, with Havelock's consent, put her into a regular mental hospital. Within a short time she was swinging from depression to such euphoria that she seemed cured, and they let her go. But as soon as she was released, she insisted on going to a lawyer and having a legal separation drawn up between her and Havelock so that he would never again have the authority to put her anywhere. She took a flat in London, tried to get some lecture engagements, decided that maybe the theatre was an easier way to make money, and dashed off a play which brought her in fifty pounds.

But she began to slip fast. She wrote a letter to Margaret saying how much she would like to meet her because Margaret was "certain to be sweet and good if Havelock said she was," but she signed it "Lady Tobias," the name of a fictional character doomed to wander around the world in search of peace. Within a few months she went into a diabetic coma and died.

It was Ellis' turn to be shattered. In his grief he clung to Margaret more than ever, clung all the more because Margaret insisted nothing that had happened was his fault.

But soon there was a turnabout. A letter from Bill Sanger, awaiting them in London, told her that he had been arrested for handing out a copy of her *Family Limitation* pamphlet to a Comstock decoy who played on his sympathy with a personal visit.

Bill was arrested by Comstock himself, who hinted that if Bill would divulge Margaret's alias and whereabouts, he would get him off with a suspended sentence; otherwise, as a distributor of the pamphlet, he would be subject to a year's imprisonment and a thousand dollar fine. Bill told Comstock to go to hell.

Like Margaret, Bill decided to serve as his own lawyer in court and to make a stirring speech to get publicity for the cause.

Another letter soon followed in an angrier tone: "The whole affair was not of my making. It is your cause I will be defending, and I would have liked it a damn sight more if you had been here to take up the work from the start, though I would not have liked you to have gone through the humility of being arrested by Comstock and thrown into a filthy jail."

Either Margaret didn't answer these rather startling letters or they, too, were destroyed. But she did immediately send dramatically worded letters explaining Bill's situation to the Socialist and I.W.W. locals who had been distributing her *Family Limitation* pamphlets in the States.

There is no doubt that my husband's arrest is but a trap of the Government, set to secure my return to the U.S.A., as well as to silence the propaganda of birth control. But we who have hatred and contempt in our hearts for these authorities whose high-handed officialism is running riot in America are not to be deterred from our cause nor trapped in our work because of sentiment; and just as I refused to go meekly like a lamb to slaughter when I saw that the Court was prejudiced against me, so now do I refuse to be tricked into rushing to the side of my comrade and pal, or to the aid of my three little ones who will be left unprotected by his imprisonment, until I have finished this work which I began to do. The sufferings of one who is loved by me could be no more deeply burned in my soul than the sufferings and anguish of thousands of other women's loved ones left alone in sorrow by death which has been caused by abortion.

Meanwhile Margaret was tired of reading at the Museum and started attending lunches with British suffragettes and members of the Neo-Malthusian League. Through Ellis, she also met important writers like H. G. Wells, Bernard Shaw, and Arnold Bennett, and leading doctors like Sir Arbuthnot Lane and Norman Haire.

How Margaret supported herself in London is a mystery; except for the money she received from the sale of her pamphlets by the radicals at home, money which came in slowly if at all, she had no discernible income. Now she needed more money in order to travel to Holland, which Ellis had told her was the most advanced country in the world in regard to birth control. For years it had been running government-sponsored clinics which told women about every known device, especially diaphragms. Indeed, one form of diaphragm had been perfected in Holland by a Dr. Mensinga, and was known as the Mensinga Diaphragm or Dutch Cap.

Ellis got her letters of introduction to the doctors and midwives in charge of the Holland clinics, and when a fair amount of money finally did come in from the sale of her pamphlets in the States, she left for Holland immediately.

Her reception there was not all roses, however. Dr. Aletta Jacobs, director of a clinic, dismissed her as a mere nurse, who was not entitled to the same consideration as a fellow doctor. Fortunately, another clinic director, Dr. Jacob Rutgers, was more cordial. He personally conducted her around, gave her samples of the Mensinga Diaphragm, showed her his records, and explained how each patient was followed up to see if the method she had chosen was successful. He then had Margaret accompany the government midwives who went to the homes of women too poor to travel to a clinic; there the midwives showed her how to insert diaphragms properly and easily.

Dr. Rutgers also gave Margaret a copy of the birth-control pamphlet given to all Dutch women on request. It was an impressive pamphlet that had changed little since it was first published in 1875. On its cover was a quotation from a Minister of Finance, who declared that "no true improvement in living conditions can be hoped for if the number of births be not considerably diminished." On the inside a description of all the known methods was divided into "Methods for Husbands" and "Methods for Wives."

Under "Methods for Husbands," the first was absolute continence. This was dismissed as practically impossible for men. The second was periodic continence or restricting intercourse to the "safe period," though the period prescribed—abstention the week before and the week after menstruation—was the opposite of what we now know to be correct.

Next came Karezza, which was poetically likened to "the ability of intelligent people to hold back tears even when deeply moved."

After that was withdrawal, which needed little description since it was widely known. And finally there was the condom, made either of sheep gut or of rubber.

Under "Methods for Wives," the diaphragm headed the list. This, the pamphlet explained, had the great advantage of "permitting the woman to be free from care during the night," and was especially valuable because the husband need not be consulted in the matter since, properly fitted over the neck of the womb, the husband would not know it was there."

If a diaphragm was not available, the rubber sponge was second best, chiefly because it was much less expensive than the suppositories containing quinine or other acid substances which French women used. Douching was next described but dismissed as useless, since it was almost impossible to use it in time.

Finally, a woman was advised to keep a supply of condoms on hand and try to slip one onto the penis of an amorous husband when he was too drunk to do it himself. This was particularly good advice in a country where gin and beer were consumed by the quart.

By early March Margaret was ready to leave Holland. But instead of going back to London as Ellis hoped, she went straight to Paris, writing Ellis that she was merely going to meet a "comrade" there. The comrade of course was Portet.

Soon she sent Ellis another note saying she would not be back in London for quite a while; she was off on a holiday to Spain. Though Ellis considered jealousy a base feeling, he was openly disturbed: "Didn't you know that Spain is one of my favorite places and that I have written a book about it? If you had invited me to join you, I could have shown you so many lovely places there."

But Margaret had no intention of inviting Ellis along. During all of March and April, she was joyously visiting first the South of France and then Spain with Portet. And though Portet, a known anarchist, was shadowed everywhere, they had a high time drinking cheap wine and brandy in the little cafés and going to museums and concerts. She was particularly delighted when he took her to a small shrine dedicated to an anarchist, Augielo, who in 1897 had been shot after he assassinated the Prime Minister of Spain. "Augielo at least sacrificed himself and did something," she wrote in her diary. "Here's to your name and your memory, Augielo. May your spirit and courage be born again—your kind is needed if the rulers and despots shall be overthrown."

Another highlight of her Spanish holiday was a letter from Stuart—the first she had ever received because, at the age of twelve, he had just learned to read and write. "Dear Mother," he wrote in childish printing: "How are you? I am fine. When are you coming home? I received a letter from Aunt Nan. I sent her a bunch of flowers."

She also received her first letter from Grant who also wondered, as Stuart had, when she was coming home.

A week or so later, after reluctantly saying goodbye to Portet, who had to get back to his Paris business, she finally returned to London where another letter from Bill was awaiting her, telling about his arrest and trial. This letter did not have the angry tone of his previous letter, but returned rather to his concern for her and her safety.

> According to Comstock, you're likely to get five years at hard labor. . . . So I can't decide whether you should or should not return. . . . Maybe you'd better remain in Europe until my trial is over and see what the outcome is, or not come back to the States at all, but go to Canada and direct the cause from there instead, as at one time you thought you might.

On May 31 Margaret replied:

> I have no intention of going to Canada. You seem to think I was planning to go there to have a lovely time. Instead, I was trying to go there to relieve you of the children & of course to be with them myself. For even tho you have given the impression I have deserted my children & have turned people against me I can wait until these storms in life pass,
>
> Allow me Bill once & for all time to relieve you of any duty toward me which you might have at one time performed, and on the receipt of this letter you may feel privileged to send the three children to me on the first boat & consider your duties to them & to me ended for all time.
>
> Your stay in Paris was one big sacrifice to me. I have no regrets, unless it be that my sacrifices were made for one too childish & unworthy to appreciate the depth of their sincerity.
>
> I am resolved to remain where I am. You may go on with birth control propaganda. All that any of them will dare to do will be done legally and when you ask me, or suggest, without any responsibility (I recognize the Sanger in you there) to come and give myself up to the United States government, I wish to reserve a decision until I see what they do with you before I do so.
>
> You will please send me any money sent to me, either through Maisel (a fellow radical) or any other people who contribute to the propaganda. Also, send the children on to me anytime you are tired of them. No doubt the same charity exists in Europe as you have solicited in America. If you can't write to me in a spirit of comradeship you will save yourself and me much unhappiness by not writing at all.

*   *   *

Margaret's anger at Bill was caused, in part, by jealousy. She realized that his arrest resulted in good publicity for the movement, but she felt it was publicity which should have come through her directly. She resented his being in the limelight.

She calmed down when she got a letter from Seattle from Caroline Nelson, a co-worker on the *Woman Rebel*. Caroline reported that the cause was moving along in America, slowly to be sure, but moving. Two Birth Control Leagues had been started on the West Coast—one in Portland, Oregon, and one in San Francisco—though these were comprised entirely of middle- and upper-class women; working women were quite uninterested.

> It seems strange, but it is almost impossible to interest the workers in this. Of course, it is because they are ignorant. I have been trying to talk this matter up among the workers. While they want to get contraceptive information in secret, they cannot discuss it in public without giggling and blushing. The Western groups will simply keep it as a semi-fashionable League. They are people who don't need the information and never did, and how we are going to get it to the workers is the problem that I constantly harp on. They wouldn't know how to use it, is the answer that I constantly get. They have no bath-rooms, they are too tired after a day's work to get up and douche, they are too timid to ask for the material in the drug-store, etc. I myself think that if the Leagues are ever to amount to anything, they must send trained nurses into the workers' districts who speak the language of the district. Our Leagues will do some good, however. When you come back they can protect you and bill you on a speaking tour through the country. . . . I hope that we will soon have you back among us. Even across the border, is better than away over in Europe.

Nevertheless, Margaret had no intention of returning to any part of America until Bill's trial was over and she saw how powerful Comstock still was. She was willing to be a prison martyr, but for a short term only. She would wait where she was.

Meanwhile, she went back to work at the Museum reading the history of the birth-control movement in England mornings and visiting Ellis evenings. He was getting more and more intimate. Since she had come back from Spain, he had taken to addressing her as "Dear Rebel," "Dear Woman," or "My sweet Margaret Woman." One short note written late at night said: "Just a goodnight kiss. You are and always will be very lovely to me!" For a man as shy as Ellis, this was progress indeed.

At the Museum she learned how in 1800, Francis Place had distributed free handbills advocating the sponge method. Though these handbills had a high moral tone and were addressed "To the Married of Both Sexes in Genteel Life," they were labeled "diabolical" by his contemporaries, and he was so vilified he had to stop distributing them. (Since he didn't date these handbills, it is hard to know whether they were written before or after he fathered fifteen children.) In 1826 Richard Carlile had printed a discreetly worded pamphlet called "Everywoman's Book or What is Love." He, too, was condemned. After being called a "corrupter of youth unfit for human companionship," he was run out of town.

By 1841 the pregnant Queen Victoria herself had gingerly advocated contraception. In a letter to her uncle, King Leopold of Belgium, written shortly after her marriage, she complained:

> I think, dearest Uncle, you cannot *really* wish me to be the mama of a *nombreuse famille*, for I think you will see the great inconvenience a *large* family would be to us all, and particularly to the country, independent of the hardship and inconvenience to myself. Men never think, at least seldom think, what a hard task it is for us women to go through this very often.

Yet, inconvenient or not, Victoria went "through with this" nine times in rapid succession, her pregnancies ending only with the death of her husband.

The same story kept repeating itself. The upper classes were trapped as much as the lower. Beatrice Webb, the wealthy co-founder of the English Fabian Society, remarked that whenever she visited one of her nine married sisters, she usually found her either pregnant or suffering from the aftereffects of a miscarriage.

Now Margaret began to read American history. In the mid-nineteen hundreds a Massachusetts country doctor, Charles Knowlton, had fervently taken up the cause of contraception, privately giving his patients advice for which they were extremely grateful. Then he wrote a book called *The Fruits of Philosophy, or the Private Companion of Young People,* by a Physician, but could not find a printer for it until he took it to New York. Still, he was prosecuted in Massachusetts and sentenced to three months at hard labor. A member of the jury remarked to him later: "Well, we brought you in guilty. Still, I like your book and you must let me have a copy of it."

Knowlton's conviction and sentence brought him so much publicity, however, that his book sold ten thousand copies in America and a British edition soon was published.

Knowlton was followed by Charles Bradlaugh, a public-spirited Englishman, who kept republishing the *Fruits of Philosophy* when its first publisher died. Bradlaugh took as a partner an equally public-spirited woman, Mrs. Annie Besant, who at eighteen had married a clergyman because the clergy seemed "such angelic creatures." But after the Reverend Besant hit her in the stomach when she was pregnant because she begged him not to make her have another child again soon, she ran away from him. Although she was penniless, she was soon supporting herself by doing "fancy work" in the Victorian tradition; meanwhile she wrote articles on "The Political Status of Women." When these articles caught Bradlaugh's eye, he chose her to be his publishing partner.

Both Bradlaugh and Besant were arrested and tried for "promoting foul and indecent literature," found guilty, and sentenced to six months in prison, although the verdict was reversed on appeal. But again the trial had gotten so much publicity that it redounded in the book's favor. Also, for forty years Knowlton's work had been selling in England at the rate of seven hundred copies a year; in the next three months sales reached a hundred and twenty-five thousand. While contraception was still a controversial issue, it had finally become a household word.

The Bradlaugh-Besant trial, too, also revived what was perhaps the best book of all on the subject, Dr. George Drysdale's *Elements of Social Science*, signed once more only "by a Physician." This had originally been published with little success in 1855; now it was swept along on the publicity wave, particularly after Dr. Drysdale's son, Dr. C. R. Drysdale, testified forcefully in favor of Bradlaugh and Besant.

At the end of August Margaret began to tire again and took a rest from her studies. She revised her *Family Limitation* pamphlet to include the information she had acquired in Holland, sold several thou-

sand copies in England, and used the proceeds to go off to Paris to visit
Portet. He offered her a three-year contract as an editor; her job would
be to find American and English books on anarchy worth translating
into Spanish or French. But while the salary was attractive and Margaret was very much in love with him, she hesitated because it would
mean staying abroad for a long time. Another series of strange dreams
were beginning to trouble her. (She had joined the Rosicrucian Society
during a trip to Ireland with Ellis, and a belief in dreams was a strong
element in Rosicrucianism.)

Her most frequently recurring dream was about Peggy. Bill had recently written her that Peggy was getting out of hand; when he
stopped by to see her evenings, he found her hard to manage. Thinking
that this might be because she was living among strangers, he had
thought she might feel better if he asked Aunt Nan to visit her. "Don't
want Aunt Nan. Want Mother," Peggy had replied.

Margaret now dreamt that Peggy was calling her. Morning after
morning she would wake up to hear "Mother, come home! Come home!"
The dream, too, was in some way connected with the number 6.

She told Portet she would not sign his contract until she went back to
England and talked things over with Ellis, who had just published *The
World of Dreams*; then, if he thought she should, she would slip into
New York on her Bertha Watson passport and try to find out what her
dream was all about.

So, early in September, she returned to England. Ellis dismissed the
dream as a "night-thought," and advised her to stay abroad until she
saw how Bill Sanger's trial turned out.

This was especially hard to do after she heard that five thousand
more copies of the original *Family Limitation* pamphlet had been secretly distributed in Chicago, and that the women in the stockyards
had kissed the hands of the person who distributed them. Despite her
restlessness, she decided to listen to Ellis and await the result of Bill's
trial.

Bill was tried on September 10 before three judges, the chief being
Justice McInerny, a Catholic. Insisting on going to court alone, without a jury, as Margaret had done, Bill had prepared a long speech on
his own behalf, a speech he had worked on for months as it was designed to express what he called his "burning thoughts of years of conviction." It started with the impassioned statement, "I am charged

with having violated a statute of the Penal Law of this State which makes it a crime to furnish information regarding the prevention of conception . . . I admit that I broke the law, and yet I claim that, in every real sense, it is the law and not I that is on trial here today."

He had barely started when McInerny cut him short: "We don't want to hear all that. Let's get on with the trial." "You don't want to hear me out?" Bill shouted. "I have been deprived of my constitutional rights to a jury. Now you want to stop me from making a statement on my own behalf?" "Sit down," commanded the judge. "I don't want to sit down. You can't intimidate me," Bill shouted even louder. Then, walking to the railing, he glared at the three men on the bench and tried to continue. But McInerny interrupted again:

Persons like you who circulate such pamphlets are a menace to society. There are too many now who believe it is a crime to have children. If some of the women who are going around advocating equal suffrage would go around and advocate women having children they would do a greater service. Your crime violates not only the laws of the State but the laws of God.

Bill tried for a last time to continue his speech but McInerny cut in with: "I declare you guilty. You have a choice of paying a fine of $150 or spending thirty days in jail." At this, Bill leaned forward, raised his fist, and declared: "It is indeed the law that is on trial here today. I would rather be in jail with my convictions than be free at a loss of my manhood and self-respect."

As he made this statement, pandemonium broke loose among the radicals crowding the listener's benches. Judge McInerny cleared the court and rapped for silence. "I sentence you to a fine of $150 or thirty days in jail," he repeated. Bill chose the thirty days, hoping that his trial might at least get the movement good publicity and make Margaret's lot easier if she decided to come home.

But it didn't get the publicity he hoped for; in fact, most of the papers ignored the matter. Under the circumstances, Bill wrote from prison on September 13 advising Margaret to stay in England; he was afraid she'd get a far longer sentence than he had gotten. On stationery headed "The Tombs" he wrote: "The walls are high and there are many keepers." Also, he would leave without a dollar to his name. He had cabled her his last hundred dollars as a birthday present. A week later he wrote her that the wealthy wife of the Public Service Commissioner, Mrs. John Sargent Cram, had offered to pay the board and keep of the children during the month he was in jail. He also wrote that Nan had been to see the "little darlings" and that Peggy, "dear little soul, wants to fly to her 'mudder' on wings." Bill was mainly worried, however, that Margaret might "have to spend a long time in one of these Hell Holes," and he didn't know what to advise her. She'd have to make up her own mind whether to come home or stay abroad.

She decided to come home.

Margaret sailed at the end of September and arrived in New York on October 4. She hurried first to the Village to see Peggy and Grant, then out to Long Island where Stuart was in school. Oddly enough she did not go to jail to see Bill, or even let him know she was back. He wrote her on October 6:

Peg Dear Soul, today the glorious news reached me thru Abbott that you had at last come back . . . a thousand emotions seize me. My memories recede back to the good old days of White Plains and . . . all past differences recede to nothing . . .

I hope the impression you receive from the news incident to my trial will be a favorable one. I shall be sad indeed if you will conclude that my thirty days in prison shall have cast a cloud over your ultimate acquittal. I come out October ninth, Saturday, 9 A.M.

You beat me to see the kids and get that first smack. I was looking forward to the time when they would recognize you and give you that first kiss in a year! But some things are denied me. I shall be curious to hear how Peggy took it all when she beheld you. Did she know you, I wonder, and Granty, little soul, he is a joy. Now sleep long and well and eat well. If on receipt of this letter you need anything write me to 277 W. 11th, (mark it hold until called for) and I'll arrange to bring over what you wish.

Love as of old from Bill.

As soon as he was released he rushed over to see Margaret who was staying at an inexpensive hotel. But she was not in a good mood. She angrily berated him for having no money to give her, as well as for letting Comstock's decoy wheedle a pamphlet out of him. He lost his temper and the meeting ended when he stormed out.

On October 13 she sent him a chilling note.

*   *   *

BILL DEAR:

As we do not seem able to talk things over without each insulting the other I am going to try to write the things I want to say to you.

First, let us *not* discuss the causes of our feelings toward each other. I recognize that you feel exactly the same toward me that I feel toward you. Just what to call that feeling I do not know for it is a mixture of memories, beautiful, ugly, disappointing, inspiring, happy & sad. It has no name, only its existing means a parting of the ways because it causes pain every time we meet. The fact is we can not forget. You have had a trying winter thru which you have blamed me for your sufferings. I have had a trying winter thru which I blamed you for my sufferings. No excuses, no intentions now can erase the scars those bitter thoughts have left in either of us. . . . I knew my feelings toward you would be this way before I came here. I could have told you the same things in February, but after your arrest I wanted to help you and I did not want you to blame my letters to you for any failure you might meet. But I find it was a foolish way to do.

I give up, Bill. Your vindictiveness & the reports & lies you have passed on in either anger or confidence (I do not accuse you of inventing them. You have repeated them, which from you stamped them with the truth) have increased the break which can never be bridged. Your insulting remarks & actions last night before the porter & hall boy only convince me that I subject myself to abuse & insult each time we meet. I should like to return your name to you or drop it, & unless you will come to a sane & agreeable or mutual understanding with me I shall be forced to proceed in a way much against my inclinations. Sincerely & affectionately,

MARGARET.

A few weeks later Peggy suddenly took ill with pneumonia. Margaret moved in with the friends who were caring for her and tried to nurse her, but Peggy became worse and was moved to Mt. Sinai where Ethel was on the nursing staff. There were no antibiotics in 1915, and the child, already weakened from her bout with polio, sank quickly. She died at midnight on November 6.

Margaret, Bill, and Grant all went wild with grief. Grant had lost his closest friend. Sixty years later he bitterly described her death: "They took my little sister up to one of the best hospitals in New York. All the hot-shots worked on her, yet four days later they handed us back a dead body."

Bill seemed to go mad. Before Peggy was buried he made a plaster cast of her body, put the cast into a suitcase and kept it with him for ten years. His second wife, Vidia, discovered it, by then broken to pieces. Bill still refused to part with it, but Vidia insisted.

"You can't keep it, Bill. You must let it go. You must."

"What shall we do with it?"

"Bury it."

"Bury it? Where? How?"

"We'll dig a grave in a place from which you can see the town in which she was born, and bury it there."

So they took the suitcase and rode to a spot on the Palisades above the Hudson River from which Hastings can be seen. There they dug the grave and silently buried the cast.

On the way back Bill spoke: "They say that Hell is a noisy place, full of cries and lamentations. It isn't. It's a quiet and lonely place. I know. I've been there." Vidia reached for his hand and rode on.

Margaret grieved too, but denied feeling guilty. "Guilt is a Freudian concept," she explained, "and I don't believe in Freud. The days after Peggy died were the darkest days of my life, but I never felt guilty at all."

Nevertheless, she ran from one seance to another hoping for a message from Peggy. In her autobiography she describes a seance:

> The room was dark and someone was holding each of (my) hands. Just before the lights went on, a woman at my left squeezed my hand and whispered, You have had a terrible sorrow.
>
> So has everyone, I replied.
>
> Yours is for a child, a little girl. She just passed before me and said, "Mother, stop grieving. You mustn't grieve any more."
>
> The lights went on. I turned toward the woman to question her further, but she had disappeared.
>
> The terrible loneliness remained. For two years at least after her death. It was impossible for me to sit across from a child in a train or a streetcar. Tears would flood my eyes and I would move swiftly away.

*   *   *

She went to a Rosicrucian meeting where she was handed a letter signed with a cabalistic symbol. It read: "We are helping with your boys largely through the influence and help of your dear little girl who is in such close touch with them. Through her closeness we can accurately sense their needs and so help better. It will be a good summer for all those at the Round Table. We are on the Rising Tide."

There was a second similar letter, and a third written in a large, childish hand: "Dear mother. We can be together a lot at Aunt Nan's so you'll know. Stuart and Grant will help each other. It will be a beautiful summer for all of this. Good night, dear mother. Love and kisses. Peggy."

Margaret wrote across the last: "Said to be Peggy's message to M.S.," and put it carefully away.

Every year for the rest of her life she crossed out the page in her diary dated May 31 with a long diagonal line, writing at its head "Peggy's birthday." She also crossed out the page dated November 6, writing at the top "Peggy's Anniversary," referring to the pious Catholic belief that this was the anniversary of Peggy's entrance into Heaven. On both these days, she canceled all engagements, secluded herself, and mourned.

After Peggy's death, Margaret became a driven woman. She drove hard in one direction and toward one goal, that of birth control, saying that this was the weapon she would have liked to put in Peggy's hands.

Undoubtedly she was driven by another reason as well. She had been warned because of her latent tuberculosis never to become pregnant again. Because Bill, too, was afraid for her, she could trust him to see to it that she did not; with her other lovers she could not be so sure. She needed to find a birth-control method better than the diaphragm, one that was as foolproof as possible, both for herself and for other women. And she would do everything in her power to see that it was found.

10

DARK DAYS AND REBOUND

Margaret could sit and mourn for just so long. Now that she had decided to stay in the States, her immediate job was to let the prosecuting attorney know she was ready to stand trial.

She had one stroke of luck. While she was away, Comstock had died; he had caught a fatal case of flu on the very day of Bill's trial. But Comstock's death didn't nullify the Comstock Law. She still had to face her trial, and for that she needed friends, money, and organized support.

The first person to whom she turned was Mary Ware Dennett, a plump, gray-haired widow who earned her living as an interior decorator. Believing that Margaret might never come back after fleeing the country, she had gotten together with Anita Block, the *Call* editor, and Clara Stillman, a wealthy society woman, to form the National Birth Control League, composed largely of the society women whose homes Mrs. Dennett had decorated. Margaret had been furious when she heard about it, but now realized she needed their help. She wrote Mrs. Dennett to ask for her support.

Mrs. Dennett responded with an invitation to meet with her and several leaders of the new league. Margaret went full of hope, but her reception was cool; she was bluntly told she would get no support. The goal of the new league was to change the law, not to defy it as Margaret had done in *The Woman Rebel*. Margaret lost her temper and walked out.

Without the league's financial support, she realized, she would have to earn money on her own. Ethel suggested she go back to taking on private maternity cases; Margaret refused. "Would you mind telling me then," Ethel demanded, "how you intend to get hold of defense money, much less make a living?" "I have cast myself on the universe," Margaret replied. "It will take care of me somehow." A few days later Ethel got a letter in the mail for Margaret from a West Coast admirer. In it was a check for fifty dollars. As Ethel handed it over, she commented drily: "Here's your first check from God."

When news of Peggy's death and Margaret's upcoming trial were reported in the papers, she began to receive more letters with money in them. These were mostly pathetic letters. Women wrote of children who had died twenty years before, but for whom they still mourned; some even enclosed pictures of the dead children or locks of their hair. The lumberjacks and miners who had known Margaret through Bill Haywood sent letters too. The contributions were small, usually from one to five dollars, but they mounted up. Then she sent out a general release to all Socialists and I.W.W. locals, asking them to hold fundraising parties for her.

Even more helpful than defense money were two open letters to President Wilson.

The first, sent by a group of well-known Chicago writers including Margaret Anderson and John Cowper Powys, asked him to "use his powerful office to help Mrs. Sanger in the interest of free speech and the betterment of the race." The second, sent from England, was signed by famous names like H. G. Wells, Arnold Bennett, and Bernard Shaw. These letters appeared in newspapers throughout the country and caused still more money to pour in.

Margaret's trial was fast approaching, however, and she was growing nervous. Wanting the best lawyer she could find, she again appealed to Untermyer. But he had not changed his mind. He told her the law might not be everything it should be, but it was still the law, and she had broken it. His only advice was that she plead guilty, and he might as a result be able to get a "deal" with the prosecuting attorney to drop the case.

Margaret refused to plead guilty. She wanted the publicity of a trial, and a deal would rule that out. She decided to go to court without a lawyer as she had done before. Moreover, she would wear the costume of the women anarchists—a black skirt and white shirtwaist with a man's black necktie.

At this point John Reed, a well-known magazine editor, made an excellent suggestion. Most people thought of women crusaders as hard-faced Amazons, but Margaret was feminine, beautiful, and could look meek as a lamb when she pleased. He advised against the anarchist costume and suggested getting Underwood and Underwood, among the leading photographers of the day, to take a picture of her in a plain dark dress with a wide Quaker collar, her hair done up in a simple coil and her two sons beside her. The release of this picture, he felt, would raise a lot of sympathy for her.

Reed's suggestion was quickly followed. Margaret posed with Stuart leaning against her shoulder and Grant in a Buster Brown suit leaning against her lap. Hundreds of papers used it, and it did more to counteract the image of the shrieking woman rebel and gain the support of important people than anything she had done before.

A dinner in her honor was also arranged with the help of John Reed at the elegant Brevoort Hotel on January 17, the eve of her trial. Among the people who attended were Walter Lippmann, the journalist; Herbert Croly, editor of the *New Republic;* Fola La Follette, daughter of U.S. Senator La Follette; and Drs. Ira S. Wile and A. L. Goldwater, Health Commissioners of the City of New York. And from the inner circles of society came women like Mrs. Ogden Reid and Mrs. Thomas Hepburn, mother of the actress Katharine Hepburn. It was the kind of turnout no newspaper could ignore.

Possibly with professional help, she memorized a short and dignified speech. Knowing that not everybody in the audience approved of her previous tactics, she tried in this speech to forestall their criticism:

> I realize keenly that many of those who understand and would support the birth-control propaganda if it were carried out in a safe and sane manner cannot sympathize with the methods I have followed in my attempt to arouse working women to the fact that bringing a child into the world is the greatest responsibility. . . . They tell me that *The Woman Rebel* was badly written, that it was crude, that it was emotional and hysterical, that it mixed issues, that it was defiant and too radical. Well, to all of these indictments I plead guilty!

Then, with a quick change of tone intended to flatter her audience she emphasized certain points:

I know that all of you are better able to cope with the subject than I am. I know that physicians and scientists have a fund of information greater than I have on the subject of family limitation . . .

There is nothing new, nothing radical in birth control. Aristotle advocated it; Plato advocated it; all our great modern thinkers have advocated it.

Yet all this scientific and technical discussion has only had the effect of producing more technical and scientific discussion—all very necessary and very stimulating to that very small group of men and women who could understand it. BUT all during the long years this matter has been discussed, advocated, refuted, the people themselves—the poor people especially—were blindly, desperately practicing family limitation—just as they are practicing it today. To them birth control does not mean what it does to us. TO THEM it has meant the killing of babies, infanticide, abortions. Women from time immemorial have tried to avoid unwanted motherhood. WE ALL KNOW the tribe of professional abortionists which has sprung up and profited by this terrible misfortune.

WE KNOW, TOO, that when the practice of abortion was put under the ban by the church, an alternate evil—the foundling asylum, with its horrifying history—sprang up. THERE IS NO NEED to go into the terrible facts concerning the recklessness, the misery, the filth, with which children have been and still are being brought into the world.

I merely want to point out the situation I found when I entered the battle. ON THE ONE HAND, I found wise men, sages, and scientists, discussing birth control among themselves. But their ideas were sterile. They did not influence or affect the tremendous facts of life among the working classes and the disinherited.

HOW COULD I BRIDGE THIS CHASM? How could I reach these people? How could I awaken public opinion to this tremendous problem?

I MIGHT HAVE TAKEN up a policy of safety, sanity, and conservatism, but would I have got a hearing?

AND AS I BECAME MORE AND MORE CONSCIOUS OF the vital importance of this idea, I felt myself in the position of one who has discovered that a house is on fire, and I found that it was up to me to shout out the warning! THE TONE OF THE VOICE

may have been indelicate and unladylike, and was not at all the
tone that many of us would rather hear.

BUT THIS VERY GATHERING—this honor you have thrust
upon me—is ample proof that intelligent and constructive
thought has been aroused. SOME OF US may only be fit to dramatize a situation—to focus attention upon obsolete laws, like
this one I must face tomorrow morning. Then, others, more experienced in constructive organization can gather together all
this sympathy and interest which has been aroused, and direct it.

Finally, having insinuated that she was seeking no personal glory,
she ended in her low, clear voice:

I THANK YOU for your encouragement and support. MY RE-
QUEST TO YOU TONIGHT is that all you social workers—so
much better fitted to carry on this work than I—that you consider
and organize this interest. THIS IS THE MOST IMPORTANT
STEP, AND ONLY IN THIS WAY CAN I BE VINDICATED!!
LET US PUT THE UNITED STATES OF AMERICA UPON THE
MAP OF THE CIVILIZED WORLD!!

The speech had the effect Margaret was looking for. Waves of applause rolled through the dining room of the Brevoort, and many stood
up to pledge their financial support. Rather unexpectedly, Mary Ware
Dennett was among them. And because Margaret was now going to
conduct her campaign more sedately, the National Birth Control
League would support her, too. As a result, so many people, rich and
poor, showed up at the trial the next morning that they filled every corner of the courtroom and spilled over into the corridor. The conservative *Evening Globe* reported that "twenty expensive motor cars
manned by liveried persons filled the streets around the court building," while the *Call* boasted that "so many reporters and photographers showed up, there was hardly room for them at the press table."

But suddenly there came a surprise. Arriving late, District Attorney
Content threw a bombshell into the proceedings by asking for a postponement to January 24. Margaret protested, but was overruled; she
and the audience had no choice but to leave. "Outside," the *Globe* story
continued, "they (the crowd) surrounded her and proposed three cheers
which were given with a gusto that woke echoes for blocks around the
Federal Building."

On the morning of January 24 she returned to court, but again Content appeared and asked for a postponement. By this time his strategy was obvious. He was representing a government that was doing everything in its power to delay a publicity-making trial. This went on for another month. Though every postponement got her name and the words "birth control" into print, the government was obviously winning by wearing down her support.

On February 18 Harold Content ended the matter by issuing a *nolle prosequi,* an order to drop the case altogether. He made a formal statement to the press:

> Since the date of the filing of the indictment, no copies of *The Woman Rebel* have to my knowledge been deposited in the mails. The defendant is in no sense a disorderly person, and is not engaged in any way in the traffic of obscene literature. . . . While the pamphlets or magazines themselves may be unmailable, the evidence is not of such a character as to establish the defendant's guilt beyond all reasonable doubt, and of such character as to warrant the expectation of a conviction in the event that the indictments should be brought to trial.

In a later release, he admitted:

> We are determined not to let Mrs. Sanger become a martyr if we can help it. We are also not the least bit interested in having a public debate on sex theories at this time.

The question of whether material relating to birth control could be legally barred from the mails and classed as obscenity was left unresolved. "The quashing of the indictment settles nothing," said an editorial in the *New York Globe.* "The right of American citizens to discuss sociological questions according to their convictions is just where it had been—subject to the mutton-headed restrictions of some post office clerk."

Still, a strategic victory had been won. Although Margaret had not been given the jail sentence she had begun to hope for as well as fear, she had become a nationally known figure around whom important people were rallying. Best of all, the matter of birth control had been well publicized. As Walter Lippmann said, "Margaret Sanger has kicked the subject clear across to the Pacific."

She realized this was the moment to follow through. Gathering her energy, she mailed letters to thousands of labor groups and women's clubs throughout the country, telling them she was ready to start a speaking tour immediately. "Write at once and tell me the capacity of the largest hall," she wrote her supporters. "Start making your town alive with interest so it will be ready for me, for birth control is the pivot around which all our social problems swing."

Indeed, she was so busy planning her trip she never thanked Marie Stopes, the woman responsible for the open letter of British support to President Wilson which the papers reported in full. Nor did she find time to write Havelock Ellis, who had written her six letters since she had come home.

In one of these, dated November 15, he told her she reminded him of a character, also named Margaret, in an old play by George Chapman. This character had told her lover she would not marry him by legal form, but by a beautiful ceremony of her own instead: "May we not our own contract make and marry before Heaven? Are not the laws of God or Nature more than the formal laws of man? Are outward rites more virtuous than the substance of holy nuptials solemnized within? Or shall laws made to curb the common world . . . halt them that are a law unto themselves?"

Ellis heartily agreed with the fictitious Margaret and ended: "So you see, dear, I knew and approved of the *Woman Rebel* many years before she took to editing a paper."

This was the sanction she needed. Ellis, her idol, was telling her she was not subject to the laws "made to curb the common world," but was a law unto herself. She kissed his letter over and over, and sent a short note explaining her silence: "My daughter Peggy was ill and died on Nov. 6." This done, she put on her most sedate clothes, sent Grant and Stuart off to separate boarding schools (probably promising to pay for their board and tuition out of her lecture fees), and started off on her tour.

THE BROWNSVILLE CLINIC
OPENS AND CLOSES

All her life Margaret was a timid and nervous speaker. Though she took a course in public speaking, she would tremble violently before every speech and was always exhausted and overexcited at the end.

She opened her new tour eagerly, since for the first time she was working through a lecture agency that arranged for groups to pay her expenses whenever possible. If they would not, she simply passed the hat, and, like Emma Goldman, sometimes got surprisingly large donations. She started in Pittsburgh and then moved on to Cleveland. She stayed in each place for a few days after her speech to organize local birth-control fund raising, laying out plans for enlisting the aid of key people. She also contacted local lawyers familiar with the legal situation, because not all states forbade the giving of birth-control information, as long as it did not go through the mails. Then she approached wealthy women directly, convincing them to give substantial sums; if she was able to start a league, as she did in Cleveland, she put it in touch with Mrs. Dennett's league, since she had none of her own. She was gaining experience as a national organizer.

Yet she was not always successful. In St. Louis, when she arrived at the lecture hall which had been booked and paid for, she found the door locked. The *Post Dispatch* explained that "protests from Catholic priests and laymen resulted in the announcement by the management that Mrs. Sanger would not be permitted to speak." But Margaret asked the waiting crowd of 1500 to follow her to her car, where she stood on the seat and began her lecture. She had just started, however, when a policeman grabbed her arm and forced her to stop, claiming that the Catholics would be incensed. She cried out, "We're not in St. Louis. We're in Russia!" and tried to continue. Fearing a riot by the crowd who had begun to shout "Go on! Go on! The Catholics run the town," her chauffeur stepped hard on the gas and drove away.

This was the first time the Catholic Church had openly used this kind of pressure against her. Yet in a way she welcomed it, for every time her opponents illegally stopped her, they helped her cause. Large numbers of new supporters would be sure to demand the free speech guaranteed by the Constitution. In St. Louis she sent out a newspaper release announcing she was suing the management for breach of contract. Free speech was something that newspapers in particular were bound to defend. The St. Louis *Globe-Democrat* warned that "to throttle free speech is to provide it with a megaphone," and *Reedy's Mirror* said, "No idea let loose in the world has ever been suppressed . . . Mrs. Sanger's exclusion from a theatre has set people to thinking and talking about her message who might otherwise never have heard about her."

In fact, the reaction was so immediate that the St. Louis Men's Club invited her to speak at a luncheon in their own meeting rooms the next day. Forty Catholic members resigned as a result, but a hundred new members joined.

In Denver, Colorado, where women already had the vote (they did not get it in all the states until 1920), she was welcomed at the railroad station by a cheering delegation that included some of the city's top officials. Among them was Judge Ben Lindsay, a man famous for his theories on trial marriage. Judge Lindsay presided at her meeting, and for the first time, Margaret found herself facing an audience composed almost exclusively of the wives of doctors, lawyers, and other professional men.

In Seattle, old-time radicals turned out in force; lumberjacks, Wobblies, Socialists, and free-thinkers filled the hall, crowding around the platform and holding out their hands as they called out, "Put it there, Margaret. We're behind you!" But in Portland, Oregon, she ran into trouble. She had just revised her original *Family Limitation* pamphlet with the help of Dr. Marie Equi, the doctor who had been riding on horseback to care for the cowboys and Indians ever since the Northwest had opened up. When three male volunteers sold copies of the pamphlet in the aisles after her speech, they were arrested. She wanted to stay and help them because giving birth-control information was not illegal in Oregon, as long as it did not go through the mails—but she had other speaking engagements and couldn't wait. When she returned a few days later, she found that the Portland mayor and city council had met secretly and passed a *post facto* ordinance forbidding the pamphlet's sale.

At this point Margaret made the Portland arrests a public issue. She and Dr. Equi called for a city-wide protest meeting at which they and three other male volunteers all distributed the pamphlet. They were all arrested and hauled off to jail. Hundreds of women marched behind them demanding to be arrested also, until the sheriff, overwhelmed, locked the jail door. When those who had been jailed were taken before the judge a few hours later, several spectators offered to provide bail, but Margaret refused; the group spent the night in their cells instead.

The next day the three men who had originally sold the pamphlet were put on trial. Several of the town's leading lawyers defended them without fee; still, all were found guilty and the pamphlets pronounced "obscene." Margaret and the women were given suspended sentences as first offenders, and the men were fined ten dollars apiece.

The arrests and fines stirred tremendous public interest. When Margaret hired fifteen men to walk through the Portland streets carrying signs reading "Poverty and Large Families Go Hand in Hand," or "Poor Women Are Denied What the Rich Possess," the reaction of the passersby was almost entirely sympathetic. Her keen publicity sense had once more made her follow through at exactly the right time.

By July of 1916, after touring steadily for three and a half months, Margaret was exhausted. When she went back to New York to rest, she found to her surprise that Sanger had left town. He had quit his architectural job and sailed for Spain to paint. A letter written before he left was waiting for her:

Now that on the opening of your tour you are entering on the still larger life, I would like you to consider that I shall do the same. For I too have aspirations—yes! You say you do not understand me. I know you don't. I was never meant for long periods of economic strife. I must have one more year in which to prove myself. I should not be sacrificed on the altar of the Perpetual Immediate (any more than you). . . . The time has come when I must have a year of uninterrupted work to accomplish anything. . . . My urge is too strong to deny it any longer.

He loved his children dearly, but if she didn't stay home to take care of them, neither would he.

There was other unexpected news, too. In New York Emma Goldman had been arrested for lecturing on birth control and had received fifteen days in the workhouse.

In April 1916, the Socialist, Ben Reitman, had been arrested for distributing birth-control pamphlets and given sixty days in the workhouse, and in May Jessie Ashley, Ida Rauh Eastman (Max Eastman's wife), and Bolton Hall, an ardent birth-control supporter, were also arrested for distributing one of Emma Goldman's pamphlets.

Still worse, a young Boston intellectual, Van Kleeck Allison, had been arrested for distributing Margaret's pamphlets to a group of factory workers; he had gotten the whopping sentence of three years in the House of Correction.

Margaret went off to Truro in July, taking along the huge batch of letters sent to her hotels during her tour, letters she had been too busy or too tired to read.

She took Stuart, Grant, and her father along to the seaside, since Higgins, at seventy, was no longer able to work. Higgins had been living for a while in an Old Soldiers' Home, but there he had talked so much and so loudly about his radical opinions that the Home had thrown him out. At Truro he was accepted as a "character"—an eccentric old windbag who went swimming with his straw hat on, insisting that the old raincoat he slipped on after a swim was enough to dry and warm him immediately, though actually it was the pint of whiskey hidden in the pocket of the raincoat that warmed him. He helped her read the letters that had awaited her in New York, letters like these:

I have born and raised six children and I know all the hardships of raising a large family. I have three daughters that have two children each, and every now and again they go and get rid of one and someday I think it will kill them but they say they don't care for they will be better dead than living in hell with a big family and nothing to raise them on.

There is a woman in our town who has eight children and is expecting another. Directly after the birth of each child she goes insane for a while, and they send her away. She comes home and is in the family way again in a few months. Still the doctors will do nothing for her.

In a few months I will again be a mother, the fourth child in five years. While carrying my babies I am always partly paralyzed on one side. Do not know the cause but the doctor said at last birth we must be "more careful" as I could not stand having so many children. I wonder if my body will survive this next birth if my reason will.

Pamphlets alone could do little for these women, Margaret realized. The only answer was a chain of clinics to which women could go and be fitted with diaphragms. As a test case, Margaret would have to start the first birth-control clinic in the country, preferably in New York, where she personally could supervise it and use it as a model for the rest of the country,

Starting such a clinic would be difficult, however. The laws on birth control in New York State were unclear. Section 1142 of the State Penal Code declared that nobody could give contraceptive advice to anyone for any reason. Section 1145 allowed doctors to give advice for the "cure or prevention of disease." Section 1145 had been interpreted by the courts, as well as the medical and legal professions, as meaning that condoms could be given to men for the prevention of venereal disease when consorting with prostitutes, but not as birth-control devices when consorting with their wives. The only way to clear up the matter was to open a clinic and see what happened.

Margaret started plans for a test clinic during the summer, after telling the New York City District Attorney and the newspapers what she intended to do.

She had three immediate goals: first, to find a location for her clinic; second, to find a doctor willing to supervise it; third, to raise enough money to open it—money for rent, furnishings, and supplies.

She started looking for a place when she returned from the Cape in September. After a long search, primarily among the worst slums of the city, she found two small rooms on the first floor of a crowded tenement at 46 Amboy Street in the Brownsville section of Brooklyn.

A check from a West Coast admirer paid the first month's rent. A few chairs, a desk for the waitingroom, a coal stove, a blackboard, and an examining table for the consulting room were provided by friends, while the contraceptive supplies came from sources Margaret didn't think it prudent to disclose.

Yet the biggest problem was still that of finding a doctor to supervise the clinic. Two women doctors tentatively agreed to help. Then they heard that Dr. Mary Halton, a staff doctor at Grosvenor Hospital in New York, had been forced to resign her post after she had prescribed a diaphragm to a woman with severe tuberculosis, whose life would have been endangered by pregnancy. This made the two women who might have helped afraid they might lose, not only their hospital connections, but possibly their licenses to practice. They bowed out.

In despair Margaret turned to Dr. Marie Equi, who had recently written her:

> Margaret, darling girl, it has been good to have you here. If I absorbed your time it was because of my mental hunger. You are the sweetest girl in the world, brave and true. . . . You little bunch of hellfire, I love you for the brave spirit you are.

But Dr. Equi wouldn't leave her established practice and come East on a gamble. She, too, declined.

Margaret's last bet was Dr. William J. Robinson, the sympathetic editor of the *Medical Critic and Guide.* He wouldn't help her either; but he did give her some sound advice:

> The American Medical Association cannot and will not in any way interfere with you. It is outside of its domain. The only Society that could have something to say would be the New York County Medical Society, but I am quite certain that you need fear nothing at their hands, because their province is only to interfere with illegal practitioners, with people who *treat* disease. As you will not deal with treatment, only with hygienic advice, they can have nothing to say to you. Neither can the Federal authorities. The only people you have to be afraid of are the State authorities, or the Vice Society.
>
> The first and most important thing is to have every woman who applies for advice sign a slip that says she is a married woman and that she wants the information for her personal use, as for

either hygienic, hereditary, or economic reasons she feels herself unable to have any more children. Of course you cannot demand that the women bring their marriage certificates, but the fact alone that they sign such a statement would absolve you from any blame and from any possible accusations of fostering "immorality." If you should publicly declare yourself willing to give that information to unmarried women you would have the law down on you at once.

If you do as I say, and if you don't charge the people anything for advice, which I know you won't, they would have great difficulty in doing anything to you, and this Birth Control Clinic might become the germ of thousands of similar clinics.

At this point Margaret gave up the idea of getting a doctor and got her sister Ethel to go in with her instead. Ethel, at least, was a trained nurse, with a Mt. Sinai Nursing School diploma to prove it. Next she got Fania Mindell, a Russian woman who earned her living as a translator and was willing to be a secretary at the clinic without pay.

Yet there was still one more problem. Margaret wanted to print thousands of handbills advertising the clinic, but printing cost money, and she had none. She asked Max Maisel, a radical bookseller who had published *What Every Girl Should Know,* if he had sold enough copies to owe her royalties. He answered that from May 1915 to September 1916 she had earned a royalty total of $580.25, but he had sent her so many cash advances during her speaking trip, that she actually owed him over three hundred dollars. Maisel would be glad to let her work off the debt the following year, but beyond that he could not go.

She had no choice except to find a printer who was willing to do the handbills on credit. Five thousand were hurriedly printed in three languages—English, Yiddish, and Italian—the most common languages in Brownsville. The handbills read:

MOTHERS
Can you afford to have a large family?
Do you want any more children?
If not, why do you have them?
DO NOT KILL. DO NOT TAKE LIFE, BUT PREVENT.
Safe, harmless information can be obtained of

Nurses
46 Amboy Street
Near Pitkin Ave.—Brooklyn
Tell your friends and neighbors. All mothers welcome. A registration fee of 10 cents entitles any mother to this information.

Margaret, Ethel and Fania shoved these handbills under doors, stuffed them into mailboxes, and tacked them up in halls.

The clinic was due to open on October 16 at 8 A.M.; by seven o'clock a line of waiting women extended halfway to the corner. Some were alone, some had brought neighbors for moral support, some were pushing baby carriages or holding onto small children, because they had no one to leave them with, and a few had even persuaded their husbands to come along. Fifty rushed in as soon as the doors were opened, and a total of one hundred and forty had been seen before closing time at five.

The next day all the Italian, Yiddish, and English papers carried a story about the clinic, and even more women came than on the first day. Within a week, women had managed somehow to get to Brownsville from as far away as Connecticut, Massachusetts, and New Jersey. And always their tales were alike: homes with only two rooms, in which seven people slept; homes where the husband earned fifteen dollars a week when he worked; wives who had had eight children, two abortions, and so many miscarriages they couldn't remember the number. Fifty to a hundred letters a day also poured in from women who couldn't get to the clinic, pleading for the information by mail.

While Fania took histories, Margaret and Ethel fitted a few women with diaphragms and told the rest about condoms and douches. Though the antiseptics recommended for douching were often harsh and dangerous, they were the best they knew. Margaret, Ethel, and Fania kept going so fast they were glad to stop for a breather every few hours and sip the hot tea Mrs. Rabinowitz, the wife of the store's owner, brought down, accompanied by free doughnuts contributed by the German baker next door.

On the tenth day a large woman who called herself Mrs. Margaret Whitehurst walked into the waiting room and told the familiar story of too many children and not enough money. Yet somehow she didn't look like the other women; her voice was too professional and her clothes too fine. Fania became suspicious and whispered to Ethel, "That's a policewoman, sure as fate." "What can we do?" answered Ethel. "We can't prove it. Send her in anyway." Fania sent her in, the woman was given the information she asked for, and when she left she insisted on handing Fania two dollars instead of the usual ten cents. Fania, more suspicious than ever, posted the two-dollar bill on the wall with a note under it: "Received from Mrs. ? of the Police Department."

Fania's intuition was right. The next day Mrs. Whitehurst strode in and went directly to Margaret. "I'm a police officer," she snapped. "You're under arrest." Three plainclothesmen from the vice squad, detectives Boylan and Mooney and Sergeant Barry, marched in a minute later and barred the door, while another policeman took up position outside. Margaret, Fania, and Ethel were handed arrest warrants, and the patients were ordered to stand in line and give their names and addresses. Slum women are usually afraid of the police, and some started to scream, while others began to cry. Margaret did her best to assure them they were not under arrest too, but it took a good half hour until the police agreed to let them go home.

Meanwhile, all the clinic's literature, contraceptive supplies, case histories, and even the examining table were thrown into the police van. The clinic had been in operation just ten days.

The next day the *New York World* reported the raid this way:

Enraged when she was told she was under arrest, Mrs. Sanger turned on Mrs. Whitehurst and cried, "You are not a woman!" "Save all that sort of thing to tell to the judge in the morning." "No, I'll tell it to you now. And you have two ears to hear me, too." "Mrs. Sanger," interrupted Sergeant Barry, "put on your hat and coat and come quietly with us to the station house." "I don't know about that. I think if you want to take me to your old station house, you'll have to drag me there."

Margaret flatly refused to ride in the patrol wagon; she insisted on marching, with head up and eyes flashing, the mile to the Raymond Street jail, with several policemen walking behind her and Ethel and Fania at her side. As the three women left the clinic they heard a loud scream behind them. It came from a woman with a baby carriage who had just arrived. The woman abandoned the carriage and started to run after them. "Come back! Come back and save me!" she was crying. She kept running until friends caught her and stopped her. The policemen and prisoners moved on.

In court, Margaret and Ethel were charged with violating Section 1142 of the Penal Code which forbade the giving out of birth-control information, while Fania was charged with selling the "indecent book," *What Every Girl Should Know*. They were told that each case would be considered separately, and the trials were put over from October 26 to November 6, when they were postponed indefinitely because of a heavy court calendar. But by November 13, Margaret had gotten impatient and decided to reopen the clinic. She did so that very afternoon, but two days later the police raided it for the second time and forced the landlord to sign eviction papers. The clinic was now closed for good and a trial date was set for November 20.

This time Margaret decided that the days of appearing in court without a lawyer were over; she definitely needed one. She succeeded in getting Jonah J. Goldstein, a man with good political connections, who was later to become famous as a judge and the founder of the Grand Street Boys. Knowing that there was little hope of getting her off without obtaining a new and favorable interpretation of Section 1142, even though doing that meant taking the matter all the way up to the Supreme Court, Goldstein readied himself for a long series of legal maneuvers.

On November 20 Judge McInerney, who presided at Bill Sanger's trial, was on the bench. Margaret quickly wrote McInerney an open letter which she released to the papers:

> In those birth-control cases at which you have presided, you have shown to all thinking men and women an unfailing prejudice and exposed a mind steeped in the bigotry and intolerance of the Inquisition. To come before you implies conviction. Now in all fairness do you want a case of this character brought forcibly before you when the defendant feels and believes you are prejudiced against her?

The next day McInerney asked to be excused from the case. Margaret smilingly posed for photographers in front of the courthouse, and a few days later, Dr. I. S. Wile held a public debate favoring birth control against the objections of several prominent Brooklyn Catholics. All of this kept the case very much alive.

Jonah Goldstein now began the legal maneuvers he had planned. While he did not succeed in getting Margaret, Ethel, and Fania the jury trial he hoped for, he did get the case postponed to January 4, 1917.

Margaret spent the extra time lining up supporters. She no longer turned to radicals, but to the kind of society women who had given her the dinner at the Brevoort. From a group of socially prominent women she formed a Committee of One Hundred with Mrs. Amos Pinchot, wife of the governor of Pennsylvania, as chairman.

The organization whose support Margaret wanted most was the New York County Medical Society. On December 26, at a meeting called especially to consider the subject of birth control, the Medical Society voted 210 to 72 against supporting any organization that called for modification of the present restrictive laws. This flabbergasted Margaret, who had expected strong backing from them, if only because Dr. Abraham Jacobi, president of their parent organization, the American Medical Association, had, not long before, come out strongly in favor of birth control. Besides, it seemed to her that getting permission to give patients birth-control information would be invaluable to doctors. How could they turn down such an opportunity?

She could only conclude that doctors were men first, and physicians second. For centuries they had had the power to decide the size of their families, by using or not using the condom or *coitus interruptus* (withdrawal). Women had never had this power; they had had to bear as many children as their husbands chose.

The Brownsville trial finally got under way on January 8, 1917, with Judges Garvin, Herrman and O'Keefe, the latter a staunch Catholic, on the bench. Ethel was called to the bar first.

The district attorney accused Ethel of dispensing illegal contraceptive information which she freely admitted. But when he charged that the clinic was a "money-making affair" because of the ten-cent charge, and that it was "anti-Semitic and anti-Italian because it was trying to reduce the number of Jews and Italians in Brooklyn," the Committee of One Hundred, who filled the spectator's benches, booed so loudly that the judges threatened to clear the court.

There was disruption again when a witness, Dr. Morris Kahn, whom

Goldstein had taken much trouble to find, testified that the clinic was of great benefit to the community and had his testimony ruled out as "irrelevant, incompetent and immaterial." Even worse, Goldstein was allowed only fifteen minutes to argue the unconstitutionality of Section 1142, though during those fifteen minutes Goldstein managed to make a few excellent points:

> The whole purpose of Section 1142 was to promote a larger population. But what if we had a similar law for fining a bachelor over thirty, who had the means to support a wife and family, but did not marry? . . . Would this clearly not be an infringement of his constitutional right to life and liberty? What if we had a law that fined all childless married couples unless they could prove they had not consciously avoided having children? Would not this also be the same sort of infringement of personal liberty as this law which forbids people the choice of how many children they will have and when?

But Goldstein was stopped short. Ethel was found guilty and told to return to court in two weeks for sentencing.

During those two weeks Margaret and Ethel did a lot of thinking. What should they do if Ethel were sent to jail? Ethel, by now a radical as dedicated as her sister, had helped Margaret with the Paterson strike; she was willing to try anything. To gain publicity they decided Ethel would go on a hunger strike.

The night before she was due in court, Ethel ate a huge meal of turkey and ice cream, and January 25, 1917, received a thirty-day sentence. She immediately made what she called her proclamation of defiance to the waiting reporters: "I shall not touch a morsel of food while in jail. I shall not touch anything they ask me to drink. I shall not do one article of work." For further impact she said she had made her will and arranged for the disposition of her children: "I made up my mind last night to die for the cause. I shall die, if need be, for my sex!" And as another act of rebellion, in the patrol wagon on the way to Blackwell's Island where she was to spend her sentence, she gave a lecture on birth control to the women prisoners who rode along with her.

When she arrived at the workhouse the warden's wife, a large woman with a brogue as thick as Michael Higgins', selected what was considered an easy job for Ethel—waiting on tables and cleaning the warden's quarters. Ethel haughtily refused the job, repeating her statement that she would not do a stroke of work in prison and would start her hunger strike immediately.

Margaret planned the publicity about the hunger strike expertly. She issued dramatic daily releases to papers throughout the country, releases that caused a host of local reporters to come and interview Ethel, while papers further away stirred up a lively debate by praising Ethel lavishly or denouncing her angrily. The *Chicago Sun Times* was a paper that praised her; the *Milwaukee Free Press* was one that denounced her. "What terrible harm misguided females, aided by masculine cranks, can work on modern society!" the *Free Press* thundered. New York Commissioner of Correction, Burdette Lewis, angered over the debate, soon barred all reporters from the workhouse and allowed Jonah Goldstein only one short visit a day. "I have no patience with Mrs. Byrne's efforts to get advertising for her cause," he blustered, "and I won't encourage such a campaign by issuing bulletins on her hunger strike."

But the papers still managed to get enough news to keep the pot boiling. On January 28 the *New York Times* headlined: "MRS. BYRNE NOW BEING FORCIBLY FED." She was indeed. Having gone 185 hours without food or water, Ethel had been ordered by Commissioner Lewis to be rolled in a blanket while a mixture of milk, eggs, and brandy was forcibly poured down her throat.

Margaret and the Committee of One Hundred were furious when Commissioner Lewis next issued a statement saying Ethel was perfectly healthy as a result of the forced feeding. They sent a delegation to Washington to try to get influential congressmen to stop the use of force, but no one would listen to them, so they called a giant protest rally at Carnegie Hall. Margaret, the Reverend John Haynes Holmes of New York's Community Church, and Dr. Mary Halton were among the speakers at the rally, and twenty of the Brownsville mothers sat impressively on the platform, while well-known people like the dancer Isadora Duncan, the writer Rupert Hughes, and the painter John Sloan applauded from boxes.

Margaret spoke eloquently.

I come to you tonight from a vortex of persecution. I come not from the stake at Salem where women were once burned for blasphemy, but from the shadow of Blackwell's Island where women are tortured for so-called obscenity.

Wild cheers came from the audience. The Reverend Holmes told his congregation later:

> I never saw another meeting like it. It had the spirit of the abolition days. Margaret took the audience and lifted it up. She had dignity. She had power. You can tell in five minutes whether a person is an actor or has the real secret of power. She had it—the power of a saint combined with the mind of a statesman. I realized that night she was one of the great women of our time.

The day after the rally, Margaret was due in court for her own trial. But when she heard that Ethel was getting weaker by the minute, Jonah Goldstein had the trial postponed. In the company of Jessie Ashley and Mrs. Amos Pinchot, who was a personal friend of New York's Governor Charles Whitman, Margaret took a quick trip to Albany where they asked for a pardon for Ethel. Whitman granted it on the condition that Ethel promise she would never break the law again.

Ethel refused to make such a promise. Margaret pleaded with her to give in, but it seems likely her reasons were compromised. Her niece reports that Margaret had become jealous of the publicity Ethel was getting and was worried that, if she herself got a jail sentence, the furor over her sister would take away some of her own ability to make news. When Ethel remained firm, Margaret declared that Ethel was too ill to think clearly and told the governor she was taking it upon herself to decide for her; she would personally see to it that Ethel did no more birth-control work.

The pardon was granted, and Ethel was dramatically carried from the workhouse on a stretcher, after which Jonah Goldstein announced: "Mrs. Sanger will sit up with her sister all night in her own apartment. We do not yet know if Mrs. Byrne will recover."

Ethel not only recovered; she lived into her seventies. Yet Margaret not only saw to it that she did no more birth-control work, she never so much as mentioned her name again in either of her autobiographies. As she intended, the reader got the impression that Ethel's hunger strike had killed her, and Margaret let it go at that.

12

PRISON

Though Ethel's prison sentence was ended, Fania and Margaret were still facing trial.

On January 29, 1917, Margaret announced to the press that she too would go on a hunger strike if convicted. But then she began to hedge. It would depend, she said, on how long a sentence she got. She realized that if she starved herself, her tubercular glands might start acting up; besides, with the war news crowding the headlines, there was little chance of her getting much publicity.

Fania's trial came first. Fania admitted distributing the booklet *What Every Girl Should Know,* so that the only matter now in dispute was whether or not the book was indecent—a matter that had been left undecided when the post office had permitted the *Call* to print several of its chapters several years before. The judges asked for time to read the book themselves, and her case was temporarily adjourned.

Margaret's case was called next. As she was the recognized star of the proceedings, the benches were crowded. Fifty Brownsville mothers came to watch and listen, many with babies, diapers, and packages of Kosher food. Near them sat a group of fashionably dressed women from the Committee of One Hundred, who had sent Margaret a bouquet of crimson American Beauty roses. She entered the court room, smartly dressed, carrying the roses in her arms.

Again there were three judges—John Freschi, a Catholic, who presided; Moses Herrman, an elderly Jew; and George O'Keefe, another Catholic. Jonah Goldstein represented Margaret; he hoped to get her off with a suspended sentence as Freschi, in particular, appeared to have an open mind.

The prosecuting attorney called as witnesses some of the Brownsville mothers who had been caught in the clinic raid. He questioned one as to whether Mrs. Sanger had given her information on birth control.

"Why did you go to the clinic at 46 Amboy Street?" he asked the first witness.

"To have her stop the babies."

"Did you get this information?"

"Yah, yah, dank you. It was gut, too."

"Enough," he snapped. After questioning a few others and getting similar answers, he rested his case.

Goldstein in turn questioned the witnesses. How many children had they had? How many miscarriages? How ill had they been with each? How much did their husbands earn?

Their answers were again similar. One thin, pale woman, for instance, said she was under thirty, though she looked more like fifty. She had been very sick when she lost three of her eight children by miscarriage; her husband earned ten dollars a week, if and when he could find work. This was more than Judge Freschi could take.

"I can't stand this any longer!" he exclaimed, pounding his fist on the desk and adjourning court for the day.

The following morning Fania was fined fifty dollars, which Mrs. Amos Pinchot paid, though the fine was later reversed on appeal. But Margaret's case was not settled so easily. Judge Freschi was willing to give her a suspended sentence if she would promise never to break the law again. Goldstein said he would ask her to make such a promise, since in any event he planned an appeal. But Margaret wouldn't agree. She kept pulling at Goldstein's coat as he dickered with Judge Freschi until the other judges noticed her and remarked to Goldstein: "Your client wishes to say something, counsellor."

"I certainly do," Margaret snapped. "I want to make several things clear that aren't clear now." The judge motioned her to take the stand.

Freschi: "You have been in court during the time that your counsel made the statement that, pending the prosecution of appeal, neither you nor those affiliated with you in this so-called movement will violate the law: that is the promise your counsel makes for you. Now, the Court is considering extreme clemency in your case . . . Do you personally make that promise?"

Sanger: "Only pending the appeal."

Freschi: "It must be without any qualifications whatsoever . . ."

Sanger: "The offer of leniency is very kind and I appreciate it very much. But with me it is not a question of personal imprisonment or personal disadvantage. I am more concerned with changing the law and sweeping away the law regardless of what I have to undergo to have it done."

Freschi: "Since you are of that mind, am I to infer that you intend to go on in this manner, violating the law irrespective of the consequences?"

Sanger: "I haven't said that. I said I am perfectly willing not to violate Section 1142 pending the appeal."

Freschi: "The appeal has nothing to do with it. Either you do or you don't."

By now the judge was obviously angry. . . . He turned to Goldstein. "What is the use of beating around the bush? The law was not made by us . . . my colleagues and I are simply here to judge the case. We harbor no feelings against Mrs. Sanger. We ask her, openly and above board, will she publicly declare she will respect the law and not violate it? And then we get an answer with a qualification. . . . I don't know that a prisoner under such circumstances is entitled to much consideration . . ."

Goldstein tried to argue for his client. He said that Mrs. Sanger's future action depended on so many factors, including a possible change in the law, that she could make no binding promises. But Judge Freschi had become impatient. He banged his gavel: "All we are concerned about is this statute. As long as it remains the law, will this woman promise unqualifiedly to obey it? Is it yes or no? What is your answer, Mrs. Sanger? Is it yes or no?"

Margaret took her time; her body stiffened and her face tightened. At last she answered: "I cannot promise to obey a law I do not respect."

The spectators bent forward tensely as the judge pounded his gavel once more. "The judgment of the Court is that you be confined to the workhouse for thirty days."

Margaret took this calmly. What was thirty days when she had been afraid she'd get a year, with a large fine in addition? As a woman from

the benches called, "Shame!" Margaret allowed herself to be led quietly to the anteroom where prisoners' fingerprints are routinely taken.
Once in the anteroom, however, she rebelled. "I refuse to be finger-
printed like a common prisoner when I have merely run a birth-control
clinic," she declared and held her arms tightly by her side.

Weary of her by now, the attendants shrugged their shoulders and
gave up. As she left the court she posed smilingly for pictures; she was
taken by patrol wagon to the Raymond Street jail, where a matron told
her to get ready for another routine procedure—a physical examination. Again she refused: "I am not a prostitute or a picket. My defiance
of the birth-control law does not bring me down to that level. I will not
be examined." She outstared the matron who, after consulting with the
other attendants, let her go. She was put into a cell for the night, and
the next day was taken to the Queen's County Penitentiary on Long Island.

At the penitentiary there were the usual forms to be filled out giving
her age, place of birth, occupation, and religion. Under occupation she
wrote "nurse," under religion, "humanity." The warden was startled
by the last answer. "What church do you attend?" he asked. "None,"
was her reply. Nonplussed, he ordered her fingerprints taken for the
second time, and for the second time she refused. He, too, gave up.

She settled down to prison routine without further protest. Asked to
choose a job, she chose the sanitary squad for the vigorous exercise of
cleaning the prison corridors. She spent the rest of her time in jail giving lectures to the other prisoners on birth control and questioning
them about the size of their families. According to the records which
she persuaded the warden to let her look at, each was an only child.
Confidentially, however, she was told that it was an unwritten law
among prisoners that they keep their families out of the picture. Actually, they had an average of seven brothers and sisters, which helped
confirm her belief that large families led to crime.

A week after her arrival, she wrote to her sister Mary:

> My days here are going fast . . . I shall be released soon. Al-
> ready I have an invitation for breakfast for the morning (of my
> release) and from then on I start a lecture trip.
>
> Stuart writes me. He is sturdy but oh! so sensible. He sets the
> table at school for breakfast for the dollar a month which is his
> allowance. He saves and spends judiciously while Grant buys

flowers and a $1.00 handkerchief for his mother's Xmas, and hides them under the pillow at night and under the dresser by day. He got a severe scolding from Stuart for such extravagance!!

Grant dreams in music, rhythm and color while Stuart thinks in dollars, food and rent. They are both darlings though, and I look forward to the days when I can have them with me again. I'll have to go next and find a widower with money and settle down for life.

Did I tell you of the Carnegie Hall meeting? That must have been when Mrs. Hepburn heard me. That huge audience rose to its feet twice in tribute to the cause and the work I am doing. I was quite overwhelmed with joy.

You are quite right about the courage of our family. I have been fortunate in having had a vision and a clear conception of what was worth fighting & dying for. With that in ones heart and brain on fire with the call to do or die—*something* had to happen.

Good luck go with you & all that you touch & my love ever.

She wrote to Ethel too, speaking among other things about Bill:

Bill seems not to have much liking for J. J. (Jonah Goldstein) but I don't feel there is any kick coming. Certainly I never expected to be acquitted nor did you, I guess. Fania—perhaps—but when once we realize that the whole force of the church was out against us—why we get some ideas of the forces behind them. Editorials in all the Catholic papers called upon the Judges "to give those lovely intellectual women a good dose of jail." It's absurd to call J. J. names now and expect he should have saved us. To me he did everything in his power to clear the issue and keep it clean. He at least kept the commercial taint out of it and that's what The Enemy tried hardest to put in. But then B. S. was always a chronic kicker, so what's the use.

Ethel answered:

I count off the days as you counted off mine. Bill S. and I are loyal friends. You will seek a level with us when you get out . . .

I saw (a) Mrs. Graves today & she expressed her pride in knowing the B. C. sisters! I looked at her all done up in her $1000 dollar worth of elegance (and thought) you should worry; you can have as many children as you want.

With lots of love to you, Margaret. I couldn't have lived or fought through anything if I hadn't known you.

Margaret was released on March 6. At the last moment they tried to fingerprint her again, this time forcibly. For two hours, until her arms were bruised and she was weak from exhaustion, she resisted. Finally an officer telephoned from department headquarters, where Goldstein had protested the delay, and the order was given to let her go without fingerprinting.

Outside it was bitter cold, but a group of co-workers were waiting. They broke into the "Marseillaise," while many of Margaret's prison friends leaned from the windows and joined in.

Margaret waved goodbye to them, then was taken, in a limousine supplied by the Committee of One Hundred, to the Hotel Lafayette where a luncheon was given in her honor. Later she had a leisurely Turkish Bath, and in the evening went to see Isadora Duncan dance.

After the dance recital she told a *New York Times* reporter jauntily: "Already I feel ready to begin work again."

NEW PROBLEMS

Jaunty or not, Margaret came out of prison with many problems. With the boys away at school, her first task was to find an inexpensive, centrally located apartment. After tramping the windy streets for days she found two high-ceilinged rooms on the parlor floor of an old remodeled brownstone at 236 West Fourteenth Street, a tacky area on the fringes of Greenwich Village. It had neither heat nor hot water. A gas stove, sink, and tin bathtub standing in a corner of the living room served as both kitchen and bathroom; the bedroom was so small it could hold only a bed and dresser. But after she had placed a Japanese screen around the bathtub, hung bright curtains at the windows and built a coal fire in the open grate, it looked cheerful. In any event, it would do, especially since Jonah Goldstein, a not-too-prosperous bachelor who had undoubtedly become her lover and was begging her to marry him, was paying the rent.

Ethel moved into an empty apartment on the floor above. Ethel was good company; besides, she knew how to hold her tongue about lovers, as she had several of her own. Ethel and Goldstein got along well, and as for the boys, Goldstein enjoyed taking them to Coney Island in his Stutz "Bearcat" during school vacations.

But once again, Margaret needed money for what she now referred to simply as "her cause." She had finally realized that the working class were interested only in fighting for higher wages and shorter working hours, not for birth control.

She found she could expect no real help from the I.W.W.'s either. One evening after pleading her cause earnestly on a speaker's platform she shared with Big Bill Haywood, Haywood got up and argued with equal earnestness against her. He drew a rosy picture of his dream state, one of whose glories would be that people would have enough money to have all the babies they pleased. Margaret was aghast. She jumped up to argue that enough money was not the answer; the real issue was women's biological slavery. She regaled the audience with stories of Hannah Grimshaw, a Quaker evangelist who had traveled through the mid-West in the 1870's holding "call meetings" on birth control in friends' homes. This mother of four, a paltry number for those days, had shocked the church elders by retorting when they criticized her: "If you are not going to believe in and practice family limitation, then practice polygamy. It is better to have a dozen wives than to kill one." But by the time Margaret went on to another story, the audience was filing out. Haywood's dream was so much more satisfying.

She next turned to the social workers for help, assuming that, as they knew firsthand the misery of the poor, they would surely help her. But they too refused, saying that their job was to relieve the misery of those already born, not to prevent new births.

She realized that her only hope lay in the educated women of the upper and middle classes, many of whom had worked for causes like civil service reform, pure food and drug laws, better public libraries, and stricter child-labor laws. These women were searching for a new cause, since most of what they had struggled for had been achieved.

Margaret had the new cause to give them, but in order to do so (her apartment was not adequate), she needed an office or headquarters. She established one in another old building at 104 Fifth Avenue, near Union Square. Again, it consisted of two small rooms—one she used as a combined office, reception room, and library, the other as a consulting room for the mothers who were sure to flock to her for advice.

Again, the rent was cheap. Margaret cleaned and painted the musty old place, then had the door lettered with the words BIRTH CONTROL. She got friends to donate a desk, typewriter, and a few chairs, and set about looking for a secretary through the classified columns in the New York *Call.*

The secretary she found was Anna Lifschiz, a tiny, timid seventeen-year-old who had never worked before. A cousin of hers had put a want ad in the *Call* for her without her knowing it. The ad read: "Wanted, an honest job of any kind." Anna had gotten exactly one reply: "If you'd like to do interesting work for very little pay, knock on the door of the top floor of 104 Fifth Avenue." When Anna nervously did so, she was greeted by Margaret, who spoke kindly but briefly. "The job I have to offer is interesting but dangerous. You may even be arrested. It consists of answering letters about birth control and sending out unlawful literature on the subject. The pay is twelve dollars a week."

"That's all right," Anna answered. "My mother has ten children, and anything to do with birth control interests me. I can spell, but I can't type. Are you sure I'm worth twelve dollars?"

Margaret was sure, especially when Anna promised to go to night school and learn how to type. Meanwhile, writing by hand would do. Anna's main job was to send out copies of a newly revised pamphlet on *Family Limitation,* for which Margaret had already been receiving two to three hundred requests a day.

Together they devised a scheme for answering the requests while eluding the post office authorities. They would send a personal reply to all inquiries, asking the women who had sent in requests to now send a handwritten self-addressed envelope, preferably stamped, and also if possible include a twenty-five-cent coin. When these envelopes arrived Anna would slip the pamphlets into them; at the end of the day she and Margaret would run around and drop batches into all the mailboxes they could find. Because of the varied hand writings on the return envelopes, the plan worked perfectly; they were never caught.

Another problem was to find a safe place to store the huge bundles of pamphlets until they could be sent out. The printers wanted them out of their hands as soon as they were run off, and keeping them in the office was too dangerous; it was difficult to guess when an innocent-looking woman who came for one in person might turn out to be a decoy. Margaret hid as many as possible under the beds in her own and Ethel's apartments, and if a large lot came in at once she asked Anna to take some home, too.

"Aren't you afraid?" her cousin asked when Anna confided the scheme to her.

"Of course I'm afraid. But if Mrs. Sanger asks me to do something, I just have to do it, that's all."

Anna's wages were a problem, too. Some weeks she got paid, some weeks she didn't. Often there was not even enough money for notepaper and stamps, but somehow the money eventually came in. Poor women who dropped by to pick up a pamphlet unexpectedly left a dollar instead of twenty-five cents. Wealthy women left fifty dollars. Anna's mother also brought in a little cash by translating the pamphlet into Yiddish and selling it to the women who were hawking vegetables and other cheap things from Bronx pushcarts. Margaret began at last to believe her boast that the universe was on her side.

With an office in operation, she turned her attention to a new medium. Remembering Ellis' advice not to duplicate the shrill tone of *The Woman Rebel,* she founded a new magazine, the *Birth Control Review,* in March 1917. It had a professional staff, shares of stock which sold at ten dollars each, and Margaret voted herself a salary as editor-in-chief. The *Review* was a long cry from *The Woman Rebel.* Instead of ranting on many subjects, it ran serious articles, on birth control only. Through the years it would publish pieces by such outstanding men and women as Karl Menninger, Pearl Buck, Julian Huxley, Fannie Hurst, Harry Emerson Fosdick, and Stephen Wise on such topics as the global consequences of birth control and the better health of women who practiced it.

To raise more revenue, Margaret featured her own book *What Every Girl Should Know,* now in hardcover, at two and a half dollars, and for four dollars she offered the book combined with a year's subscription to the *Review.* Nor was she above selling a pamphlet by James Waldo Fawcett on *The Trial of William Sanger* for ten cents. The magazine also included in every issue pathetic letters from readers asking for contraceptive information, and a Calendar of Events telling how "Mrs. Sanger lectured at Convention Hall in Atlantic City to an overflow audience," or "Mrs. Sanger held the Women's Club of Passaic, New Jersey, spellbound," and her name alone was splashed across the front page as editor. But the chief value of the *Review* lay in the publicity it gave to the cause. Because the very words birth control were shocking, no newsstand would carry the magazine. It had to be sold either by subscription or on the streets; it did better on the streets. Seeing these words displayed day after day in crowded places, like the front of Macy's department store or the entrance to Grand Central Station, helped make passersby think about the issue, at the very least.

On the streets the *Review* was held up silently by a tall handsome blonde who stood at her post day after day. Born Rosa Schneider, in Germany, she had a stern Prussian father who heaped guilt upon her both because her mother had died in childbirth and because she was a girl. The severity of her Catholic upbringing, along with a confessor who kept asking her questions like: "Do boys try to put their hands up your skirts?" long before she had thought of such things, forced her to run away. At fourteen she left home and Church and managed to get to England, where she changed her name to Kitty Marion. In London she sang briefly in music halls, then became a militant suffragette who had been imprisoned so many times and undergone so many hunger strikes and forced feedings she could hardly remember them all.

At twenty she had emigrated to America and shifted to the cause of birth control, where for a small salary she stood on the streets holding up the *Review* in rain, shine, or snow. Old ladies shook their umbrellas at her; policemen ran her in, only to have to release her because there were no charges against her they could sustain. A few men and women bought copies and hid them in their pockets or under their arms while they hurried on. As the years went by, Kitty Marion became such a familiar New York sight that one day a small boy, seeing her standing tall and silent as ever with her hand upraised, exclaimed, "Oh look! There's the Statue of Liberty!"

But a birth-control office and magazine were only a beginning. Margaret also needed an organization behind her. So on March 20, 1917, after much postponement, she founded the Birth Control League of New York, whose main purpose was fund raising. She hired Frederick Blossom, an experienced fund raiser, to head it, asking him to raise a minimum of five thousand dollars to support the cause of birth control. Blossom started to work fast. In no time he had persuaded a number of influential organizations including Mary Ware Dennett's National Birth Control League to stand behind Margaret, but she refused to join hands with any of them.

Mary Ware Dennett's organization had given a luncheon to which she was invited, but Margaret declined the invitation because by now she considered birth control her exclusive territory; it was as if she had drawn a magic circle around herself over which no one could step. As Elizabeth Grew Bacon, a dedicated birth-control worker, put it years later: "As far as her cause was concerned, Margaret Sanger counted 1,

3, 4, 5. She was number one, and there was no number two; she would let no one approach her that closely. When Mary Ware Dennett had the effrontery to claim to be another number one, she became Margaret's enemy who had to be vanquished at all costs." For all practical purposes, Margaret's Birth Control League became synonymous with her cause.

The new League grew fast. She weathered public denunciations from Billy Sunday, the evangelist; from John S. Sumner, head of the Society for the Suppression of Vice; and even from ex-President Theodore Roosevelt who kept thundering about "race suicide." While Roosevelt admitted, when challenged, that birth control might perhaps be good for the poor, he was sure it was not good for the rich. The rich, he declared, should breed as fast as they possibly could.

Busy as she was, Margaret also proceeded with her negotiations to get a divorce from Bill Sanger. On March 21, she wrote him a letter accusing him of publicly insulting her.

I want to return your name to you in the same condition I obtained or accepted it, and I call your attention to the fact that in fourteen years of public life that name was not assaulted until you assailed it last Friday night.

I will appreciate it if you will name your part in the support of the children. And also to name any articles or property of yours in my possession. I wish to wipe from my memory all thought of connection with you and shall appreciate any effort on your part to further that end.

Bill answered her diatribe with only a short note. In it he told her again how agonizingly lonely he was, following up his note with a bouquet of her favorite flowers. Unimpressed, Margaret wrote again on March 24:

Your flowers came this morning, and it is needless for me to say that I appreciate their beauty and the spirit in which you sent them. But if you could only realise that such expressions from you, coming at this time, give me greater pain than the pleasure you hoped they would give. If once you could realise this, I feel certain that you would try to co-operate with me in granting my last request for a complete separation. Just as you say it is impossible to be alone, so do I say it is impossible to go on like this. My work is piling up and it is impossible to do justice to it or to give the thought and attention it requires while I am in this unsettled state of mind. Won't you please help me? Won't you put yourself aside? Won't you let go that straw of hope that you have clutched to so long, and let me have the freedom and future happiness which I think is my right? Will you insist that I use all the cruelest means of society in order to protect my self-respect? If you continue to write me and attempt to see me, I must resort to this most drastic method. If the affection which you feel for me is deeper in your being than your love for yourself and the pity that you have for your own loneliness, you will either grant me a separation at once, or go away where we will not be tormented by the presence of each other . . .

Unless you can settle this matter (of our complete separation) immediately and to my satisfaction, I shall leave the country within the next few weeks and leave everything to those who are carrying on the birth-control work. My kindness to you has only prolonged an agony that should have been dealt with two years ago. Please think this over and let me have an immediate answer and a final one.

Bill replied by chucking his job, reminding Margaret that she owed him money from the mortgage payments on the Hastings house, and setting out again to Spain to paint.

But a few months in Spain made his spirits sink even more. In Vigo, broke and exhausted, he wrote angrily:

Whoever said one could live in Spain on $4 a week? Yes, in a place full of filth, crying kids, bawling women, and food steeped in so much garlic it makes me sick. I've certainly had enough of poverty in America and Bank Street without going to Spain to get the local brand yet. *I want no more of it,* and I've quite decided I'd rather be without a penny in America than here in Spain any time.

He wanted the mortgage money she had promised him but not sent, and quickly. He needed fifty dollars immediately and fifty dollars a month allowance for the next few months—and would she please take enough pains to find out about the steamer sailings to make sure he got the payments soon?

Margaret probably sent him the money on the condition that he give her a divorce on the grounds of desertion, because on August 15, 1917, she received an unusually formal letter from him in Spain.

Dear Peg, let this be the last you shall hear from me. It is best that you go your way and I go mine. It is impossible for me to live with you. I have thought it all through and have decided I shall live my life alone. Yours, Bill.

She did not hear from him again until December, when, weary and ill, with little work to show for his six months abroad, he was back in New York. He offered to cooperate further toward a divorce if she sent him a statement admitting that the desire for a final separation came from her, not him. "I do not want to hand down a heritage to my children that I took the initiative that we should pass out of each other's lives. I want above all to abide in their hearts as love."

Margaret now bought a small inexpensive cottage in Truro and spent the whole summer there. She didn't answer either of Bill's last letters as she had gotten what she wanted from him. Across the envelope containing the statement that he was in effect deserting her, she wrote: "This is the letter on which my divorce was granted." But she did not use the letter immediately. She put it away and waited until it suited her purpose to use it, which was not for four long years.

14

MORE FRUSTRATIONS

Margaret's need to be the sole leader of birth control created conflicts with men as well as women. When she hired Frederick Blossom as a fund raiser and office manager in 1917, it did not occur to her that he would try to replace her.

He had seemed, at first, a lucky find. Because his wife had money, he could afford to work for a smaller salary than other men. He also had a great deal of experience in office management. In a very short time, he drafted a series of form letters that reduced Anna's need to answer each incoming letter separately; he also organized the many volunteers who had heretofore dashed haphazardly in and out of the office. His social connections made him a first-rate fund raiser, and he understood the intricacies of politics well enough to direct a campaign to nullify the Comstock Law in New York State. Remarkably, he even found the time to coedit the *Birth Control Review*.

Still, Margaret chafed, because it was soon evident that he had the ability to take the leadership away from her. And with his handsome face, polished manner, and excellent cultural background (he had done some translating of Proust), it looked as if he would succeed.

The antagonism between them grew rapidly. It climaxed over a comparatively small matter: a difference of opinion about a *Review* editorial Margaret had written. In a fit of anger Blossom moved out of

104 Fifth Avenue late one night, taking with him all the office records and vouchers, and even some of the furniture.

When Margaret arrived the next morning she, too, lost her head. Though she had long since resigned as an organizer for the Socialist Party, she was still a member. In this situation it would have been customary for her to lodge a complaint with the Socialist special-investigating committee. Instead, she went straight to the office of New York City's district attorney, though dealing with the government was something no good Socialist was supposed to do.

While the D.A. was willing to try to help her, she realized her mistake might alienate her from Party support. She went now to the Socialist committee only to find that Blossom had also gone there. The result was a series of charges and countercharges that went on for months. Eventually she won, but the Socialists, angry because she had gone to the government, formally ousted her from the Party. She found herself without both a first-rate office manager and whatever benefits Party membership might bring.

This threw her into a particularly deep depression. She could neither work nor sleep. She declared she could not even *think* about birth control.

Her depression lifted in January 1918 when Jonah Goldstein won a strategic victory for her. He got the New York State Court of Appeals to declare that the law permitting information on contraception to be given to men "for prevention or cure of disease" applied to women as well. The court's opinion was so broadly stated that doctors could now give advice to any woman, provided they found even the smallest evidence of bad health.

It was a stunning victory, and had Margaret followed through on it, she could have immediately opened a legal clinic in New York. Since New York and California usually set the legal pace for the rest of the country, such a clinic would probably have been followed by similar ones throughout the country.

But for reasons that are not clear, she did not follow through. Perhaps at the age of thirty-nine, her small taste of battle and fame had left her with a taste for larger battles and greater fame. Perhaps she enjoyed the kind of plotting and planning it took to work illegally—to continue to defy the Postmaster General and sneak pamphlets through the mail.

Most likely, however, she simply did not have the funds. Opening a clinic where women could be helped individually by competent professionals would take a lot of money, and Margaret's income was barely enough for her own needs. She had given up nursing; her main source of income was her lecture fees. And while Goldstein may have still been paying her rent, she certainly couldn't ask him to contribute clinic expenses as well.

Then there was the continued cost of the private schools in which she insisted on keeping Grant and Stuart. Though she claimed the private schools gave them a better education, the truth was she had neither the time nor the inclination to keep them at home, and she knew it.

Indeed, time after time she disappointed the boys by failing to visit them as promised. In February 1918, Grant, ten and as shy as ever, wrote wistfully from school that he knew how busy she must be or he was sure she would have come down when she had promised. He had waited in for her all day and she had never arrived. A month later he wrote to ask if he had permission to come home for the Easter holidays, or if not, would she come to see him instead? And in November he was wondering where he was supposed to go for Thanksgiving. All the other boys were going home. Where was he supposed to go?

As for Thanksgiving, she told him to go to her apartment in Greenwich Village where Daisy, the black maid who had replaced her Irish helpers, would cook him a nice dinner. It was the answer of a crusader who didn't have time for her own child.

Stuart took the matter of her visits more firmly in hand. At fifteen, he was already an outstanding athlete, and the admiration traditionally showered on athletes made him into a different kind of boy. While at the Peddie School on an athletic scholarship he got the mumps, and promptly used this as a reason to ask his mother if he could come home to visit her. "Dear mother," he wrote,

> I am glad you are sending down some magazines as it is tiresome laying in bed doing nothing. . . . As soon as I am well, can't I come into the city for a day or two. All the fellows (regularly) go home for three or four days.
>
> P.S. Please send the money to come home if you decide in its favor. I will need about two dollars and will give the change to you. I will be alright so you won't have to meet me. I will come right over to the office. What is the phone number there? Just send me a thought wave.

P.S. 2. I just looked at myself in the mirror and I am not a well boy.

A week later he was thanking her for the two dollars she had sent, adding: "I am glad I can come home and get fat. I am very thin and a little pale. It will be a change and I will have something to dream about and look forward to."

Yet Margaret could disappoint Stuart, too. When Margaret didn't go to Truro for the entire summer, Ethel took charge there. On a day that Margaret had written she was surely arriving on the early afternoon train, Stuart thought he would surprise her by walking to the railroad station to meet her, then share her taxi back. It was a blistering day, and Stuart, blond and fair-skinned, set out in bare feet and bathing trunks. The station was several miles away, and by the time he got there he was badly burned. He waited for one train, then another; Margaret did not appear, and he had no choice but to walk all the way back. As a result, when Margaret arrived a day later, she found Stuart in bed, badly swollen from sunburn and in great pain. She felt sorry for him, she said, but things had worked out in such a way that she couldn't get there when expected; she would try to do better next time.

At the end of 1918, the tubercular glands in Margaret's neck acted up again and required surgery. While recovering, she decided to write a book. With the help of a young newspaperman named Billy Williams, whom she met in Truro, she began writing the book called *Woman and the New Race*. It was a far cry from the hysterical *Woman Rebel* or anything she had done before. It used quiet language, quoted recognized authorities, and gave stirring historical material. It told how allowing newborn babies to die from exposure had flourished in China and India for centuries with the tacit consent of the government, while on the other hand penalties for abortion in Japan, Greece, and Rome were so severe they included death for the mother. She described how medieval Germany had added torture to the death sentence for abortion, the penalty being to throw a woman alive into a river tied into a sack that also contained a serpent and a dog who would struggle with her, and thus prolong her agony.

She told, too, how in 1917 fifty-seven percent of American families had a yearly income of eight hundred dollars or less. Here she used a quote from Senator Borah: "Tell me how a man earning $800 a year can provide shelter for his family. He is an industrial peon. His home is scant and pinched beyond the power of language to tell."

There was also a recent report to the Public Education Association of New York: "An overwhelming proportion of classified feeble-minded children in the New York schools come from large families living in overcrowded slums." She concluded: "We must not permit an increase in population we are not prepared to care for. . . . We must set motherhood free. For then motherhood, when free to choose the father, free to choose the time and number of children from the union, will refuse to bring forth weaklings, refuse to bring forth slaves."

It was the book of a zealot that based the entire progress and quality of the race on birth control. Published in 1920, it sold over two hundred thousand copies, a record none of her other books approached.

Aside from this, it was not a fruitful time for the cause. The First World War had just ended, and people were far more interested in eye-witness accounts of the war and the Russian Revolution that followed than in birth control. Margaret's lecture engagements were few indeed.

Yet there was one lecture of importance; this was in Elizabeth City, North Carolina—a landmark of its kind for the South. Eight hundred men and women turned out to hear her; some women had driven with their husbands fifty miles by horse and wagon to get to the lecture hall. Margaret spoke for an hour and a half, phrasing her material in such delicate language that no one could possibly be offended, and afterward so many women crowded around to ask specific questions that she requested the men to leave so that she could spend another hour discussing birth-control techniques, something she seldom did from the platform.

By now she was tired. On February 7, 1919, she wrote in her diary "I must get away and out of the reach of the phone . . . J. J. (Goldstein) dear generous one, took me to the Hotel Commodore for a bite." Then she descended on Grant, scooped him up without notice from his school, and took the train to California.

"It is all a new world to Grant," she wrote in her diary as they rolled along, "especially the invention of making a bed out of a seat . . . It's good to lie down and rest. There is a joy in resting with the motion of the train." As she looked out on the snow-covered Rockies, she felt "just lazy. Nothing to do, and I don't feel like doing even that . . ."

In San Diego the scent of the orange blossoms filled her with joy, reminding her of Spain.

But no sooner had she rented a cottage in California than her mood changed. "I am in the grip of despondency today. Changes have their effect on me so often. It may be the changing climate, but anyway it is a most awful anguish one suffers. Peggy and (the sudden death of) Portet, everything seems to loom up before me like a nightmare. Birds are singing and goodness knows one should be happy but I'm not."

On March 8 a "nice letter from J. J." cheered her, leading her to speculation on love: "These chemically fascinating men must needs be dismissed from our consciousness. I often wonder if love is not based on chemistry, and that is why married people grow so indifferent as age advances."

A week later she was in Los Angeles trying to rouse interest for birth control. "But B.C. seems to have fled from the minds of the people. Russia is the all-important subject. Louise Bryant (one of the old Village group who had just returned from Russia) is in Frisco speaking and drawing big crowds."

She had a moderate success in Los Angeles nevertheless, then gave several successful street-corner lectures in Fresno on April 1. On April 2 she gave several more Fresno street-corner talks, but these were interrupted when a group of Socialists in the audience heckled her. "They repeat the same old argument that people can have all the children they want under Socialism . . . It never dawns on them that women shall no more desire to be breeders under a Socialist Republic than they want to today."

In San Francisco, her next stop, she found upsetting mail from home. She referred cryptically in her diary to "one letter in particular which makes a new look on the future imperative." This probably was a letter from J.J. asking her to finally decide if she would marry him. If she refused, he would find someone else because he wanted to settle down. Forced into a corner, she wrote in her diary: "It did not seem one could suffer so intensely. . . . My heart is so heavy it seems difficult to go on at all."

She felt better when she got an answer to a letter she had written to Bill Haywood, who was in the Federal Prison in Leavenworth, Kansas, awaiting sentence for his part in a recent I.W.W. strike.

Your letter post marked Jan. 27th is just received. I first saw the account of the death of Jessie Ashley in the papers and at once wrote to Anita (Block), realizing how deeply grieved she would be. Jessie was much like a mother to her, wish it were possible for me to see Anita—and offer the condolence and sympathy that is in my heart. . . . I could never tell how much I will miss Jessie. Though I never wrote to her often I communed with her frequently in my thoughts. I knew where she was, occasionally heard what she was doing, could imagine what she was thinking. Jessie was the one best woman friend I ever had, a greater tribute I cannot pay her. I only hope I was as much to her life and being as she was to mine. A real friendship is a much more wonderful thing than passing love.

Margaret, all my dreams are coming true. My work is being fulfilled. Millions of workers are seeing the light. We have lived to see the breaking of the glorious Red Dawn. The world revolution is born, the change is here. Remember me kindly to any friends you meet. Come when you can.

But Margaret never did get to see him again. For after his release he was soon sentenced to a new jail term for his anarchist activities. Not being able to face the ordeal of still another prison sentence, he skipped to Russia, which turned out to be sadly disillusioning. His dream of a New Dawn unfulfilled, Haywood drank himself to death.

Margaret was homeward bound, arriving in New York in early May and being met at the train by Billy Williams: "Dear old Billy. One can be proud of such a loyal friend as he. Often I think we women scarcely deserve that men be fair to us—when men so big and generous and devoted offer their strength, labor, energy, talents, love at our feet."

On May 7 she was back in her apartment on West Fourteenth Street, trying to make a decision about marriage to Goldstein. When he called the next morning to ask for her answer, she told him she'd have to have more time to think about it. Then she sat down with Daisy and wept, knowing finally that she couldn't marry him even though it meant losing him. For though she knew she needed him and would miss him both emotionally and financially, she couldn't take the step. Marriage to her meant giving up her freedom, and she valued that freedom too much to give it up.

A few weeks later she was raring to go again. Because the movement needed publicity badly, she began planning a national conference on birth control to be held the following winter. In the meantime she wanted to have a farewell dinner with Goldstein, and another dinner with a group of old-time radicals: "It was good to sing the old songs and get a message from Peggy. Old songs and old friends always seem to bring Peggy back."

She spent the fall and winter lecturing to any group that would listen to her, then suddenly had a longing to see Havelock Ellis and plan her new conference with him. Having saved what she could from her lectures, plus the little she had put aside from the salary she had voted herself as head of her cause, she got a passage on a small boat for England, bought a few clothes in the fashionable "boyish form" style that suited her slender figure, and wrote him a note saying she was happily on her way.

A MOMENTOUS MEETING

Back in London, Margaret renewed her relationship with Havelock and told him excitedly about her work's progress, her continued grief over Peggy, and her great plans for the future. He told her about his books in progress and his plans for books to come. She felt as if their five-year separation had never occurred. Havelock, at sixty, was no longer with Amy Barker, making Margaret more welcome than ever. And, in turn, Margaret was always at her best in England: At home she felt constantly that Mrs. Grundy or the Church was peering over her shoulder, so that as a result she must present as serious a public image as possible. The columnist Heywood Broun once accused her of a lack of humor in her lectures. "To the people to whom I speak, birth control is not a humorous subject," she retorted. But in England she could laugh as much as she pleased. "Margaret is fond of teasing," Havelock wrote to a friend, "very Irish and playful." In England she was indeed.

Soon Havelock was planning a trip to Germany for her; he had heard that an anti-spermicidal jelly had been perfected there, which would make the diaphragm far more effective. Margaret would have to find out about it. But first he wanted to introduce her to some of his chief admirers. They had formed a group called the Wantley Circle, led by the dashingly handsome man Hugh de Selincourt.

Hugh de Selincourt was of French descent. His father, founder of the well-known firm of de Selincourt and Sons, furriers, was, however, an odd combination: a strict Baptist who made his seven children take turns singing hymns with him on street corners, he was not above seducing the family cook. As a result Hugh developed a lifelong hatred of what he called the "hypocrisy of organized religion" and turned into a hedonist instead.

After studying at Dulwich College where he was captain of the cricket team, he went to Oxford determined to become a writer.

He wrote one commercially successful novel about cricket, followed by a few unsuccessful novels with sexual themes. The last were either too frank for the times or written in such florid style that no one was sure if they were meant for children or adults. Soon he married Janet Wheeler, a former concert pianist whose substantial income rounded out his small family allowance, and settled down to the leisurely life of a country gentleman devoted to literature, sports, and music. Janet continued to play the piano while Hugh became engrossed in poetry, especially the romantic poetry of Shelley and Blake. By good fortune, he found the perfect romantic home to rent—a thirteenth-century stone house in Storrington, Sussex, called Wantley—which had once been owned by Shelley's father. Wantley, with its handhewn beams, deep recessed windows, hand-wrought hardware, and sunken gardens filled with roses and fine old trees, made Hugh feel an authentic country squire.

Early in their marriage, Hugh and Janet had agreed that each would be free to have outside affairs; jealousy was an ignoble emotion they would never permit to enter their lives. In doing this they were following the example set by the original Shelley Circle of a century before; Shelley had a lover named Claire Clarmont who later became Byron's lover, while Shelley's wife Mary took on Jefferson Hogg. Hugh and Janet were happy to follow the Shelley Circle's practice. After their marriage Janet had taken one or two lovers, while Hugh had taken as many as he could find, reciting poetry to them while he flashed his romantic good looks.

He intrigued Margaret by first appearing to disdain her, then suddenly capitulating to her charms. On her first visit to Wantley, Hugh made fun of her feet, shoes, dresses, hands, and voice. Yet, as she told Havelock later, she had a "whisper inside her that kept on liking his laugh, even when he objected to everything I said and did." On her next visit they had a long quiet talk in which she told Hugh: "If you like my religion—birth control—we shall be friends." He replied with his favorite line from Shelley: "The good life consists in living as if life and love are one." To him, the highest kind of love was sexual love, which suited Margaret perfectly.

Soon she was begging Hugh for another meeting, preferably in London. He replied that he had no plans for going up to London in the near future, but invited her to come back to Wantley soon.

She couldn't go at once, however, because she had a series of speaking engagements in Scotland that had been arranged for her by the Neo-Malthusian League. After her first lecture there she wrote Juliet Rublee, now the chief financial backer of birth control and Margaret's most intimate female friend: "Oh Juliet, never was there such a Cause. Those poor, pale-faced, wretched wives. The men beat them. They cringe before their blows, but pick up the baby, dirty and unkempt, and return to serve him."

In Glasgow she gave lectures on birth control, the problems of marriage, the hygiene of pregnancy, and the dangers of abortion. Following Havelock's advice, she had changed her public stance on abortion. She gave no more outcries about "the right to destroy," only about the right to create or not create new life.

In Glasgow, too, she spoke to two thousand male shipyard workers and was amazed at the size of the turnout. But it was the poverty of Scotland that made the strongest impression. "Oh, I am busy and tired," she wrote Juliet. "Things are hard here—*terribly* hard. Try to move a mountain with a shovel and you have an idea what it is like here—but it is *moving*."

A week later she wrote Hugh a letter headed: "Glasgow, a damn cold dirty place," continuing,

Yes, dear Mister Man . . . love and life are one. You will like to learn that every meeting here this week has been packed. Oh, the sorrows of womankind, Hugh; really it's enough to want to die. When I see these women always carrying a baby in a shawl; when I see them crowded up before windows where trinkets are displayed (It's my own weakness) I *know* that the hunger for beauty and charming things is just as great in them as in me.

This is a gloomy place—but then your house is the only place where I loved it to rain.

On July 12, she made a laconic diary entry: "Nice letter that J. J. and Harriet were married in London on their way to Poland." Getting

this news after a hectic lecture schedule may have accounted for her
entry the following day: "Left for London, very tired and weary." Margaret never seemed to understand that at least half her fatigue was
emotional. She may have refused to marry Jonah Goldstein, but the
fact that he had married someone else hurt badly; she felt lonely and
abandoned. She tried to counter her loneliness by making another
terse diary entry: "I am the Resurrection and the Life."

Back in London she tried to shake off her depression by writing
again to Hugh:

> To think you were in London only a day or two ago and I have
> missed you. Came back from Scotland almost ill—too messy in
> head and neck to leave London until I saw my X-Ray specialist to-
> day. I must get a rest and live in the open before I go to Germany.
> But I will not come down now, Hugh, to Wantley. I will wait and
> see how the plan for Germany works out. If it does not go well, I
> will hope your plans will allow of my coming for another weekend
> sometime later. But I don't like these weeks slipping into months
> and not seeing you at all . . . I long to lie in the sun quietly
> while some one nice—very nice—reads Shelley to me.

When Hugh didn't answer, she consoled herself by accepting an invitation to visit Easton Glebe, the country place of H. G. Wells. She had
met Wells briefly before, but this was the first time he had invited her
to his home to meet his family. A weekend there bounced her back. In
her diary for July 25 she notes: "Most heavenly day. Walk with H. G.
in garden. Most interesting chat." And on July 26: "H. G. took me to
the train in his car which he calls Pumpkin. He has twinkling, laughing eyes and is a sort of naughty boy-man."

She described July 28 as "a big day. Breakfast with Mrs. How-Mar-
tin, an old-time suffragette. Lunch with Mr. and Mrs. Clinton Chance,
wealthy Britishers most interested in birth control. Tea with Harold
Cox, former member of House of Commons and now editor of Edinburgh Review." And on July 29 she told of having a delightful tea at
Rebecca West's, followed by a dinner with Havelock.

Again a reaction set in, however. After two more days of running to
luncheons, teas, and dinners she noted, "Dreams of night bad and disturbing ones. Hope all is well."

When the dreams persisted, she consulted a "psychic" who told her

"Uncle Tom is here, signing a paper to your benefit." The remark of the "psychic" about a benefit she took as a good omen; she brightened up, called Hugh, and invited herself to Wantley for the weekend. When she got back to London she underlined a new man's name in her diary: "*Mr. Harold Child*. Had a nice visit with him on the train on the way back to London from Wantley."

She wrote Hugh telling him how delighted she was to meet Harold Child, and how Havelock had read some of Child's poems to her in front of his fire. "I liked the swing and run of the first two poems very much and wish your lovely Janet would put them to music. If I were a painter I'd do them in colors, such were the emotions they stirred in me."

Harold Child, a friend of Hugh's, was a small, plain-looking man with bright eyes, a hooked nose, and a winning smile. He had been first an actor, then a feature writer for the *London Times*, and was now editor of *The Times Literary Supplement*. For years he had been keeping his mentally disturbed wife in a private sanatarium. He lived at Wantley and commuted to London more as a matter of economy (Hugh didn't charge him much) than because he shared all of Hugh's views. When the talk in the garden turned to the kind of sexual freedom in which Hugh so strongly believed, Harold would draw aside quietly and puff at his pipe.

Harold was as quickly attracted to Margaret as she was to him; he was delighted to meet a woman who was both involved in a serious movement and radiated personal charm. Not long after their first meeting, he began regularly inviting her to dine with him in small London restaurants, where they sat and talked for hours much as she did with Havelock.

On August 22 Margaret left for Germany hoping to find the man with the anti-spermicidal jelly, though Havelock had forgotten his name. She was shocked to find Berlin, two years after the war, still a dead city. People spent most of their time searching for food, particularly potatoes, and when these couldn't be found, settling for turnips. She was fed so much turnip soup, turnip salad, turnip coffee she began to hate the sound of the name.

Even worse than the terrible food was the condition of the women and children. Men came first, as always. Whatever food was available was offered the men; women and children got only what was left. At the same time the women were told they must produce as many children as ordered to. When Margaret spoke to several doctors about birth control, they shouted, "Nein, Nein! No birth control in Germany! It is abortions here only. With abortions it is all in our hands. Never will Germany give control of its population to women. Never will it let women control the race." At last she met a doctor who told her there might be a firm in Dresden making the contraceptive jelly she was looking for. But in Dresden they told her to try Munich, and in Munich they gave her an address in Friedrichshaven.

In Friedrichshaven she was met at the station by a small, shabbily dressed man holding a bunch of wildflowers wrapped in newspaper as his greeting. He admitted it was his father's firm who was making the jelly, but no, he couldn't take her to see the factory, and no, he couldn't sell her a sample. The best he could do was to refer her to his sister in New York who might become the firm's agent there. It might be possible for Margaret to make a deal with her if the price was right.

When later she did contact the sister and get some samples of the jelly to test, they did not turn out to be particularly good. But the search had exhausted Margaret again; she returned to England with a hacking cough. She was also broke and had to cable home to Mary and Nan for a loan.

Then as usual she made a comeback. After a week's rest in bed she was enjoying a concert with Havelock given by the Italian opera singer Tetrazzini, which she summed up as "glorious!", and lunching with Harold Child, whom she described as "delightful." She was also dashing down to Wantley for another gay weekend, after which she wrote Hugh:

It was such a treat to be with you these lovely days, dear man. This is the very first morning for weeks that I have felt well enough to want to get up when called . . . When you come to London won't you let me know and let me have an hour or two with you while here? I am happy and grateful to know you.

Another letter followed soon:

Hugh, I'm in love with everyone in Wantley, even the cat. Your grass smells sweeter than other grass anywhere. You *are* making that force you spoke of—and it effects the bloom of the flowers and the song of the birds as well as making you a—well—rather nice person—ahem."

She had obviously fallen deeply in love with Hugh, so much so that she refused a second invitation from Wells so that she could go to Wantley once more instead. But Hugh pretended not to notice how Margaret felt about him. On October 21 she sent him a long letter shortly before leaving for home.

> Those horrid words of yours keep teasing me. Do you remember? You said you would not care if you never heard from me or saw me again—you did say it—honest you did. Of course I know you were trying to tell me that you were master of your own destiny so far as other individuals are concerned—especially women. But I have tried to squeeze in a day to get down to see you in spite of your not caring. Now I know it can't be done.
>
> I sail on the *Olympic* the 27th from Southampton. Won't you send me a note there and say you would like to see me when I return in the Spring? It has been a joy to me to be with you and to know Wantley too. It's all a delightful memory—a soul memory.
>
> I send you my love and a hug to top it off. I'll be thinking of you often, far oftener than I'll write to tell you. But you'll know . . .

She relived her days at Wantley over and over as she sailed for home, though as she neared New York she was wondering in her diary whether "the darlings Stuart and Grant" would be at the dock tomorrow to meet her, adding "perhaps not." And the day after that, November 12, maybe because thinking about her sons made her think about their father, her diary contained a single line: "Bill's birthday."

On impulse she invited Bill, Ethel, Stuart, and Grant, to a Thanksgiving dinner at her Fourteenth Street flat. The dinner was not a success. The boys were awkward with their father, whom they hadn't seen in a long time, and Bill became so upset he left early, writing Margaret, "Please don't invite me again. I sat across the table from you and still loved you so much I couldn't bear it."

One man loving her to distraction while she was in love with another. It was a pattern that would repeat itself for the rest of Margaret's life.

VICTORY FROM DEFEAT

The beginning of January 1921 found Margaret in a slump. She wrote Havelock that she was "sad at life." She had learned while she was in England of the deaths of Billy Williams and John Reed. The combined loss, added to the fact that Hugh had answered none of her letters, made her again feel deserted and old, and her lectures changed with her mood. She began to speak less on birth control and more on marriage. She recorded in her diary lectures titled, "Is Modern Marriage Conducive to Happiness?," "The Sex Problems of the Unmarried," and "Marriage a Failure." Other lectures were simply written off as "missed" or "called off because of Catholic protest," and there were many days that had no entries at all. Clearly her spirits were down.

Then came an upswing. At the end of January Hugh finally wrote to her.

> Your letter reconciled me to your absence. The loveliness of you! We read fairytales as kids to have our minds quickened to appreciate the marvels of nature—the bulb, say, and the tulip in flower. We dream dreams to have our imagination quickened to feel the beauty of reality, transcending any dream. When you say, Margaret, he (Ellis) is not well, I want to wrap him close in my arms. I worship that man.

You bring me nearer to him, nearer to your dear heart. You
quicken my eyes to beauty, and all I really want to do in the world
is to write a beautiful book which shall warm men's hearts to
love. Thank God I have actually kissed your feet, though only for
a moment.

Margaret answered at once:

What a letter—I have read it at least ten times and always
there is some new meaning in it for me. I can see you standing so
tall and wicked beside me, eyes laughing, always laughing, and
asking yourself what was in that letter to make the busiest woman in New York—no, America—read a letter ten times. You
might well ask and then be careful.

I am thinking of getting that splendid essay of yours on "vice"
out in booklet form like those we got up for Havelock's articles.
What do you think of that idea? I am waiting to publish it until
our *Review* is changed into its new form. Then too I have called up
Physical Culture until I'm blue and red in the face to get an answer on your article. I got Williams one day who said he had received it and liked it too well to give it up. He was trying to see if
his magazine *dare* publish it. He hoped so and would do all that
was possible to put it through . . . Do you forgive bold women
who do things like that with your articles?

Mrs. Brandt (Margaret's literary agent) and I had dinner
together a few evenings ago and she talked of you . . . She likes
your work. She said it can be published privately and done well.
Oh Hugh, things are coming for you . . . It's zero weather; I long
to be in England.

Revitalized, she began to plan the opening of a birth-control clinic on
Manhattan's lower East Side. She also started work on the long-
delayed National Birth Control Conference to be held in New York in
October or November. She resumed her lectures, and the *Review* reported "overflow meetings" once more.

On February 16, she came down with tonsilitis from her spate of
meetings, and wrote Hugh from bed:

Were you with The King on his birthday? What a man he is—
and now that he has broken the silence of ages by his work & vision others are coming on with books that astound one . . .

I went to a Feminist gathering last night . . . They are trying
to put over a Feminist magazine here but I'd never buy a copy if it
was to be no more inspiring than that group of 30 women were. I
decided after I came home that night not to go out in "Society"
any more. I don't belong. Nobody wants the truth. They hate you
for telling it, & for trying to sell it. But I have just had an article
in *Physical Culture* on "Mobilized Motherhood." So many magazines are asking me to write that I am wondering in a dazed way
why? There is so much I want to talk to you about, dear dear man.

I think of you often often often, & love you with the kind of love
that always is.

In April she went to Truro for a few days, then hurried back to New
York to keep a date with a man who was different from any she had
ever known. On April 5, 1921, the initials of this man appear for the
first time in her diary: "Dinner with J. N. H. S."

J. N. H. S. was J. Noah H. Slee, a stocky, ruddy-faced Dutchman
from South Africa. In his middle sixties, he had worked his way up
from a penniless boy to a millionaire. He was president of the Three-
in-One Oil Company, and hopefully, the "rich widower" Margaret for
years had dreamed would come along and solve her financial problems.

Unfortunately, however, Slee wasn't a widower; he had a wife.
Worse, his wife was Mary Roosevelt West Slee, of impeccable social
standing but few other charms. After thirty-five years of marriage,
during which, each time J. Noah made love to her, she called up her
mother the next morning while he was listening and reported, "He did
it again, mother, he did it again." He had stopped "doing it" and was
now living mainly in the Union League Club in New York while she
puttered about in her garden up the Hudson. His only friend was the
minister of the Episcopal Church he attended, and his only hobby was
trying to make more money than the nine million he already had.

Slee had made his money largely through skillful promotion. He was
especially proud of the fact that he had invented advertising on the
sides of barns. He told Margaret how, as he rode along, in the country,
he had often spotted a dilapidated barn and offered to paint it free on

condition that the owner would also let him put on it a big ad for Three-in-One Oil. He figured that if the farmer couldn't afford to paint his barn in the first place, he probably would not be able to afford to repaint it; Slee's ad would therefore stay on indefinitely.

Margaret met J. Noah, as most people called him, at Juliet Rublee's home. Because Juliet was also a multimillionaire, she usually entertained multimillionaires. At these parties she would try to steer the conversation around to birth control. When she was successful, heated arguments would follow, during which, as if by sudden inspiration, Juliet would call up Margaret and ask her to join them to answer questions. Margaret, wearing a simple dark dress (Havelock had taught her that the more radical one's cause, the less flamboyant one should look), would end up charming Juliet's guests so thoroughly they would promise substantial contributions to her cause.

After one of these parties, J. Noah took Margaret home in his chauffeur-driven limousine. Soon he was attending all her birth-control lectures. While his conservative background made him oppose everything she stood for, he found Margaret herself irresistible. He was fascinated by her burnished red hair, wide hazel eyes, and slender figure. In addition, her frank talk about sex and her ebullient manner and quick wit astonished him. Soon he was as dazzled by her as Bill Sanger had been.

Since Margaret liked to dance, J. Noah took dancing lessons. Since she loved flowers, he sent her fresh bouquets every day. Margaret's secretary Anna and the other volunteers were working on old battered typewriters; J. Noah sent in new ones. Margaret called marriage an outdated institution; J. Noah begged her to marry him as soon as he could arrange a divorce.

J. Noah's money was tempting, but "What do I want with a man like that?" she would say to Anna. "I don't want to marry anyone, particularly a stodgy churchgoer who isn't interested in art or anything. Yet . . . how often am I going to meet a man with nine million dollars? . . ."

Although she continued to see J. Noah throughout April, she decided abruptly to sail for England on May 2 with the intention of surprising her friends, Hugh, Havelock, Harold Child, and H. G. Wells. While aboard ship, she wrote to Juliet: "I am borrowed to the hilt."

Despite the fact that she was ill and tired when she arrived in Lon-

don, she told her friends that she had come abroad for the excitement—and to line up at least one "big name" to come to her National
Birth Control Conference in the fall.

She first asked H. G. Wells, but he was much too busy; he did, however, offer to write an introduction to a book she was planning to write.
Next, Harold suggested she try Dean Inge, Archbishop of Canterbury,
as he had openly begun to express sympathy for birth control; Inge also
declined. Havelock himself wouldn't consider traveling as far as America, not even for Margaret. Finally, Hugh suggested Harold Cox, who
agreed to come. Cox was not particularly well known, but he was an
excellent speaker and had the added prestige of having been a Member
of Parliament. Cox became her "name."

Now Margaret was free to run down to Wantley to loll on the lawn
with Hugh and to spend a few days in London with J. Noah who, having been in Paris on business, had flown over to London. J. Noah was
still entreating her to marry him as soon as they were both legally
free. Margaret promised to consider it, though as soon as he left she
wrote Juliet: "I am *not* inclined to marriage. Freedom is too lovely, and
I mean to enjoy it for some time."

There is little doubt that Margaret and Hugh became lovers in the
summer of 1921 and that Margaret was delighted when she discovered
he was an expert at Karezza. But no romance, no matter how delightful or diverting, could prevent her from fighting to maintain the leadership of the birth-control movement. This leadership was now threatened by an English woman, Dr. Marie Stopes.

Marie Stopes was both an intellectual and a mystic. A short, plump
woman in her late thirties, she held doctorates in paleontology from
German and English universities. But she was so sexually naive that
it had taken her six months after her marriage to realize her husband
was impotent. Yet after an annulment and a remarriage, she found sex
so surprisingly delightful she wrote a book, *Married Love*, extolling its
pleasures. Margaret met Stopes on her first visit to England, just after
Married Love was completed. When Stopes could not find an English
publisher (it was very frank), Margaret took the manuscript to America where she did find a publisher. It was so successful it was soon published in England too, where it became an instant success. In gratitude, Marie had written the open letter to President Wilson asking
him to intervene in Margaret's federal trial. Marie had also written
Margaret at the time: "Keep joyous, for, my dear, whatever happens

now, tens of thousands of American women will bless you later. . . . Remember, I am with you all through. God bless you and strengthen you." As a result, the two women had been on very friendly terms for a while.

But now Marie Stopes had gone on from praising the joys of sex to campaigning for birth control; she even claimed that God had spoken to her and told her to do this. At the moment she was in the process of starting a clinic in the London slums, heralding it as "the first legal birth-control clinic in the English-speaking world." Margaret was so angry at her becoming a rival she planned to undercut her whenever she could.

First, however, Margaret had other things on her mind. Ellis had finally convinced her to go to a throat specialist, whose diagnosis of her tubercular infection located the infection, not in her neck, but in her right tonsil. He recommended that both her tonsils be removed.

But Margaret procrastinated, using the excuse that she had to attend a conference on birth-control techniques in Holland, and left at once for Amsterdam. She wrote Hugh from Amsterdam, asking him if he would arrange to go to Plymouth with her for two days after her return and the operation was over as she wanted very much to see him alone before leaving for New York.

> And go I must Hugh. The few dear ones, the faithful ones, are in a panic. If things were going well I would stay. I shall be patched up like the horses in the bull ring for a while anyway. But it's life to live and to love and to fight for ideals—and to work. Come back to America with me for a few months, can't you, adorable one?

After Margaret had her tonsils removed in London, the results seemed amazing. "Think of being rid of my T.B. after twenty-three years of suffering," she wrote Juliet. "Though my throat is still sore and I cannot speak. I'm sailing soon to get going on the (New York) conference, and I told Havelock to make me a sign to hang around my neck saying in large letters SHE IS DUMB."

Though Hugh did not go to Plymouth with Margaret, he did spend her last day in London with her, going along to the doctor's office while she got her final checkup.

The voyage home was rough and tiring however, and as soon as she got to the States she left for a week's rest at Juliet's summer home in Windsor, Vermont, where again her first thought was of Hugh. On September 30 she wrote him from Vermont:

> It was glorious to have you that last day, even in the horrid city. I know you hated it all—I could feel it in the air, tho you did nobly in hiding it in your face and voice. I can see you now standing outside that five-guinea man's office waiting, and looking bored, bored, bored!!
>
> The King came with me to the boat, he is just the dearest creature ever. Did all the little big things for me—sent letters, licked stamps, did all the thousand things I forgot to do. Now his letters are full of remorse that he didn't do more. Blessings on you both.

From Vermont she went to Massachusetts to attend to the divorce from Bill Sanger which she had been postponing for a long time. She picked Massachusetts because she owned the cottage at Truro, and was a legal resident of that state. Desertion was also grounds for divorce in Massachusetts.

She was still hesitating about getting married again and certainly wasn't the least bit in love with J. Noah. Yet marriage to him would solve all her financial problems, and having her divorce would leave her free to marry or not, as she chose.

Bill's letter saying he was deserting her convinced the court. On October 4, 1921, her decree came through, though she told only a few close friends, making them promise not to tell anyone else lest the Catholic Church hear about it; she was having trouble enough with the Church without adding this.

She must have written Hugh, telling him of her divorce and implying a possible remarriage, because in a November fifteenth letter she talked to him at length on the subject:

> Of course marriage does not mean a thing to us in one way. It certainly makes not a whit of difference to me toward anyone I've ever loved, only to be happier toward everyone . . . I've learned, Hugh, dear, of spiritual laws that to obey mean peace of heart. You sense them too. And tho our dearest ones do not see these laws, it's scarcely our work to point them out unless asked to do so.

*   *   *

Now Margaret set to work in earnest planning a November birth-control conference. She rented a room at the Hotel Plaza to display current birth-control methods to the doctors and nurses who would attend. The large auditorium of Town Hall on West Forty-third Street was hired for her public lecture entitled "Birth Control! Is it Moral?" The lecture was heavily advertised in the *Review*.

The first two days of the conference were successful enough, though most male doctors shied away lest their hospital connections be jeopardized. As the evening of the public lecture approached, Margaret began to worry. She dreamed of trying to carry a baby up a steep hill, describing the dream in her diary:

> I came very abruptly to a side hill which became a mountainside of rock and slippery shale, and I had nothing to hold onto to keep me from slipping. The baby kept crying and I tried to comfort it but I dared not use my right hand, as it seemed to be held up like a balancing rod which kept us both from falling. The wretched dream kept me drowsy all day. Always when I dreamed of babies there was some troublesome news not far away.

The Town Hall lecture was due to start at 8:30 in the evening, and the doors were to open at seven. Margaret had supper at Juliet's home with Harold Cox who had arrived from England, while Anne Kennedy, managing editor of the *Review*, went on ahead to Town Hall. At 7:45 Mrs. Kennedy phoned to say that practically all the seats were filled.

A few minutes after eight, Margaret, Juliet, and Cox left for the hall by taxi. As they got to Forty-third Street the taxi had trouble getting through the street because the roadway was jammed. "An overflow meeting!" Margaret exclaimed happily. "Look, Juliet, a wonderful turnout!"

Cox and the two women left the taxi and tried to push their way through the crowd toward the doors, but to their suprise two policemen blocked their way, and when they looked around they saw still more policemen. Soon they were told that the doors were locked; there was to be no meeting.

Margaret phoned the Police Commissioner to find out what was happening but was told he could not be reached.

She was trying to reach New York's Mayor Hylan instead when she

saw that a policeman at the door had opened it momentarily to let a
few people out. She saw her chance. Ducking under the policeman's
arm with Juliet and Cox following her, she rushed straight to the platform where a tall stranger boosted her up.

The hall was in a turmoil. Margaret knew that the lecture meeting
could be closed under the fire laws if the aisles were blocked, so she
shouted to the audience, "I'm Mrs. Sanger. Get in out of the aisles."
Then she tried to address the crowd. She had spoken only a few words
and given a quick nod to J. Noah in the second row, when two policemen stopped her. She sat down and motioned Harold Cox to try instead. He got no further than, "Ladies and Gentlemen, I have come
across the Atlantic . . . ," when a policeman standing on the platform
took him by the arm and hurried him to his seat.

By this time a man in the crowd had begun to shout "Defy them!
Defy them!" Another was calling out: "What's the charge? Where's the
warrant?" The policeman didn't answer, but Anne Kennedy explained
to Margaret what had happened before she came.

A man had come up to her as she was waiting on the platform and
asked who was in charge of the meeting.

"I am," Mrs. Kennedy had replied.

"This meeting must be closed."

"Why?"

"An indecent, immoral subject is to be discussed. It cannot be held."

"On what authority? Are you from the police?"

"No, I'm Monsignor Dineen, Secretary to Archbishop Hayes."

"What right has he to interfere?"

"He has the right."

At this point Monsignor Dineen turned to Captain Donahue: "Captain, speak up."

"Who are you?" Anne Kennedy demanded of the police officer.

"I am Captain Donahue of this district. The meeting must be
stopped."

"Very well," Mrs. Kennedy said, "we'll write this down, and I'll read
it to the audience for you, Captain. 'I, Captain Thomas Donahue, of the
Twenty-sixth Precinct, at the order of Monsignor Joseph P. Dineen,
Secretary to Archbishop Patrick J. Hayes, have ordered this meeting
closed.'"

Mrs. Kennedy now pointed out Monsignor Dineen to Margaret. By this time he was standing at the back of the audience directing the police by a nod of his head, or sending messages to the Captain, still standing on the platform, through a runner.

In spite of the noise in the auditorium, Mary Winsor, a former suffragette, next tried to speak. The Captain stopped her. The crowd yelled louder. Then Margaret tried again. She was also stopped and told to "get off the platform before you cause more disorder." Instead of obeying, Margaret tried to speak several times more, since her aim now was to get herself arrested. She knew that unless she was arrested she could not make a test case of the principle of free speech.

This strategy worked. On her tenth try Captain Donahue arrested her for refusing to get off the platform. He also arrested Mary Winsor and Anne Kennedy, and when Juliet, who had also tried to speak, asked, "Why don't you arrest me too?" Donahue agreed.

The street outside was a jam-packed mass, with men, women, and police reserves pushing this way and that. Though several wealthy women of the audience such as Mrs. Dwight Morrow, Mrs. Charles Tiffany, and Mrs. Otto Kahn offered their limousines, Margaret and the other prisoners refused to ride. They marched from Town Hall to Broadway and up to the West Forty-seventh Street station with police flanking them and several hundred men and women marching behind them singing, "My Country 'Tis of Thee." At the police station Margaret, Mary Winsor, Juliet Rublee, and Anne Kennedy were ordered into a patrol wagon and taken downtown to Night Court, where they were released without bail and told to appear in court the following morning. After that they went back to Juliet's apartment, with Harold Cox, followed by several reporters.

The reporters expected a routine story about police stupidity, but Mrs. Kennedy insisted that there was much more to it than that. Archbishop Hayes himself, she said, had ordered the meeting closed. In order to check her story, a *Times* reporter phoned "The Power House," as the Archbishop's Madison Avenue residence was colloquially called, and got through to Monsignor Dineen. "Yes," the Monsignor admitted, "We did it. We got the meeting closed."

When Margaret fell asleep at dawn, she was plagued by the same dream in which she was trying to carry a baby up a steep sliding mountain. She couldn't know then that the Town Hall incident had done more for her cause than five years of struggle. When she woke the next

morning, she found she had made the leading newspaper in the city—
page one, column one, of the *New York Times*. It ran a headline no
reader could ignore:

"BIRTH CONTROL RAID ON TOWN HALL MADE BY POLICE ON ARCHBISH-
OP'S ORDER. CAPTAIN DONAHUE'S ONLY INSTRUCTIONS FROM HEAD-
QUARTERS, 'LOOK FOR MSGR. DINEEN'"

Other New York papers responded as strongly. The *Tribune* called
the breaking up of the meeting "arbitrary and Prussian to the last degree." The *Post* warned that "without an open way to debate, our boasted freedom of speech is a mockery," and the *World* summed up the general feeling when it said "the issue is bigger than the right to advocate
birth control. It is part of the eternal fight for free speech, free assembly and democratic government, which must always find defenders if
freedom is to survive." Even papers which had called Margaret a
crackpot and fanatic fell into line.

Riding the crest of the wave, Margaret at once engaged another and
much larger hall for November 19—the Park Theatre at Columbus
Circle.

The theatre had fifteen hundred seats but four thousand people
wanted to get in. Despite this, the crowd was quiet and orderly once
those who could be seated were inside the hall. Harold Cox spoke for
almost an hour on the history of the fight for birth control. Then an actress, Mary Shaw, gave a short, dramatic talk, ending with the reading
of a scene from *Ghosts*. Next Margaret, as always the main attraction,
took over. She tackled the question, "Birth Control: Is It Moral?"

Responsible sex-action requires forethought, and irresponsible
action is immoral. Every civilization involves an increasing forethought for others, even for those unborn. The reckless abandonment of the moment and the careless regard for the consequences,
is not morality . . . It is not only inevitable, but it is also right
that we learn to control the size of our family, for by this control
and adjustment we can raise the standards of the human race
. . . Nature's way of reducing her numbers is controlled by disease and famine. Primitive man achieved the same results by infanticide, abandonment of children, or abortion . . . Contraception is a more civilized method, for it involves not only a greater

forethought for others, but finally a higher sanction for the value of life itself.

Her speech lasted only ten minutes, but she was interrupted by applause nineteen times.

Margaret had invited other speakers to take the opposite side and argue against birth control. To a man, they advocated continence and self-control. Margaret ended the evening in a low, intense voice:

> The law requires a married woman to give of herself to her husband or forego his support. This makes self-control by women impractical, if not impossible . . . And the argument that the use of the marriage relationship is only for the purpose of procreation would conceivably have to limit unions to only a few times in the course of a marriage . . . This last is perfectly absurd because it places man on the same level as animals . . . There is another side, another use of the marriage relationship. I contend that it is just as sacred and beautiful for two people to express their love when they have no intention of being parents, and that they can go into that relationship with the same beauty and the same holiness with which they go into music or to prayer. I believe that it is the right understanding of our sexual power and of its creative energy that gives us spiritual illumination. I say that there is more than one use to make of it, and that is the higher use, the development of our soul and soul growth.

This was the kind of speech Margaret was to give for many years, and it became the philosophy by which she was to live her life.

While waiting for the trial of the arrested women, the Church tried lamely to defend its action by saying that the Town Hall meeting had been canceled only after Monsignor Dineen became shocked when he saw four children being admitted. Margaret's lawyer proved that the four "children" were eighteen- and nineteen-year-old Barnard College students, who had been sent there by their sociology teacher, and saw to it that the papers played this up.

The trial itself was a comedy of evasions. The police had made an enormous mistake in arresting Juliet Rublee, whose husband, George Rublee, was an extremely knowledgeable lawyer. He demanded that Commissioner Enright punish Captain Donahue for acting without specific police orders, though Donahue was not even at the hearing. The papers played this up too, and Rublee then insisted that Enright appoint a commission to investigate the raid.

The investigating committee did more evading. Instead of investigating the raid, they delved into the whole birth-control movement, starting with the Brownsville Clinic five years before. When they had to admit under Rublee's questioning that this was beside the point, still another court hearing was held. At this hearing the presiding magistrate spoke as if Margaret had been arrested for selling contraceptives at Town Hall. "Just what was she selling? Where are the articles?" he kept demanding. When none could be produced, the magistrate dismissed the case and announced that the matter was closed.

By now it was obvious that the police were ducking the subject of the unlawful raid itself; they were trying to hush up the matter, and had no intention of bringing in either Captain Donahue or Monsignor Dineen as witnesses. To try to force their hand, George and Juliet Rublee held a meeting in their East Forty-ninth Street apartment, inviting some of the most prominent people in New York, including Henry Morgenthau, Paul M. Warburg, and Herbert Satterlee. The group sent an open letter to Mayor Hylan demanding a further investigation, or as one newspaper called it, "an investigation of the previous investigation."

The second investigation was no better than the first. Though Captain Donahue was finally forced to appear, he testified that he had merely responded to telephone instructions to stop the meeting from his superior, Lieutenant Lahey. And when Lahey, who was the officer in charge of the precinct, appeared, he said he had received telephone instructions from someone at police headquarters. From whom exactly had Lahey received them? "As far as I can remember, from the telephone operator on duty that night."

It was clear that the name of Monsignor Dineen was never going to be mentioned, much less that of Archbishop Hayes, and that Captain Donahue was never going to be punished. In fact, Donahue was promoted not long afterward, then quietly retired. With evasion following evasion, the matter was allowed to drag on for months in the courts until it finally fizzled out.

But it did not fizzle out in the newspapers. Letters pro and con kept pouring in, and the newspapers, enjoying the controversy, kept printing them. But because of this remarkable publicity, though Margaret had won no legal victory, she had again won a tactical one. Her name, too, had become a household word. Better yet, she had gotten the middle class almost solidly lined up behind her. She had gotten the support of the upper class when she formed the Committee of One Hundred after the Brownsville raid. Now many more of the middle class, who if possible were even more insistent on the separation of church and state because they dreaded the thought of the influence of "Popery," came over to her side. If a representative of the Pope could stop a perfectly legal discussion, they realized, free speech could go down the drain.

Now Margaret got ten times as many invitations to lecture on birth control as before, and at many times the price. While before the Town Hall incident she had been glad to speak for traveling expenses and a fifty-dollar fee, she was now offered anywhere from a hundred and fifty to a thousand dollars to speak. Prosperous at last at the age of forty-two, she moved from her dingy flat on Fourteenth Street to a much finer one at Eighteen Gramercy Park. She decorated this apartment with "golden walls, golden silk curtains, Chinese blue rugs and hangings, red cushions, vases, books, and loads of flowers—all very simple and restful."

Yet her peaceful surroundings did not lessen her anger against her rival Mary Ware Dennett, who continued to work for contraception through her own league. After a bitter exchange of letters, Margaret compelled Dennett to drop the words "birth control" from the title of her league on the grounds that Margaret had coined the phrase, and to change it to The Voluntary Parenthood League. (On November 15, after Hugh wrote suggesting that she stop feuding with Mrs. Dennett, she answered tartly: "Hands off, Mr. de S. No, I won't be gracious to Mrs. D.—so there!") Next, she turned her anger against Marie Stopes, who was at the moment lecturing in America on both contraception and her book *Married Love.* She wrote Hugh on November 27:

> The most amazing thing was the very bad impression Marie Stopes made here. While she was in the States for only four days she advised people to support the Voluntary Parenthood League instead of my organization. She (also said she) came to open the *first* American B.C. Clinic!!!

Poor Marie—her egotism will be her downfall. She looked very pretty and has a certain charm, but conceit runs like the babbling brook—on forever.

Hugh answered with a mixture of common sense and the kind of flattery that Margaret adored.

To think that you were bothered by such a matter as Marie. But it got me a jolly letter—oh bless your darling heart! I'm planning an article on the B.C. question from the Catholic point of view. *ESSENTIAL*, dear & beloved Margaret, that you should *understand* their point of view—by so doing you take the wind out of their sails. Of course the gnats bite and are infernal accursed nuisances, but that is to be expected. A cause is always won by its enemies. You, oh flaming eyed Lioness, must have a tremendous enemy. But your enemy is declared. He is in the open. Half the battle is won!! I wish I could put my hand on some of their actual words written or spoken against. Send me along all you can. Please. And you won't be angry with me for seeming to give YOU advice. I'm only reminding you of the fact that *what you touch you enliven* whether you touch to strike or bless.

Margaret sent him all the clippings she had about the raid, telling him to pass them on to Havelock and Harold, then on December 16 she dashed off an angry letter to Dennett, who was now trying to form an International Council on Contraception and had invited both Margaret and Stopes to join. Margaret refused to be part of any council started by Mrs. Dennett. She also objected to Marie Stopes becoming a member:

I return the names of the nominees for the International Council with Dr. Stopes' name crossed out. As I always work in the open, I will give my reasons for my objections to her on any international or American council.

Dr. Stopes has not been a happy influence for the Birth Control movement. Her intense egotism, her ridiculous conceit, have rendered her obnoxious in England, where the *real* pioneers of the movement like the Drysdales et cetera will have nothing to do with her. And her visit here has done very little to further the cause.

I might also add that it has required very little courage for Dr. Stopes to join the Birth Control movement, because she joined it at the tail-end when the movement had become well established in every civilized country, and even after it had acquired a stamp of respectability.

Also, Dr. Stopes has brought very little sacrifice to the movement. On the contrary, she never in all her life made so much money as she has since she became identified with the movements of Birth Control and Rational Sexology, to both of which movements her original contributions are nil . . .

Not being a physician, a fact unknown to a great many people, she has the assurance and the aplomb of the layman with a little knowledge. All of her writings contain foolish and erroneous statements; but she is so conceited that she wouldn't permit anyone to correct her.

In "Married Love," which she asked me to publish and which I did with considerable hesitation, I did eliminate and correct some of her errors. But of course, I could not do so in her other writings . . .

For the above reasons I vote against Dr. Stopes as a member of any International Council and particularly as Chairman of that Council. She has neither the knowledge nor the poise nor the unselfishness necessary for such a position.

This was not only an angry, but an untruthful letter. Margaret did not "publish" Stopes' book *Married Love*; she merely found a publisher for it. Birth control had not been "accepted in every civilized country." And Stopes did not wait to make a lot of money until she worked for birth control; she had earned a substantial salary as a university professor before that time, then married a wealthy man who gave far more money to the cause than she took out of it.

But Margaret was far too distracted, at the moment, to think straight; she had two other exciting projects at hand—a trip to Japan the following year and a new lover.

She had been invited to Japan by a group called Kaizo, a society of young progressives opposed to the ruling military clique which advocated a larger population in order to get more soldiers. The Kaizo group also invited three other lecturers—Albert Einstein to explain relativity, Bertrand Russell to discuss the consequences of the Peace of Versailles, and H. G. Wells to elaborate on his ideas for bringing about world disarmament. Margaret realized she would be moving in fast company; she needed speeches more carefully planned than ever, and would have to set to work writing them immediately.

Her new lover was Wells, whom she had met briefly in London the year before.

Wells lived pretty much as Hugh did. He claimed he was not for "free love" but for "free-er love"—a fine distinction since he had induced his wife to give him almost total sexual freedom, letting him disappear from home whenever he pleased, stay away as long as he pleased, and return at will, with no explanations asked.

Margaret was definitely Wells' type of woman. In his thinly disguised autobiographical novel *Ann Veronica*, he described a young woman with whom he had once been passionately in love.

> Ann Veronica had black hair, fine eyebrows, and a clear complexion; and the forces that modelled her features had loved and lingered at their work and made them subtle and fine. She was slender, and sometimes she seemed tall, and walked and carried herself lightly and joyfully as one who habitually and commonly feels well. . . . Her lips came together with an expression between contentment and the faintest shadow of a smile. Her manner was one of great reserve, and behind this mask she was wildly discontented and eager for freedom and life.

This described Margaret almost perfectly. It wasn't important that Margaret wasn't young anymore; at forty-two she still seemed so to Wells who was fifty-three. And it certainly didn't matter that her hair was red instead of black. She had the two qualities he cherished—complete freedom in sexual conduct, and an endless curiosity about life. Indeed, her curiosity was something her friends particularly noticed: "When you tell Margaret something, she *listens*," they said.

Wells and Margaret had many other things in common as well. They had both been brought up in poverty-stricken homes; they were both intelligent but without the benefit of a formal education; they had both suffered from tuberculosis as well as depression, and they both had an irresistible urge to crusade.

At the end of 1921, Wells came to the United States and wrote to Margaret from his hotel in Washington:

> Dear little Mrs. Margaret, I think I shall be through here about the 10th or 12th (of December). Then I shall probably come to New York. I'd like to be somewhere convenient to you but I'll probably stay with the Lamonts. Have you any ideas? I'm very much at your disposal. Ever glowingly yrs. H. G.

On December 7, he followed this with another note.

> Dear little Margaret Sanger. My plans in New York are ruled entirely by the wish to be with you as much as possible—and as much as possible without other people about. I don't mind paying thousands of dollars if I can get that—I'm really quite well off you know. I'm offered Mrs. Lamont's hospitality all the time I'm in New York & if you were not in the case I'd go to her all the time.
>
> So far as the Rublee's go, it will ruffle dear Mrs. Lamont if I go there, but I'll go there gladly if it means a sure, sweet access to you. But not if it means just tantalizing glimpses. If I take my own apt. could you come to me abundantly? If so—secure it. I can come and go to it for a few days at a time . . .
>
> You know how things are in N.Y. and the dangers that are about you. It's much better that you arrange things than I do. I want to sit about with you in the costume of your tropical islands more than anything else in the world.

Margaret undoubtedly got an apartment as Wells suggested, and met him there frequently. Still, Hugh remained her most beloved. She thought of him on Christmas night:

> Hugh dear, Japan seems positive. I hate to go until the B.C. situation is better protected. . . . The Catholic Church is desperate, the Police of late have been insulting to the limit. . . . Sometimes I think I'll accept the nicest & richest man I know, marry him & leave all the miserable people to wallow in

their own misery & learn to fight for themselves. It's glorious to do constructive work but this negative kind is discouraging.

H. G. Wells has been to my house for tea. I know you don't like him, but he came out for birth control at the Disarmament Conference which was very decent of him.

I'm very tired these days—but very well. No neck trouble. That operation was worth two trips over. I'm a booster for tonsils out with gland troubles now. . . . More later, blessed one.

As she sealed her letter in her Gramercy Park apartment, she decided that all in all it had been a good year. She had made the final break with Sanger. Her cause had leapt ahead and moved her closer to the national spotlight than ever before. She had a millionaire eager to marry her plus several adoring lovers. It had been a very good year indeed.

JAPAN, CHINA, AND A SECRET MARRIAGE

Margaret's moods rose and fell dramatically, especially during the first few months of 1922. She was elated when she finished editing the February edition of the *Review*, celebrating Havelock's birthday. She wrote to Hugh about it on January 27: "Hugh dear—no *darling*—looking over the page proofs all evening in which is your splendid birthday tribute to Havelock. The King will die of joy over it."

Her joy was heightened by the success of her lectures in half a dozen cities (one of these cities even founded a new birth-control league as a result). But her mood changed abruptly when an Episcopal bishop reneged on a public endorsement of birth control he had promised to give.

A worse blow was the failure of a rally she had arranged for February 5 at the Lexington Opera House. Tickets were a dollar each or twenty-five dollars for a box of four, and she had advertised it heavily in the *Review* under the grandiose title of "Farewell Mass Meeting in Honor of Margaret Sanger who is Leaving for Japan and China Where She Will Take the Message of Birth Control." In her excitement she forgot to say there would be other speakers there too, and the advance sale was so disappointing the rally was called off with the excuse that she was "too busy and fatigued to attend."

This excuse was partially true; she *was* tired—tired of trying to make a decision about marriage to J. Noah. She jotted down one of those revealing notes she was in the habit of putting into the files: "I'm not sure I'm really fit for marriage or its responsibilities. My only real interest is my cause." Nevertheless, she decided to let him accompany her on her trip as he had been begging to do. She said she might even consider marrying him in Paris on their way back.

But because J. Noah was joining her, she would have to take a chaperon along for the sake of appearances; the chaperon she decided on was Grant. She ran down to the Peddie School, where Grant was preparing for college, and told him to get ready at once to leave with her and a "friend" for Japan. She also asked Grant to call her friend "Uncle Noah." Before Grant had a chance to explain why he'd rather not go, she dashed off. Grant, who was a new boy at Peddie and was just beginning to make friends, did not want to miss a whole term at school. But she didn't take the time to listen.

Deciding to tell Hugh a little more about J. Noah, she wrote on January 27:

> For some strange reason two very fine men have been thrust my way. One a millionaire and sixty, a terribly American type of respectable business man, church-going, widower, generous, happy, thinks I'm *sensible*—likes me for that stupid quality. He could with his wealth make life very comfortable & insure the financial success of my cause. Shall I accept him?
>
> The other a bachelor about 42—a eugenicist, good birth, fairly wealthy. Not enough to make cause successful, but believes in woman's advancement. He's very pressing for marriage. I don't believe in that institution particularly—but I could have such a beautiful time if that cause were won. I'd buy Wantley for you. I want to live in London near Hill Road.

In writing that J. Noah was a widower she was less than honest. But a widower would sound much better when her own divorce became public, as it eventually would have to. As for the second suitor, if he existed at all, he must have disappeared quickly, because no one in her family ever heard of him.

She then wrote Bill Sanger, asking whether, if she did marry again, she could keep the Sanger name. Also, she asked him to keep their divorce a secret for a while.

Bill replied from Truro:

* * *

I am visiting with your father and have told no one of our divorce as yet. I've always left good enough alone, so to speak. A public scream of our separation could not hurt me—we artists are out of the pale of Society anyway—but it could hurt you.

As to keeping my name after a possible re-marriage, certainly you can. In fact, I am proud to have been married to a woman who carried that name so high.

Margaret, Grant, and J. Noah took the train cross-country to San Francisco. From there, they intended to sail to Japan on the *Taiyo Maru*, but complications arose. In her haste, Margaret had forgotten to get a Japanese visa, without which the steamship line refused to sell her a ticket. They also advised her that the Japanese Consul was unlikely to issue her one.

As the ship was almost ready to leave, she rushed to the office of the Japanese Consul and demanded that he tell her why he would not give her a visa. Was she an undesirable person who could not be admitted into his country? Or was it her subject that was taboo? He bowed politely and murmured, "both." His Imperial Majesty had heard something about a Town Hall arrest; she was therefore personally undesirable. And her subject was not a proper one for his people to hear.

When the Consul was through explaining, a Japanese official who happened to be standing nearby suggested to Margaret that, since their ship was also going to China, she try to get a Chinese visa instead. In any event, other Japanese officials would be sailing on the *Taiyo Maru* as well; maybe she could talk to one of them during the voyage and convince him to intercede on her behalf. She felt the exhilarating effect that the prospect of a battle always gave her, hurriedly got the Chinese visa, and trooped up the gangplank with Grant and J. Noah just in time.

Yet none of the Japanese officials on board could or would intercede for her. When the ship arrived in Japan, she had to send a message to the American Consul to ask for help in getting a permit to land. While she awaited his reply, a tender brought more Japanese officials on board; they questioned her endlessly. What was the purpose of her visit? Who had invited her? If the American Consul did succeed in getting permission for her to land, would she sign a statement saying she would give no public lectures on birth control, but speak only to the specific people who had invited her? She said she would sign such a statement, and did.

In her diary, she noted:

> In two minutes after the door was closed upon the government officials, I was besieged with reporters. Every male reporter expressed his regrets that their government was acting this way & said the people of Japan desire to hear about birth control. Mrs. Kohashi, the reporter for *Woman's Magazine*, came & also a delegation of six women representing the New Woman's Society of Japan. These doll-like New Women are the instruments to carry out the real dreams of an emancipated womanhood.

The delegation from the New Woman's Society explained:

> When leaders say women need vote, most women do not listen. When they say women need economic equality, most do not listen. But when they hear of birth control, then like lightning we understand.

At last the good word came: the Japanese Chief of Police would let her land. The U.S. Consul had refused to become involved, but because of her signed statement that she would not speak publicly she could come in.

But Margaret was not one to accept a finger when she could get the whole hand. After a good night's sleep in Tokyo, she was ready to fight again. She went personally to see the Chief of Police in order to wheedle: Couldn't she speak more freely than he had sent word she could? No, she couldn't. There was a new law called the "Dangerous Thoughts Law," passed by the Japanese Diet under pressure from the military clique who wished to exclude all thoughts that did not conform to ancient tradition. No specific thoughts were cited, but everyone at Police Headquarters had read Margaret's *Woman and the New Race* and was sure it contained dangerous thoughts.

Undaunted, she rickshawed to the Minister of Home Affairs. "Alas!" said the man at the door, "the minister is out." She hurried on to the office of the liberal Kaizo group who had asked her to come. They suggested she go directly to the Imperial Diet, which luckily was in session. There she argued the importance of her cause, citing figures on

Japan's exploding population. How it had mounted from twenty-six million in 1846 to thirty-three million in 1872, then doubled to sixty million in 1922, and how these numbers of people were crowded into their tiny island at the rate of 2600 people to the square mile of arable land as compared to 466 in England. It may have been her statistics, it may have been her charisma; the Diet gave her permission to speak publicly.

Soon she was visiting hospitals and lunching with doctors, discussing current birth-control methods and suggesting new ones. There are brief diary notes:

> Dr. Koji told of the methods he found successful—plain soft Japanese paper folded & inserted against the cervix—then as this absorbs the sperm it is removed & a clean piece of paper wet in antiseptic solution wipes the vagina dry. 1000 cases, no failures. Count Kowarori and I spoke very frankly both of methods and the art of love.

She couldn't pass up a visit to Tokyo's red-light district where she grieved over girls barely in their teens, who had been sold by their parents to the brothels, and were made to accept nine or ten visitors a night. If they were caught trying to run away, she was told, the madam who ran the brothel broke the bones of their legs so they were truly trapped.

Though Margaret was exhausted by now, she had to press on to Yokohama where she had other speaking dates. From Tokyo and Yokohama her next stop was to have been Kyoto, but the Kaizo group canceled her Kyoto lectures because the police authorities had frightened them. Two days later, however, the police relented and agreed to let her lecture on condition that she speak to professional groups only. On March 30 she spoke to three hundred members of the Medical Association of Kyoto. They were so enthusiastic that she followed up the three-hour lecture with a two-hour demonstration.

She was able to rest and tour in Kyoto, going with Grant and J. Noah to look at a collection of rare embroideries in a shop celebrated for its fine kimonos. The owner bowed extremely low as he told her he was a faithful "Sangerite," and Margaret bought "two glorious kimonos, a red one and a blue one, plus an evening coat of rare, old purple." When the proprietor said he had sold the Metropolitan Museum in New York forty-seven thousand dollars worth of similar kimonos at the same price, J. Noah beamed; he was both getting a bargain and dressing up his beloved. Also, the Kaizo group had paid her two thousand yen ($1800) for four lectures, so his pocket hadn't been emptied by the trip as much as he had feared.

As her Japanese visa was good only until April first, she had planned to go on to Korea on that date. But for some reason she could not get a visa for Korea; she had to stay in Kyoto waiting to see if the authorities would change their mind. Meanwhile she turned to her journal:

> One hears much of the "New Woman" here but one seldom sees her. It seems only those women who have turned Christian are able to think independently or to do anything with their lives. It also seems that to be a Christian means to be a rebel or a radical of some kind. One tells it with great secret pride.

Despite this, she got very angry at a dinner where some missionaries among the guests came up with the old argument that self-control was the only acceptable means of birth control. She argued forcefully to the contrary, especially after a doctor sitting near her told of the tremendous number of abortions performed each year in Japan, and an Australian official told how Malay women sprinkled the acid juice of pineapple on tampons as contraceptives, or drank egg mixed with sake hoping to bring on a missed menstrual period. Obviously in every country in the world women were desperately trying to find some means of birth control.

Having finally gotten visas to Korea, Margaret, J. Noah, and Grant sailed across the China Sea to Korea at the end of May. Before they left, Margaret had finally received an eagerly awaited letter from Hugh. She had written him and Havelock very short notes from Japan because of her hectic schedule, but instead of answering her they had written each other about her. Ellis wrote Hugh a perceptive analysis: "What you say of her is very true . . . She is a combination of the shrewd, practical, hustling American with the elusively fascinating Irishwoman."

When she got her letter from Hugh, who called her "sweet as bell heather, sweet as a rose," she responded at once:

> What an enchanting letter writer you are, old goose. So you had

a glorious day with the King and he told you that I was not wanted in Japan. Well by this time you have heard how I went anyway
just to see, and what a welcome I got!! I gave fifteen lectures &
then up & got sick. I was *weak*. I hated myself for not being a
mule or a goat or something *hardy*. But here I am all well again,
having finished in Japan, organized a League in Tokyo, and
another in Peking and Shanghai . . . I'll be in London with
Grant July 10th or perhaps earlier, with Grant in his first pair of
long trousers making me feel old and lonely.

She also said she had formed birth-control leagues in China, though
this was as fanciful as some of her other stories because she hadn't yet
left Japan. But then, as she had once told Hugh, "Being Irish, I never
tell a story the same way twice."

The Korean women impressed Margaret mainly by their costumes;
she didn't think they had the strength to fight for their own emancipation: "One man told me he wanted to have twenty children. He said he
already had two. He was stunned when I suggested that perhaps his
wife had had the two!"

She made only one speech in Korea, to the New Family Reform Association.

The hall holds 800 people and was filled, though their rules are
no smoking, no drinking, no gambling, so their membership is
quite small. I was surprised that men, women & children were
there together. The women seemed to attend for some reason but
not for the birth control message. As in Japan, the work will have
to be done thru the men.

A young woman interpreted the address; she had lately returned from America and was considered good. But one had only
to listen a few minutes to recognize she was not an expert. When I
asked the chairman if I was to give the theory or practice of B.C.
he said "both." But when I came to speak on the practical side my
translator's courage took flight. She could not go on. She turned to
me & said "I will get a doctor to say that." But the only doctor
available had been talking to someone & had not heard the practical side. I suggested giving the Family Reformation Association
a good supply of my pamphlets, and all were satisfied.

* * *

In Peking, Margaret spoke at the University, where twenty-five hundred men crowded into the hall but, again to her surprise, only a few women.

> For 2½ hours I held forth—crowd very enthusiastic—quick to get the point. At dinner later, one of the Professors says he is going to do work on mules to see why they don't breed. Maybe that will be a clue to B.C.!!

In Hong Kong, where she went next, she was upset when she saw women coolies carrying coal on their backs to the steamers. "I was shocked not only by their strained faces and emaciated bodies but by the fact that, unlike the men, they did not sing."

When her lecture tour ended in May, she and Grant and J. Noah set off on a vacation trip by boat through the Mediterranean. On May 31, when they landed at Aden, Egypt, she made a stark diary entry: "Peggy's birthday. Twelve years old today." As usual, she stayed in bed that day to mourn.

After traveling through Italy and Switzerland, they finally arrived in Paris. Grant begged to be sent home. He insisted he had done plenty of sight-seeing and wanted to spend the rest of the summer with boys his own age, instead of with an "uncle" of sixty-two. So off he sailed, and Slee, whom Margaret had decided to marry, set about the serious matter of getting a French divorce.

He had prepared his way carefully. When he had gone to Paris the year before, his "business" had been renting a small office, ostensibly as a branch of the Three-in-One Oil Company. He had also registered at the Trade Registry of the Department of the Seine, paid his business-license tax, and declared he "intended to make Paris his home forever."

Now he petitioned the court for a divorce on impeccable legal grounds. He declared that "his wife, Mary West Slee, had refused to accompany him to Paris and to cohabit with him in spite of the fact that he had informed her that he had taken up his abode in Paris definitely and permanently, and that, were she content to do so and resume the conjugal life, he would forgive and forget their years of misfortune, but that because of this obstinacy on the part of Mary West

Slee, and also because of her terrible temper, he was now deprived of the conjugal life."

He soon received his divorce, having given Mary Slee a large settlement. He and Margaret celebrated the occasion, then set off on a shopping tour. J. Noah insisted she buy a trousseau of the finest clothes, complete from handmade lingerie to a floor-length ermine coat. With these stowed away in a handsome new trunk, they took the boat train to London where, still for appearance's sake, she went to the Hotel Russell and he to the Savoy.

In London Slee outfitted himself with expensive new clothes, while Margaret spoke at a neo-Malthusian and birth-control conference in London. Immediately afterward, she got in touch with Hugh. After telephoning him, she sent him a rather odd note, odd because it still did not mention Slee.

Hugh dear—Since my return there has been nothing I have wanted to do more than to see you . . . But your voice was so bored on the 'phone, dear Hugh, especially at first. Still it was good to hear you—oh what a darling voice it really is. I am feeling very blue & discouraged with Mrs. Sanger. She is unable to do the things she loves to do. She is unable to be with the friends she adores—while she finds all her time taken up talking to very horrid disagreeable people she does not like at all.

But Hugh, the Cause is moving. It will really come to pass. We will see it too. I spent a nice day with the King, but I feel someone has captured his heart. He was dear & lovely to me, oh so dear. Yet I feel a pang of separation I never felt before.

The (London) Conference was a success, (though) I am not emotional enough to stir a British audience. I am afraid of them, these Britishers who sit so silently & move not. But you are there in Wantley, lovely Wantley and I am here in this hotel-barn where wild & crazy people think they live. I shall marry for wealth someday soon & come to live near you—yes? When I am fit & strong I shall come leaping across the world to you.

Oddly, Margaret tried again to postpone her marriage to Slee, but he was too impatient to wait. Dressed in his new black lounge suit with white quilted vest, he placed a gardenia in his lapel and escorted

Margy (his pet name for Margaret), luminous in green silk and jade jewels, to the registry office of St. Giles Parish where the marriage was quietly performed and recorded. Both gave their status as divorced, but while he gave his correct age of sixty-four, she lowered hers from forty-three to thirty-nine.

She had, however, drawn up another document that was not recorded. It was an agreement saying that, after marriage, she would be free to come and go with no questions asked. She would also have her own apartment and servants within her husband's home, where she could invite and entertain only those friends she chose, as the door to the apartment would be locked. He would have to telephone her from the other end of the house even to ask for a dinner date.

Slee was taken aback when this agreement was handed him just before the wedding. But Margaret was firm. Either he sign or the marriage was off. She clinched her argument by pointing out that Havelock and Edith Ellis had married under a similar agreement and, as far as Slee knew, the marriage had worked well. He signed, then took Margaret to the best silver shop in London and bought her a sterling silver dinner service as a wedding gift.

Margaret had told Hugh that marriage would make no difference in her life. She started at once to see that it did not.

She sent Slee sight-seeing alone all over London. When he got bored with museums, she suggested churches. When he had his fill of churches, she suggested Kew Gardens or Windsor Castle or outlined nice long walks. When he had had his fill of this, she suggested he go see Oxford, he finally lost his temper and began shouting at her, but she reminded him that he had signed an agreement. So he packed and got ready to go to Oxford, his consolation being that the nights he spent with her made up for the days alone.

They had undoubtedly become lovers on the trip to Japan and China, because, as Stuart bluntly put it, "Mother wouldn't marry anyone she wasn't sure could come across as a lover." But this was different. He had looked forward to an unbroken two weeks of what he expected to be a honeymoon, for their sexual life together was a constant surprise and delight. Though in his sixties, he was as eager and almost as innocent as an adolescent boy, and Margaret was an expert who enjoyed teaching him; she was as different as could be from Mary West Slee who, as the years went by, had become not only more frigid but mentally disturbed. His new marriage, J. Noah had to admit to himself, was infinitely better than the old, though there would be no honeymoon.

Indeed, Margaret succeeded in getting him out of the way whenever she wanted to, leaving her free to visit Hugh and Havelock, neither of whom did she tell about her marriage.

She even managed time alone with Wells. She had dropped a note to him from Paris, telling him she would be in London soon, and received one of his characteristic short replies: "Tell me exactly where you shall be and when a letter will find you . . . Warmest desires to you." That was all she needed. They spent an exciting evening together in his London flat, while Slee sat alone in his hotel lounge and waited for her as patiently as he could.

Finally she grew worried about her long absence from the birth-control movement in New York; in late September they sailed for home. Yet when they got there she continued to keep her marriage secret, as she was determined to keep hidden as long as possible the fact that the public Margaret Sanger had become the private Mrs. J. Noah Henry Slee.

THE RESEARCH BUREAU ON
SIXTEENTH STREET

Before he married Margaret, J. Noah had divided his time between his office, his club, and a cavernous old mansion up the Hudson near Fishkill, New York. Even after his three children were grown and gone and he and his wife separated, he spent weekends there because, with little education and no cultural interests, his chief pleasure came from living the life of a country gentleman. Eating huge meals, taking tramps and horseback rides through the woods, playing an occasional game of cards with a neighbor, he was content.

But Margaret would have nothing to do with the old house. She said it was too gloomy, too Victorian, too everything. Until they could replace it with something smart, she wanted an apartment in town. So they took a fine place in a new building at 31 Fifth Avenue near Washington Square, bought new furniture, and settled down to enjoy it, while Slee went about selling the old house.

Meanwhile, Margaret plunged back into her birth-control work. Ten thousand letters a month begging for contraceptive advice had poured in to her office while she was away. They came from all classes of women and cried out for replies.

The first thing she did was to rent Carnegie Hall for the night of October 22, 1923, and advertise "A Public Meeting to Welcome Margaret Sanger Home After Her World Tour in the Interests of Birth Control." But this time she had the sense to charge very little and to let her readers know they would get their money's worth. She promised tales of the fascinating places she had visited and said the witty *New York World* columnist Heywood Broun would serve as chairman. As a result, eighteen hundred of Carnegie's two thousand seats were filled and the evening was a great success.

Next she asked Anna to reply to as many letters as possible and soon set out on a round of speaking tours that covered the entire East. Though traveling at this pace by train wearied her, and she was using potent painkillers like morphine to ease her nervous stomach pains, she couldn't resist the temptation to go. She went even though the fee was sometimes only fifty dollars—a figure she accepted because in a rash moment she had boasted to J. Noah that she would be able to pay all her personal expenses out of her lecture fees, letting fall a rare check for twenty-five hundred dollars from her pocket to prove it. But it was the boost to her ego, plus her eagerness to promote her cause, demonstrated by the streams of tragic letters that poured in, that kept her running.

These letters were full of desperate cries, like:

> Excuse me for writing you this letter but after reading your book *Woman and the New Race* I can't stand it. I never had much friends as I am a orphan from the age of two years, mother dying of cancer of the breast and father putting me with strangers. It just about breaks my heart to think of the past but my future isn't much better. Living with strangers up to seventeen years, I decided to marry and have a home of my own. But Oh, the wrong I done I know now, Mrs. Sanger. Being married about four years have 3 children and seem as I am pregnant again and so weak can't hardly get around and just think three babies to take care of . . . I know if I wouldn't have to have any more babies I would get strong and pick up again, but being pregnant every year makes a sick woman out of a healthy one. Please, Mrs. Sanger, be so kind and advise me how to take care of myself so I couldn't get pregnant so often or never again.

> I have went to doctors and had illegal operations performed until I couldn't afford it any longer and then tried doing it myself until I'm afraid I'll have myself ruined . . . I am so nervous I just think I would lose my mind.

*   *   *

My husband don't want more (babies) either because I suffer so much. We tried so many things but I get that way any time, no matter how careful we are. Our Dr. told my husband to get a divorce as I could not stand having children, but we are happy together with our boys and won't do anything like that. But if there is something that will keep me from getting that way I would be glad.

Will you please help me? You speak in your book of some methods being more dependable than others. Would you tell me what they are? No matter how expensive they must be cheaper than a baby every year.

She ran letters like these in the *Review* each month, as well as items like this reprint of a story in the October 27, 1922, *New York American*:

Mr. and Mrs. Fred Scott moved from La Porte, Indiana the other day, taking thirteen children with them and buying only two railroad tickets. The oldest of the 13 children, triplets, were four and a half years old. The youngest, twins, each six months. That mother in ten years has had triplets five times and twins twice, and lost six children. You can't add anything to that.

Occasionally she even ran a humorous letter like this one from Africa's Gold Coast:

Dear Friend: I have the honor most respectfully to apply for your special and particular catalogue. I have married two women, so try your best and send me some of catalogue. Send it to me very instantaneous.

Anna and a few volunteers kept answering the letters, enclosing a copy of *Family Limitation*. Because they could now refer the writer to the nearest doctor friendly to the cause, they were again answering letters one by one.

J. Noah wanted to help. When he heard how inefficiently the letters were being handled, he worked out new form replies. Next he took on a huge backlog of unanswered letters from doctors and devised an easy way to answer them, bringing to the job all his years of managerial experience. But he received little thanks from Margaret, who wanted him kept out of this part of her life and had no more intention of sharing the limelight with him than with anyone else.

But sharing his money was another matter. She needed money and a lot of it, for she had come to realize that sending out pamphlets through the mail was both a risky and unsound method of giving advice. The chief contraceptive she recommended was the diaphragm, yet women couldn't easily learn how to insert it properly themselves, much less teach others. Diaphragms came in different sizes, graduated according to the size of a woman's cervix and the number of children she had borne; they had to be individually fitted. Because of this, the need to open a clinic where she could dispense information "for reasons of health," as the law now allowed her to do, became pressing.

But there were other obstacles to opening a clinic. She needed a quiet place free from the noise of clattering typewriters; she needed a licensed physician to run it.

Finding a doctor was the harder job. Several tentatively agreed to help but at the last minute got frightened and begged off. Dr. Mary Halton took two women, obviously unfit for pregnancy because of health (one had advanced tuberculosis and the other a serious heart condition), and drove them around to every municipal hospital in town, all of whom refused contraceptive help. What's more, the hospital with which Dr. Halton herself was connected found out about what she was doing and threatened her with immediate dismissal if she went ahead.

Next Dr. Anna K. Daniels hinted she might take the job, but the Town Hall raid, plus again the possible loss of her hospital connection, scared her off.

At last Margaret found Dr. Dorothy Bocker, a young woman who was working for the Public Health Service of Georgia. Dr. Bocker admitted she knew nothing about birth control but was eager to learn, persisting even after Margaret warned her she might land in jail. But as a compensation for giving up her secure government job, Dr. Bocker wanted a two-year contract at five thousand dollars a year, a large sum in 1923.

Margaret asked J. Noah for the money. He refused, chiefly because he kept hoping that Margaret would "give up all this blooming nonsense" and become the companion for whom he yearned. Besides, Margaret had to admit to him that she was already in financial trouble.

She was, for instance, greatly in debt to the printers of the *Review*; the bills for the last half-dozen issues were long overdue.

Also, the *Review* made very little money as its small ad revenue came mainly from three-liners for books on subjects like *The History of Woman's Slavery*, brought out by little-known publishers like "The Truth Publishing Company," "Health & Life Publications," or by men who operated solely from box numbers. Other ads came from companies which had nothing to do with birth control, like the Carbozine Laboratory that sold things like Carbozine Goiter Cream or Carbozine Tonic Pills "certain to stimulate gland function in men."

Mixed in with these were ads for Margaret's own books, and full-page ads for Three-in-One Household Oil. Yet it all brought in so little that, at the Birth Control League's Annual Meeting in February 1923, the financial report for the previous year was dismal: The total income from the *Review* had been $18,551, half of which came from ads and sales and the other half from donations, while the expenses were $17,734, leaving the slender balance of $817 in the bank.

As for her Birth Control League, its receipts for 1922 were $20,175 and its disbursements $19,954, leaving the even smaller balance of $221. The league money had gone mainly for printing 213,500 birth-control pamphlets given away surreptitiously at various meetings, usually at no charge. The rest had gone for postage on the 112,775 pamphlets mailed to women who failed to enclose stamped return envelopes along with their requests, as well as for propaganda leaflets distributed to what Anna described as "carefully selected mailing-lists," meaning doctors and clergymen who could be trusted to spread the word.

In addition to lack of money, there was also a curious legal obstacle to starting a clinic. This was the use of the very word "clinic." In New York a special license was needed in order to use this word, because a clinic was considered the equivalent of a dispensary or place where state-supervised drugs were given out. The Birth Control League could not get a dispensary license unless it was associated with a hospital and no hospital would be associated with birth control.

Another obstacle was the fact that the word "clinic" meant, to poor women especially, a place where things like drugs could be had for free. Margaret couldn't possibly give away contraceptive advice or supplies for free. She had to pay rent for a place to operate in, as well as Dr. Bocker's salary. She would have to charge at least five dollars a visit, though hopefully, rich women would volunteer to pay more. Also, for that minimum of five dollars she would have to provide an initial vaginal examination and explain the various kinds of contraceptives available—the best ones were the Dutch cervical cap, which was shaped like a large thimble and fit snugly around the opening of the cervix, but was hard to insert, and the diaphragm which was flatter and had a thin wire in its rim making it easier to insert. Then, if the diaphragm was requested, she had to see that it was fitted properly, give a second examination a few days later to see if it was comfortable, and a third a few months later to see if it was working well. And if the woman didn't come back on her own for these examinations, she had to send out a paid social worker to find out if anything had gone wrong.

On top of all this, she would have the expense of keeping records because she wanted her clinic to be a research facility as well as a consultation center. This meant keeping a complete file on each patient, including the patient's age, nationality, number of children, number of abortions whether done by a midwife or self-induced, as well as the answers to questions on the patient's attitude toward sex. Did she enjoy sex? Was she indifferent to it? Or did she dread it for fear she might be "caught"?

Opening a place that would do all this would take a lot of money, and with Slee refusing to donate it, she didn't know where to turn. Then she remembered Clinton Chance, a wealthy Englishman she had met in London who had promised her a large amount of money for a specific purpose connected with birth control—if she ever needed it. In response to a long telegram explaining her situation, Chance sent her five thousand dollars to cover the first year of Dr. Bocker's salary, plus an extra thousand for an examining table, instrument sterilizer, and the other equipment a good facility needed. While she was delighted to receive his contribution, it was only a beginning. Remembering what she had said years ago when she had "cast herself on the universe," Margaret was determined to stay afloat.

Originally she had rented two small rooms on the top floor of 104 Fifth Avenue for her headquarters. Now she added two rooms across the hall and had the entrance door lettered: *Clinical Research*. These words were just vague enough to get around legal restraints on the use of the term "clinic," yet they conveyed the idea to the women who came to seek her service. With only word-of-mouth advertising these women came in great numbers. Mainly Jewish, Italian, and Irish, they crowded into the tiny waiting room with the broods of children they almost invariably brought along, and a harried volunteer interpreter ran from one group to the other to keep them placated. In the first two months a staggering total of twenty-seven hundred women came. Of these Dr. Bocker found nine hundred she could conscientiously fit with contraceptives for "health reasons." Diaphragms proved to be by far the most popular contraceptive, as soon as women were assured that a diaphragm was fitted with great care and that there was no chance it would get "lost" and wander up into their bellies.

The demand for diaphragms was so great that it led to still another problem: Where was Margaret to find enough to meet the demand? A few could be bought in drug stores, but because the law was still so vague that no American manufacturer would publicly acknowledge making them and no drug store display them openly, they had to come from mysterious places and were, therefore, extremely expensive. A few had been smuggled in from abroad, hidden in copious handbags or under the girdles of friends of the cause, who would call up the Research Bureau and murmur, "Your jewels have arrived." But keeping a good supply on hand was very difficult. Then she had a break.

When Margaret was living in her cold-water flat on West Fourteenth Street she used to buy coal for her fireplace from a red-cheeked Italian named Vito Sillechia. Since she never could bank a fire well enough so that she could return to a warm flat at night, she paid Vito a few cents extra to drop in at various times during the day and keep her fire going, giving it an especially good stir just before she was due home. She often brought along several birth-control advocates as her guests, and Vito, when he had the time, would stay and listen to their conversation. One evening he asked her, "Mis' Sanger, what are those little things you and your friends talk about so much?"

"Those?" Margaret laughed. "Those are what a woman uses so she won't have too many babies."

"You mean bambinos? I got too many bambinos, my friends got too many bambinos, everybody got too many bambinos. Where you get those little things, Mis' Sanger? How much they cost?"

When she explained that they were expensive because they came mainly from Holland, Vito hesitated. Then he volunteered a bit of information. He didn't make a living just from selling coal and wood. Ever since Prohibition he had been doing some rumrunning on the side. "I got the connections in the States, Mis' Sanger. You make the connections in Holland and I run them for you in liquor bottles. It cost you a little something extra, but I manage if you like."

Margaret had no extra money, but she did manage to persuade J. Noah to lend her some, promising to pay him back out of her clinic fees. Slee capitulated, on the condition that Vito also bring him a supply of the good Holland gin he needed as a "health tonic."

So for the next few years Vito smuggled in diaphragms for Margaret and gin for J. Noah from ships anchored outside the twelve-mile limit, transferring the bottles to swift motorboats. As a result, Vito not only made some extra cash but he also learned to limit the size of his family and save up for the candy store he had long dreamed of owning. In discreet Italian he passed on the word how to use "those little things" to his neighbors. Later, at the height of Margaret's battle with the Catholic Church, Vito, a good Catholic, tried to get an interview with Cardinal Hayes to tell him how wonderful Mis' Sanger and her birth control were. Here, however, he did not succeed.

After finding a way to get a plentiful supply of diaphragms, Margaret had two other lucky strikes. First, a brownstone town house at 17 West Sixteenth Street was put on the market for seventy thousand dollars in cash, a low price for an imposing place on an excellent street right off Fifth Avenue. Slee recognized it as a good buy at once. Pouring money into a nebulous movement was one thing; acquiring a chunk of fine New York real estate was another. Because the plot was twenty-eight feet wide instead of the usual twenty, and because it was five stories high instead of four, he decided to buy it. It was an ideal place to which to transfer the Clinical Research Bureau. He raised the cash in no time and gave the beautiful old house to Margaret as a gift.

Margaret got busy remodeling it for her purpose. She made the basement floor into a storage room, divided the first floor with its high ceilings and black marble fireplace into a waiting room and consulting room, and made the next floor an office. Then she added several bathrooms and fixed up the top floor as a cozy apartment for herself, where she could rest during the day or sleep overnight if she chose.

Next a convent near Slee's old Hudson River mansion burned down, and the Church, wanting to find another place for the nuns immediately, offered J. Noah a hundred acres of beautiful hilltop land with a large private lake in exchange for his house. Slee accepted. On a hundred acres he could build an English manor-type house, resembling

Margaret's beloved Wantley, and become the squire of a lordly domain.

He engaged a firm of Italian architects to build a grand house, hired a neighboring farmer to head a crew of men to gather fieldstones for the exterior, got a team of skilled decorators to plan the interior, and another of landscape architects to design a garden. The total cost was many hundreds of thousands of dollars, but while Willowlake, named for the dozens of willows planted around the lake, was being built both he and Margaret were gay as larks.

Bill Sanger was dismayed, however. In February 1923 he had finally learned through Margaret's father, with whom he was staying in Truro, that Margaret had remarried, "and so respectably, too." He wrote her that he was astonished she had suggested he continue going to Truro under the circumstances, even though it was only to paint her father's picture. He would leave at once. More, he should like to be spared the embarrassment of further correspondence with her, adding that her father had given him "some detailed and illuminating knowledge about her" which he declined to discuss. As a result, he might even change his mind about her keeping his name, and for the first time he ended his letter formally: "Good luck to you, Margaret. William Sanger."

Bill seldom saw his sons after this, and when he did, he acted strangely. To celebrate the Thanksgiving of 1923 he invited Stuart and Grant to his studio for dinner, promising to meet them at Grand Central Station, but when they arrived he was nowhere in sight. Not knowing what else to do, they went into the vast waiting room and sat for hours waiting for him to fetch them. When he finally arrived, he took them to his Christopher Street studio where he announced that if they would wait some more, he would see if he could find a delicatessen that was open so he could buy them something to eat. They asked him if he couldn't warm the place first, as the studio was freezing. He said he was sorry but he had no wood for the fireplace, though he thought he knew where he could get hold of a little. Grabbing an axe, he cut down the flagpole from the roof of the building and chopped it up and threw it into the fireplace. Then he went out and came back with some potato salad and cold cuts. For the boys it was a bizarre holiday. Stuart decided that Bill "wasn't much of a father," and Grant didn't know what to think.

Meanwhile, Margaret finally announced her new marriage to the press, though she said she would continue to use the name of Sanger in public, hyphenating her name to Sanger-Slee in the English manner in private life. In 1923, she moved her research clinic to its new home on Sixteenth Street. On the front door she installed a prominent brass plaque that proclaimed: *The Margaret Sanger Clinical Research Bureau.*

Soon the place was a beehive of activity. Hundreds of women came each day to its open door. Dr. Bocker saw them all.

One thing that surprised Dr. Bocker was that fully a third of the women were Catholic, some blurting out stories of being so desperate over unwanted pregnancies they had considered suicide, holding back only because of the fear of hell. One twenty-one-year-old Irish girl told the heartrending story of how her husband had tried sleeping on the floor to avoid sexual temptation but it hadn't worked; she soon became pregnant with her fourth child. The child was delivered by cesarean section after she almost died during prolonged labor, yet though her doctor told her she should not have another child under any circumstances, he refused to tell her how to avoid another pregnancy. At confession her priest had said, "God should strike you dead for even thinking about such a thing." Finally, her husband had spoken to a nurse who told her to look up the Sanger Bureau in the phone book. That's how she had gotten there.

Other women told how they had heard about the Bureau through neighbors. A grapevine of whispered information was fast becoming the magical passport to knowledge of birth control.

In advising such women, Dr. Bocker considered she was rendering the finest service a doctor could. Yet she resigned when her two-year contract was up because Margaret bossed her much as she had the workmen remodeling the Bureau's new home—something almost no doctor will accept from a lay person. Indeed, just before Dr. Bocker quit she and Margaret had such a terrible fight she walked out with nearly a thousand records, falsifying some, though later she returned them and corrected the altered ones.

Margaret didn't particularly mind Dr. Bocker's leaving because she was trying to get the American Medical Association behind her. An unknown doctor from Georgia heading the Bureau would never attract top flight medical support. Besides, as Margaret kept saying, a battle always excited her, and the one with Dr. Bocker gave her a tremendous burst of energy. She used this to resolve the problem of finding a more acceptable doctor as well as to supervise the finishing of Willowlake.

And Willowlake was coming along fast. A handsome fieldstone carriage house, almost as large as the main building, was in the process of being built as a servants' quarters. A Japanese tea house was being constructed in one of an elaborate series of gardens, and a special tree house, nestled high among the willows and elms, was being built as a retreat for Margaret. As for servants, she still had old Daisy as her personal maid, and J. Noah was lining up an additional maid and butler for her, a valet and butler for himself, a chauffeur for his three cars, and several experienced gardeners. In any event, Margaret couldn't have fired Daisy even if she had wanted to. As Robert Parker tells it, Daisy liked her liquor, and when she'd had an extra glass or two, she would show a mean streak and taunt Margaret with: "If you fire me I'll start talkin'. And don't forget, I know a lot. I'm the one who used to let Mr. Goldstein in."

To replace Dr. Bocker, Margaret found Dr. Hannah Stone. Dr. Stone was a handsome woman with dark hair tied in a simple bun, skin as clear as Margaret's, and a fine, firm figure, adding up to a commanding presence. She was also backed by her husband, Dr. Abraham Stone, a highly respected gynecologist and editor of the medical journal *Fertility and Infertility*. On top of all this, she was a woman of courage, willing to take on the Bureau even though it meant losing her connection with the Lying-In Hospital. The very fact that she had a husband and a child made her more accessible than the spinster Dr. Bocker. When she sat down and talked with a patient, saying things like, "How often do you have sex relations with your husband? Do you enjoy them? You should, you know," they were less embarrassed than before Dr. Bocker.

Dr. Stone also was courageous in another way. She hated to withhold birth-control information from anyone who asked for it. When she could find no accepted medical reason for fitting a woman with a diaphragm, she would pencil the letters NHR on the corner of her record. The letters stood for "no health reason." She was running a grave legal risk in doing this, but she did it just the same.

Hannah Stone never asked for or accepted a salary from the Bureau, a feat which Margaret endlessly boasted. But she got paid in other ways. After a while she worked at the Bureau mornings only; afternoons she was to be found at her private office on lower Fifth Avenue to which Margaret referred the women who could afford private care. Her fees weren't high—seldom over ten dollars—but again she lettered most cards NHR. Also, in collaboration with her husband, Hannah

Stone soon wrote *Marriage Manual,* the first, and in some ways the best, book on sex, reproduction, and birth control, a book so comprehensive and delicately phrased it is still selling. All in all, Margaret could hardly have found a better doctor to head her clinic.

Because of the combined demands of both getting the Bureau going and settling into Willowlake, Margaret had to skip her regular trip to England during the summer of 1923, a trip she sorely missed. But she continued to make news in England. Seventeen hundred copies of her *Family Limitation* pamphlets were seized by the police from a London bookshop, and even after so eminent a doctor as Sir Arbuthnot Lane appeared in her defense, they were destroyed.

Something else began to upset her. Hugh was writing her more and more about a new friend, Françoise:

> Françoise is an absolute dear. Her little ridiculous boys are here for a fortnight getting brown and well. They are little pets. . . . The first day, of course, the youngest fell plump into the pool with all his clothes on. Françoise grows more adorable as I know her better.

Françoise? Françoise who? All this talk was a bit too much. Margaret was used to having her pamphlets seized, but she would have to get over to England as soon as she could—to learn more about Françoise.

QUEEN OF THE DRAWING ROOM TOO

While Hannah Stone was getting established at the Bureau, and Willowlake was nearing completion, Margaret stayed in her town apartment and took a rest. She wrote letters to England telling Hugh, Havelock, and Wells only that she was still considering marrying J. Noah, not, for some unknown reason, that she already had.

Hugh answered:

> Shall I like this Mr. Slee? I don't see how I can help it (much as I want to hate him out of natural spite and envy) if he is much with you, for your beauty is so infectious.

Havelock was perplexed. He congratulated her, but at the same time wrote Hugh.

> I have also had a recent letter from (the prospective) Mrs. Noah H. Slee, though I do not know if that is how she wishes to be addressed. I am not sure, however, that I should myself like a husband who was "a good churchman," while if I were the good churchman I should be rather nervous about marrying the Woman Rebel.

And Wells sent one of his characteristic short notes:

206

* * *

If it makes you happy, then marry Mr. Slee. But all sorts of people who adore you will regard him with watchful and envious eyes.

But soon Margaret realized it made no sense to keep up the pretence, so she wrote Hugh, Havelock, and H. G. again, telling them the truth. In addition, she told Hugh she would like to set up a series of poetry readings for him in America, if only as an excuse to have him near her. But he answered that he couldn't possibly make the trip as his wife had lost quite a bit of her money lately through bad investments. He was also busy packing; he would have to leave the comparatively expensive Wantley for a smaller and less impressive place called Sand Pit. He enclosed a picture of Sand Pit as well as one of himself in a dreamy and romantic pose, wearing an open-collar and pearl tie pin. In return she sent him one of herself dressed, as Hugh described it, in "a cruel great thick dress, so tremendously distinguished and obscuring." She agreed that she did look distinguished, adding: "And I'll have you know I'm Queen of my drawing-room too!!"

Hugh also sent her a wedding gift, a selection of Blake's poems copied out in his own hand with explanatory notes between the lines. The gift, he wrote,

> . . . is to carry around in your purse as a sort of spiritual powder-puff, or some other little accessory to your loveliness, and a little means by which perhaps I may be kept warm in your heart.

He included a long article in praise of Havelock which he hoped she would publish in the next issue of the *Review*. When she did, he wrote her:

> You darling Margaret. It makes my heart glow to be connected with such a magnificent number—really generous; so refreshing in this meagre world.

Then suddenly he struck a different note; he wrote again about Françoise, ending arrogantly:

> Françoise is my friend, but I've told you *that* in letters that

have crossed with yours. I love you more than ever, only, if you
will allow me to say so, less hungrily. However, that is my affair,
really.

His affair? Her heart sank. She decided to find out more about Françoise at once. Her jealousy drove her to more than a little investigating, and she learned a good deal.

The summer before, Havelock had told Margaret about a new friend,
a French woman, who had come into his life, but in his usual shy man-
ner he had hinted she was more than a friend. Now it looked as if
Hugh's friend and Havelock's friend might be the same person. Indeed,
Margaret found, this was the case. In fact, the story went back to
Edith's death in September of 1916.

Soon after Edith died, Havelock had received a letter from a young
Frenchwoman, Françoise Cyon, who was living in London. The letter
said that Edith had promised her thirty pounds as payment for a trans-
lation of a book of hers into French, but as the job wasn't quite finished
when Edith died, Françoise would take as little as five pounds if Ellis
would give her the French rights and allow her to try to get the book
published herself.

At the moment, however, Ellis didn't have five pounds to spare. The
publisher of his *Studies in the Psychology of Sex* had gone into bankruptcy, depriving him of an important source of royalties. He replied
that he would send her a little money as soon as he could, and in the
meantime would think about an article she had written which she had
also enclosed. The correspondence between them went on for months,
during which Françoise gradually unfolded the story of her tragic life.
Not long afterward, Ellis, who was used to getting letters from distressed women, invited her to visit him. In May 1917, she did.

When Françoise entered his flat, Ellis saw a woman young enough to
be his daughter and almost as shy as himself. As petite and charming
as Margaret, though not as beautiful, she had one son by a man she
had left because he did not live up to her pacifist ideals, and another by
a Russian named Cyon, whom she had married in England under the
impression he was a compassionate man. But Cyon had disappointed
her too. She found him to be a materialist, a warmonger, and an extremely domineering man. She had left him, taking both her sons with
her, and was trying to support them on her own.

Since she had few skills other than translating, supporting two boys and herself turned out to be very difficult, yet Cyon refused to give her any money unless she came back to him and lived with him as a traditionally submissive wife. She had refused to do this and eventually became so desperate she considered suicide. When she told Cyon about her suicidal thoughts, he grew frightened and suggested they seek advice on how to live together in peace. It was at this point that she had written to Ellis, hoping he might give her the advice she so badly needed.

She arrived at Ellis' flat wearing a shabby blouse and skirt, a pair of borrowed shoes that were a size too large, and a thin coat. The moment she saw Ellis, she was relieved because he was dressed almost as poorly as she. And she felt even better when she left because, while he had said very little, she realized he had liked her for herself and that she had at last found a sympathetic friend. Yet, strangely enough, she hadn't seemed to know that Ellis was both a doctor and famous, and this pleased him greatly because for the first time in years he also felt that someone was accepting him on his own.

At their next meeting, Françoise sensed that Ellis too was in emotional turmoil. He was fifty-eight, and while he was still magnificently handsome and in excellent physical shape, he was even more despondent than when he first met Margaret. He felt guilty about his wife's death; he was so poor he had sold his furniture and was sleeping on a camp bed; and he was again afraid he had nothing more to write. Françoise told him she wanted to give him some of her strength. She had given up all thoughts of suicide; instead she was looking for a part-time job to supplement her translating income. She was sure that she would soon be successful, and he would too.

But within a month Françoise was upset again. Cyon had been sending her a little money from his well-paying job as a columnist on a London paper, but now she heard he had returned to Russia. Worse, a friend told her that Cyon was separated from another wife and child in Russia, and no one knew for sure if he had ever divorced this Russian wife. Was she, therefore, legally married to him or not? Did she and their son have any legal claim on him, or he on her? She realized he had told her many other lies too; he had for instance rejoined the very Russian army he had claimed he despised. More, he wrote her that because he was in the army, he was sending his Russian son to England for her to take care of as well as her own boys.

Françoise was so shaken by all this she went to visit Ellis more often than ever, and compared to the other men in her life, she found him the image of perfection. On April 3, 1918, she wrote him:

> Dear friend, I am going to write a very difficult letter. Yet it must be written if I am to have peace of mind. The truth is, Havelock, that I love you . . . Yesterday I came away from you in a state of high emotion. I went to bed and shouted, "Havelock, I want to be your wife!" If the wind could have carried my words you would have heard them, though they were only said in my heart.

Many women had fallen in love with Havelock after he had given them greater self-confidence, and he had received many similar letters as a result. But these other women were usually far away; he had never met them and never would. Françoise was close by. He was no home wrecker; he honestly believed he had been working with Françoise toward some kind of reconciliation with her husband, using what he called a "friendship cure" in the same way that analysts use a psychiatric cure.

He knew he must clarify the situation at once, especially since he found himself falling in love with her too. He sent her a reply he described in his diary as written "in full honesty and full caution":

> Dear, I had your letter this morning. It is very, very beautiful, and I am glad you wrote it, because it will help us to understand things and to have everything clear and right. I wanted to put my arms around you when you lay on the sofa half asleep, but I did not want to do anything you might misunderstand, and I should be sorry for you if I do anything you might feel afterwards was not right and that might make you unhappy. I would like to soothe you and comfort and help you, and it is very good for me too to be near you, and I felt much better for your visit. I am sure we could be loving friends, real affectionate and intimate friends. But I wouldn't be any good as a passionate lover or husband. I am not a bit like the virile robust men of the people in your dreams! I have several dear loving women friends, married and unmarried, but there is not one to whom I am a real lover. That is how I would like to be with you . . . As a lover or husband you would find me

very disappointing. When you know me more you will feel that as
an affectionate friend you will have all the best that I can
give . . .

If you feel that this kind of affectionate friendship (with me) is
not possible, then it would be best for us not to meet. But I think it
is possible, and that you will find it quite easy and beautiful and
natural and helpful. I am in some ways understanding, as you
say, but I am also like a child, and it is lovely to me to be able to be
like a child.

When Françoise received his letter, she was puzzled by its vagueness. Still, she replied: "I will have nothing but what you offer; it is the
very flower of love."

Ellis was brought sharply back to life and vigor by Françoise's attitude. For the first time in years, he was happy. He met her children
and found to his surprise that he enjoyed them; he had thought of children mainly as nuisances or hindrances to his work.

Françoise, too, was happier than she had been in years. She found a
job as a junior French teacher though she continued to live in a tumbledown house furnished with orange crates. Gradually she and Ellis
gave up the idea of restoring her marriage; instead they became lovers
themselves. And strangely, Havelock found that at sixty he was able to
become what he had never been before, a potent male. He was sure
that it was her unquestioning love that had brought this miracle
about.

His friends noticed the change in his personality, and hearing rumors that it was caused by a passionate Frenchwoman, they asked to
meet her.

Hugh as always was the most insistent. In his own mind he was "The
Perfect Lover," and he simply had to learn for himself whether Françoise was as good as she was rumored to be. After asking Havelock and
Françoise to lunch at a smart West End restaurant, he invited Françoise down to Sand Pit alone. She hesitated, afraid she wouldn't be up
to his brilliant conversation. But Havelock thought differently; he told
her it would be good for her to get out of her shell and move in a wider
world. She went to Sussex, where Hugh at first restricted his conversation to praise of Havelock. Soon, however, he began concentrating on
Françoise. He whispered to her the same poetic phrases he had whis-

pered to Margaret. He was in effect seducing her, though he refused to think of himself as a seducer; seduction was ugly, and all was supposed to be beautiful in the magic world of free love.

Yet, seduction it was. Havelock, a man of fixed habits who refused to believe that Hugh would do anything to hurt him, went off for the winter to Cornwell as always, leaving Hugh to break down Françoise's resistance by telling her that "theirs would be a beautiful physical union between two souls drawn close by their love for the great teacher who had freed men and women from the bondage of obsolete moral laws."

Françoise, overwhelmed, slowly yielded, especially after Hugh showed her a letter from Havelock saying,

> I hear of you from Françoise, and am delighted to know she so enjoys your visits, for her vigorous vitality is under so crushing a weight that she has no energy left to seek for herself the contact with the larger atmosphere you give her.

It wasn't long, however, before Havelock began to sense from Hugh's glowing letters what was really happening. At first he felt merely sad, feeling it his duty to suppress his jealousy. Then he returned to London and to his surprise slipped into a bitter quarrel with Françoise. He wrote her a note reassessing Shelley and James Hinton, the great prophets of free love: "Both had beautiful visions of life, but when they tried to carry them out they made a terrible mess of their lives."

Françoise understood, though by now it wasn't easy to retreat. Havelock might have become potent, but he never could match Hugh's expertise. Hugh also quoted Shakespeare and Blake at table, while Havelock kept his fine phrases for his books.

Nevertheless, Françoise realized that her deep, long-term relation lay with Havelock. She gave up Hugh, and she and Havelock were reconciled, though Havelock also started a quarrel with Hugh that he never completely resolved. Later, in his autobiography, he wrote bitterly about "sexual athletes who stab their friends in the back"; this devastated Hugh, who could not help but recognize himself, yet never understood what he had done wrong.

Margaret too became saddened over the situation. She loved Hugh more than she had ever loved anyone, but for a while she stopped corresponding with him. Havelock, who still sent an occasional note to Hugh on literary matters, had to give him news of Margaret. In July

1923 Havelock wrote Hugh, "This afternoon I heard from Margaret, she says, 'How's Hugh? I have not written to him in ages, but I take delight in reading over and over again some of his old letters. I do this when I get blue.' But Margaret seems very happy at present and her husband very devoted to her."

And Slee *was* devoted. In the summer of 1924 he took her on a long, luxurious trip to Lake Louise, stopping only at the best hotels. Still, with Grant and Stuart he was apt to be tightfisted. Though Slee paid Grant's tuition at the Hun School, an exclusive prep school in Princeton, New Jersey, he balked when it came to a personal allowance, sending Grant only a dollar a week. In November, when Margaret was back on the road lecturing, Grant complained to her. Slee defended himself: "Grant is catching the extravagant disease. I am sorry he has a roommate whose parents are so unwise they doubtless will pay the penalty later on. I will leave it to you to keep Grant within reason. In fact, the school recommends a boy's allowance be a dollar to a dollar and a half a week."

He also made Grant keep track of every penny of his allowance and give him a monthly report. One month Grant simply couldn't account for thirty-six cents. He complained again to his mother: "I'm just not good at figures. That 36¢ probably went into my stomach. I'm always hungry."

Slee was just as firm with Stuart, though Stuart was now captain of the football team at Yale. Even Stuart, who had always been money conscious, couldn't satisfy Pater, as he had been taught to call his stepfather. Slee wrote Margaret on the subject: "My field is finance-accounting and marketing, specialties which I know best. Stuart has never shown me his figures. However I could write reams and get nowhere with a *mother*. I could with a masculine mind."

Mainly, however, J. Noah wrote Margaret about his health. He went into great detail about his food, drink, and exercise. He had joined the Life Extension Institute and was getting himself examined regularly to ward off even the possibility of disease. When Margaret was lecturing in St. Louis just before Thanksgiving, he reported: "Darling, you know I have a wretched cold and don't feel very happy, my nose is in a constant state of eruption." Yet in the same letter he described the fine dinner he had just eaten: onion soup, fried chicken, and cake with whipped cream, followed by "a bottle of Kianti which cost only $2.50, though my bootlegger usually charges $3." And for good measure he told her exactly how much time he had spent that morning cleaning his teeth.

Margaret by now was terribly bored with this kind of letter, but soon she was back planning the decoration of Willowlake, keeping a careful list of the furnishings to be ordered, noting exactly where she wanted each piece placed. Her upstairs bedroom was to have a single bed with the best quality box spring hair mattress, a fine Chinese rug, a tall, painted fruitwood highboy, a French dressing table, and a velvet arm chair. Her upstairs living room was to have a loveseat, a Chinese rug, both a chaise longue and a daybed, and fine brass fittings for the fireplace.

The boys' bedrooms and the guest room were to be much simpler. A plain bed and dresser would do for them; J. Noah was to have, instead of a bedroom, an outdoor sleeping porch furnished with a double brass bed and a single iron cot, presumably to give him the widest latitude in selecting appropriate sleeping accommodations for his health.

When finished, the main house at Willowlake was a handsome place. It had deep recessed windows ending in arches of pointed stone and furnishings in Margaret's favorite colors, blue and red. Peacock-blue tiles bordered the huge living room fireplace, while blue satin easy chairs, a red brocade sofa, and a hand-painted red Korean chest complemented the thousand-dollar blue and red Chinese rug.

For the library adjoining the living room, she chose another red brocade sofa and blue Chinese rug, as well as two thousand leather-bound books which she proudly described as "catalogued," though they were the kind usually kept more for display than reading. She commissioned a full-length portrait of herself, wearing a rose-colored gown for above the fireplace, and a smaller bust-length portrait of J. Noah. Her portrait was to cost fifteen hundred dollars, his two hundred.

The dining room, which was surprisingly small, was furnished sparsely; it contained only an oak refectory table and buffet, a grandfather's clock, and six Early American dining chairs. This was perhaps a reflection of how little the house was intended for living. In the winter Margaret expected either to be off traveling, staying in their town apartment, or dining alone in her upstairs sitting room. Nor would the boys be dining much at Willowlake. J. Noah was frankly upset by the noise of adolescent boys and their friends, and he resented the expense they entailed too. Once when Stuart had been driven home from Yale in a friend's car, and had, as a matter of courtesy, filled up the gas tank with a dollar and a quarter's worth of gas, charged to Pater's account, he was roundly scolded; next time such an expense would have to come out of his own allowance.

While Margaret kept track of the expense of furnishing Willowlake, J. Noah kept track of the building costs. He drew up an expense account that included fifty-three thousand dollars for the builders, five thousand dollars for the architects, twelve hundred dollars for electric power, and seven thousand dollars for miscellaneous items, including excavating the site and adding a slate roof and central heating. This totaled sixty-six thousand dollars—a lot of money in 1923. And since he had received nothing in exchange for his former house except Willowlake's land, and the cost of landscape gardening was still to be added, he realized how expensive the house was. On the other hand, Margaret's rejuvenating sexual enthusiasm made him decide it was worth the cost.

He even tried to compose romantic love letters to her while she was away from home lecturing.

> My adorable wife, I've had you much on my mind all afternoon. I am truly lonely without you and miss you terribly. Each time you go away it seems more so. I love you so ardently that no one is interesting and I long only for you. . . . Come home soon please. I need you to clasp in my arms always, and love divinely always more and more.

This kind of letter bored her too, so instead of answering him she wrote to Hugh, enclosing a picture of herself in knickerbockers and mountaineering shoes "bought for poking around the building-operations in Willowlake." Hugh answered in characteristic form: "Of all the dainty delicate exquisite people—the contrast of those thick tweed bags and stout imposing shoes, oh you are an enchanting person."

Margaret answered that she liked being called dainty and exquisite "but never call me sweet. Sometimes sweetness and dearness are weaknesses. Always remember that when people speak of Margaret Sanger as sweet, that word is likely to make me start something."

She went on to tell him that she had just run a portion of his confessional book *One Little Boy* in the *Review* and gotten vigorous complaints. She was afraid that in the future she would have to confine herself to birth-control subjects only, using stories like one told by Kitty Marion titled, *Ye Who Pass By:*

After crying in the wilderness, in other words selling the *Birth Control Review* in the streets of New York for 6 years, I am very well satisfied with the result of my efforts. Some of the best, most intelligent and most influential people from all parts of the earth have got in touch with the movement through buying the *Review* on Broadway and have taken the glad tidings back to their homes.

Most of the people who talk to me agree that birth control is the only thing that will save the human race and civilization from destruction, but quite a number are sure it is against nature and against God. I recall a man who came up and said, "Aren't you advocating murder?" I said, "No, there is no one to murder," and explained what we are doing. "But that is interfering with nature," said he, and I told him he interfered with nature when he shaved, had his hair cut and put clothes on, that nature had brought him into the world naked and that to live according to nature he should run around naked and live in a cave or up a tree instead of in a house with all the latest comforts and conveniences. He admitted it was a good argument but insisted that "we were here to reproduce ourselves," and I asked him to think of the thousands of human beings in and outside of institutions incapable of looking after themselves. Did he want those to reproduce themselves? He replied quite vehemently, "No, I don't, you are right, you're right!" He left wishing success to the cause.

I had a similar discussion with an Irishman who called it the "slaughter of the innocents." I told him there were no innocents to slaughter, but he insisted that birth control meant taking life. I explained that it was not taking but preventing life. Oh, but that was intercepting God and nature. I asked him did he think it natural to be taken ill? He did—and did he think it wrong to get a doctor to intercept, prevent or cure sickness? No, that was all right. And I suggested to him that it was even more right to intercept and prevent the spread of poverty, disease, feeble-mindedness, etc., by prevention of conception. Well, he admitted perhaps I was right.

After thoroughly explaining to some people what we are trying to do, they asked very anxiously, "And does this paper tell how to prevent?" I groan inwardly and explain again that it is against the law to give such information.

One day last November, a woman in passing said, "You vile creature, you ought to bury your face in the mud, you dirty thing!" Later she returned and knocked some papers out of my hand which were promptly picked up for me by other passersby.

I have been subjected to every expression of disapproval, contempt and scorn imaginable, including making faces, expectoration and crossing themselves. But that is water on a duck's back, and more than compensated for by wonderful compliments on my courage and perseverance.

May all who see me sell the *Review* have the same impression as one of a group of little urchins who, seeing me holding up the paper, called out "Aw, lookit, the Statya of Liberty!" For birth control stands for liberty—liberty far more concrete than the Lady in the harbor herself.

SAINT AND RAGAMUFFIN

On New Year's day 1924, Harold Child wrote Margaret whom he had met at Wantley in 1920.

Harold had moved with Hugh to Sand Pit, from which he again commuted daily to London. When Margaret sent him a New Year's card from New York signed "with love," he answered immediately:

That card was a most delightful surprise. And with Margaret's love, too! It made me very happy, because I so feared I had lost sight of you—what with your work, and your getting married, and my work, and one thing and another! And I often think, with curses loud and deep and horrible, of the last meeting of ours— the lunch at the Monico. Shall I confess? Yes! I was hideously jealous. You were just rushing off to catch a train, and I said to myself that of course as she's going off with Havelock Ellis she's counting every minute till it's time to start, and she isn't enjoying herself a bit and the whole thing is a failure . . . So when there came a card with your love, I just bucked up like anything. And if only you'll come over here again soon, and have lunch or something with me, I shall be ten years younger and six inches taller.

Margaret did not answer his exuberant letter at once; the annual February issue of the *Review* honoring Ellis' birthday had her in a flurry of activity. This issue contained tributes by such well-known people as Ruth Hale Broun, Ellen Key, and Ruth St. Denis, as well as an especially reverent article by Hugh. As usual, Margaret considered Hugh's article the best and told him so. She had also succeeded in finding an American publisher for his novel, *One Little Boy*.

Any kind of publication delighted Hugh, and when Margaret was able to get a review of his book in *Physical Culture*—a review she had written and the only one it ever got—he became ecstatic.

She tried to be ecstatic too. But she had begun to complain of insomnia, headaches, and constipation, plus overweight from joining her husband at his abundant meals. In a few months her weight had gone from 115 to 131 pounds, her waistline from 20 to 29 inches. As a result she didn't like either the way she felt or her image in the mirror.

Also, now that news of her divorce and remarriage was out, she was terrified that the Catholics would use it as a new weapon against her. Then the papers had given her vanity a stiff blow when they revealed that Grant was sixteen and Stuart twenty-one. She could no longer subtract years from her own age and claim to be any age she pleased.

But it wasn't long before she did a turnabout. When spring came to Willowlake she described the place as "a gem." The newly planted annuals had started coming up and she wrote Hugh that she was "simply mad with joy." She added that she even occasionally went into a cathedral and knelt down "just because I feel like it." As to J. Noah, he was a darling who "gives in to my every wish."

J. Noah was indulging himself as well. With Margaret away so much, he went off to luxurious hotels like the Homestead in Hot Springs, Virginia, where he could socialize, ride horses, and eat very well indeed.

Soon he was begging her to join him at these luxurious places, but Margaret had arranged her life so that she could come and go as she pleased. She used "doctor's orders" and new lecture engagements as excuses to stay in New York or Willowlake, and tried to mollify J. Noah with notes that started: "Darling of my soul," and ended with "All my heart is thine, beloved. My heart belongs only to you."

As Margaret wouldn't come to J. Noah, he had no choice but to go to her. Time and again he would suddenly pack up and go home because he found himself lonesome as ever. To placate him, she made him treasurer of the Birth Control League, the kind of job he enjoyed. He at once got busy trying to organize the league's finances in a businesslike way by breaking Margaret of the habit of raising money when she needed it, then spending it as fast as it came in. But aside from letting him become treasurer she kept him out of her cause. That, she insisted, was hers alone.

With the thought of Françoise still disturbing her, letters from Havelock and Hugh soon were not enough. She told J. Noah in June 1924 that she simply had to take a quick trip to England to see them. She had persuaded J. Noah to stay home the last time she went by using the argument that he was needed to personally supervise the building of Willowlake. But this time J. Noah was adamant; he insisted on going along as he wanted to meet Hugh and Havelock himself. But when he did, to his surprise, he was not the least bit impressed. After Hugh admitted he was willing to come to America and give poetry readings just for the expense money, he dismissed Hugh as "impractical and wholly sentimental." And he couldn't see the greatness in taciturn Havelock at all. He might have been impressed with Harold, who at least was a businessman who kept regular hours and held an important job on a famous paper, but Margaret never phoned Harold to say they were there.

Back at Willowlake within a month, Margaret rested, then began thinking of a new plan to publicize her cause. After a few weeks she hit on it; she would hold not merely a national conference, but an international one the following year. There had just been a big breakthrough in contraception: Hannah Stone and James Robinson, working together, had perfected an anti-spermicidal jelly which, when put inside a diaphragm as well as around the rim, doubled its protection. She would demonstrate this jelly to doctors from all over the world. She would also hammer home her statistics on self-induced abortions and tell how, out of a sampling of 1655 women who had come to the Bureau, 1434 had admitted to regularly aborting themselves; one woman had done this forty times.

But to hold a successful international conference with doctors attending from many countries, she needed internationally known Big Names, and Big Names wouldn't come unless they knew that other Big Names would also be there. In addition, many European doctors would expect their travel expenses to be paid. She realized that an international conference was going to be both difficult and expensive to put together; she would have to look for Big Names in England first.

In the fall she sailed for London, this time writing in advance to Harold: "I've got to bag two or three important men for my Conference. Can you help me? Will you be in London? It will be glorious to see you again." She added a significant P.S. "No husband will be present."

Margaret took Juliet along now to meet Hugh and Havelock, and this time she persuaded J. Noah to stay home, using the argument that if he didn't supervise the landscaping at Willowlake he would be cheated for sure. Besides, they could cable each other every day from the ship.

Just before she sailed, she received an unexpected letter from her old friend Alexander Berkman. She had often thought of Berkman and tried to find him, though to her friends she never mentioned either socialists or anarchists because such people, she insisted, were part of her distant past.

Berkman had written her from Berlin, addressing her as Peggy, the name the I.W.W.'s used:

My dear Peggy, You will probably be surprised to hear from me, and perhaps even more so at the familiar appellation. But that is the way I think of you, an old habit (do I hear you say "a bad one"?).

The occasion of this writing? Well, since my letters to you—one to London, and later on one to N.Y.—remained unanswered, I stopped writing. But now a letter of yours came to hand. . . .

I see by your letter that you have not forgotten me, and that pleases my—shall I say vanity? Anyhow, I am pleased to know it, though I have heard that you have proven unfaithful to me and went and got married. The nerve of you! Without consulting or even telling me! Seriously, is the report true? I am so generous-hearted, that I should forgive you even if it were true. And if he is a decent fellow, then you have probably done a very sensible thing . . .

But I cannot think of you as anyone's "wife," and I am writing to you as to the Peggy I used to know of old—the one I used to take dinner with at that Hungarian restaurant in the basement of Second Avenue, or spend time with somewhere else in the old environment. I wonder whether you still remember?

* * *

He went on to say he was completely broke, as he had written a book about Russia that no one would publish. He signed himself "As of yore, 'Sasha.'"

Margaret answered Berkman immediately, and he replied:

> My dear Peggy: It was no small pleasure to get the letter from you, dear friend. It is like talking to you in the days gone by. . . . You say in your letter, "Well, well, I've found you again!" Did you ever lose me? . . . You will not lose me again, will you, dear? I am happy to get a line from you now and then.

Berkman's book on Russia was finally published, but it turned out to be a dismal failure. A few years later, despondent over both the book's failure and the fact that he couldn't get readmitted to the United States after being deported during the Big Red Scare, he committed suicide in Nice. Though he had gone to Nice with another woman, it was still Emma Goldman who mourned him most deeply, hurrying down from Paris to arrange his funeral. As she had been permanently exiled from America, too, Emma in time wandered back to Canada and died there.

Meanwhile Margaret arrived in London to find an encouraging letter from J. Noah. He was doing something, of which he was sure she would approve, to increase the supply of diaphragms. Vito Sillechia, having saved up enough money to open his candy store, had dropped out of the rum-running business, and J. Noah had hit on the idea of having German doctors send diaphragms to the Canadian factory where he was manufacturing Three-in-One Oil more cheaply than he could in the States; he was getting these European diaphragms across the American border in a way he'd tell her about later. "Dr. B. has already gotten thru 275 pessaries to me from Berlin at a dollar each," he exulted. Then, in an abrupt change of thought: "I hate B. C. that takes you away."

The day after she landed in London, Margaret as usual rushed down to Sand Pit, noting in her diary:

> Hugh was perfect. He seems to have a new look in his eye, a look which means he has seen through the mist and beyond to the

light. . . . Juliet was very silent most of the visit. I was elated
and noisy. Sunday evening I saw Havelock and he toned me down.

Now she was ready to start seeing the men whom she hoped to get
for her conference. The first of these was John Maynard Keynes, who
said he would help indirectly by publicizing the conference, but that he
was terrified of coming to America since he wasn't a public speaker.

Next, she saw Harold Cox, "a perfect angel of a man who has been to
America before but would make no promises." Then she received a
much-desired invitation to lunch with the distinguished Sir Thomas
Horder, who said, "maybe he'd come and maybe he wouldn't." After
that she met with J. O. P. Bland, who definitely promised to come "but
only to smile."

If only as a change of pace, she began seeing much more of Harold
Child. By now they had undoubtedly become lovers. "My Margaret," he
wrote on October 9,

> I want to cover this whole page with sweet names for you but
> they are all summed up in just that—My Margaret. It's so lovely
> to think that there is a My Margaret—no one else's—a real whole
> lovely being, a woman, friend, that is mine because you give it to
> me. But the mystery of what you can see in it and why you're so
> gracious as to accept it is beyond explaining.

The intensity of this letter surprised her. She had started a mild flir-
tation with Harold and she found herself receiving an adoration so
complete it reminded her of the early days of Bill Sanger's courtship;
she was walking on air.

She was also continuing her affair with Wells. In an undated note
sent from Easton Glebe he begged:

> Please keep as much of your time as possible for me, because I
> want being taken care of just now. I shall be back in London (Flat
> No. 4 Whitehall Court) on Thursday night. Can't I carry you off
> somewhere for a day or so? Anyway Friday belongs to me, and
> Saturday—and I can stop in London Sunday also.

In another note he wrote:

                              *   *   *

What are you doing next week? . . . Will you have Monday or
Thursday evening free? For perhaps a little dinner somewhere
about 7:15, and afterwards we could see how we wish to spend the
evening. A music hall or so forth?

And on October 8, 1924, he sent an unsigned note from his London
flat that consisted of just two words: "Wonderful! Unforgettable!"
Their affair had evidently reached a peak.

It added up for Margaret to a free-love dream—three English lovers
at once, plus an ardent husband waiting at home. Not long before,
J. Noah had met a reporter at a party who asked him why he had married a woman like Margaret. He replied testily, "That's an impertinent
question, young man." But a moment later he called the man back and
said, "She's the adventure of my life. Nothing interesting ever happened to me before."

To her lovers, too, Margaret was an adventure. She was beautiful,
charismatic, and involved in important work. The child who had been
the plainest of the four Higgins sisters had blossomed into a bewitch-
ing woman who was famous worldwide.

All was not perfect however, for soon, his affair with Françoise practically over, Hugh was again on the prowl, making a play now for Juliet. True, Juliet had thyroid eyes, a fluttery manner, and the annoying
habit of always dressing in flaming red or pink. But she was extremely
rich, extremely bored, and quite obviously taken by Margaret's Noble
Lord. Hugh decided Juliet would do.

Margaret sensed what was happening and countered by spending
more time with Harold. On October 10 she told him she wanted to see
Oxford where she'd never been. He promptly rented a car and they
drove there, lunching at the famous Mitre Hotel and having a drink afterward at the Monks' Retreat pub. They had barely returned when
Harold sent around a note by messenger to her hotel: "I've been kissing
my own hands! Can you guess why? They smell of *your* perfume. 'Gold-
en Sunshine,' was it called? or 'Margaret's Laughing Eyes'?"

The next day another note arrived: "It's exactly nineteen hours since
I've seen you and touched you. It seems like nineteen years. Are you alright? And do you love me? . . . Oh, but I love you, sweet sweet girl."

At the same time she was receiving almost daily letters from
J. Noah who insisted that she come home and never leave him again

Margaret as a nurse
probationer, when Bill Sanger
first saw her.

Margaret Higgins, the Irish
colleen, with Corey, her first
beau at Claverack College

Margaret Sanger with Stuart,
her first-born son.

Grant and Peggy Sanger in
Greek costume

Bill Sanger, Margaret's first husband. Though he adored her, their stormy marriage finally ended in divorce.

Margaret mourning for her
daughter Peggy

Margaret, in smart British
costume, awaiting trial with
her sister Ethel after the
Brownsville raid of 1916.

Margaret, caught in a rare
moment of peace, in 1932.

Havelock Ellis, the
famous British
proponent of "free
love." He was
Margaret's mentor
and lover.

Hugh de Selincourt, the would-be poet, in 1925. His intimate, passionate relationship with Margaret lasted for many years.

J. Noah Slee, Margaret's wealthy second husband, with Michael Higgins, her father, at the Truro cottage.

Willowlake, painstakingly designed and built by Bill Sanger for Margaret. He sold it with deep regret when she tired of it.

Margaret, living in Tucson, the wealthy hostess of elegant parties.

"or I might do something foolish due to my utter loneliness."
But Margaret wasn't planning to return home. She had told J. Noah
she was going abroad for only a week, but she was having far too good
a time to keep her promise. She answered that she was too busy pursu-
ing Big Names; she never knew when one might consent to be a speaker at her conference. J. Noah would simply have to wait.

Wells, eager to help, gave a big dinner for her on October 15, seating
Bernard Shaw on her left and former Chancellor of the Exchequer
Lord Buckmaster on her right. The novelist Arnold Bennett and the
playwright St. John Ervine were among this distinguished group.

Her particular targets that evening were Shaw and Buckmaster.
But Juliet so monopolized Shaw's attention that Margaret couldn't get
in a word. More, the conversation moved so fast she couldn't get Buckmaster's attention either, even though Wells leaned over and whispered, "Have you got Buckmaster yet? You're an American. Go faster!"
She had to content herself with writing to them later, and while Buckmaster replied cordially that he thoroughly believed in birth control,
the date of her conference conflicted with the opening of Parliament,
making it impossible for him to go. Shaw, who couldn't go either, wrote
her such a classic statement on birth control she ran it as the lead article in the next issue of the *Review*.

Birth Control should be advocated for its own sake on the general ground that the difference between voluntary and irrational
and uncontrolled behavior is the difference between an amoeba
and a man, and if we really believe that the more highly evolved
creature is the better we may as well act accordingly. As the amoeba does not understand birth control, it cannot abuse it, and
therefore its state may be the more gracious, but it is also true
that as the amoeba cannot write, it cannot commit forgery. Yet
we teach everybody to write unhesitatingly, knowing that if we
refuse to teach anything that could be abused we should never
teach anything at all.

She did have one bit of success however. She managed to heal, at
least temporarily, the rift between Havelock and Hugh caused by
Hugh's affair with Françoise. When Hugh told Harold about it, Harold
wrote Margaret joyously from Sand Pit:

I've been walking round and round the little pool in the sunken garden: the place was full of you. Who but you could have planned that meeting between Havelock and Hugh, and who but you could have brought it off? I can see you to the life—sly, mischievous, triumphant, bubbling with inner laughter, then serious all at once—as enchanting a picture of a great and exquisite woman and an adorable little girl as ever I've seen or imagined.

Finally she told J. Noah bluntly that she was delaying her trip home, though she tried to soften her letter with fibs and endearments:

Today I received your cable for $300. You said you had sent another too. It is perfectly adorable for you to send them on so quickly. I dislike asking you for money and only sheer desperation made me do it. Had I come to London alone without Juliet I would have gone to a boarding house, but having started in style I got into the ways of London before I knew it . . . I am here tongue-tied and lonely. I want my sweetheart husband more than I want anything else. But work detains me, and the treatment on my neck can only be gotten in London.

J. Noah had no choice but to bear it. Lonelier than ever, he busied himself with birth-control work, tackling again the problem of the dwindling diaphragm supply. He succeeded in persuading the German manufacturers to lower the price of the diaphragms from fifteen to twelve cents apiece. Though Margaret was delighted by this news, something else had begun to upset her.

Not long before she came to London to look for her Big Names, Janet de Selincourt had taken a trip to Paris with Harold, and Hugh had approvingly told Margaret, "Old Harold is in Paris having, I hear, a high time with Janet. He is more a darling than ever."

But soon afterward Harold told Janet of his love for Margaret. On October 17 Margaret received a distraught letter from Janet:

Darling Margaret—Do you remember once at Wantley when you said you would like to hold me in your arms? Perhaps you have forgotten, but you were being Heavenly to me. I should like you to hold me now, and tell me you love me.

When Harold came to me all glowing to tell me about you, it

gave me a great pang & opened up an old wound that I thought I had cured. I forgot everyone but myself & everything turned to bitterness inside. I was rebellious that new life & happiness came to others while my own had come to hopeless grief & felt there was never to be anything more for me but being glad for others. And I went all dead & frozen & hurt Harold. Can you forgive me? So much love is poured out over me, I should be satisfied you would think, but the old longing came pushing up again. It is awful to feel dead. I am coming alive again now & I do love you & Harold.

On October 20, feeling better, Janet sent a second letter:

Darling lovely Margaret. You have got hold of the wrong end of the stick altogether & if I can't make you feel that you have, I shall curse myself forever for writing that letter. Either there was no need for me to have told you of any pain or I should have been much clearer. There is *no hurt* to me in the fact of your love for Harold. My pain didn't spring from that; it wasn't his having found you & your love that hurt, but that I had lost someone to whom I had gone out in the same way . . . Why you adorable lovely person, what man could help falling in love with you?

Don't, don't go (home) on Saturday if you can possibly stay. Hugh is longing to see you quietly & it would be *heavenly* if you came back Thursday.

Margaret stayed on in England gladly; she ran down for a quick visit to Sand Pit, and on October 25, she received a note from Harold: "You are love incarnate . . . You incredibly darling mixture of the Saint and ragamuffin."

Saint and ragamuffin! He had caught her to a T. To her admirers she did seem a Saint, sparkling and gentle; one letter had reached her merely addressed to "Saint Margaret, New York." But to her lovers she was a ragamuffin, always hungry for sex and love.

Years later when she was an old woman she told her sixteen-year-old grandaughter:

Kissing, petting and even intercourse are alright as long as they are sincere. I have never given a kiss in my life that wasn't sincere. As for intercourse, I'd say three times a day was about right.

Undoubtedly one reason for her interest in birth control was its connection with sex. She enjoyed sex so much that she wanted all women to enjoy it too—without having to bear children they didn't want.

By mid-autumn of 1934 J. Noah was *demanding* that she come home, but she cabled him for still more money, saying she needed an expensive new nightgown. He sent it, receiving studied and effusive thanks:

> I have been very, very soul-lonely, Noah darling . . . I'm of course disturbed to know you have been lonely too . . . It will be paradise to be in your arms again . . . No other man could satisfy my urgent passion. That belongs to you and to you alone.

Nevertheless she insisted, she had to wait around to see Lord Dawson of Penn, the king's physician, because Dawson had recently come out strongly for birth control; he had startled a British medical meeting by declaring, "I'm sure you give birth control information to your rich patients, why do you withhold it from the poor?" But Dawson, who was off shooting grouse in Scotland, was not due back until the end of the month. As she wanted him to be the keynote speaker at her conference, she would have to stay on.

When finally Dawson returned, Margaret got her appointment:

> At last the hour came to see Lord Dawson. I felt disgusted to think I had taken champagne for dinner the night before, fearing my brain would be dull and not respond properly. But when his secretary opened the door and announced Lord Dawson and I saw him I felt all was well as far as champagne was concerned. He is a handsome gentleman about forty-five. *Marvellously* handsome. He took me along the spacious hall to his private office where a fire burned cheerfully and he sat not at his desk in formal fashion like our American men would do, but lounged on a sofa and acted as tho there were hours and days in which to discuss B.C. (Yet) he would not promise to come to the conference. He wants to have famous American doctors like the Mayo Brothers with him.

* * *

Getting the Mayo Brothers was hardly likely, so she caught a train to Southampton and made the next sailing of the *Berengaria*.

Before sailing, she sent a goodbye letter to Hugh:

Hugh, darling old thing, Harold came with me to the boat. What a friend and god that man is. I feel sad because I have not seen enough of you. Juliet took your time, Françoise your heart, Havelock your mind. Nothing left but a stingy little pecking kiss on the neck for ME.

Oh why can't we love & let our love grow unfettered? I am a poor one to talk of love, I know, but I am sitting at the feet of those who know. I want to cry because I could not get you on the phone today. I wanted to hear your "grunt" so I could laugh the cry away. Kiss me, hug me, good night.

Once on the seas, however, she suddenly felt homesick for J. Noah, uncomplicated J. Noah, who presented no problems: "I miss J. N. terribly," she wrote in her diary. "I've almost promised myself not to go anywhere without him again."

Once home, she had another bright idea. Havelock would soon be seventy, and she wanted to give him a special present for the occasion. Perhaps it would be possible for Françoise to give up her teaching and translating jobs, move in with Havelock, and become his full-time secretary. If Hugh could find out how much money Françoise was earning, she could give her an equivalent amount each year so that she could devote herself exclusively to The King.

Hugh did the detective work, and reported that Françoise was earning about three hundred pounds a year (fifteen hundred dollars at the time). J. Noah, delighted to have his Margy back, promised to contribute the fifteen hundred starting in February 1925.

All in all, 1924 had been a good year, Margaret reflected. It seemed even better when she got a letter from Hugh telling how Harold had also told him of his love for her, and "it has made Harold not only look more dear and shining but *be* more dear and sensitive to me than he has been for years." The circle was seemingly going round and round, with love conquering all.

Hugh's letter so excited Margaret that she decided to celebrate by giving an impressive Christmas dinner at Willowlake, inviting not only some of her wealthy friends, but Grant, Stuart, and her sisters Mary and Ethel.

Everything went fine at first. J. Noah beamed in his best black Langdon suit at one end of the laden table; Margaret glowed in blue silk and turquoise jewelry at the other. But just as the butler was about to serve a fine roast goose, Ethel, who had begun to drink quite heavily, saw a chance to get back at Margaret for excluding her from the birth-control movement. Ethel babbled, "Remember how in Corning we had good things only at Christmas time? Just one little orange each?" Margaret tried to hush her, but Ethel kept repeating, "Just one little orange? And we ate it in hand-me-down clothes."

Margaret saw to it that Ethel was never invited to Willowlake when guests were present again.

SMUGGLED DIAPHRAGMS

A long freight train slowly moved toward the border between Canada and the United States. One carload had been shipped by J. Noah Henry Slee from his Canadian oil factory to his head office in the States. An inspector weighed the load and wondered why it seemed so light. He opened the car and examined its contents. The cartons inside were filled not with oil, but with cans containing flat rubber objects which were identified as diaphragms or contraceptives; the cargo was confiscated. Since J. Noah Slee had been in business so long and had such a respectable reputation he was not punished; a "cease and desist" order was issued against him instead. It was the end of his smuggling operation, an unhappy end, since getting diaphragms through the Canadian customs had been easy. Getting them through the American customs would be something else again.

But Margaret and her husband refused to be daunted. Julius Schmid and Company, a German firm with a branch in the United States, had been manufacturing a few diaphragms in addition to their well-known Ramses condoms which could be sold legally "for the cure and prevention of disease." But making diaphragms was a risky business and prices were correspondingly high. They could not afford to deal with Julius Schmid. They had to find a cheaper source.

Margaret found that source in Herbert Simonds, a man who was willing to make diaphragms for Margaret in the United States, and also help her cause in other ways.

Herbert Simonds was a chemical engineer from Spokane, Washington. He and Margaret had met many years before when she was in Spokane on a speaking tour. They met in an unusual manner. As Simonds told it later:

> Margaret and I met under water. She was an excellent swimmer and diver, and someone pointed her out to me as an interesting woman who was sitting on a raft in the middle of a lake. As I was a bachelor of 28 and she an exceedingly pretty woman of 35, I swam out to join her. When she saw me coming, she dove off the raft into deep water, daring me to follow her. I took the dare, dove in after her, and we shook hands, laughing, under water.

In 1917 when Simonds was an army captain getting ready to sail to Europe from a camp near New York, he phoned Margaret and they made a date to go dancing.

> The friends she introduced me to on these occasions were all Villagers, in spirit at least, and I was too. Strangely enough, she never talked about contraception on evening dates. We just danced and laughed a lot.

In 1920, when Simonds came back from Europe, he settled in Boston where he got a job as editor of the New England branch of a firm that published engineering books. He dropped Margaret a card from Boston and she answered saying she was planning a lecture on birth control in Boston but was having trouble finding a hall. Could he find her one? Simonds answered "of course," not realizing how hard this might be to do.

He went first to a minister whom he knew through family connections; the minister wouldn't even listen to him. He tried other ministers; the results were the same. Even radical friends shied off, refusing to rent her their union halls. Finally the manager of the Copley Plaza agreed to let her have a basement room. Not the Grand Ballroom to be sure, but a downstairs room where she and her audience could sneak in and out.

Simonds' next job was to find ushers for the lecture. This proved hard too, though eventually he found a few. And though only fifty people showed up, including the usual hecklers, he observed that Margaret was "masterly at handling people; she knew just how to parry the hecklers and hold them down."

More interested than ever, Simonds offered to drive Margaret to Providence, Rhode Island, where she had scheduled another lecture before a small group of doctors. He found it a momentous trip. Margaret was very affectionate and he very vulnerable. Almost immediately, according to Simonds, they became lovers. When he stayed on for the lecture he discovered that she didn't have enough diaphragms to hand out to the doctors who asked for them. He tried to help her once more. As a respected engineer, he might be able to get a personal interview with some of the big New England chemical companies and try to persuade them to manufacture diaphragms. But none of them would touch the job at any price. He traveled all over the East whenever he could find the time, only to meet with failure. Making diaphragms was just too dangerous; the companies were doing fine without risking their money on that.

Finally he decided to take the risk himself. He kept his Boston editorial job as a front and founded a . . .

. . . wacky company, consisting of a playwright whose name I forget, a man from the Associated Press whom Margaret had met at an A.M.A. convention, and me. We called our company the Holland Rantos Company, the Holland part because Holland was the first country to make diaphragms, and the Rantos part because it sounded like Ramses. I dug up a couple of hundred dollars, the other two guys dug up $400 between them, and Slee added a little more. We hired a secretary and installed her in a dinky room in the basement of an old house on 20th Street near the Research Bureau, fixed up a second room as a factory, and were off. Our place had to be near the Research Bureau because under the Comstock Law we couldn't ship the stuff by either mail or truck, but we experimented until we perfected a quality of rubber that would withstand all kinds of climate, and volunteers would walk up town every day with empty suitcases and go away with them full.

Things went on like this for a long time. We couldn't supply the bureau with as many diaphragms as they needed, but we did our

best. Finally the law was changed. We expanded and moved to a
fancy uptown location. In time we opened branches in Chicago
and Los Angeles, and I must confess we ended up doing pretty
well, though Margaret herself never made a cent on the deal.

Margaret and Simonds remained friends and occasional lovers for
the next thirty years, and, as always, she gave more than physical
love.

Thanks to Simonds, by 1925 Margaret was assured of a fairly regular supply of diaphragms from his tiny factory. But she had trouble
getting them to the few doctors outside of New York who were willing
to recommend them. Most doctors still derided her as a "mere female
nurse" and wouldn't come near her or her lectures. If she sought them
out, they all but slammed the door in her face. She would have to find a
man, preferably one with a medical degree, to travel and make con-
tacts for her within the medical profession.

She found him in Dr. James Cooper.

Dr. Cooper, who at one time had been a medical missionary in China
and now was a successful internist, entered the birth-control movement full of zeal. Nonetheless, since he would be giving up a good practice to accept the traveling job, he wanted a two-year contract at a substantial salary. Margaret's only steady source of money was J. Noah,
and he was growing more and more impatient with the whole birth-
control cause. What was the use of having a charming wife and maintaining a beautiful country estate, when that wife was off early every
morning to a New York clinic sixty miles away that was "run by a
bunch of crazy women." Worse, when his wife was home, likely as not
she would be secluded alone in her private apartment. True, all this
was part of their marriage agreement, but it was beginning to get
badly on his nerves.

On February 2, 1925 Margaret wrote him a letter that was part business, part seduction. It read:

To J. Noah H. Slee, 1925 is to be the big year for the breakthrough in birth control. If Dr. Cooper's association with us is successful, I feel certain the medical profession will take up the
work. When the medical profession does this in the U.S.A., I shall
feel that I have made my contribution to the Cause and can with-

draw from full-time activity, (though) I shall still want to publish the *Review* and take some interest in it and write articles and books on subjects allied with B.C.

Even should this not occur in one year, I shall be satisfied having a Committee taking responsibility off my shoulders.

It is estimated that Dr. Cooper will cost about $10,000 salary and expense for 1 year. His work will be to lecture before Medical Societies and Associations—getting their cooperation and influence to give contraceptive information in clinics, private and public.

If I am able to accomplish this victory with Dr. Cooper's help, I shall bless my adorable husband, J. N. H. Slee, and retire with him to the garden of love. Sealed, signed and delivered, Margaret Sanger.

She never did retire to his private garden of love, but just the fact that he was giving the cause ten thousand dollars—a much larger sum than he had ever donated before—gave J. Noah greater self-confidence in dealing with Margaret. One night after she had held a big meeting at their house, she hinted that she was very tired and wanted to retire immediately to her own apartment, and to bed.

"Oh, no, you are not tired," declared J. Noah. "This is one time when you do not lock the door!"

Dr. Cooper stayed on for two years and seven hundred lectures, traveling by train, bus, horse, and mule into the remotest parts of the country. He insisted he enjoyed every minute of it, even when, in places like Nashville, Tennessee, he had to ring doorbells all day trying to find doctors friendly to the cause. "These one-night stands are certainly the life," he wrote Margaret from Marshall, Texas. And from Paris, Texas, "One hundred miles by bus today. Real covered wagon stuff." He was very proud of those doctors who were brave enough to admit their interest in birth control publicly and attend a lecture. "The president of the medical society is the boldest man in town," he wrote from Greensboro, North Carolina. "He sponsored my meeting." He summed up his travels: "I glory in the pioneering work."

Before he was through, he had covered practically every state in the union and collected a list of twenty thousand doctors sympathetic to the cause.

Margaret continued to take pride in her work for the cause as well, especially when she had to accept lecture engagements from groups like the Ku Klux Klan. In Silver Lake, New Jersey, the woman's branch of the Klan had invited her to speak because they were virulently anti-Catholic. In her autobiography, she described the eerie experience:

My letter of instruction told me what train to take, to walk from the station two blocks straight ahead, then two to the left. I would see a sedan parked in front of a restaurant but was to wait ten minutes before approaching the car. I obeyed orders implicitly, walked the blocks, saw the car, found the restaurant, went in and ordered some cocoa, stayed my allotted ten minutes, then approached the car hesitatingly and spoke to the driver. I received no reply. She might have been totally deaf as far as I was concerned. Mustering up my courage, I climbed in and settled back. Without a turn of the head, smile, or a word to let me know I was right, she stepped on the self-starter. For fifteen minutes we wound around the streets . . . We took this lonely lane and that through the woods, and an hour later pulled up in a vacant space near a body of water beside a large, unpainted, barnish building.

My driver got out, talked with several other women, then said to me severely, "Wait here, We will come for you." More cars buzzed up the dusty road into the parking place. Occasionally men dropped off wives who walked hurriedly and silently within. This went on mystically until night closed down and I was alone in the dark. A few gleams came through chinks in the window curtains. Even though it was May, I grew chillier and chillier.

After three hours I was summoned at last and entered a bright corridor filled with wraps. As someone came out of the hall I saw through the door dim figures parading with banners and illuminated crosses. I waited another twenty minutes. It was warmer and I did not mind so much. Eventually the lights were switched on, the audience seated itself, and I was escorted to the platform, was introduced, and began to speak.

Never before had I looked into a sea of faces like these. I was sure that if I uttered one word outside the usual vocabulary of these women they would go off into hysteria. And so my address that night had to be in the most elementary terms, as though I were trying to make children understand.

In the end, through simple illustration, I believed I had accomplished my purpose. A dozen invitations to speak to similar groups were proffered. The conversation went on and on, and when we were finally through it was too late to return to New York. Under a curfew law everything in Silver Lake shut at nine o'clock. I could not even send a telegram to let my family know whether I had been thrown into the river or was being held incommunicado. It was nearly one before I reached Trenton, and I spent the night in a hotel.

In Brattleboro, Vermont, she had a quite different experience. Here she spoke to three hundred sturdy farmwomen:

honest, strong, capable housewives who made their pies and doughnuts and preserves before they came. When I had finished there was not a murmur from the three hundred. The minister of the church had asked me to stand beside him to say how-do-you-do when they came out. They just went by, eyes straight ahead.

On the telephone afterwards, however, each was asking what the other thought. The cases I had cited were typical of their own community. "Was she referring to this one or that one?" they queried.

I returned two days later to lunch with a doctor and four or five social workers, and was surprised to hear, "The women want to start a clinic." But there wasn't any enthusiasm when I suggested it.

The people around here don't express much openly. They were moved to quietness. But just the same they're starting a clinic in Brattleboro.

Another lecture had a humorous twist. She spoke at the Yale Divinity School, and the toastmaster introduced her as the mother of one of their divinity school students—meaning Stuart who was a medical student. She didn't correct him. "If it will help to be associated with a Divinity School, a Divinity School it shall be," she laughed to herself as the applause broke forth.

Yet she wasn't always that lucky. When Harvard's Liberal Club gave a luncheon for her in their private clubrooms, Mayor Curley of

Boston was furious. "I will declare war on birth control," he thundered, "and revoke the license of any public hall in which Margaret Sanger speaks." She spoke just the same. Mayor Curley was still threatening revocation a few years later when she was invited to speak at Boston's Ford Hall Forum. She got around him by sitting on the platform with grinning eyes and a large piece of adhesive tape stretched across her mouth, while Arthur Schlesinger, Sr. read her speech. The stunt made for great publicity. "The more they gag me, the more I am heard," she boasted.

Uppermost in her mind in early 1925 was her planned international conference. To her horror she found it would cost about twenty-five thousand dollars to bring European speakers to the United States, hire Town Hall for a week, print the programs, and get out the publicity. When she asked the Birth Control League (now the American Birth Control League) to raise the money, she found herself embattled; they flatly refused. She proceeded with her arrangements in her usual style—spending money first and worrying about getting it later.

Eventually Juliet Rublee paid most of the conference bills, but Margaret was worn out from the struggle with the league. Nor did she feel any better when Hugh wrote her on January 10 that the fight with Marie Stopes was going full tilt again:

> So Marie Stopes is going to warn Havelock about you. Poor man, he needs the warning. It's awful to think of him being deceived by an unscrupulous woman, him so sensitive and childlike and trusting. Couldn't I help in some way? My God Margaret, there are women who literally make me want to vomit. The Stopes book smelled, as I told you on the Downs the first walk I took with you. I can hardly smile even over Stopes' impertinences and follies, egregious creature.

Harold Child also sided with Margaret against Stopes, but no matter how hard he tried he couldn't compete with the effervescent Hugh. Margaret even forgave Hugh for both taking Juliet as a mistress and accepting a large sum of money from her.

> Margaret, what do you think! Juliet has sent millions and millions of pounds scattering over me like rose-leaves. "It's not a

thing that's ever done," one says. "Isn't it?" she answers. "Well that's another reason why I should do it." And all one's little respectable dignity that would leap to resent such an action is melted up. You had a hand in it, Margaret. It bears your stamp. You egged her on. Or at any rate your silent influence is there. Such a fairy godmother!

I say, ought she to do it? I'm not *deserving* you know; I'm not *in need*. But how much difference it'll make—more freedom, more fun. Heavens! I'm all in such an utter excitement, I think I shall burst. Why are you all so adorable to me?

Margaret found Hugh's excitement so infectious she sailed for England at once, planning to stay only two weeks and spend most of it with him. By February 15 she was in London, settled in at The Ritz, and Hugh was welcoming her from Sand Pit.

A few days later they had met and made love, and he was sending her a note hinting at possible trouble to come as a result:

I wept in the train to think I had missed enjoying being with you. I ought to have been really strong to bear the sight of you . . . I spilled a lot, so to speak, being disgracefully flabby, sickening bad luck. Makes me ashamed of myself.

Let me see you once more, if possible . . . I hope H & W (Harold and Wells) are doing you good. Oh I loved seeing you. Love me always. Love me always. Let it grow and grow.

Whatever it was that Hugh feared—maybe a failure in the practice of Karezza of which he was so proud—there are no letters from him to Margaret between February and September of 1925, an unusually long period of silence.

Hugh was going through a difficult period at this time in any event; he simply could not find a publisher for his books. He had also just turned fifty, an age when many men suffer a crisis of confidence, and to a man like Hugh it must have been even more traumatic than to most. For try as hard as he could, Hugh had not been a success, and he knew it. Living on a wife's income or accepting an occasional gift from a wealthy friend is more common in England than in America, but nonetheless, Hugh must have found this more bitter than he cared to admit.

* * *

By early April of 1925, Margaret was back home from England and off visiting Juliet in Vermont. J. Noah had to write her that the clinic bank balance was down to a low of $649.18 and that he could authorize Hannah Stone to pay only those bills which were absolutely necessary. He ended telling her, as always, how very much he missed her.

But much as J. Noah missed her, Grant missed her more. In 1925 he was seventeen and still painfully shy. After waiting for an expected visit, he wrote, "I waited all afternoon for you to come out but it was all in vain." The next day he wrote again asking for a raise in his allowance because, "I am spending too much on things like stamps and shoestrings." A week later, having thanked Pater for giving him the raise, he wrote that he still wanted badly to see his mother but warned her "not to make any rash promises you can't keep." And on September 12, Margaret's birthday, he sent her a card hoping she'd live forty-eight years more. As she was only forty-six, this didn't please her a bit.

Weighed down with lectures and arrangements for her upcoming conference, Margaret wasn't giving much thought to Grant, anyway. She had started her diary again on March 7:

> For the past hour the same old nervousness has been upon me. That same gripping in the pit of the stomach (Solar plexus) that I used to experience in the past. I expected I would get over it, but it seems to be with me yet. I am going to speak at John Hayes Holmes Community Church, 34th Street & Park Avenue.
> Later: This feeling did not leave me all evening. I did not inspire my audience. I felt a load, a difficulty in getting my words to fit the ideas. Never a harder lecture, Church packed to the doors.

Because the medical profession in general shied away from the controversial subject of birth control, the advisory board of the Birth Control League was made up almost exclusively of sociologists and eugenicists. This meant that at a meeting with members of the Catholic hierarchy, Margaret had to rely on a sociologist for support.

> Today Dr. Garth arranged for a meeting at the Bankers' Club where the B.C. people were able to meet the Roman Catholic Hierarchy. Dr. Murray Cooper, the spokesman from the R.C. Church, was present. Nothing but "moral" & "altrustic" arguments presented. Middle age minds. Where can we meet? On

what common ground can one meet with minds that think there is more altruism in raising children beyond your strength & health than there is in keeping abreast?

For the rest of the month she worked at details of the conference which was due to open in a few days. She worried about hotel arrangements for the hundreds of delegates from seventeen countries who had agreed to come. She worried about getting volunteers to meet the boats of the various delegates. Indeed, one scientist from France was almost missed.

There were other complexities. Though the league had hired a team of expert translators, some of the delegates had had their papers translated in advance by people who were less than expert. One of these was Dr. Fru Thit Jensen of Denmark. Speaking of the difficulty she had trying to arouse enthusiasm among fellow-doctors in favor of birth control, her remarks were translated: "When I gave my greetings to those boneheads as I am to you." The audience tittered, and by the time Dr. Thit finished speaking, they were laughing so hard they hardly could hear what she was saying.

Despite the fact that the speakers were primarily eugenicists and demographers, the conference went smoothly. The demographers gave statistics on the alarming growth of population all over the world; the eugenicists preached that, by encouraging the "fit" to procreate and discouraging the "unfit," the world would become a better place in which to live. Because no one knew exactly who were the fit and the unfit, or how to encourage one group to reproduce while discouraging the other, the results of the conference were not far-reaching.

Still the conference did move the cause along. Ministers and rabbis of various denominations attended, and the medical session attracted a few doctors, including the eminent gynecologist Robert Latou Dickinson, past president of the American Gynecological Society of New York, and William Allen Pusey, past president of the American Medical Association. Dr. Pusey told the press: "It is women who bear the penalties in injury, disease, death, and mental torture that are involved in unlimited childbearing. They have a right to know how they can intelligently—not crudely and dangerously—control their sexual lives." Eight hundred papers across the country printed his speech. "It was worth holding the Conference," Margaret exulted, "just for this. Wonderful helpers everywhere. Noah the dearest of them all."

Indeed, when the conference was over, she and J. Noah were so elated they contemplated having her biography written immediately. The first choice as author was still Hugh. "Why don't you write my life?" Margaret pleaded with him. "That would bring you to the U.S.A. and we could spend days and days together always talking about ME." But Hugh was clever enough to refuse. "Oh what fun to write your life! What joy!" he answered, then gracefully bowed out: "At about 190 years of age I shall have got cool enough to do it dispassionately."

But it was too early in Margaret's life for a biography. True, she had opened one birth-control clinic and been the inspiration for a few more. She also had organized the first important world conference of scientists interested in population problems, getting men as prestigious as Pusey and Dickinson to endorse her cause; but that cause still had far to go. Pusey, for example, had not gone beyond his one statement, and Dickinson's remarks had been extremely guarded: "I have attended thirteen of the fourteen sessions, and they were conducted with dignity and propriety." This was the most he could bring himself to say. None of the other doctors who attended were willing to make any public statement.

The doctors had reason for their caution. The nineteenth century was the golden age of diploma mills, quacks, and patent medicines. American women gulped down Father John's Medicine and Lydia Pinkham's Pills in huge doses. Naturopaths, hydropaths, bleeders, and mesmerizers did a thriving business, especially in the rural districts or the newly opened up West.

In 1847 the American Medical Society was organized to combat these influences. Its aim was to arouse public confidence in licensed doctors from recognized medical schools and in tested remedies, and to discourage people from patronizing quacks who promised miraculous cures. The newspapers had little truck with licensed doctors however, as the press thrived on ads for cheap patent medicines. Given the strength of their opposition, responsible physicians often resorted to what they called "negative therapeutics," prescribing nothing rather than drugs they considered potentially harmful.

When Margaret arrived on the scene, therefore, she was met by strong resistance. Many doctors felt that much of their push toward respectability would be jeopardized if they endorsed the contraceptives being offered by a laywoman, and a notorious one at that. Thus as late as 1921 only a few doctors gave birth control any kind of support. One was Dr. Abraham Jacobi, a pediatrician who saw for himself the effects of hopelessly large families among the poor—undernourished children susceptible to every childhood disease. Another supporter was Dr. William J. Robinson, publisher of the *Medical Critic and Guide*, who left two pages blank in his book advocating contraception to dramatize the fact that he could give no specific advice in print. The third was Dr. Dickinson, who, though thoroughly convinced of the necessity for birth control, had been elected president of the Academy of Obstetricians only when he was ready to retire from practice, and its members felt that he would be too old to be of much influence.

Altogether, it was not a happy state of affairs for Margaret and her cause; her struggle for public acceptance continued to be extremely difficult.

Meanwhile, of course, she continued her private life and whenever she could she made that private life extremely private. She would send J. Noah off to his favorite health resorts while she stayed in New York or at Willowlake on the pretext of taking mysterious "health-injections," and no amount of pleading could persuade her to join him.

She also continued giving lectures and these lectures, which were never boring no matter how nervous she felt, continued to captivate her audience. Ellen Watumill, a wealthy woman married to a Hindu who ran a gift shop in Hawaii, remembered twenty-five years later the excitement of hearing Margaret speak in Portland, Oregon. It is a typical recollection of a Sanger speech:

I was intrigued by the delightful, petite, extremely feminine woman with lovely red hair who poured out her heart to the packed audience. She never spoke about methods or intercourse or used any of the language so freely used over the air or in public addresses nowadays, but talked of her work as a public health nurse in the lower East Side of New York, and of her frustration when she had nothing to tell her patients when they asked how to prevent unwanted births. Everyone listened with rapt attention and she received a great ovation at the conclusion of her address. It was not delivered as a militant crusade, but with the sincerity, the appeal, of a woman's compassion for all women who were longing to be free from slavery to their biological functions, as well as be free from the oppression of the Comstock law that considered even the words "birth control" and "sex" obscene.

After being quickly introduced to Margaret Sanger, I went to the table in the foyer where someone was selling a little book entitled *Family Limitation*. She had not written this particular book although she must have given the author a great deal of the material it contained. But as I stood there Margaret came down the aisle and was not more than four or five feet away from me when police closed in, arrested her, and took her off to jail to spend the night. Had I been affiliated with any group in Portland at the time, I would undoubtedly have insisted on going to jail with her. Unfortunately my work took me back to Honolulu, and I did not see her again for all these years when we became fast friends.

After the 1925 Portland lecture, Margaret experienced another of her deep depressions. When she got back East, she tried to relieve it by more work—planning a new book and staging a still bigger conference, this one in England. She worked once more to ask the Birth Control League to pay for the delegates' travel expenses. She was dumbfounded when she found the league had less than three hundred dollars in the bank. "Write to Mrs. Thomas Lamont at once and ask for help," she told Anna Lifschiz, without bothering to look up the date when Mrs. Lamont had sent in her last contribution. Mrs. Lamont, who had just mailed in a good-sized check, was indignant, but she relented and posted another that at least tided them over their immediate office expenses.

On September 12, 1925, her forty-sixth birthday, Hugh, Havelock, and Harold sent Margaret a joint birthday cable. She answered Hugh with mixed happiness and dismay:

> What a wonderful trio telegram to receive on my birthday! How did you know? And remember? Havelock always remembers the fatal day which brings me nearer to gray hairs, but no one else is allowed to know, fearing they will keep track of the years. But you would not be so unkind.

She followed this with remembrances of her first meeting with Hugh five years before:

> I remember a letter that missed you. I wrote about *you*, about

dressing up to meet you and for the first time in my life purchasing a powder puff & rouge & trying it on my face, nose, chin according to directions in a book. Then washing it all off again & going forth bravely, *unpowdered* to meet you. Then the queer feeling at not finding you & the talk to myself about such childish feelings—& then meeting you. The adorable funny hat—your lanky frame like our Abraham Lincoln, your strange English, oh very very English words—which with you is always like my favorite music.

Oh I can't remember all the things I wrote. My memory is flooded with our first visit. I hope you find that letter because the writer had been smitten with some wildness at one time.

I am well. Reading lots, two kinds of reading at same time—popular & real. For instance while I was reading Life of Duse & Olive Schreiner's Letters, I was also reading Job, Herodotus, Odyssey & The Autobiography of Benvenuto Cellini. Now I must get back to Population reading, reports, magazine articles etc. etc. for winter's work.

Do you ever dream that the day may arrive when I shall live in England? I'm really a lost soul wandering about in America.

The boys—Stuart called to Yale for football practice & Grant plugging at an Algebra exam. So the winter soon begins. My asters are beautiful for a first year. It will be even better in later years I hope. Thank Janet & naughty neglecting Harold for the cable and thank Havelock too.

This letter is Maggie-Margaret in essence. It is the little girl telling no one about her birthday for fear they may find out her true age—only forty-six, but already afraid of the gray hairs. It is the great lady trying to impress Hugh with the serious books she is reading, when she much preferred light magazines, and dug up material for her speeches herself only when she had no other choice. And it's the woman who calls Harold faithless when he didn't write often enough because her need for flattery was boundless; no matter how much he gave her, she always demanded more.

Juliet Rublee, Margaret's best female friend, was often shown Hugh's letters and seemed to understand him better than Margaret did herself. "Hugh is a dear, but he is also abnormal and morbid and so terribly introspective he destroys himself," she wrote in an undated fragment. It was this kind of keen observation that probably made Margaret hold Juliet close.

Juliet's impulsiveness also bound the two women. On one of her wild escapades, Juliet had been in Italy trying to dig up sunken wrecks, reputed to be full of gold, from the Bay of Naples. When she thought her secretary had been rifling her private papers, she dashed off to Rome to ask the personal advice of the American ambassador. When she didn't get to see the ambassador she wrote Margaret: "(Since then) some instinct or protecting spirit has made me cable Mr. R. to send me a letter to the ambassador . . . Don't let us ever travel again without letters of introduction to the American Ambassadors of every country we visit!"

Yet after George Rublee gave her an introduction to the Italian ambassador, she used it mainly as a way of importing some of her favorite English cigarettes into Italy duty-free. She thought up the ruse of having Margaret send them to the ambassador marked "by diplomatic pouch," with her address on both the inside and outside of the wrapper so he would know whom they were for and forward them. It was a niggardly saving for a woman of her wealth—just as niggardly as Margaret's demand for travel expenses for herself and conference delegates from a league that was barely able to survive, while she herself was a millionaire's wife.

Then too, both women were insomniacs with mystical, often frightening dreams. In London while waiting for Lord Dawson, Margaret had a dream which she reported to Juliet:

> Met two queer persons able to read past incarnations. I seem to have been a nun in an Italian convent three hundred years ago. These men are very ordinary men yet they are serious. It is hard to believe they are "fakirs."

Juliet replied quickly:

> I was *greatly* interested in your extraordinary dream. What *do* you suppose it means? Is someone in deep trouble? Was the feeling one of despair—or prayer or what? You did not write half enough details. Do put down *everything* that comes.

This dream may have foretold death. Not long afterward, Margaret received a letter from her sister Mary who was ill with bronchitis in a Buffalo hospital:

Dearest Margaret
    Could you not spare one day of your busy life to come up to see a rather sick sister? It would give me much comfort and relief. If you feel you can't do it, don't send anyone else as the point would be lost.

Mary died on January 11, 1926. Margaret's notation in the margin of this letter reads:

    Darling Sister Mary!!! died shortly after. She talked of her will & left me sole executor. She was greatly loved—& a GENIUS born.

Hugh, meanwhile, had also developed an inexplicable fear; he was afraid that Margaret had thrown him over. With his fear came an uncharacteristic greediness. He had once told Margaret, "Surely there must be some place for me in your great Cause." Now in November 1925 he was writing in a different vein. Suddenly he was indignant because he had never been paid for any of his sketches in the *Review*. "This is absolutely *obligatory*. You will please remind Mrs. Boyd, the managing editor, about this. Only do it tactfully—and do it soon. I won't be fobbed off by any naughty little millionairesses' cold forgetfulness."

As Margaret had never paid for any of the material that appeared in the *Review* she was astounded, all the more so because she had recently sent Hugh a substantial gift of money with which to build a small cottage which he could rent out for additional income. She had also sent him a special check earmarked for sunbaths for him to take or, better yet, to buy himself a sunlamp if there was electricity in Sand Pit. And she had ended her accompanying letter in an outburst of love: "I want to hug your dear head and kiss your blessed eyes and laugh with you and romp for very joy that you are so dear."

And now came this demand for money for long-ago essays.

She apparently forgave him, as usual, ignoring his greed and replying from Willowlake:

    Darling Hugh: Cheereo!!! It's raining out here where J. N. and I came for a weekend. But I like to walk in the rain tho J. N. said this A.M. as I trudged him up the road two miles in the wet & drizzle that anyone liking such a walk must be crazy.

We go back to town in a few days, and hope to see Juliet soon. She is still in Italy and asks you to write to her. She thinks that J. N. poisoned your mind against her. Please write her a nice letter. J. N. is such a treat 'em rough person when one is flighty that he gives one a horrid impression of his thoughts.

By mid-December, Hugh was doing better than writing Juliet. He was continuing his affair with her and boasting about it:

Oh you darling Margaret, the telephone bell rang; Juliet was in London. Could I see her at lunch? Of course; she *must* come down here. Absolutely and utterly and completely out of the question: so much to do and she sailing on Wednesday. So I hire a car, and drive up to the gorgeous hotel in St. James Place to fetch her quietly down. No; adamant. So I drive home alone—after a really lovely lunch—anyhow I swore to myself the little dear person should emerge while I *was* with her; and the time from 12:30—6:15 (most generously allotted) should be enjoyed quite to the full. And out this little enchanting person stepped at about 12:50 from oh such a very tired and almost crestfallen Juliet Rublee and remained out till I left, though every now and then she shook her wings to fly away—but only flew enchantingly round the room . . . So delicious it was coaxing her out and seeing her emerge: her laugh changed, her face changed, her voice changed . . .

Then, cleverly giving Margaret the credit, he concluded: "It came of course through speaking about you. She couldn't speak long enough about you to me as the grand accomplished lady."

By December 29 Juliet was back home, ready to tell Margaret about Hugh and show off her new clothes. She found Margaret, who was waiting for her in her Turtle Bay Gardens home and writing to Hugh:

Here I am at Juliet's waiting for her to tell me all about her trip to Naples, Geneva & Sand Pit. Juliet will insist upon dressing & redressing & trying on various flame-colored gowns before a long mirror trying to get them short enough to show her beautiful knees. They must be shortened to be fashionable. So there we are . . . In the meantime I write to you to wish you a Happy New Year & a Lucky 1926. Is 9 your lucky number? Five is mine, but 3 and 5 are sympathetic. I am so glad she did get to see you alone at Sand Pit. Paradise indeed without the bread or wine.

Though this letter was cheerful, it was soon followed by one in which she spoke about a woman she envied. "Oh what poise! I'd give years to be like that but I never shall be able to come even miles near its outskirts." The letter following this was a mixture of dreams and regrets:

The cold days or rather evenings are here. Today I am blue & depressed. It is so hard, Hugh, to organize human beings into helpers—they are so egotistical that it takes a like person to meet the breed—Greek meets Greek. If only one could wander about in a garden & think, dream, love & work & find life's fullness there how glorious that would be. In fact I think it would be easy to be *Great*. But this struggle with personalities—with friction—with diseased desire to "boss" grows harder & harder. I have begun to feel that no one can stand praise or encouragement without losing balance. What & why is it Hugh?

I am writing in knickers—I know Harold would like them on me. Where & how is the adorable darling? I think of him oodles of times & always with regret that he could not fall in love with me.

This last statement was pure fantasy, as Harold had recently written her again, calling her a saint as well as a great lady and adorable child. At year's end, Margaret was seeking poise and surcease from her recurrent depression through astrology, numerology, sex, religious cults, and friends. No wonder, despite all the talk of her twinkling laughter, most of the pictures of her taken after 1925 reveal her as sad.

GREAT PLANS

The year 1926 started as badly for Margaret as 1925 had ended. Mary's death left Margaret feeling empty. Mary had raised her; when she needed Mary, she was always there. Margaret took her death particularly hard.

To ease her pain, Margaret plunged again into her diary, though the entries were desultory and vague. On January 3 she sent off a thoughtful note to Hugh about Juliet: "She is really a lovely person, Hugh, seeking her ideal love as all women seem to seek (except me) and I doubt she will ever find him or her because——Did you love Juliet or adore her? Which? She's worthy of both."

On January 5, 1926, she notes that she was at the Sixteenth Street clinic the entire day; on January 10 there was "Dr. Petty's Forum." But then comes the *non sequitur*: "Sister Mary died," followed by "Shop for clothes."

She had tried to dispel depression by sex, travel, Rosicrucianism, numerology; now she tried a new panacea, astrology. She subscribed to a personal daily horoscope by Evangeline Adams. On a day that her horoscope predicted would be bad, she wrote Hugh:

Today I bought the cutest little "dinky" Peter Pan hat that you ever saw. I went out on a real "bust" like I do whenever I want to break up the blues.

I was absolutely *sick* sick, way down, when I learned that Havelock did not get the (birthday) flowers. I felt like choking, beating, pushing someone—somewhere.

Havelock was perfectly dear about it, but I was *furious*. I am so spoiled you see, Hugh, that I cannot tolerate existence when I ask a thing to be done & it is not done. I need a few rebukes to cool me down perhaps.

Hugh was distressed too:

Life can be damned sad and inexplicable, Margaret. I seem to have struck a specially bad patch with publishers at getting my stuff in print. It shouldn't be so, I confess: one should just go steadily on without minding about the unpublished work—but there it is; I am afraid I resent these difficulties and am furious at set-backs. Still I do plough on, somehow. . .

On February 3, there was also a sad letter from Harold Child, though expressed in his own newspaper "light leader" style. He had been ill and overworked, and his father had recently died at ninety-two. He wanted Margaret to come back so he could hear her laugh and see her eyes twinkle. "Come soon, before I get too tired and old and stuck to be of any use to you. I was 975 years old last birthday."

The news about Harold's father sent Margaret back to her diary, this time reminiscing about her own father. "Father had stroke on Dec. 20, but pulled through. But Mary died after midnight that day. She knew she was going to die." She went on to relate another queer dream. In the dream she was walking the street with hundreds of people approaching her, including the eugenicist, Dr. Little. She smelt the strong smell of mice.

Dr. Little works among mice . . . It was queer. Two nights later Mary died. This is the second dream I have ever had when I smelled a smell and death resulted in a few days. Mary was the stable sympathetic member of a large family. Her passing looses up the foundation. A dear and loving person. A universal mother. Peace to her!

Soon Harold wrote that he was worried about a book Margaret was in the process of writing, a sex-and-marriage manual to be called *Happiness in Marriage*.

> I think it ought not to be published yet, because it would rouse more opposition than it would do good. I don't know whether you want a row just now; whether it would help or hinder B.C. These are questions no one can answer who doesn't know your country pretty well. Can you trust Juliet's opinion on these things? Evidently she is dead set against the book being published just yet.

Margaret wouldn't listen to either Harold or Juliet. She knew that Hannah Stone was about to start a series of lectures on sex and marriage, and wanted to get her book out first. So she hurried and finished it, though most of what she said was opposed to everything she believed.

For instance, she upheld the double standard that gave men sexual freedom before marriage but denied it to women. Chastity for women was a "must"; even premarital kisses were forbidden. She argued that "a girl is more attractive when modest and hard to conquer," and that "the one who is playfully elusive is bound to attract men of more sterling worth."

Her picture of the wedding night is particularly amusing:

> The ardent lover who helped his bride overcome her initial shyness by turning out the light, who gradually, step by step, removed each article of apparel, expressing his tender rapture at the revelation of each new loveliness found, who finally took her in his arms and carried her to a couch sheeted with rose petals, who then knelt beside her and told her of his abiding and undying love and adoration—of his prayer to hold his love for her above his passion—this man was sowing the seeds of undying devotion and life-long happiness.

Published in 1926, the book was received with a chill. Writing in *The Masses*, Floyd Dell criticized her sharply both for her duplicity and her gush, calling them qualities not to be expected of Margaret Sanger.

Aside from *The Masses* and the *Call*, which gave it perfunctory notices, most papers ignored *Happiness in Marriage*. The poor reception sent her spirits down.

At the same time she received a strange letter from Hugh—strange because he usually sent her unqualified declarations of love. This letter was different:

> Surely you know by now that I am a hopeless freak and never love or adore anyone. I'm not a great passionate nature—give me kindness and tenderness and truth and out of that what glories may grow! My love to you always—a queer brand of love but my own.

J. Noah soon decided to retire completely from business so as to have more time alone with Margaret. He sold the Three-in-One Oil Company to Standard Brands in exchange for stock worth four million dollars, using part of the proceeds to buy himself a seat on the New York Stock Exchange.

But retired or not, J. Noah was not to get his wife to himself. Soon she was back at her birth-control work. When her energy gave out she went to Truro to rest and visit with her father, who was seriously ill.

Ethel was taking care of Higgins in Truro, and he was proving a handful. In his eighties he was as obstinate as ever, even from a wheelchair. One day when the house was cold, and Ethel busy elsewhere, he got up out of the wheelchair and went down to the cellar for an extra bucket of coal. Ethel returned, heard him shoveling in the cellar, and ran after him. By this time he had the bucket full of coal and refused to drop it. Ethel ended up carrying him upstairs with the coal bucket still in his hand.

All this weighed on Margaret's mind. She felt, too, that her cause seemed to have run out of gas. She was enmeshed in the same round of lectures to small groups, sneaking *Family Limitation* pamphlets into the mail, and referring patients to Hannah Stone—either at the Bureau or in her office. True, she was winning a good deal of support among the wealthy and middle class, but things were moving without the splash she craved. Suddenly at a board meeting of the league, with the eugenicists telling each other for the hundredth time that birth control would eliminate disease and deformity as well as empty the jails and orphanages, she determined to stage a huge international conference on birth control and population problems as soon as possible. She chose Geneva as the site because it was the home of the League of Nations; she was sure the League of Nations would be so impressed it would take over the international work.

Yet the very effort of deciding to stage such a difficult conference gave her stomach pains. She checked into the Columbia Presbyterian Medical Center for an exploratory operation which showed she had gall stones but did not need immediate treatment. She scribbled in her diary, the repetitive phrase: "Juliet, Juliet, Juliet!" and retreated to Willowlake and bed. But soon she was up again, trying to convince J. Noah she needed her most potent anodyne—a trip to England to see Havelock and get his help with the proposed conference. J. Noah could even come along.

But J. Noah wasn't sure he wanted to go. After all, he was seventy and all this running back and forth tired him too. Then Hugh sent her a photograph of himself looking more poetic and handsome than ever. That clinched it. She would go to England, J. Noah or not, to see only Hugh and win him back.

The only problem about making the trip was money. J. Noah was sometimes generous, sometimes tight. But he was obsessed with health, both his and his wife's. And like many people of his time, he thought a "change of air" was good for everybody—sea air in particular. He would hand over money for a boat trip as a rule more readily than for anything else. Enough to travel first class, too.

So off she went to England, though this time visiting Hugh and charming him as in the old days didn't help; depression settled on her like a pall. She did no birth-control work at all that summer and returned home in bad spirits. Though J. Noah was also ready to pay for moving from their New York apartment at 39 Fifth Avenue to a more prestigious address at 230 Park Avenue, the very thought of the work involved depressed her further. On September 28 she wrote Hugh that since her return, she had been "hanging around like an apple on a tree, with no go or pep or anything." She had also been in an auto accident and hurt her spine; an osteopath was treating her—he'd fixed her lower back and shoulders, but the tubercular trouble in her neck had definitely shown up again. "It's a game of hide and seek," she told Hugh. "The husband longs for me to run off to Italy with him, get a house on the Riviera where the sun shines, but I'm too lazy and undecided even to think."

Not knowing what to do, she did the obvious. She sailed for London again in early October. Again she went without J. Noah, whom she had convinced to stay home and supervise the winter covering of the plants and shrubs at Willowlake. The flowers in her exquisite rose garden would die, she assured him, if they weren't properly protected; the deer would come down from the hills and eat her evergreens. And J. Noah, who welcomed anything that would keep him busy now that retirement hadn't proved so blissful after all, stayed home.

For a change she let Harold know she was in London, and on October 6 he humbly begged her to lunch with him. He apologized for asking her, as if he had begun to fear, from what Hugh had told him, that he couldn't hold her much longer:

Will you come to lunch (very simple) with me here on Wednesday or Thursday; or any time before the evening? *Do*. Forgive me for bothering you, but you know how much I want to see you! Dear Margaret, your Harold.

A week later he was no longer begging. She had had a long lunch with him, after which they had gone to her hotel and stayed together for a night of love. He was intoxicated again:

I walked back under the moonlight across the Park with the love of you and the thought of you and the scent and the feel of you rushing through body and soul like the very water of life. And so I went to sleep, and when I awoke I didn't have to say my prayers. I was already in the arms of God, who is Love. Margaret my own, *stay in London till the end of the month*. You came so suddenly, and love flowed out so suddenly that we haven't been able to plan things as we should. *Stay, stay, stay*. Dear, I can't say what I feel. Words won't do it. So I'll shut up.

Hugh, whom she also saw on this trip, was humble as well. He wrote from Sand Pit to her London hotel telling how his knees would quake if ever he found her "too grand and glorious. Poor little frightened Andrew Ant (a name Hugh used for himself)—you would be kind to him, wouldn't you? And not stand on your toes and lorgnette him from the midst of the latest Parisian confection!" Then, more seriously: "I plod on, not really discouraged, having the faith of darlings like you. I perpetually pray to write *a good book*. One musn't complain about the way in which one's prayer is answered."

Margaret responded by giving Hugh all the faith she could, though she couldn't stop him from being jealous of successful writers like

H. G. Wells: "I want to hear you laugh," Hugh wrote. In another note he said: "It is an awful obsession—this wanting to hear you laugh. I think I ought to be analyzed and be free from it, and be nice and normal like H. G. Wells or any other of your grand friends. Real he-men! Sweaty beggars! Never mind!"

At the end of October Margaret sailed for home, even though it meant passing up an invitation to Wells' country place to meet some prestigious people who might be useful to her cause. She probably sailed because an even more tempting opportunity awaited her—a luncheon in New York from a woman she called in her diary "Queen Marie Romaina." She took J. Noah along to impress him, as a queen was certainly a Big Name.

Her diary entry for November 6, the anniversary of Peggy's death, is almost unreadable. That day, and the week following, she stayed in bed and mourned, emerging only for a meeting on the planned international conference at which "Mrs. Selzburger" (probably Mrs. Arthur Sulzberger, wife of the publisher of *The New York Times*) was another Big Name guest.

"My father married the whirlwind," Grant Sanger used to say. He was right. Her mourning for Peggy over, she went right back to England to see Hugh, Wells, and Havelock. This time J. Noah went along, flatly refusing to stay home alone any more. But she persuaded him to go to Paris for a while as "the season" was in full swing in Paris, and from there to the Riviera to catch some sunshine for his health. Since she was planning to stay abroad for several months in order to get the Geneva conference underway, she also suggested he look for a villa on the Riviera for them to rent for the winter.

Once in England she rushed down to Little Frieth near London to see Havelock, but since in her excitement she had forgotten to tell him she was coming, he had left for Cornwall. So she hurried to the Mayfair Hotel and immediately wrote a mollifying letter to her husband: "Dearest Noah. Darling. It is really always lonely to be away from you for even one day."

On December 7, she wrote him again:

> Dearest love: This is a busy day . . . I had lunch with Julian Huxley and got from him his ideas and found him deeply interested and willing to help in a limited way . . . I may have to go to Edinburgh and I will have to go to Cambridge. I am glad you are

not here! I can work better and get things done quicker when I can concentrate all my energies and time like this than to do otherwise.

She *could* concentrate and work better without J. Noah. She enjoyed having him fuss over her health, but only up to a point. She became furious when he told her to go to sleep when she wanted to stay awake; to wake up when she wanted to sleep; not smoke because it was bad for her lungs when it was a cigarette she craved. As she had once confessed to Grant when she was ill and away from home: "Don't tell Pater I'm not well because he will come flying down here, and you know how that nervous old dear grates on my nerves."

On December 9, she took the time to write her husband a long, thoughtful letter:

> There is much fear on the part of the Scientists that I have come too late to get help, that I should have been getting them started to work on this last October. There is genuine willingness to help me, but a fine honesty in the English which refuses to take on what they cannot do well. It makes me almost sick when I think of it, for Dr. Raymond Pearl told me I should have come sooner or it would be too late. You see Noah dear, all my life I have acted on an inner voice & when that speaks to me it speaks wisely and never fails me.
>
> When I disobey it for one reason or the other, I always suffer. If only I could help you to believe this & help you to understand it, you would, I know, add to it your splendid powers & make everything I do a glorious success. But when we put our own man made minds against God's will & God's advice then disruption & disaster results somewhere. It will be a busy week next & I shall hope to have seen every worthwhile Scientist in England. I will then decide if I can do the Conference anyway.
>
> The sun shines here today. It is not cold & I am well. I love you dear one, you know, & I will write you a loving letter later.

Loving letters or no, J. Noah was so angered by her absences that he stopped writing her. For a change, she became worried. Still, after spending Christmas and most of January with her husband at the Villa Bachlyk—a beautiful eight-room villa between Nice and Monte Carlo with a spectacular view of the Mediterranean—Margaret went back to London to continue her work on the conference, while J. Noah, reluctantly, stayed on alone. Her letters start again from the Stafford Hotel on February 1, 1927.

I have been deeply depressed today & yesterday over the affairs here. I know that were I free to work & keep on the job I could put over a conference that would astound the world—BUT—here I am, interests divided & diverted and I cannot know what to do. The movement now needs one dominating force to drive it to success. The interest is alive, the time is ripe, but I shall need to give time to it if it is to succeed. No one else can do it, so·it seems. It will crown my past efforts & repay my sacrifices to see this Conference a success. Will you help me? Not by money, darling one, but by seeing this thing eye to eye with me & giving me the time I need to work it up properly. I know how hard it is for you to let me be away from you & I shall try to arrange it so there shall be few separations, but there must be some and unless you say you can help me, I will not go on.

You have done so much to help me make it the success it has become, that I believe you will help me again—forever. I can never believe that you have come into my life to hold me back, you who are so vigorous & glorious in your love and splendid in your ideals and generosity! You have helped others to attain their life's work, you have given support and inspiration to others you love less, and I believe with all my heart, with all my faith that you will help me to victory and success. My heart is sad, but yours.

Obviously the course Margaret had taken at Claverack in "epistolary communication" was standing her in good stead.

The question remains, however: How much did J. Noah know of the real reason for her long stays in England and her insistence on keeping him away? Had he resigned himself to honoring indefinitely his marriage agreement to let her come and go at will, asking no questions, and being content with the little he received?

How much, too, was Margaret deceiving herself, believing that all her hard work had no other purpose than to advance her cause? Did she realize that the admiration and flattery she received from men and women everywhere were vital factors to her? How well did she understand herself?

In 1926, perhaps in an effort toward self-understanding, she began to search for an epitaph. She found it years later when she chose a verse by Arthur Guiterman called "Harlequin," and marked it "For my tombstone."

It read:

This body, now a gallant robe, is frayed:
I must withdraw a while to put it by
And don a new, wherein I'll masquerade
So well that none will guess that I am I.

THE CONFERENCE THAT HURT

When Margaret arrived at the Villa Bachlyk to spend Christmas of 1926 with her husband, she invited Hugh to be their guest.

In the twenties, the French Riviera was full of writers, poets, and painters who thought it the most glorious place in the world. Margaret, J. Noah, and Hugh were soon caught up in its excitement. They took long drives on the Grand Corniche, ate at the most deluxe restaurants, gambled at Monte Carlo, bet on horse races, drank magnums of champagne, and altogether had unforgettable weeks.

Hugh even ingratiated himself with his host. One morning as J. Noah was emerging from his bathroom, Hugh placed a wreath of lemon-vine leaves fresh from the garden on his head, dubbing him "the poet in blue pajamas." After that J. Noah was sure that Hugh was a charming gentleman, impractical or not.

Hugh pleased Margaret as well by finding out how much money Françoise earned and arranging to pay her an equal amount from Margaret, so she could devote herself full time to Havelock.

Back in London, Hugh received a letter from Françoise that showed both her gratitude to Margaret and the fact that she had not gotten over her feelings for him. "Big Brother." Françoise wrote:

I am not dead. Only too many beautiful things are happening.

It almost makes me ill. So excuse silence and silly letters. I will see you *soon*.

The fact that through Margaret I may give up my post at Easter, giving notice next week on Havelock's birthday . . . I can't be articulate. I will explain when I see you. I am knocked silly. It is all *through you too*. Life is too much at times. So this is my poor love, rather silly, stunned. Still! La Petite Soeur.

Ellis also thanked Margaret, but he put his literary efforts into his books; his letters, especially now that he was getting older, tended to be brief and rather businesslike. Besides, he was so shy that generosity and praise bothered him, and at the moment, he was at the height of his fame. Two laudatory biographies of him had recently been published, bringing him letters from all over the world. Margaret's offer, even though made through Françoise, made him hesitate at first. Then he capitulated, and wrote her with more fervor than he had done for a long time. Margaret wrote Hugh a glowing letter. "Hugh old thing—darling—the King accepts the secretary. Now isn't he a lamb?"

Yet in spite of her love for Havelock, she was upset when she read that he had made some derogatory remarks in public about Jews and Americans. She wrote Hugh:

It shocked me to have *him* speak in that way. A real shock—an inside thing jumped and left me sad. After all is said, it was in Puritanical Philadelphia that his studies were published. And in America by Americans and Jews, too, that his works were and are most appreciated . . . I know he appreciates this fact, and doubtless his sentence was written in one of those moods when he likes to be considered "smart" in the sense of being in the "push" or in line . . .

Then she returned to an old theme: wouldn't Hugh write her biography, "The Life of Margaret Sanger the Typical American—no Irish, too, to make it worse."

Hugh once more was smart enough to decline. True, he needed whatever profit it might bring, but he knew he was not the man for the task.

Margaret and J. Noah celebrated the New Year of 1927 at the Suvretta House in St. Moritz, skating, skiing, and eating, for Margaret liked good food and wine as much as J. Noah did. Indeed it was one of the few enthusiasms they had in common and they had chosen to stay at the Suvretta House because it was famous for its international cuisine. There Margaret indulged herself in her favorite foods, especially caviar, to her soul's content, and washed them down with endless bottles of the champagne that made her laugh.

Yet, as often in the midst of gaiety, her mood changed quickly. On January 17, she recorded in her diary a frightening dream:

> Dreamed last night that a large glossy, spotted snake lay full length in my bed, head up, looking defiantly at me. I looked for a weapon and found a large *saw* which I took and struck at him with, but alas struck the baby who was in the bed—hurt it severely—cut him. The snake glided away—the baby cut and in a fever. I awakened anxious and worried.

Ellis had written a book on dreams, and she was now more eager than ever to see him, both to celebrate his birthday and talk about her anxiety. She planned to leave for London alone as soon as possible, sending J. Noah on to the Villa Bachlyk at Cap d'Ail. As a further inducement, she added that she would also try to get Ellis a series of lectures in the States so that he could earn some big money. "I shall begin rounding up a proper agent as soon as I get home . . . one who takes on *Important Englishmen*."

She stopped her packing long enough to write Hugh, and beg him again to write her life, adding a few glimpses of what he would discover to entice him.

> Yes, you will write the life—I shall begin to toss things together for you as they come along. Won't you be shocked to know me really!! How I smothered my innocent little sister with a pillow when ever my mother left us alone! Goodness, but you will shudder. How I stole money to buy flowers to put at the feet of the Virgin Mary! Oh—oh—what fun we shall have. You must promise not to publish it while I live—or at least while I am young enough to care.

Margaret arrived in London and saw Hugh and Havelock immediately. Hugh again declined to write her biography, and Havelock cautiously interpreted her frightening dream. Actually, he might have told her the dream could be symbolic of castrating a male child, possibly one of her sons, as the snake in psychiatry is equated with the penis. But knowing how much this would upset her, he said it was another of her "distressing night thoughts," and let it go at that.

Reassured, she plunged energetically into work on her conference, planning a trip to Paris to round up French delegates. She wrote J. Noah:

> The flu is raging in London and I am taking all precautions against it. I am trying to push things here so I can leave for Paris Sunday or Monday. I must have a preliminary meeting of the Conference Council and these busy people lecture at universities and are engaged months ahead in their work. Someone has got to put time and intelligence into the thing or it stops. Huxley said yesterday, "You are wasting your time if you think we can go on without your constant direction. It won't go with less and if you can't do that you had better not attempt it at all." So there it is.

From Paris she wrote:

> . . . I went to an expert on headaches and several of them agree that my hair is absorbing all my strength. Do you think you could stand it if I had it cut? I'll await until Tuesday to hear and if I have courage I'll go ahead . . . Mrs. Jones and Mrs. Delafield (Acting President and Vice-President of the American Birth Control League during her absence) are greatly upset because you have cut down the *Birth Control Review* (money) to $300 a month. They think it is hard on them!! I think Paris is lovely tonight, tho' wet and not too lively. I wonder why we live in the U.S.A. at all!!! It is nearly midnight . . . I'd like to have a long talk to you on the Conference. I've simply got to dig in and take hold. It's such a burden to carry, but I can make it if you will help me. No one can take your place in this world . . .
>
> I attended a lecture on Population by Jean Bourdon (lecturer at the Sorbonne and Director of International Studies at the Medical Musée) and have my eye on him for the Conference. If only I spoke French I could help to change public opinion here!! I must

wait to see the man with the flu, and if he can see me Wednesday,
then I'll have started something here anyway . . .

It will be heaven to see you . . . I'll be home soon and make
you as happy as you make me.

Soon she was on her way to Cap d'Ail to spend a few days with
J. Noah. There she received the shocking news that she was no longer
president of the American Birth Control League. She had been away so
long that the league, unsure when or whether she would return, had
elected Mrs. F. Robertson-Jones president for the current year. Margaret was beyond herself with rage over the defeat, but tried to pass it off
lightly: "I can devote more time to play and J. N. and to you," she wrote
Hugh.

She left for Geneva alone a week later to arrange for a conference
hall and accommodations for the hundreds of delegates and secretaries
who would attend. This done, she hurried back to Cap d'Ail for a few
days, then to Paris once more. From there she wrote Hugh:

Hugh, dear—Paris is cold. I am *discouraged*. Not because the
Conference does not go faster, but because I am so torn between
the things I want to do. Harold did not come to the train (the last
time I left England) and I was blue and horrid. Of course I realize
that one with only one idea like myself should shut myself up in a
convent and never come out! Attractive minds like Harold's get
no stimulation from mine, and all the darling can do is *listen* to
my prattle . . . I shall miss you horribly at the Villa at Cap
d'Ail. I have no right to miss you but I shall just the same!!"

Grant, now nineteen and a premedical student, missed her too. In
February she received a series of letters from him. In one he said he'd
heard she had bobbed her hair, and if she hadn't she shouldn't because
she was too old. The last word was underlined, which she didn't like a
bit.

Another letter called her ridiculous for expecting him to remember
how he'd spent his pre-Christmas allowance. He'd kept accounts for a
month and showed them to Pater who had a fit because they were fifty-
eight cents off; without a doubt her younger son was going to the dogs.
But if she and Pater insisted on spending their winters three thousand
miles way on the Riviera, what was he to do?

On May 31st his tone changed. He doubled-headed his letter PEG-

GY'S BIRTHDAY and admitted he had been depressed all day. He was also worried about whether Margaret was coming home for Christmas. He had heard both that she was and was not.

In her answer Margaret dodged his complaints and tried to placate him in her usual way—sending him money. She added that he should be sure to hear Toscanini "as he is a genius, and music becomes spiritual beauty under his direction." She also became motherly enough to remind him to wear his fur coat at football games so he wouldn't catch cold. She didn't say a word about Christmas, as she had no intention of coming home. The Geneva conference was too much on her mind.

In April, after more conference-planning trips to London and Paris, she and J. Noah closed the Villa Bachlyk and set off to Geneva to open permanent headquarters there.

At first she was intoxicated with Geneva, reporting to Hugh:

> I have had my hands kissed by every nation of Europe and Asia except Italy (whose ambitions are not ordinary). I got close contacts with Mussolini and have now decided never to live in U.S.A. longer than I can help it. I adore Geneva!! One grows and expands there and lives but does *not* grow fat.

Still, news of trouble in Pennsylvania upset her. Dr. Stuart Mudd, who was battling to have the local Comstock law repealed, had at first been promised help by Dr. James J. Heffernan, a member of the Pennsylvania legislature. When Heffernan received countermanding orders from his Cardinal, he began to lobby against the bill, calling it "the abortion bill." Heffernan claimed the bill was sponsored by druggists who wanted to sell more contraceptives and by the Ku Klux Klan. Dr. Mudd was sure Margaret could have scotched such accusations with stirring speeches and well-placed publicity, but he could not.

Margaret was having romantic trouble too. She had not heard from Harold for a long time, and when she did, his letters were disturbing. For the first time he was questioning the ethics of their relationship. Hugh was her confidant as always:

> Harold is a difficult darling . . . Comes the question: shall we let (our love) be known? That in the negative seems to disturb Englishmen and delight American women. We like the secrecy.

We like keeping the secret until it grows out beyond our holding it back.

Then always foolish men will bring up the husband. "He should know—I don't like taking something which belongs to him. He's a decent fellow and it's rotten of us to butt-in, etc., etc." All nonsense and spoils everything this babble. Too much talk and too little feeling spoils romance.

As if this wasn't enough, the entire board of the ABCL (American Birth Control League) had become angry with Margaret. They did not think international work was their function; they were having enough trouble raising money for work in the States without taking that on too.

As usual when emotionally disturbed, Margaret got ill, this time with more pounding headaches. She decided to make a quick trip to New York to try to settle matters with ABCL. Sailing with J. Noah on the *Olympic* on May 22, 1927, she wired Grant that they were coming. He wired back: "Will be home this weekend. All hopes, prayers, dreams and love."

Arriving in New York, she learned that Bill Sanger had recently remarried. His wife, Vidia, had been a member of the Provincetown Players but Bill made her quit, announcing he would have no more "career women" in his household. To ease her various aches, Margaret began toying with a new religious cult called *Unity* which advertised for the first time that summer in the *Review*. Unity described itself as a "mental treatment that was guaranteed to cure every ill the flesh is heir to."

She put off joining Unity, however, until after she returned to Geneva in July. The conference dates had finally been set for August 31 through September 3. With her assistant, Anne Kennedy, a redoubtable woman who had long been active in the cause, she now started vigorously planning the publicity without which the whole Geneva affair would mean nothing.

First, however, she would run back to England to see Hugh, as she found being on the European continent too tantalizingly near to resist seeing him again. At the last minute, however, she almost changed her plan in favor of a visit to Wells. Wells had told her how he had been staying in Grasse near the Villa Bachlyck with a young woman named Odette Kuhn who fell in love with him sight unseen, through his writings, and invited him to visit her, naming an evening. Unable to resist any woman who promised the excitement of what, at sixty, he still called "the glittering black magic of sex," he had gone to her house and found it quite dark. When he knocked, a voice had called "come in." He soon found himself in a bedroom which was almost completely dark, though he could make out a form lying in bed. "Get in," the voice commanded, and there in the blackness, without either having so much as glimpsed the other, they immediately made love.

"I didn't care if he was fat or thin, a giant or a pygmy," Odette had told friends. "I wanted him at any cost." He had been staying with her on and off for a year, describing her to Margaret as "an interesting Levantine writer who adores me and is a little too desperate to be jealous." Some time ago he had invited Margaret to Grasse, calling her, "My dearly beloved," and adding, "Please keep this address a perfect secret as almost no one else knows I am here."

Margaret hadn't answered Wells' invitation because she was too busy with her conference. Now just as she was about ready to accept, Wells wrote her canceling the date; he was leaving for London because:

> my little wife has to die of cancer & I want to spend what time remains of her life with her . . . My wife's illness came upon us all very suddenly. I left her in London not three weeks ago, smiling & alert, but looking a little tired. Then came an X-ray examination & this . . . Odette will keep on with the home, but I shall have to leave her very much alone for a time. Come to see her if you pass this way again.

So Margaret went to England to see Hugh. When he heard she was coming he wrote her in his effusive way: "Darling Lovely Pet. How I rejoice that you are coming! Be forever blessed! I'm bivvering to know if I shall like your hair. I did so adore your great rolls. Oh joy! Oh joy! Margaret is coming." He arranged music-and-poetry evenings, nights of sleeping on the lawn at Sand Pit as they had at Wantley, and told his best stories to make her laugh. Still, she sensed that something was troubling him.

Back in Geneva, she wrote him:

> I recognize you as one of my adolescent dreams, the man I looked for in books—on the stage—but never found. Always you

send out *Beauty*. I was amazed at that fact when I first felt the thrill of you on the way from the (London) station years ago. What is it lovely one that troubles you? What friendship? Do I know him or her? That is why I am so happy in a cause, Hugh. All the world of human beings are a passing show. They come and go—but the ideal of human freedom grows ever closer around one's heart and comforts and consoles and delights. Oh Hugh! Do send me word that you are not troubled or grieved at the loss of a friend. New ones come as old ones fulfill their places in our lives—that's all. Let go in order to get seems to be the Law. My love to you. *Ever and Ever Amen.*

After this, as time was getting short, she paid strict attention to the business of the conference. At the last minute, she couldn't get the man she most wanted, Lord Dawson of Penn, to chair her conference. So, possibly impressed both by his title and the fact that his wife was a Lady in Waiting to the Queen, she got Sir Bernard Mallet instead. Mallet was correct as only a minor British lord can be, complete to monocle, waxed mustache, jaunty cane, and gray spats. Although Margaret did not agree with him on the speakers, the central theme of the conference, or, indeed, on anything, she took him on in desperation. She did get Julian Huxley and John Maynard Keynes to agree to come as English delegates, and she also persuaded Dr. F. A. E. Crew of Edinburgh University, a man whose hormone experiments in making hens crow like roosters were making headlines, to come from Scotland. From America she got Dr. C. C. Little, President of the University of Michigan, Professor Henry P. Fairchild of New York University, and Professor Raymond Pearl of Johns Hopkins. It began to look like an impressive list.

She was less successful in getting the men she wanted from countries like Spain, Italy, and Germany. The Siamese Minister in Geneva, though known to be interested in eugenics, graciously declined. Margaret wrote across his note: "From a charming Prince, father of eighty children."

Serious trouble about the subject matter of the conference began brewing in mid-August. Dr. William Welch of Johns Hopkins, another delegate from the United States, warned Margaret:

*   *   *

You may think everything is settled but it isn't. Sir Bernard Mallet has undercut your invitation to liberal Italians like Guglielmo Ferrero, and allowed the Fascist government to substitute the arch-conservative Corrado Gini instead. The same thing is happening in Spain, Belgium, France, and Catholic Germany. Sir Bernard wants no confrontation on the crucial issue of birth control.

Still another blow was to come. A few days before the August thirty-first opening, the proofs of the official conference program came in. Margaret had put her name on the front page in bold type as the chief organizer, followed by the names of her associates. As she was reading the proofs, Sir Bernard leaned over her shoulder, picked up a pencil and crossed out all the women's names, including her own. They did not belong on the program, he insisted; only the names of the actual delegates should be there.

He may have been technically right. Conferences of this kind are usually organized by scientific bodies or drug houses, not by individuals. But there was no scientific association or drug house in the world in 1927 which would have organized a population meeting. Besides, Margaret had raised the money; she had done the spadework; she had garnered most of the delegates. No matter who she was or what her status, she argued that it was unthinkable that her name be kept off.

Sir Bernard countered that her name was far too well known in connection with birth control to be used. In fact, the term birth control would probably not be mentioned directly at all, because if it was, the whole conference might fall through.

Margaret was livid, but she knew when she was beaten. Her entire staff threatened to resign in protest, but she persuaded them to stay, and she did win a compromise that her name be listed in the final printed record of the proceedings as a member of the general council.

There was still another temporary setback. On the day of the opening session she had set up a table in the lobby of the conference hall on which any delegate could display a book he had written. Naturally some of these were on birth control. The men from the Catholic countries created a scene by demanding loudly that these books be removed. But this time Margaret stood firm, with the imposing J. Noah at her side. "This hall is for rent next week," she declared. "Meanwhile, we will take no dictation from anyone as to what shall be displayed here."

The table remained as arranged.

From then on things proceeded smoothly. Not only had the liberal Lord Dawson of Penn joined the speakers from Great Britain, but Lord Horden and Dean Inge had done the same. These men read papers arguing that their country needed fewer people, though at Mallet's insistence, they didn't say how this was to be brought about. These papers helped offset those read by delegates from the conservative countries, Italy and Germany, which declared that they needed more people. Surprisingly, the French delegates came out against limitation of population too. Most French men practiced birth control in private, but since France was nominally a Catholic country, they refused to endorse it in public. When the French paper was read, Margaret could do nothing but listen and grind her teeth.

She felt better when, at the closing banquet, Sir Bernard stood up and congratulated her for her superb organization, and the entire assembly of some eight-hundred delegates and visitors followed him in rising to hail her. The Englishmen burst into the traditional "For She's a Jolly Good Fellow," while the Europeans who understood hardly a word of the song, knew only that it was a gay tune, something to bang spoons to.

Although she was very excited at having pulled off a prestigious meeting, and Albin E. Johnson, the *New York World's* Geneva correspondent to the League of Nations, had been gracious enough to play up the full name she had given it: *The Sixth International Birth-Control and Neo-Malthusian Conference*, still, the delegates from the League of Nations had not, as she hoped, been impressed.

Nevertheless, ready to go back to work, she packed J. Noah off to England and stayed behind to edit the proceedings. Her diary reflects the highly nervous state in which she was functioning. As she believed in astrology more strongly than ever, she was convinced that part of what had gone wrong was due to the fact that she had not listened to its voice.

On August 21, 22, and 23 her diary records: "Careful."

On August 24: "Poor period."

On August 26 and 27: "Strenuous criticism."

On September 11 through 15: "Start nothing new."

On September 16,17, and 18: "Careful, careful, careful."
On September 20: A rare "Good, good."
On September 29, 30, October 1: "Heavenly rest."
On October 7: "In bed all day."
On October 8: "Depressed."
Her letters to J. Noah mirrored her feelings: On September 21, she wrote him:

I have been under great tension & high pressure. What a woman needs is to be alone, absolutely alone with God for a few days or weeks, until she has filled up the reservoir of her soul again with faith, hope & courage. I have been impatient I know and really horrid at times. You have been tired and disappointed so I should have been kinder & dearer to you than ever, but I was too unhappy to be anything but miserable. Now I shall get the papers to the printers & then go to the mountain top alone & meditate & think. I need solitude as much as food & I thank you for making it possible at this time. . .

On September 27, she wrote him again:

Are you thinking about us and our future? I am. It is not all clear sailing yet, I'm afraid, because we are so much alike and yet so different. It is our interests that are so wide apart. There are none that you have that I can take up so as to bring us into closer harmony, and you do not like me to expand my own. Yet there is all the attraction between us that the world counts essential & necessary. It's really complicated.

My heart is troubled to have you lonely & apart from life's activities but I should wither up & die to be shut off from the intellectual currents of my contemporaries. All I want is a little more freedom. That is not much to ask, but I must be able to feel that I can waste a whole night or day or week if I feel it good for me to do so without explanation or asking. I'm too grown up & too developed to not be free. My actions so far have been tempered with intelligence & I can't go back to chattel slavery. For that is what it really is dear when a woman is not made to feel that she can act without asking her husband's consent. Outside of financial affairs (which is & should be a joint affair between them) there should be utter liberty for both parties to enjoy tastes & friendships utterly free from the other. You will never see this I am certain, but until you can see it there will be no real happiness for the modern woman. If you could only be made to see what riches a woman can bring into your life, not only in outside forces but in the joyousness of her own being when she is fully conscious that freedom & love, faith & respect are the foundation of her marriage.

I know darling Noah that one must not expect you to plunge into the depths of these thoughts but think them over now & then & talk about them to me & we will make our future. . . I want·to make your every day one of golden sunsets . . . Those are my desires. I worry because I am failing (in them) so I am analyzing the causes which underlie the problem. Now you can write me just as you think & what you feel about the difficulties. It will help me to see the other side. Devotedly & lovingly ever & ever—no matter what we say.

This unusually articulate letter is the closest she had yet come to a statement of her personal credo.

Slee answered wondering whether she would ever be at peace, then became irritable and said he obviously wasn't as young and spry as she was and so couldn't keep up with her. She countered tartly by reminding him he was seventy-two and might as well make the best of things and not try.

Any husband would undoubtedly have provoked Margaret, as well as been provoked by her, even her adored Hugh. The best part about her relationship with her lovers was that they were in the main far away; she could take them or leave them as she pleased. It was she who controlled the relationship. It was lucky that her plan to have Hugh at Willowlake for an extended period to write her biography had fallen through; otherwise, she might never have maintained the passion for him she continued to have for the next twenty years, even after he had cooled.

Alone in London, J. Noah's patience had by now completely run out. He knew no one there, owned all the made-to-order suits, coats, and hats he could possibly use, and had no interest whatever in museums or high culture. (In all his careful records of expenditures, there is only one mention of a book.) He became so persistent that Margaret realized she had little choice except to give in and join him in Paris.

In Paris they went to the races and ate in the best restaurants, J. Noah posing jovially in front of an outdoor cafe in his new finery, and Margaret looking absent-minded and sad. She soon persuaded him to visit Zurich, while she hurried back for the nth time to see Hugh in London. After a luxurious lunch of sole, grouse, and wine at the Mayfair, she got from him a rather cool note of thanks:

I have visited Havelock and he is beginning to like me again, though Françoise is in a black swamp of misery because I didn't love her and she didn't know me, though of course you know I don't love anybody. I only enjoy being in the presence of people I'm fond of; a maddening sort of impossible male, as impossible to catch and hold and have as a smell.

A few days later she joined J. Noah in Germany, in part to fulfill a speaking engagement with the Society of German Medical Women, in part to vacation some more. In Germany, feeling chipper because she was doing what she knew how to do best—lecture—she had a saucy picture taken with J. Noah in front of the castle of Frederick the Great. On the back of it she scribbled, "Not bad this cottage. He was a great old boy, had a special room for Voltaire which shows his good taste and free mind." After this came a train ride back to the Suvretta House at St. Moritz to celebrate another Christmas.

Her Christmas letter to Hugh was nostalgic:

Never shall I forget the glory of the Villa Bachlyk with you there. It was like a dream. Do you remember the dull day when I had a tantrum? Several days I have had the same thing. It's a slump. J. N. is so patient. I am never well when loafing more than 2 or 3 days.

Her letter to Grant was mainly dutiful.

When this letter reaches you it will be 1928. We both wish you a happy & joyous & fruitful New Year.
We attended the Ice Carnival today, and as I have taken to skating, all their tricks and turns are more wonderful than ever. I am keen to learn how you enjoyed your holidays & especially to

hear just where you and Stuart went. It will soon be time to think of returning. But just now time hangs heavy on my hands. I am no good as a loafer.

Then, despite her protestations she proceeded to loaf some more. To regain the energy that the conference had depleted, she settled in at the Suvretta House with her husband for another two carefree months.

BITTER BATTLES

Margaret celebrated the year's end at the Suvretta House. After an exhilarating sleigh ride, she dressed in the new silks and sapphires J. Noah had given her and danced and feasted through Christmas Eve. On New Year's Eve she reveled in a letter from Hugh that referred again to J. Noah as "a poet crowned with blue flowers in striped silk pajamas."

Noah was so impressed he answered in kind: "My dear Poet," he wrote on January 11, returning to a persistent theme, "would you like to write my Margy's life? But there are so many angles. Do you mean to write biographical or about her work? I am so very ignorant of literary efforts. My mind is entirely commercial."

Hugh replied as usual that he would think about it, so J. Noah and Margaret continued to dance, feast, and sleigh ride until February 15, when they had had enough of the mountains and set off for Zurich, Paris, and London. Finally, they sailed for home on the *Ile de France*, landing in New York on March 13. Grant, Stuart, and J. Noah's three children were waiting on the dock.

They had been away for eighteen months.

It was another two weeks before Margaret got around to visiting the Research Bureau. For ten days, she came in every morning, then retreated to Willowlake and bed rest in the afternoon.

Life at Willowlake was luxurious. There were nine servants, including a chamber maid, laundress, butler, chef, chauffeur, head gardener, and two assistant gardeners. Margaret still had her private apartment, making a retreat to bed afternoons and dinner alone later, both easy and delightful.

As soon as she was feeling her oats she began a bitter battle with American Birth Control League (ABCL), especially with Mrs. Ellen Robertson-Jones, the new acting president. The bone of contention between them was the fact that Mrs. Jones, a woman with long-time experience as a member of the League of Women Voters had been trying to put the league on a sound financial basis, instituting yearly dues of ten dollars instead of relying on haphazard donations. In addition, every disbursement over five dollars was to go through the treasurer; there were to be no more big expenditures jotted down as "petty cash." These changes, Mrs. Jones said, were necessary because the league's bank balance, always in a precarious state, was especially low at the moment. It ran both the Research Bureau and the *Review* at a loss, and now was being asked to foot a significant portion of the bill for the Geneva conference as well. Margaret countered by speaking of "the apathy that comes from a fat bank balance," and insisted that she alone should control the ABCL funds; as she was the chief money raiser, she should be the sole money dispenser—with no questions asked.

The battle came to a head over a small matter. An ABCL booth had been engaged for a propaganda display at a Parents League exhibition to be held at Grand Central Palace in New York. William Shea, the Catholic Superintendent of Schools, heard that the birth-control group was to have a booth and threatened to pull out his booth unless theirs was canceled. Hearing this, without notifying the ABCL board, Margaret rushed to a lawyer and offered him a substantial fee to get an injunction against the entire Parents League exhibit. The ABCL board members insisted that since they would have to pay the lawyer's fee, they should have been consulted. Margaret defended her right to act on her own. She went ahead further, and rented space for an exhibit in a building across the street from Grand Central Palace, again saying the ABCL would foot the bill. The board was furious and asked for her resignation as president, though it would let her continue as a member if she chose.

She resigned as president at once, claiming with veiled sarcasm that she was sure they would do very well without her. True, she admitted she was accused of being a fanatic, but "what some call fanaticism is never dangerous to the life of an organization such as this one. Apathy and languid convictions are."

The ABCL ignored her rude remark and proposed a compromise. Margaret would manage the Research Bureau, while they would run the *Review* under professional management.

This so infuriated Margaret that she wrote the ABCL saying she was not only quitting entirely, but taking with her a group of social-ites, including Mrs. Frances Ackerman, Mrs. Walter Timme, and Mrs. Thomas Hepburn—all of whom had not only called her "our beloved leader" and "a singing symbol," but insisted they would be happy to follow her wherever she went. Slee gave the league a gift of a few hundred dollars, vowing it was his last. It was almost the last of the league as well. Deprived in one stroke of Margaret's growing fame and Slee's contributions, it never fully recovered.

Geared for fight, Margaret waged still another battle in 1928. This fight was with Mary Sumner Boyd, the regular assistant editor of the *Review*, but editor-in-chief during Margaret's absence. Out of the fifty thousand heartrending letters received by the Bureau during the past few years, Mrs. Boyd had, at Margaret's suggestion, selected a few hundred for a book to be called *Motherhood in Bondage*. Due for publication in 1928, the book contained letters like these:

I was married when a girl of only 17. There were 13 children of us. My father always drunk and we had to go to work very young, myself when I was 11 years old caring for the boarders in a large boarding house. I am now only 21, and already have four children. How can I stop?

I have been married eight years. My first child was only a six months baby. She lived three days, born in July and the next January I had a miscarriage. The next January a little boy was born; in about four months another miscarriage, and then the next January 27 another girl; 21 months and a boy who is now two years old; and I have had two miscarriages since then. I never had a chance to regain my real strength. When my second child was born I said then if I was ever that way again I would commit suicide. I'm almost ready to do it now.

* * *

Others spoke of being the mother of ten children after twenty pregnancies, or of having delivered fifteen children, only to have eleven die
during the first year.

"I just want to rest," one woman summed up her life. "I want one
night's real sleep before I die."

All the letters were not tragic, to be sure. A few were humorous (one
woman asked for another diaphragm because she had hidden hers in
the barn and the cow had eaten it), but most were pitiful pleas from
women truly in bondage to their fertility. Mrs. Boyd had culled the
best and edited them with great care. The battle began when she asked
Margaret to give her credit on the title page, or at least a thank you in
the preface. Margaret argued that since Mrs. Boyd had been paid for
her time, nothing more was due her. When *Motherhood in Bondage*
was published merely as "by Margaret Sanger," Mrs. Boyd was under-
standably aggrieved.

The book did not sell well in any event. A few heartrending letters
sprinkled between articles in the *Review* were highly effective. They
were equally effective when Margaret included them in her speeches,
holding up the original handwritten copies and adding dramatically,
"What an orgy of agony!" But a whole volume of them was deadening.
It merely gave Margaret one more title to add to her list of publications, plus several thousand unsold copies to mail out for propaganda
purposes.

Meanwhile she complained to Havelock: "Mrs. Boyd has a martyr
complex and her inflated ego had gone to its limit. Politics, jealousy,
selfishness, desire for glory and power, kill the spirit always." It was a
fine example of projection, since it was Margaret's own ego that had
caused the fight.

She summed up her feelings in her diary: "I'm left weak with the
sadness of it." Reacting in what was now her typical way, she became
ill and retreated to Truro for a long summer of rest.

At the same time, Juliet went off to Mexico with her husband, taking
a house near the Dwight Morrows, parents of Anne Morrow Lind-
bergh. The two women wrote each other often, usually about diets
which they undertook to "purify their systems." Some of these diets
were odd indeed, like one which consisted of nothing but lettuce, spin-
ach, and soup. Juliet wondered whether two weeks on nothing but water wouldn't be even more helpful; she had heard of a place in England
where people went for water diets which made them feel wonderful.

But Juliet, like Hugh, could be practical on occasion. She saw a chance to do Margaret an important favor: to get her the support of a foundation that would give regular contributions to the cause, and thus lessen her dependence on haphazard donations.

Margaret had worked for this for years, applying to one foundation after another, only to be turned down. But in August 1928 Juliet succeeded; she persuaded the Brush Foundation to promise a definite yearly sum.

Charles Brush was a wealthy uncle of Juliet's whose son had died the year before. The young man had been interested in scientific research, and his father had set up a publishing trust in his memory. The trust had published a few papers on child development, but the bulk of the money was untouched. Juliet heard that her uncle was becoming interested in population problems, and wrote Margaret immediately.

My uncle asked what you thought would be the best thing to do with about 25 or 30 thousand a year. I said that I thought the most important part of the work was to establish clinics, as the real aim of the movement was to give immediate help to the women who needed it and also thereby help save the world from the menace of the hordes of the defectives. He said he thought so too. I told him there were about 22 states that had no laws against them, and clinics could be established at once if we had the money to send out the workers and get them started. He pointed out that there were thousands of women on farms who could not be reached by clinics but only by mail, and that we must continue to work to get the law changed. So telegraph at once about the $25,000 and the best use for it. Love! Health! Wealth! Juliet.

Margaret was elated; a plump bank balance was just what she wanted. And, another important matter had been mentioned by Charles Brush. Margaret had been thinking of getting not only the local or "little Comstock laws" changed in those states that still had them, but also mounting a full-scale attack on the federal law. She had tried this in Washington in 1925, but had given it up when Anne Kennedy reported that more educational work was needed first. In 1926, Mary Ware Dennett's Voluntary Parenthood League, faced with the same problem, had folded completely. But now, with Brush's support, Margaret decided to mount a federal legislative campaign, beginning with an intensive cross-country lecture tour.

She also devised what she hoped would be another coup. Mrs. Den-

nett had long advocated an "open bill"—that is, one that would legalize
the giving of birth control information to any woman who asked for it.
Margaret decided to advocate a "doctor's only" bill, meaning giving information only through doctors. Margaret realized that, in the climate
of public opinion in the twenties, such a bill had a far better chance of
being passed.

The chief pitfall here was her relations with the medical profession.
At her Town Hall Conference in 1921, her birth-control exhibits had
created great controversy. Many of the doctors violently opposed the
methods demonstrated, calling them "foreign contraceptions that were
filthy, untested, and unsafe."

Her *Family Limitation* pamphlets were equally suspect. She had
written the first pamphlet in 1915 before fleeing to England releasing
it through her radical friends, so doctors never got hold of it; there is no
copy of it in the files. But there are copies of a pamphlet dated 1916,
which told women not to wait until they "came around," but to keep a
chart and take a laxative four days before their periods were due, as
this would "expel the semen from the uterus." She suggested laxatives
like castor oil, Beecham's Pills, or quinine followed by hot water.
(What taking a harsh laxative like castor oil every month, whether
needed or not, would do to the women's intestines, she did not say.)

In the 1916 edition, she also condoned abortion, declaring: "No one
can doubt that there are times when an abortion is justifiable," though
she qualified this by saying "abortions will become unnecessary when
care is taken to prevent conception. (Care is) the only cure for abortions." Later she stopped condoning abortions, but meanwhile the very
use of the word scared doctors because medical men were regularly being sent to jail for performing them.

In the same edition she had a section titled "Douches and Their Importance." Here she advocated various chemicals to be added to water
and used after intercourse. They included first Lysol, which was potentially harmful when used in large amounts; second, bichloride of mercury, which could be absorbed by the vaginal tissues, distributed
throughout the body, and if used over a long period of time, do enough
damage to kill a woman; third, chinosol, which she admitted was less
hazardous than bichloride, but harder to come by; and fourth, vinegar,
which every woman had at home on the shelf.

In an undated edition there was also the curious advice to use
douches, particularly astringent douches containing boric acid, alum,

citric acid, or hydrochlorate of quinine, *before* intercourse as a preventive of pregnancy. How these could become contraceptives, other than by slightly tightening the tissues at the entrance to the womb, was not explained.

Something else that put doctors off was her advice that women use their index finger to explore the vagina and clean out whatever remaining semen might be left after a douche had been used. Using a finger this way seemed dangerously close to masturbation and was distasteful indeed. Even more distasteful was her advice concerning the use of the diaphragm or pessary. (Both are words for the same thing.) "Any nurse," Margaret said, "can teach one how to adjust a diaphragm; then women can teach each other." Now "any nurse" did not know how to adjust a diaphragm, much less how to choose the correct size. And the vision of women teaching each other was especially horrifying. Doctors called this "lay gynecology" and opposed it strongly.

At least, in none of her pamphlets did Margaret repeat the advice of the Dutch physician, Dr. Mensinga, who advised his patients to leave the diaphragm constantly in place except during the menstrual flow. Margaret advised her clients to leave it in only for a few hours after intercourse, then to remove it, wash and dry it, and put it away until needed again—a far more sanitary practice. But then, doctors didn't read her pamphlets carefully. They simply continued to dismiss the whole matter of birth control as "filthy and indecent," ignoring even her revised material, where she no longer spoke of using douches as contraceptives, but suggested they be used for cleansing purposes only. Or when, in her eighteenth edition, she advised women to put a contraceptive jelly inside the diaphragm to double its effectiveness. No matter what she said, doctors turned their backs on her.

To be sure, in the light of modern knowledge her pamphlets weren't very good, but they contained the best that she, or anyone else at the time, knew. But women didn't turn their backs. They were grateful for her persistence in getting illegal material printed, and her cleverness in getting it into the mail without being caught by either Comstock or his successors—both achievements of no small order.

ONE STAUNCH SUPPORTER

Dr. Robert Latou Dickinson was a peppery man with a triangular face, a pointed Van Dyke beard, and eyes as blue and bright as Havelock's. But he couldn't have been more different. Havelock was tall; Dickinson was small. Havelock was shy; Dickinson was bold. Havelock was cautious and old beyond his years; Dickinson was a vigorous man who jumped around on the lecture platform like a hurried grasshopper and took nature-hikes along the Palisades above the Hudson River for relaxation. (He insisted he had even been born in a hurry while his mother was on her way home to Brooklyn from New Jersey.) After studying medicine in Germany and Switzerland, he had become a doctor in 1882, just three years after Margaret was born; in the late 1920's he was still practicing, as well as holding down the prestigious posts of President of the American Gynecological Society, Director of the American College of Surgeons, and Senior Gynecologist and Obstetrician at Brooklyn Hospital.

Born of a well-to-do family, wealth was his natural milieu, yet he refused to think of his patients either as a source of money or as mere "cases." When his nurse would announce, "Doctor, your next case is ready," he would rebuke her with, "You mean that pleasant Mrs. Miller with the auburn hair?" And to lessen his patients' embarrassment during a gynecological examination, he would hang pictures on the ceiling to distract them. He was also a skilled sculptor. To demonstrate the differences between men and women, he sculpted two models which he called "Norma" and "Norman," complete with frank sexual details that shocked his colleagues. Indeed one reason he was made president of the Gynecological Society was to "kick him upstairs," where the conservatives thought he would become harmless. But he went on. Next he sculpted a series showing the progress of a baby as it traveled down the birth canal, the photographs of which became the high points of his *Birth Atlas*, still the chief attraction at classes in "natural" or educated childbirth. These sculptures earned him the title of the "Rodin of Obstetrics."

Above all, Dr. Dickinson was an enthusiastic champion of birth control After he traveled to the Far East during World War I as assistant chief of the medical section of the National Council of Defense, he said: "When the Far East becomes industrialized, its excessive population will be the greatest danger the world has ever known." He repeated this to everyone who would listen. But he was for birth control primarily because he saw it as a basic feminine right. Year after year at the annual AMA convention, he would ask for a corner in which to set up a birth-control demonstration. "Just a little corner?" he would plead. "Just a little one?" But year after year his colleagues turned him down, just as they had ignored Abraham Jacobi, AMA president, who had been at the very top of what doctors themselves call " the power structure," and had come out in favor of birth control many years before.

In 1921 the majority of doctors were still shutting their eyes and ears and hoping the whole subject of birth control would just go away, even though by now the law in many states allowed them to give contraceptive advice for four reasons—if a woman had heart trouble, kidney disease, tuberculosis, or gross malformation of her genitals—all of which made pregnancy dangerous for her to undertake. Some of them didn't even know they could give this advice; the rest insisted it was none of their business. If women didn't want babies, they said, let them practice continence or be sterilized. They reasoned that there were no tested, surefire contraceptive methods, and that tested methods of doing things alone separated science from quackery.

In all likelihood, there were other reasons for this medical indifference. One probably was that the vast percentage of doctors were male, and products of their time and class. When they dismissed the subject of birth control as "filthy and indecent," they were merely echoing the Victorian sentiments learned from their fathers. Men might *do* certain things in private, but they certainly didn't talk about them in public. In public, they were models of decorum who wore severe, tight clothes and stiff, high collars to show they were upright gentlemen. If one oc- casionally sneaked upstairs to seduce the maid, at least he had the de- cency to do it in the dark.

Also, many doctors were extremely money-minded. "It takes at least half an hour to explain the different methods of birth control to a wom- an," one obstetrician put it, "and the most I can charge is around ten dollars. During the same half hour I can do a hysterectomy, or super- intend a delivery and charge three hundred. Why should I change?" And many doctors simply went along with the economic theory that "all babies were potential consumers who would keep money in circu- lation," and that on general principles more of anything was better than less.

There were a few who thought differently. Dickinson was one. But he was in a spot. He knew as well as his colleagues that there were no proven contraceptives. As early as 1916, the very year that Margaret was opening her Brownsville clinic, he had handed out circulars to all the men who came to a meeting of the Gynecological Society, asking:

> What serious study has ever been made upon the harm or harmlessness of the variety of birth-control procedures, or con- cerning the failure or effectiveness of each? Who has or can ac- quire any considerable body of evidence on these matters but our- selves? What indeed is normal sex life? What constitutes excess, or what is the penalty for repression among the married? Do we still have to hark back to Luther for an answer? . . . . Some time a start must be made.

Yet he didn't quite know how to make that start. Margaret and her cause seemed the only answer, and yet he hesitated lest he alienate his colleagues even more. For, while he admired Margaret as a woman of courage, he also saw her as a political radical and a patent-medicine barker, especially when she continued to claim that birth control would not only end poverty, disease, war and crime, but keep a woman forever young and beautiful, and her hair in curl.

Because he admired her, he had attended her 1921 Town Hall Con- ference. She promised him then that, as soon as possible, she would open "a first-class research center." But he had been sorely disappointed when she hired Dr. Bocker as her director. Bocker's records were ill-kept and uneven, and she had done practically no follow-up to see which of the methods her patients had chosen were helpful and which were not. Unfortunately, Dr. Stone was no better at research and record-keeping than Dr. Bocker.

So in 1925 he came to the conclusion he would have to open a study center himself. "We all know that contraceptives are being used," he kept repeating at gynecological meetings. "The question is, are they harmful? Are they harmless? Do you know? I don't know." He determined to find the answers quietly, experimentally, scientifically. His colleagues had a choice. They could either back him or let him join some Sanger group.

The words "Sanger group" did it. His colleagues agreed to help. He gave his study center the innocuous name of the Committee on Maternal Health, and said he hoped it might eventually proceed to open its own clinic.

But where could he open his study center? Because he had promised he would do it quietly, the only place seemed to be his upstairs office at the Academy of Medicine at 4 East 103 Street, New York, a tiny room which had been given him for use as president of the Obstetrical Society. It would be merely a referral center, moreover. Women would come there for a preliminary interview, then be referred to one of seven hospitals which had promised to cooperate with him and his committee on the strength of his prestige. The hospitals would give the necessary examinations to see if contraceptives could be legally given, keep the records, and hand out the supplies.

His plan proved too timid to work. Though he passed the word around through his patients that his center was open, the very women who needed it most—poor women, workingwomen—were overwhelmed by the vast halls and formal atmosphere of the Academy of Medicine building. They were equally turned off by the impersonal hospitals where they had to sit for hours on hard benches waiting for their names to be called. And when their turn came, they were upset because the information was whispered to them by embarrassed interns. To add to this, they found more often than not that there weren't enough birth-control supplies to go around. The best that could be offered were condoms which they had to persuade their husbands to wear, or spermicidal jellies, or douche ingredients—all of which the doctors doled out like conspirators. One intern even confessed he felt he had to slip the women what supplies he had in an alleyway next to the hospital rather than within its own walls. Diaphragms, the device Margaret had promoted most vigorously in her pamphlets, were usually unavailable because they had been cornered by the lady herself.

Dickinson was therefore in a bind. He had endeavored to sow a few seeds of independent research, yet he had been unable to do it. When he admitted this to his fellow academicians, his hard-won Committee on Maternal Health drifted apart, and the women went back to Margaret's clinic, where they at least felt at home.

Margaret was in a bind too; she knew that to gain the respect of the medical community, her clinic needed a dispensary license. This license, granted by the State Board of Charities, simply permitted a clinic to dispense information. Every state requires one, and there are three standard requirements: proof of public need, proof of the good character of the people behind it, and proof of enough funds to carry on. In the case of the Sanger Bureau, the New York State Board acknowledged that these three requirements had been met. But unexpectedly, they came up with a fourth requirement—a waiver from "certain religious groups." Many religious groups gave this waiver without hesitation. The Roman Catholics would not, and months of negotiations could not make them budge. The license was withheld.

This was less because the members of the state board were unfriendly than because they were afraid of public opinion. One observer, though convinced that the Bureau's getting a license was an impossibility, had the impression that the state board members would really welcome a way out of the situation. If, for example, a Dickinson group took over the Bureau, they would let it operate without a license, as did 125 of the 350-odd other New York City clinics.

Dickinson was undaunted; he tried to form a new study group called by the slightly different name, the Maternity Research Council, which he hoped would be able to persuade Margaret to cooperate. He cajoled three doctors into visiting the Bureau personally, among them, the Catholic gynecologist George Kosmak. But Dr. Kosmak was shocked by the lurid propaganda posters showing the horrors of abortion. Doctors, he said, did not use such posters for any reason. Further, when he discovered what poor records the clinic kept, he stormed out, claiming: "The whole Sanger research thing is a sham. It's both a violation of the law and a public menace."

When Margaret promised to take down the abortion posters, Kosmak was somewhat placated. He even admitted that maybe doctors should join her, but only if she could get a dispensary license. She agreed: "I can see the good a license will establish. I can see the fight practically won by such an achievement."

Kosmak now went further. He said that if Margaret would let his group take over the Bureau entirely under his direction, he would be willing to go along with a full heart. Surprisingly, she agreed again.

Dickinson was delighted, especially when the Academy of Medicine got the Rockefeller-backed Bureau of Social Hygiene to give the Maternity Research Council a ten-thousand-dollar grant. He applied immediately for the elusive license. To his chagrin, he was once more refused. This time the excuse was that his Research Council should either join Margaret's Bureau or start its own clinic before a license was granted, though privately a member admitted, "The board is too much afraid that *any* license will be widely exploited as a victory for Margaret Sanger."

There it was again. Dickinson could get nowhere if he associated with Margaret. His colleagues would not do anything without the license. Dickinson's short-lived delight turned to disgust; he even found himself being publicly censured by some of his own medical societies. Instead of quitting, however, he began to think of another strategy.

Margaret meanwhile continued working. She recognized the need to legitimatize the Bureau and appointed a distinguished advisory board made up mainly of social scientists and eugenicists. But soon the board members were openly fighting with Dickinson and his colleagues. They wanted to use the Bureau records to do their own kind of research; they argued that "medical men have no right to take over a field that has been tilled for them by others." The Bureau at this point had become a political football, with the social scientists determined to win the day.

Undaunted, Dickinson pursued his original goal. He came up with what he called an "interim plan," which called for doctors to take over the Bureau immediately, on the premise that this would somehow gain the coveted dispensary license. For though he had begun privately to despair of getting that license, he thought that once doctors were in charge, it would be too late for them to drop out. It was a shrewd plan, but at the last minute Margaret did a turn around and blackballed it. She came up with an interim plan of her own which would admit a few doctors to the board, but keep the social scientists in command. When she sent Dickinson a letter outlining her plan he was so furious he left it unanswered on his desk

Margaret continued. To please her board she revamped her patient records to include information like nationality, heredity, religion, occupation, even trade-union affiliation. When the public health doctor Ira. S. Wile heard about this and told her that this mixing of medical and social matters didn't make sense, Margaret ignored him. And, of course, she left everybody up in the air when she went to Europe in 1927 to stage her Geneva conference, and stayed away for eighteen months.

When she came back in the fall of 1928 and resigned from the ABCL, Dickinson was waiting for her. As she had separated herself from the ABCL, he thought she would be more pliable. He told her that he had really pulled off a coup; he had gotten the prestigious New York Hospital to promise to cooperate with him. Also, on his urging, more doctors had joined her Bureau board while she was away, and all were jubilant at the thought of working with the New York Hospital. But again Bureau board politics came into play. At a hastily called meeting, the social scientists outvoted the medical members; they would not cooperate with any hospital at all.

Margaret was in the midst of writing a letter to Dickinson telling him this when Grant had a bad motorcycle accident that made her think only of family affairs.

As soon as Grant recovered, she wrote Hugh that she was "off on a motor-trip to Quebec and Montreal with my two handsome sons," adding: "I can see that devil of a fellow Harold at the wheel—bless him. He can go as fast as likes when he takes me for a drive—tell him that. He never writes to me & has forgotten that I ever walked around the sunken garden with him once upon a time."

By the end of August she was back at Willowlake, energetic enough to plan a new series of lectures. She had heard from Françoise that Hugh had been ill, and wrote on September first commiserating with him, and hoping he had behaved better than she did when she was sick: "I am positively horrible to everyone who comes near me, so it behooves me to keep well or I shall be sent to a pest house."

She also told Hugh she was planning another surprise for Havelock. When Françoise moved into the small Brixton flat Havelock had kept all these years, there was enough space for her in the room he used to keep for Edith, but not for her boys, so they had taken a larger flat in Herne Hill, on the outskirts of London. But Margaret wanted them to have a country home as well, a place where Havelock could have a garden to sun himself in, as well as build a special three-sided writing hut that revolved to catch the fugitive English light.

In September she wrote:

So if ever you hear of his finding the kind of country house he likes, send me a S.O.S., and I will take an inventory of my wares in bankery and I will let you do the rest. You're such a wizard at manipulating the wires of good will & loveliness that I know you will arrange this too some day.

Hugh started looking for another house for Françoise and Havelock at once. Margaret thanked him in an outburst of love: "I want to hug your dear head and kiss your blessed eyes and laugh with you and romp for very joy that you are so dear."

But almost immediately she became depressed. Her September birthday had arrived, reminding her of what she hated most to remember—her age, now forty-nine. Her beauty was going; her chin was beginning to sag, and crow's feet were forming around her eyes.

To cheer up, she took a solitary cruise to the Caribbean, but she didn't stop working. She wrote a new series of speeches for a December lecture tour in California; new arguments were needed because her audience had greatly changed over the years. No longer was she speaking to the radicals and the poor, urging them to stop breeding both to lessen their own misery and to "frighten the capitalist class." Now in 1928 she was speaking primarily to that very capitalist class, urging them to stop breeding themselves and to try to restrain the lower class, because the lower class bred the "unfit." She defined the unfit as "the retarded, the feeble-minded and the insane," adding "illiterates, unemployables, paupers, criminals, prostitutes and dope fiends," pointing out that the fit had to support the unfit. The theme she tried to hammer home was that the unfit should be segregated or sterilized if they refused to practice birth control.

Emma Goldman's biographer accused Margaret of deserting her radical friends. In a sense she did. But by 1928 she felt she had to use the kind of lectures that would curry favor with people of wealth, those who could donate the much-needed cash to her cause as well as supply the expertise they had learned in their long battle for woman suffrage.

By now Margaret was determined to become an adroit politician. And she knew that her middle- and upper-class audience would be as much taken by her political know-how as by her fame, charisma, and fervor.

She was right. On one occasion in 1928, the manager of a lecture hall in Hartford, Connecticut, tried to back out of his contract with her at the last minute on the familiar plea that if he let her speak his license would be revoked. She sued him and won, seeing to it that the papers got all the details. The result was that when she did get to speak, her upper-class audience was excited to fever pitch, and applauded loud and long before she uttered a word.

Her new speeches roughed out, Margaret began to rethink her offer to buy Havelock a country home. Would he accept her gift with the same eagerness with which she wanted to give it? She wrote Hugh on November 16: "I know the darling man is terrified of getting into deep water. He is happy when he feels he is not living up to his income, and God forbid we should push something onto him even from generosity." She also told him that her book *Motherhood in Bondage* was finally on the market, "only they left out a picture I wanted on the frontispiece of a pregnant woman facing death. Now they will hear from me, and catch hell too!!"

J. Noah was catching hell too. When Margaret started on her lecture tour, she shot off a letter to him from the Fairmont Hotel in San Francisco berating him for not having written her for several days. She went on to insist that he stop telling her private affairs to the birth-control people back home. "I am afraid you are a *sieve*! Everything goes through you." Then she did a quick turnabout and finished in her most soothing manner: "Devotedly and lovingly, adorable one. Your wife and sweetheart, Margy."

Margaret's increasingly extreme mood swings may have been due to the fact that she was still going through her menopause. Especially high-strung women like her sometimes react strongly to it—often fearing the loss of love. When she complained, "Too bad Harold never fell in love with me," she was expressing the fear that she might lose his love, not that she never had it. Also, without hormone replacements or tranquilizers to temper her menopausal reactions, she had become open to every crank diet suggestion and every cult leader's far fetched promises.

She would swing especially high in 1929 when two incredible blunders played into her hands.

INCREDIBLE BLUNDERS

"It's going to be great fun," Margaret Sanger had written a friend when she resigned as president of the American Birth Control League, gave up management of the *Review*, and took over sole management of the Research Bureau instead. It didn't turn out quite that way. Under professional direction, the *Review*'s motto changed in 1929 from "To Breed a Race of Thoroughbreds," to "Babies by Choice, Not Chance." The *Review*'s editorials, heretofore written mainly by Margaret herself, now included guest editorials, some of them praising Mary Ware Dennett. And Margaret's own name, heretofore on the front page, was relegated to the inside cover along with the names of the entire professional editorial staff.

She had sworn to herself she would not be upset by these changes, but she was. She had another intestinal attack and took out her pain and anger on J. Noah, writing to him at Willowlake from her New York hotel: "The surgeon doctor says I am O.K. No need of an operation . . . *Not nerves.* So stop telling people this is my fifth breakdown of nerves and such drivel . . . I am ashamed to have you running around out of captivity talking nonsense." Then, becoming contrite: "I don't know why I talk to you like this, but I just do."

At this point, and many others, in fact, one may wonder why J. Noah stayed on with "his Margy." But he probably still considered their marriage his life adventure. Difficult though it might be at times, it was never in serious danger of breaking apart.

Now occurred the first of the two thunderstorms. Mary Ware Dennett was arrested and sentenced to a year in jail.

In 1922 Mrs. Dennett had written a little pamphlet called "The Sex Side of Life." She did it for her two adolescent sons, but word of its existence had gotten around to her neighbors, who asked for copies. Then *The Medical Review of Reviews* heard of it and published it, thus bringing it to the attention of the Y.M.C.A., several churches, theological seminaries, and social work agencies. These in turn had found it so sane and sensible they had begun distributing it through the mails to their members at the nominal cost of twenty-five cents. Using the mails did the mischief, for the mails were still being closely watched by John S. Sumner, Comstock's successor, and his powerful Society For the Suppression of Vice. Sumner was particularly offended by three statements the pamphlet made: one, that sex relations can bring great pleasure; two, that venereal disease can be cured; and three, that masturbation is a harmless activity that will not drive a person out of his mind. Such statements, he insisted, simply could not be made to young people in the year 1929.

Mrs. Dennett was tried in a Brooklyn court for violating the Comstock Law. William Sheafe Chase, Canon of the Episcopal Church, was seated at the counsel table next to John S. Sumner and James Wilkinson, the prosecuting attorney. The counsel for the defense was Morris Ernst, a distinguished liberal lawyer in his late thirties. Ernst had on hand a group of witnesses from organizations like the Y.M.C.A. that had distributed the pamphlet, all of them ready to testify that it was one of the finest they had seen. But Judge Warren Burrows refused to listen to their testimony, ruling it out as irrelevant. On the other hand, he listened carefully to Wilkinson, who merely asked the prospective members of the jury if they had ever read anything by Havelock Ellis or H. L. Mencken. One prospective juror had read some of Ellis' work; he was considered prejudiced and excused. The rest said they were "plain family men" who had heard neither of Ellis nor Mencken; they were retained.

Mrs. Dennett took the stand in her own defense. The *New York Herald Tribune*, in reporting the trial, described her as "a slight and benign figure with a soft voice, quick smile, and carefully waved white hair, who made her living as a maker of decorative leather wall hangings, though she occasionally wrote for *The Century* and other magazines. When asked what age she considered the pamphlets suitable for, she answered 'any time between twelve and twenty-five.'"

Ernst cited similar pamphlets now being distributed by the United States Public Health Service, the State Department of Health, and the Board of Education, but Judge Burrows ruled this out as irrelevant. He also refused to let any of Ernst's supporting authorities take the stand. "I object to having a galaxy of persons paraded here to air their views on the subject," Judge Burrows declared, after which Wilkinson, a big red-faced man, sneeringly read aloud from the pamphlet, calling it "pornographic and obscene on the face of it." He ended his speech to the jury with the exhortation: "I ask you as fathers, would you allow this to be placed in the hands of your own children? Would you let your daughter read it?"

Ernst countered with the argument that pornographic and obscene materials were "doled out in dark corners" while this was sold openly, "and that to convict Mrs. Dennett was to condemn the children of the next generation to getting their information from the gutter."

He got nowhere. The jury found her guilty. Her crime, they declared, was nothing less than "corrupting the youth of America." For this she was sentenced to a year in jail or a one hundred and fifty dollar fine. Hearing the sentence, Mrs. Dennett stood up very straight and declared: "If I have corrupted the youth of America, a year in jail is not enough for me. And I will not pay the fine!" She was released on bail pending appeal.

The trial of Mrs. Dennett was an incredible blunder; it only succeeded in making people aware of her pamphlet who had never heard of it before.

The *Birth Control Review* ran a statement on its front page praising Mrs. Dennett's speech, while Margaret enclosed the *Tribune* clipping in a note to Havelock:

I know you will laugh at the Dennett trial notes. You will see what your name means to the 100% juryman. It's outrageous that she should be convicted . . . She has more nerve in her old age than she had when she was in the B.C. fight. She said I was "posing" then. It's encouraging that people do change—and for the better.

Havelock scrawled across the clipping: "How the Y.M.C.A. has changed."

Then, on April 13, a Mrs. Tierney came to the clinic requesting contraceptive advice. Dr. Stone examined her, found she needed a diaphragm for medical reasons, and gave her instructions for using it. Three days later Mrs. Tierney returned, using her right name, Mrs. McNamara and flashing a police badge. With her came another policewoman, Mary Sullivan, and six policemen. The officers charged into the waiting room, where fifteen frightened patients were sitting, and bullied them into giving their names and addresses. Then Mary Sullivan, who knew that the clinic was now asking for information on nationality and religion as well as strictly medical details, began to seize all the available birth-control supplies as well as over a hundred doctors' records.

Margaret rushed to the Bureau, angrier than she had ever been in her life. A policeman tried to keep her out. "This place is shut. You can't come in," he shouted, opening the door a crack. "Oh yes I can," she shouted back, putting her whole weight onto one foot, sticking it into the crack, and refusing to budge. Seeing that things were at an impasse, another policeman let her in.

The place was bedlam. Margaret calmed the frightened patients, then strode over to the police who were busy scooping up records. though they stopped occasionally as if to look for special names.

Margaret demanded to see their search warrant. When she read the signature of Chief Magistrate William McAdoo, she became visibly shaken. Still, she fought back.

"You're going to get yourself into more trouble than you suspect if you interfere with those records," she shouted at Mrs. McNamara.

"Trouble? What about you?"

"I can take care of myself."

By this time the police were becoming restless. Having arrested Dr. Stone, Dr. Cooper, and three nurses, they pulled up the patrol wagon and tried to force them in. Margaret demanded that she be allowed to call taxis instead, but was refused permission to do so. They were all herded into the wagon and taken to the Jefferson Market Court in Greenwich Village.

Once there, Margaret telephoned Dr. Dickinson, whom she knew would give her good advice. He recommended that she engage Morris Ernst as her lawyer, both because of his spirited defense of Mrs. Dennett and his success in the Bours Case some years before. Margaret phoned him, and he hurried to court.

Dr. T. Robinson Bours was a Chicago physician who specialized in women's diseases. In September 1912 he received a letter in a woman's handwriting asking if he would perform an abortion on the writer's unmarried daughter, "to relieve her of her disgrace." Bours answered cautiously; he would "first have to see the patient before determining whether he would take her case or not." The letter from the "mother" was, it turned out, a decoy written on Comstock's order, but Bours was found guilty for merely answering it. Ernst had made the appeal for Bours and got his conviction reversed.

When Ernst got to the Jefferson Market Court, he was startled to find a group of young girls seated in the last row. In 1929 the subject of birth control was so taboo that young girls were not allowed even to hear it discussed, but they told him they had been arrested for picketing in a garment worker's strike and felt they were in great luck because they could listen while waiting for their own case to come up.

After some preliminary arguing, the Bureau case was postponed and transferred to the Mulberry Street Court, where Magistrate Rosenbluth was sitting on the bench. Ernst gathered a panel of physicians, among them the distinguished neurologist Dr. Foster Kennedy, to testify that the clinic doctors were lawfully acting to prevent disease when they gave information to Anna McNamara. Two hundred spectators, clergymen as well as laymen, were shunted out of the courtroom when they laughed as Dr. Foster Kennedy testified that, to his knowledge, Mrs. McNamara had said during her examination that she had been married six years, had three children, and her husband "drank some." The spectators were soon readmitted, however, and heard Ernst go on to question Dr. Kennedy:

"Now these birth-control supplies are very often recommended to prevent or cure disease?"

"You say very often, I say always," answered Dr. Kennedy. This brought a cheer from the spectators, some of whom burst into "My Country, 'Tis of Thee." Kitty Marion sang "Land of dumb driven cattle" instead of "Sweet land of liberty."

Next Dr. Louis I. Harris, former Health Commissioner of New York City, took the stand. His testimony was similar to that of Dr. Kennedy, but Magistrate Rosenbluth objected to it on the grounds that not enough care had been taken to find out if Mrs. McNamara and the other clinic patients were married or not.

"It was more important to take pains to find out if these patients were married than if they were ill," he declared.

"Do you know of any case in medicine where a doctor sends out detectives to find out if a patient is telling the truth about her marital status?" Ernst asked Dr. Harris, making the spectators laugh loudly again as Dr. Harris answered no.

By now Magistrate Rosenbluth was thoroughly aroused. "Another demonstration and I'll clear the room," he declared. "I think I'll clear it anyway. Everyone out."

The courtroom cleared, Dr. Dickinson took the stand for the defense, testifying that he had inspected both the Bureau and its records on several occasions and found that fully one third of all applicants had been rejected because they did not come within the health specifications laid down by the law. After that Dr. Max Meyer, head of the gynecology clinic of Mt. Sinai Hospital, testified that the clinic had acted as carefully in these matters as did his own. Several other doctors gave firm support as well.

The prosecuting attorney now took over the cross examination. He called each doctor who had testified and held up a diaphragm. "Do you believe this can cure disease?" he asked sarcastically. They answered of course not; it might prevent disease but not cure it. Regardless of the state of a woman's health, medical witnesses agreed that it was best for both mother and child if there was a space of two to three years between one delivery and the next.

At this point the prosecuting attorney excused the witnesses, and Ernst moved for dismissal on the grounds that "licensed doctors who had given advice in good faith to cure or prevent disease had been arrested." He insisted that it was the burden of the prosecution to prove lack of good faith. "Otherwise," said Ernst, "physicians might be hailed into court to justify their every act, and be subject to a re-diagnosis of their cases by lawyers." He also stressed the fact that, in seizing 150 record cards, the police had violated the time-honored relation of confidentiality between doctor and patient.

The seizing of records was the crux of the matter. Once the police admitted doing that, Chief Magistrate McAdoo, who had signed the warrant, had no choice but to publicly back down and admit that Mary Sullivan's "party" had been another serious blunder. Police Commissioner Grover Whalen, McAdoo's superior, had to apologize to the Academy of Medicine for McAdoo's issuance of the search warrant in the first place. As in the Town Hall incident, there followed much passing-the-buck between the two, with neither side admitting whose idea the raid had been in the first place.

When the press, led by the *New York Times*, reported the story in full detail, the Sanger Bureau on Sixteenth Street found itself receiving the best publicity it ever had. Heywood Broun did a witty column for the *New York Telegram*, calling Grover Whalen a "gardenacious popinjay" for his habit of wearing a gardenia in his buttonhole. The conservative *New York Daily News* ran an editorial comparing the blunder in both the raid and Mrs. Dennett's arrest. The *News* prophesied:

> Both cases will probably blow up in time. And with what results? Birth control and the Clinic will have won some more free advertising. And everyone now knows that one book at least exists in which young people have some hope of learning the facts of life without hysteria or dirt or bunk . . . Some day we will learn to treat a human instinct as a human instinct, instead of making a fetish of it and fools of ourselves.

The News was correct in its prophecy. Mrs. Dennett's conviction was reversed on appeal, and the Bureau was totally cleared. Besides making the newspapers indignant, the trials offended their readers too. Margaret reported to Havelock that she heard people heatedly discussing the matter on the street, in the subway, everywhere she went. At a dinner given soon after, eight thousand dollars was raised for birth control, while the League of Women Voters, who had been standoffish before, petitioned the New York legislature to permit doctors to give contraceptive information to women regardless of health.

Margaret gave more details to Havelock:

> I think at last the stupid District Attorney sees that prevention of conception is a means to prevent disease. . . . His poor mind was so full that all he could see & say was that the pessary did *not* cure disease. He kept on asking every Doctor, "Do you see this? (pessary in hand) Do you believe this can cure disease? Do you not advise it to prevent conception?" Then he smiled to the court as if to say "I'll get them."

The Chief Magistrate was a dub whose wife paid a fat sum to get him on the bench so we do not expect him to think except as he is told. The newspapers have been wonderful to us & backed us 100%. But it put us ahead ten years, especially because of the medical testimony that from two to three years should intervene between births of children in the vast majority of cases.

Better yet, the medical profession was thoroughly involved; the seizure of the records, which they rightly regarded as a breach of ethics, had made them furious. Aware of how much medical support had helped her and how much she needed more, Margaret gave Dickinson the most encouraging word yet, telling of her desire "to have closer cooperation between the members of the medical profession and the Research Bureau," adding specifically that she wished to "enlist the supervision of the Bureau recommended by the Academy of Medicine."

Dickinson was elated. This clearly indicated Margaret's willingness to let go of her tight grip on the Bureau, and he worked during the entire summer of 1929 to bring this rapprochement about. Dr. Stuart Mudd of Philadelphia encouraged Margaret, pointing out how medical supervision would help in the establishment of other clinics and open up Hannah Stone's reports to the finest medical journals (coming from a lay clinic, these reports had been almost impossible to place), as well as enable both recognized gynecologists and interns to serve on the Bureau staff. "It's an opportunity not to be missed," Mudd summed it up.

Maddeningly, Margaret took a step backward again. "I do not want to release too quickly the control of a work it has taken years to develop," she shot back to Mudd. At one time she had accused Dickinson of personal motives, writing James Cooper: "Dr. D. is wildly anxious to get in control." Now she went further. "Contraception is not medicine," she said.

Dickinson had sensed a new storm coming before it broke. After making more statements welcoming medical supervision and direction, Margaret did still another complete turnabout.

She forgot she had started the Bureau, not for research, but to bring birth-control information to the women who came and asked for it. The word "research" was initially a way to get around using the word clinic. In letting the social scientists control it for their own uses—that is, write papers on the patients' ages, nationalities, or even the trade union affiliations of their husbands (another way of determing economic class)—was clearly in contradiction of her original plan. Yet, at this point, she was either so muddled or so flattered by the social scientists that she fought the very people she and her patients needed most—the doctors.

She proceeded to call a secret board meeting, excluding the medical members; at the meeting the plan to let the Academy of Medicine supervise the running of the Bureau, as now they were at last ready to do, was vetoed.

Dickinson, who had worked for seven years to win over the Academy, was pulverized. He had to go before them with bowed head and confess, "It is hopeless to get Mrs. Sanger to cooperate with other groups." She, astoundingly, retaliated with the statement that her board had practically begged the academy to come to her aid. "I refused however to hand over a service of humanity to be a football in a political setup and finally abolished, as the clinic would have been" was the way she made the statement.

David M. Kennedy in his book *Birth Control in America* interprets this last series of turnarounds as a victory of her emotions over her intellect. To her the social scientists did not seem nearly as much of a threat to her position of number one as the doctors did. The clinic was her "baby," in a way taking the place of her long-lost Peggy. She felt she had to hold it tight lest it slip away.

Meanwhile Havelock had moved with Françoise to his new house in Haslemere, which Margaret badly wanted to see. She soon succumbed to the temptation and took off for England, taking J. Noah along, but planning to send him off to Paris to sightsee; she herself planned to squeeze in a few visits to some Berlin clinics as an excuse for going abroad in the first place.

As soon as she got to England, she visited Hugh, and then saw Havelock. She undoubtedly saw Harold too because he wrote: "How thrilled I was to see you again & hear you laugh & feel your presence. After such ages, I felt still as if I had been with you only the day before!"

But after she left England to join J. Noah in Paris, she became desolate because she heard that Harold and Hugh were about to break their long friendship over the matter of Helen, Harold's future wife.

Helen or "Nell" was a friend of Hugh's who lived near Sand Pit with her husband, Jack, and two daughters. A tall, thin woman with a quick sense of humor, her marriage to Jack had been very unhappy, and Harold, though he still dreaded the thought of remarrying, longed for a home of his own. Gradually, he had become attracted to her, as Nell visited back and forth, even becoming godfather to her youngest child.

Hugh, already jealous of his daughter Bridget's affection for Harold, now envied Nell's affection for Harold, especially since Nell was one of the few women who had turned him down as a lover. In a fit of rage, Hugh accused Jack of trying to seduce Bridget. Nell later explained.

My first did like women, but he was *not* a seducer of seventeen-year-old virgins. The main attraction was, they were both mad on cars.

Hugh was certainly a queer one. I remember his going off the deep end because I said, "Of course if people can afford it, they should have a honeymoon." "Rubbish" says he, "whatever for? We didn't have one," and look what happened to that marriage. Every year a new woman, then the old one cast out when the next happened along. Such an off-putting spotty man.

When Harold and I decided on marriage Hugh was quite intolerably rude to me in front of his wife, Janet, poor lamb. She was very unhappy about it. I didn't mind, but Hugh just ceased any communication with Harold and finally bullied poor Janet into doing the same.

Hugh was a selfish cad, and Margaret was deceived . . . (But) you would have loved my dear little man. Such humor and so sweet. He adored my children, and they adored him. Children and animals made a bee line for him. He loathed puritans with a quiet rejection of all they stood for.

I didn't meet Margaret at Sand Pit. Hugh kept her hidden away when anyone was around. But afterward I heard her speak a few times, and at a birth-control reception I attended (Harold couldn't come) she stood in the foyer receiving the guests and saw me coming and gave me the most gorgeous wink . . . I'm quite sure that Harold didn't keep any of Margaret's letters. He would have destroyed them before marrying me in 1939. And any she wrote after we were married he always shared with me. He always spoke of her as being great fun. (I knew they had been lovers.)

One of the reasons I don't think Margaret can have loved Harold as he deserved was his surprise & joy at any little thing I did for him, such as getting up and shutting the window when I knew he would be feeling it. That this should so enchant him proves that no one had ever really loved him in every possible way.

Margaret sailed home from Cherbourg in August, dashing off a note to Havelock before she left:

*   *   *

We are off on the *Mauritania* today . . . In Berlin I found the clinics thriving under Communist direction, and the clericals and conservatives grinding their teeth and throwing mud at them all.

She would go to Russia in a few years to see for herself how clinics were doing there, and come away a disillusioned woman indeed.

While Margaret was away, Juliet was producing a movie in Mexico. The two women had kept up a constant flow of letters, and as soon as Margaret got back, Juliet begged her to run down to Mexico immediately. She asked for a loan to finish her movie: "I don't suppose J. N. would ever consider for half a second gambling on it, would he?" but it was Margaret herself whom Juliet wanted more than money. Margaret couldn't go however, because she was set to leave on a cross-country speaking trip.

27

BATTERING AGAINST THE FEDERAL WALL

The great American Depression hit the country in October 1929, on a day remembered as Black Tuesday. Banks closed, financiers jumped out of windows, and J. Noah lost a substantial part of his fortune. Yet on the very day the stock market broke, he called up his investment manager from the Union League Club in Manhattan and commanded: "Sell anything you can, only make it enough to buy my wife the mink coat she's always wanted." If he had to go down, his Margy would go with him in style.

Margaret, meanwhile, was ready to tackle her biggest challenge—getting the federal Comstock Law repealed by Congress. This time she decided to get advice; she chose the John Price Jones Corporation to help her.

The Jones Corporation gave her expert counsel on how to lobby, organize, and raise funds for a national endeavor, with all of which she agreed, but she was shocked when they suggested she join forces with Mary Ware Dennett to consolidate the birth-control movement. Mrs. Dennett had gotten a lot of publicity as a result of her sex-pamphlet trial, and while she had disbanded the Voluntary Parenthood League, she was receiving almost as many invitations to lecture as Margaret. Besides, the sedate Mary Dennett was far more acceptable to the medical profession than the volatile Margaret Sanger. But, for Margaret to belatedly admire Dennett was one thing—join forces with her? Never.

A second shock came when the Jones Corporation declared that a nation-wide campaign would take far more money then Margaret had anticipated. The Depression, instead of ending quickly, as most people had expected, was getting worse. As a result, the Jones people were afraid she would never be able to raise enough funds. Here Margaret was cocky. During the past few years some of the richest people in the country had become her admirers—not only men like Juliet's uncle, Charles Brush, who now contributed even larger gifts to be used at her discretion, but George Eastman of the Eastman Kodak Company, and John D. Rockefeller, son of the man she had blasted in the *Woman Rebel*. In a pinch, of course, she could always call on her husband as well; J. Noah might complain loudly about his financial losses, but he would dig into his pocket when Margaret smiled at him. Indeed, during the height of the Depression years, while bankruptcies were breaking out all over the country, Margaret and her main financial assistant, Mrs. Ida Timme, managed to raise $150,000 for birth control, no mean sum during those bad years.

Yet perhaps the most shocking suggestion of the Jones Corporation was that Margaret step down as leader of the campaign. They stated frankly that she had become not only famous, but notorious; the Catholic opposition stiffened perceptibly whenever her name was mentioned. Her reaction to this was as expected. She shot off a blistering letter saying that under no circumstances would she retreat from a position, "which years of study, work and consecration have made unique." She immediately gathered scores of volunteer Washington assistants about her and hired a doctor, a minister, and a social worker to lobby at conventions of their colleagues. In 1931 she formally opened a headquarters for her national publicity drive at 1343 H Street—with herself as undisputed head.

Still, she was essentially a general without an army. She needed hundreds of assistants throughout the country—women to organize cities, counties, and states; volunteers to ring doorbells and keep going the kind of grass-roots endeavor that is needed in a political campaign. After a few months, she had organized enough people to mount a campaign.

The best-known was Mrs. Thomas Hepburn, mother of actress Katharine. Mrs. Hepburn was born Katharine Martha Houghton in Corning, New York, though she was so far socially removed from Margaret, they had never met. Katharine's uncle, Amory Houghton, was president of the Corning Glass Works, and Katharine's mother was one of those ladies with parasols whom Margaret envied. Yet Katharine Houghton had been brought up to be far more than a socialite. Her mother was the first woman in Corning to start a social discussion club, and she had stated in her will that she wanted her three daughters to go to college. When Amory, the family patriarch and will executor, disagreed, refusing to dole out college money, Katharine, though only sixteen, threatened to take him to court. "He can run a big factory, but not me," she stormed.

At Bryn Mawr she majored in political economy, supplementing Amory's stingy allowance by tutoring. She put up a sign in the washroom offering to teach anyone in any subject.

Soon after graduation, she married Dr. Thomas Hepburn. They settled in Hartford, Connecticut, where the young Mrs. Hepburn founded the Woman's Equal Franchise League, which later became The League of Women Voters. Attractive, red-headed, and feminine under her starched shirtwaists and mannish ties, she spoke about woman's suffrage on street corners and before men's clubs. Her league won women the right to vote in Connecticut in 1919, a year ahead of the national victory.

Fully aware of the need for birth control as well, she bore two children a year and a half apart, decided this was enough for the time being, waited four years to have two more, and then took another four years to complete her family.

Prostitution and venereal disease attracted her attention, when she found out that the biggest brothel in town was located next to the police station, on property owned by the Catholic Church. She trumpeted her findings so loudly the brothel was closed. Later, when a friend died of acute gonorrheal salpingitis caught from her new husband, Mrs. Hepburn founded the American Social Hygiene Society with Harvard's President Eliot at its head.

She had met Margaret at a birth-control dinner in 1928, laughed with her over the coincidence of their coming from the same town, and now joined the anti-Comstock campaign as Federal Legislative Chairman.

In Washington, Mrs. Hepburn was peppery. If she thought a Congressman was talking too long and boring his listeners during a Congressional debate, she moved to a seat behind him and pulled at his coattails until he sat down. But when she decided to run for the Senate herself, her husband objected so strongly she gave in.

The campaign under way, Margaret suddenly came to another decision. She would dismiss Anna Lifschiz, her longtime secretary, and do it as ruthlessly as she had divorced Bill Sanger. She summoned Anna to the living room of the house she had rented in Washington as her personal retreat and announced: "All things wear out their usefulness in time. Typewriters, desks, people. I'm sorry, but you have lost your usefulness to the movement. You'll have to go."

In Anna's place she took on Florence Rose, a stout spinster with what her friends called a passion for push. "You can talk and talk to Florence Rose but she doesn't budge," was a common remark. (She would dismiss Florence Rose as abruptly when Rose proved too obstinate and pushy for the staid university crowd Margaret began to associate with.)

Later, Margaret became contrite over her dismissal of Anna, and found her a job as manager of the newly opened branch of the Holland Rantos Company in Los Angeles. When she told Anna she was doing this, Anna protested that she had no more experience managing an office than she originally had in typing. But Anna took in misfits and oddballs who worked so hard for her that the operation became a success.

For the New Year, Hugh, knowing her passion for diaries, sent her one as a New Year's present, interlarding the dates with poetic quotes in his tiny handwriting. Margaret, meanwhile, planned an intensive speaking tour of the West Coast as well as a Western states conference in Los Angeles.

The conference was held on February 20 at the Los Angeles Biltmore. Margaret's diary records Mrs. B. P. Schulberg, wife of the movie producer and mother of Budd Schulberg, as a member of its committee, "plus at least four Doctors of Divinity, two Ph. D.'s and two M.D.'s, the last being the hardest to snare."

J. Noah joined her in Los Angeles, perhaps because he had no other way of filling his time. Summers he still made the round of fine hotels, reciting to Margaret the details of every meal. But winters he stayed at Willowlake with nothing to do, except chat with the gardener or visit a neighbor if his chauffeur could manage to get one of his cars down the icy slope. The Christmas before, Grant had sent him a box of fine cigars, and he admitted, "I am so bored I have been smoking a big one three times a day."

Out West, they rented a small house in Pasadena, complete with cook, butler, maids, and chauffeur. Juliet visited them on her way home from Mexico after her movie proved an abysmal failure. She was thoroughly downcast. Margaret thought it would cheer Juliet up if she, Juliet, and J. Noah formally became members of Unity, a religious cult they had been toying with for some time.

Unity was an obscure cult founded in 1887 by Charles Fillmore, a crippled and bankrupt man, whose wife was ill with tuberculosis. He announced he had discovered "a mental treatment that was guaranteed to cure every ill the flesh is heir to," though he declared it was neither a church nor a denomination, but "a non-sectarian educational institution demonstrating that the teaching of Jesus is practical as a way of life seven days a week."

Fillmore admitted that sin and sickness were real but taught they could be overcome. Health was natural, he said, sickness unnatural; if one avoided anything that injured the body such as anger, hatred, self-interest, alcohol, or tobacco, he could tune into the Universal Mind and get whatever he desired.

Then, having declared against self-interest, he reversed himself and had the audacity to rewrite the twenty-third psalm:

> The Lord is my banker—my credit is good.
> He giveth me the key to his strongbox.
> He restoreth my faith in richness.
> He guideth me in the paths of prosperity
> for His name's sake!

This psalm had strong appeal, because the Depression was now in full swing and Fillmore asked for no dues, only "love-offerings" and subscriptions to his paper.

Margaret in particular got a great deal from Unity, staying in it for the rest of her life. It seems she sought many substitutes for her lost Catholicism. In her 1930 diary she reminded herself to buy a book called *The Christian Science Practitioner*, and another called *Egoists, a Book of Supermen*. She gave donations to the American Tagore Association and, at the other extreme, attended a Socialist get-together on New York's lower East Side. At the same time, in an interesting juxtaposition, she rated her favorite hotels and Parisian shops.

She remained generous to her old friends and family, too. Vito Silecchia and his children got their annual Christmas present. The

Board of Child Welfare of the Corrado Children's Home and the Poughkeepsie Children's Home regularly got fifty dollars each, while her sister Nan got an allowance of one hundred dollars a month and her brother Joe, out of work, was given one hundred dollars a month, as well. And when Grant graduated from Princeton Medical School, sending her a telegram saying, "Passed everything with flying colors," she rushed him a return letter: "What wonderful news, dearest son, your telegram brought us. Pater was so proud and happy he began telling everyone as though *he* did it." She deposited five hundred dollars in Grant's name to start a savings account. At the same time, Stuart got a gift of two hundred dollars. All this, plus the eighteen hundred dollars a year for Havelock, and a special sum to Robert Parker for helping her do an article for *Parents' Magazine*, were duly entered in her check book. A whopping one hundred seven thousand was paid to Tripler and Company, New York's most exclusive haberdasher, for the made-to-order clothes J. Noah needed to accommodate his extra weight. All in all, unlike many of the formerly wealthy, Mr. and Mrs. J. Noah H. Slee were not singing, "Brother, can you spare a dime?" during the Depression.

Yet with all her high living and religious strivings, Margaret was often sad. She had odd dreams, one of which she related to Havelock:

> Last night I dreamed about Bernard Shaw. I was lying on his bed (innocently) with him. His hands were bandaged from broken wrists and he was pink and fat—very jolly with children (his own) running about. Later I dreamed that like a flash of light came a picture of the Madonna & Child on a wall in front of me, a beautiful painting filling all the side of the wall. The queerest thing was that when the flash came I made the sign of the cross on myself as the Catholic children are taught to do. Then at once I was amazed that I did that—so that I seemed to be in two states of consciousness at once. It was a nice dream so full of color and motion. All because I started to dream of Shaw.

She dreamed about Bill Sanger too, writing Grant:

> Some day when you are in N. Y. I want you to look up your father and let me know if he is in a bad way. I've been dreaming about him for several weeks off and on and think you or Stuart

should look in on him and give him some money if he is ill or very hard up.

Margaret undoubtedly felt guilty about Bill and through Grant, who had remained his father's favorite, sought to remedy the situation. Grant found Bill living on the top floor of a walk-up tenement at 277 West Eleventh Street, not ill but hard up indeed. If help was offered him, he would certainly have refused.

Margaret as usual was the chief speaker in behalf of her campaign. In addition, she used a lecture bureau to arrange nearly two thousand speeches for her associates. The best of these speakers was Hazel Moore, a charming Southerner who had left the Red Cross to go after senators, congressmen, and organizations like the General Federation of Women's Clubs.

Groups like the General Federation of Women's Clubs took special efforts to reach. When Mrs. Moore, for example, showed up in Detroit to attend one of their national conventions, the delegates wouldn't let her in. Refusing to be fazed, she waited outside and handed out pamphlets to the delegates as they emerged. Even after she put on her best Southern accent, it took her weeks to win over the South Carolina delegation, months to win over a half a dozen other Southern clubs, and a full year to get the Federation itself to appoint a committee to report on the "doctors-only bill." After three years, Mrs. Moore got what she was after—a vote of 493-17 in the bill's favor.

Religious groups were similarly wooed, though here, Margaret usually preferred to do the wooing herself. For five minutes on the platform of a religious convention, she would travel hundreds of miles. When she heard that Rabbi Sidney Goldstein and Reverend Charles Francis Potter might be receptive to her cause, she hurried to see them and plead with them to contact other ministers. When she got the support of the American Unitarian Association followed by the Special Commission on Marriage, Divorce and Remarriage of the Presbyterian Churches, and the Federal Council of the Churches of Christ (a parent body representing twenty-three million Protestants), she sent out jubilant press releases. And when the United Churches of Christ gave her bill an overwhelming backing by declaring it was "in the interests of morality and sound scientific knowledge and the protection of both parents and children (to) repeal both Federal and State laws prohibiting the communication of information about birth control by physicians and other qualified persons," she sent out more releases, quoting the Churches of Christ word for word.

"I couldn't have put it better myself," she exulted, and the *New York Herald Tribune* and *World Telegram* agreed.

All this activity, of course, stirred the Catholics to even stiffer opposition. A strident foe was Father Charles Coughlin, the so-called "radio priest," who thundered: "We know that contraceptives are bootlegged in corner drug stores surrounding our high schools. Why are they around the high schools? To teach them to fornicate and not get caught. All this bill means is how to fornicate and not get caught." When this last harangue was made before a congressional hearing at which were present many of Margaret's associates, they felt as if they had almost been called prostitutes to their faces, and Margaret had to restrain them from throwing their inkwells at him.

The Reverend Wendell Corey of Notre Dame used his own highly emotional approach: "Continue the practice (of birth control)," said Reverend Corey, "and the sons of the yellow man or the black will some day fill the President's chair in Washington." And a large group of Catholic doctors in Brooklyn and the Bronx quickly organized a campaign of their own against the bill, with Methodists and Baptists joining them. This caused the *Milwaukee Sentinel* to protest: "The spirit of the guarantee of religious liberty has been forgotten apparently by the very churches which throve under its protection." And so the battle raged.

The Federal Legislative Committee now went into heated action. If twenty thousand letters had to be sent to men and women throughout the country asking them to urge their congressional representatives to support the anti-Comstock bill, the Washington volunteers stayed at their desks all night and got them out. If they became so weary they wanted to quit early, Margaret took them all out for coffee, and laughed them into a new surge of effort that kept them working long into the evening. Her laugh seldom failed to recharge them; it still had a magic all its own.

If it were not for the haven of Willowlake, however, she could not have kept going. England had been her escape valve for years. During the hectic campaign time, Willowlake took its place. When she became exhausted, she retreated there, ate her breakfast on the porch that overlooked the lake's blue waters and holed up in her private apartment for lunches and dinners. J. Noah became more and more furious over her seclusion, screaming at her over the house phone, but she refused to budge. "I always tell him that Ellis once said there ought to be a league for the husbands of famous wives," she confided to one of her associates. Slee wanted no league. He wanted his wife, but she couldn't be had.

Only her old maid Daisy was allowed to penetrate her seclusion. Daisy indeed had become practically a member of the family. She would march into the living room whenever she felt like it, and slump into an armchair to listen to the conversation. "What are you doing here?" Slee would demand furiously. "Just gettin' an education. Just gettin' an education," Daisy would reply

Always, though, Margaret was quickly back on the campaign trail, with Slee usually going along. From the Western states conference, Margaret had written to Grant, whom she now seldom saw, "It's a lot of work. I wonder I don't stop and play with life a little while I have the golden opportunity to play. I guess a queer driving force gets hold of us, isn't it? You have it too, I think."

After the Western states conference, she reported to Grant that it was a BIG success and detailed to him a few days later a typical schedule:

> Am going hard, lecturing every night. Pater *wild*. We leave Thurs. March 13 for Denver—I speak there and leave for Chicago the same night. Wild again! Arrive Chicago the 17th and leave for Madison, Wis. at once. Then up to Minneapolis (to speak) for 18th & 19th—then back to Oberlin College and cross again to St. Louis for the 23rd and leave that night for home via Penn. R.R. Pater will go on to N.Y. alone from Chicago.

Grant answered wistfully from the university that he was dying to see her; didn't know when he'd missed her more. He guessed it was because, "as I grow older I appreciate you more."

At this point Margaret got the politically naive idea of trying to get lame-duck congressmen to sponsor her "doctor's only" bill. If Comstock had his bill passed by lame ducks, she could too. But Comstock's success had been a fluke; generally lame ducks, knowing their political careers are through, mainly linger around Washington until their time is up. They may occasionally try to get something accomplished, but they don't try too hard.

The first lame duck whose help Margaret thought she had won over to her cause was an eighty-year-old senator from Massachusetts, Frederick Huntington Gillette. He had been around for many years and distinguished himself by doing nothing. He did nothing for her either. Three other lame ducks did little more. They each went so far as to introduce the "doctor's only" bill, and each time they did she wrote Havelock jubilantly: "I'm sure we'll win this time." But she was always let down; they couldn't get it out of committee, for their fellow congressmen might act one way in private, another in public. Birth control was just too touchy a subject to be aired. Margaret had done a survey showing that few congressmen had more than three children; clearly birth control was being practiced. Still, one senator summed up his feelings: "The whole business is so damn nasty I can't bear to talk about it or even think of it. If I were the Creator and were making the universe all over, I'd leave sex out of it!"

And even when some of the more liberal legislators were willing to open up the debate, the Catholics opposed them so vigorously they were overpowered. When Mrs. Dennett had campaigned, the Catholics had given her merely lukewarm opposition. When Margaret or her followers appeared, they became fiery. The National Catholic Welfare Council set up its own lobby in Washington on the grounds of "protecting morality and the family," and matched every group that backed Margaret's bill with one that opposed it. They even stooped to personal attacks on Margaret, using an old tactic called "ad hominem," meaning "if you can't attack the subject, attack the person behind it."

Some non-Catholics joined them. The Canon, William Sheafe Chase, an Episcopalian, once more denounced the doctor's bill as a "crook's bill," insinuating that Margaret and her husband were making huge profits out of manufacturing contraceptives when actually the opposite was true. They were buying them at any price and reselling them at cost, just to keep up with the demand.

Slee, who was in charge of buying diaphragms, was very particular about quality. A 1930 letter, from an L. Halsenbad of the Ramses Company in New York, does its best to answer his complaints about faulty diaphragms. Halsenbad has been abroad and compared his diaphragms with those of German make. He is sure his are better—"less blisters, less cloudy, more transparent," yet Slee is dissatisfied.

Slee wanted the shape changed: Halsenbad has the forms altered. Slee has complained the diaphragms are too heavy: Halsenbad has them made thinner. The rings aren't right: He has them corrected. Other firms use compound rubber but he uses pure rubber "which is as much different from using low grade axle grease as Three-in-One Oil." Halsenbad is sure that when Slee and his wife get his diaphragms, they pound them, pummel them, step on them, and send them back as defective. But he's been a rubber manufacturer for forty years, and to please the successful Mr. Slee whom he respects, he'll try again.

Margaret responds in her own way to the Catholics' attacks on her. She went so far as to accuse one woman who appeared as a legislative witness for the Catholic Church of knowing nothing about birth control because she was a "childless woman." Indeed, when Pope Pius XI issued his 1930 encyclical on birth control *Casti Connubi* (On Chaste and Christian Marriage), Margaret went after him too.

The Pope issued his marriage encyclical in response to the British Lambeth Conference held on August 15, 1930, where the Anglican Bishops cautiously endorsed birth control as an alternative to abstinence "as long as these measures are carried out for sound reasons and done in the light of Christian principles." Pope Pius XI refused to go that far. For the first time, to be sure, he declared that intercourse between married persons during pregnancy or after the menopause (or at other times when conception was impossible) was not an act "against nature." But in all other cases, abstinence was still the only permissible method of birth control.

In an article written in answer to the Pope, which was published in *The Nation* and widely distributed in reprint form, Margaret declared abstinence "positively harmful to health." It could, she said, bring on serious nervous derangement. As her authority, she cited "medical science," though she never defined the words "medical science" any more than the church defined the word "natural," except to say that natural meant "something that appealed to the natural reason of all men."

If Margaret had been a better scholar, she would have said that contraception had never been specifically mentioned in either the Old or the New Testaments. Nor had there been official church opposition to it until Sixtus V issued an encyclical against it in the sixteenth century, and even then, he rescinded his encyclical two years later.

The prohibition against contraceptives, the Pope stated, was mainly to protect women, as the male user of contraceptives was apt to undergo moral degeneration. "It is also to be feared that the man growing used to the employment of contraceptive practices, may finally lose respect for the woman, and no longer caring for her physical and psychological equilibrium, may come to the point of considering her as a mere instrument of selfish enjoyment, and no longer his respected and beloved companion." Considering this statement, Jesuit historian Garry Wills points out that it might as well be said that frequent repetition of communion would lower respect for God.

Margaret took a break from her campaign work while Congress was in its summer recess, writing to Havelock about the Bureau: "We are now grand as can be. Your picture hangs on the walls as always and blesses and graces our work." After a summer at Willowlake, she told him, she was planning to take a trip to London, then go on to Zurich in September to attend an international birth-control conference she had organized there, "to include all the things that Geneva left out." But she postponed her trip when she heard that Havelock was ill. "It simply made me shudder to think of your losing consciousness even for a few minutes. I was so relieved to learn you are O.K. again. Pray keep well & don't do anything but *SIT*!!"

J. Noah was in the hospital too, recovering from surgery for a double hernia.

Still, Margaret soon changed her mind again. She would go to Europe earlier than planned because she heard that Hugh, practically broke, was thinking of selling Sand Pit:

> I can't bear for you to even think of giving up Sand Pit!!! The idea is preposterous . . . I wrote you yesterday that I should likely not find time to go to Sand Pit (while en route to Zurich) and asked if you could meet me at the boat & drive me to London. Now I *must* see you that's all . . . Don't for God's Sake sell Sand Pit without first giving your friends a chance to help you . . . We have all been having a difficult time financially the last six months. But something must be done & can & will be done.

She sailed for London on the *Europa* on July 23, leaving J. Noah at home to recuperate. When she received a cable from him soon after she arrived, saying: "Return. Every day is like a week. Cruel to leave me," she scribbled across the cable her intended reply: "How can you send such a selfish message to me when I am so far away?"

After a month in England with Hugh and Havelock, Margaret left to attend the Zurich conference. There, Margaret impressed Anna K. Daniels, an American doctor, as a "neatly dressed woman who looked always sad." But when Dr. Daniels flirted with a bachelor whom Margaret considered her exclusive domain, Margaret informed her that, when a desirable man was in the offing, she had first choice. As Dr. Daniels knew nothing about Margaret's personal life, she concluded that Margaret had no husband or children. She was quite surprised later when she was working at the Columbia Presbyterian Hospital and casually asked Grant Sanger who was on the staff: "Are you by any chance related to the famous Margaret Sanger?" He replied quietly: "She is my mother." It hadn't occurred to him to mention the fact.

Margaret had many reasons for appearing sad during 1930. Hugh was broke and Havelock was ill, and as an added slap in the face, or so it seemed to her, the *Birth Control Review* had quite changed. The magazine was now regularly using articles and reviews by Mary Ware Dennett as well as advertising a free copy of her pamphlet "The Sex Side of Life" with each new subscription. Equally outrageous to Margaret, it was listing Marie Stopes' book *Sex and the Young* as suggested reading on sex education, instead of recommending only Margaret's *What Every Boy and Girl Should Know.*

She countered these personal blows in many ways. One was to get J. Noah to send a check to Hugh, who she said was as ill as Havelock. J. Noah sent it on left-over stationery from his former business, decorated with brightly colored pictures of Three-in-One oil in cans and jars. "My dear Poet," he wrote:

> I am so truly sorry to hear of your illness and that you are so utterly miserable, that it becomes a pleasure to me to enclose a small check so you may go to the sea shore or elsewhere as I am a great believer in a change of surroundings to be one of the best panaceas for right hopeful thinking . . . I know how very depressed one must get to be out of sorts. As today is M.S.'s birthday have been reading proof with her all morning for her new autobiography. I am glad to report her health better than usual, imag-

ine her taking a swim in the lake every morning, especially these autumn days, and while I take a cold shower the year round, I want a warm bathroom. Dear man get well soon.

The Zurich conference proved quite different from the Geneva conference three years before. Birth control was openly discussed now—a significant advance.

Back at Willowlake, Margaret reported her success to Havelock:

> Just returned from Zurich. The Conference was good. About 125 persons, mainly doctors and other chemists, all experienced in B. C. techniques. *I had a good time too*. I'm planning another Conference for Geneva soon, getting to be known as a good conference organizer so it's time to stop.

She went on to boast to Havelock of speaking to nearly twenty thousand people in various places in the two weeks since her return, and spending eight nights in a row on sleepers shuttling from town to town. "I'm getting so I like to sleep on trains. So, like Johnny Walker, I'm still going strong."

She had a laugh when the *Review* ran a humorous story by Heywood Broun describing his visit to a home for unmarried mothers to which many young women came back regularly year after year. A social worker he spoke to explained, "We try to rehabilitate them but in certain cases we fail over and over again." "Why," asked Broun, "don't you think it would be a good idea to give these unmarried mothers contraceptive information so they wouldn't be such steady patients?" "Oh," answered the worker, "that wouldn't be moral!"

As for Margaret's biography, once Hugh had refused to do it, Margaret decided to write it herself. She made copious notes, then engaged Rackham Holt to do the actual writing, though it was signed predictably "By Margaret Sanger." Not knowing it was in preparation, Ellis had been approached by Dutton to do a book that would be about her and the entire subject of birth control. He declined, commenting to Margaret on October 21:

> Such a book is badly needed, and it is very nice indeed that I should be thought of in connection with it. But I have written them to say that with my increasing years and diminishing

strength, I cannot. Even if I could, the really important part of
the whole story can only be told by you. By simply telling your
own experiences it would be fascinating material. The dry mat-
ter-of-fact history of the movement does not seem to me important, and might be rather dull for the ordinary reader.

Margaret was modest with few people. Havelock was one. She replied that she could tell about her personal role in the struggle, but
was neither "learned nor scientific enough to do more." It was an admission she would seldom make again, except to Dr. Robert Latou
Dickinson. It seems both Havelock and Dickinson were men of such
compelling character they elicited from Margaret a kind of humility
she would never reveal to others.

THE BATTLE RAGES ON

For once the medical profession and the Church were in agreement. Priests declared that abstinence was the only allowable means of birth control. The Journal of the American Medical Association kept repeating: "We do not know of any effective method except complete abstinence."

Yet women sought something better. In the 1930's they wrote by the hundreds of thousands to Margaret's "mother department" begging for contraceptive advice. Others bought any kind of useless or even harmful commercial preparation advertised for "feminine hygiene."

So Dickinson kept working. Under his prodding, a few colleagues had begun exploring many devices. One of these was the stem pessary or "gold pin," a thin metal device that extended up into the uterus, then curved out to cover its opening.

Women clutched at it eagerly not only because of the magical connotations of the word "gold," but because it was comparatively cheap and promised to last indefinitely. Unfortunately, however, it was discovered that the pin did not fit snugly; it kept the area constantly open to infection and let sperm enter the uterus as well as bacteria. It therefore performed no magic at all.

Dickinson next asked doctors to explore the "silver ring," a device that slipped over the outside of the uterus and was supposed to hold the entrance closed so tightly that no sperm could enter. This too proved valueless. Next he urged them to examine the rumor that Russian researchers had developed "an almost ideal immunologic technique for men that provided up to a year of sterility"; this too proved false. Margaret, meantime, was spending her own money to persuade Edinburgh researchers working with mice to try to develop a chemical that suppressed ovulation. This research eventually developed "the pill." Yet when the Scotsmen reported their preliminary findings at the Zurich conference of 1930, they admitted fears of their experiments' social implications. "It is doubtful," they stated, "whether we shall ever wish to obtain a point where these dangerous weapons will fall into the hands of women and men."

The problem was indeed complex. If anyone recognized this, it was Dickinson. He saw that more and more people desperately wanted to limit the size of their families, and were trying any and all ways to do it. But as yet there was no contraceptive that was at once safe, inexpensive, aesthetically acceptable, and easy to use. There were, for instance, many cheap douche ingredients around, but some of these were unsafe and some useless. There were also several kinds of cheap condoms, but many husbands refused to use them. The best method, the diaphragm plus jelly, needed not only a correct original fitting but a refitting after the birth of each child, making it too costly and difficult for the majority of women.

In 1933, however, new hope appeared with the discovery of "the rhythm method." Many investigators had for a long time suspected that women could conceive only on certain days of the month. Indeed, during World War 1, two men, Ogino in Japan and Knauss in Austria, had independently observed from examining birth dates that the days of conception coincided quite precisely with the days of soldiers' leaves. Put another way, the days of the soldiers' leaves had been "ovulation days." They noted also that these ovulation or conception days occurred twelve to sixteen days before the start of a woman's next menstrual period, or about the middle of the menstrual month. It was then evidently that an egg or ovum burst forth from the ovary and traveled down one of the Fallopian tubes where the actual joining with sperm took place. They found too that if there were no sperm to join an ovum, it lasted only about thirty-six hours, before it shriveled up and died. The conclusion was plain: If a woman avoided intercourse during the crucial time that the ovum was alive, she would not conceive. Best of all, since avoidance of intercourse was not an artificial means of contraception, the Church approved of its use.

After the excitement of this discovery, however, researchers realized that calculating the safe time was not easy, since ovulation had to be figured as occurring at so many days *before* the next menstrual period, not after the last one. This figuring in advance was difficult.

The chief proponent of rhythm, Dr. Leo Latz, recommended that a woman determine her ovulation date by taking her temperature every morning of the month before breakfast, as he had found that on the ovulation day it shot up as much as half a degree. But women often forgot to take their daily temperature, so Dr. Latz suggested instead that they abstain from intercourse for a whole week around the middle of the month. He also devised calendars showing a woman how to determine the week of abstinence according to the length or rhythm of her particular cycle, as menstrual cycles can vary considerably, and he sent "rhythm calendars" flying through the mails. Complicated as the practice of rhythm was, the medical profession nevertheless called it a "ray of light," though a few years later it had to admit that the light was a feeble one. A common story went: Question: "What do you call people who practice rhythm?" Answer: "Parents."

So birth control plodded along. In 1934 Margaret was still sending Dr. James Cooper around the country to show those doctors who would listen to him how to fit diaphragms. She also sponsored another conference in New York in 1934, though the medical profession in general turned a deaf ear to it. Most of them dubbed anything connected with her or her clinic "sensational contributions by fanatical propagandists or hysterical ladies." In addition, editors of medical journals continued to close their columns to Hannah Stone's reports, and only thirteen of the seventy-five top-graded medical schools were giving any regular instruction in contraception. A few gave incidental instruction, but as late as 1936, nearly fifty percent still gave none at all.

Nevertheless, the public kept clamoring for birth-control information. When they saw that most doctors were either ignorant or silent, they turned once again to the quacks. And when in 1935 a federal court decided that contraceptives could be both advertised and shipped through the mails, if intended for legal use, such a rash of ads broke out in national magazines for what were cautiously called "feminine hygiene" products that almost a million dollars a year in revenue poured into the cash-boxes of their manufactures. Over twenty-one million a year was paid out for the products themselves. Even mail-order houses like Sears Roebuck and Montgomery Ward participated. One unscrupulous firm, hoping to trade on Margaret's fame, took the name of "The Marguerite Sanger Company" and jumped from state to state until the law caught up with it.

Many of the "feminine hygiene" products were quite worthless. In 1938 *Fortune* magazine reported that "millions of women have been duped and secret tragedies enacted," and that "the medically approved portion of business in female contraceptives is pitifully small." This made the Federal Trade Commission step in to stop some of the more flagrant abuses and the commission issued a statement laying the blame where it felt it belonged: "Neither the government, the AMA or any other organization will give a woman any advice as to the relative merit of these products." The commission obviously did not consider the few clinics in operation throughout the country important enough to mention. Where then was the average woman to turn?

Margaret herself was partly to blame for the current state of affairs. True, she sent out her pamphlets. True, she gave information to the women who came to her Bureau from New York and nearby cities, as well as instruction in techniques to the few doctors who sought her out. But she continued to frustrate Dickinson and the medical profession by listening to the social scientists and echoing their statement that "social and economic distress are more vital reasons for using contraception than medical ones"—a strange statement from a woman who was vigorously promoting a "doctor's bill."

Nevertheless, Dickinson persevered. Several months before, he had succeeded in getting the AMA section on Obstetrics and Gynecology to appoint a committee to see how doctors and social scientists could pull together to get the laws that hampered them changed. The AMA section had procrastinated by referring the matter to its Board of Trustees, who handed it back quickly, using the excuse that the matter was "too controversial to be looked into." Later, a Dr. J. D. Brook practically demanded that an AMA committee look into the subject, but the AMA now refused even to consider appointing a committee to think about it. Matters had come to a complete impasse.

Dickinson was puzzled. Being the kind of man he was, he found it difficult to realize that, in addition to the AMA's old fear of quackery, there were remnants of male chauvinism in the organization's obstinate stand. One doctor had actually started a textbook for nurse-midwives with this sentence: "I myself have never delivered a baby but I will teach you how. After all, a gentleman never soils his hands."

HUMBLE PIE

In 1931 Margaret was campaigning for passage of her "doctor's only" bill, though she was getting nowhere. She wrote Havelock:

> The bill was introduced in the House & we are now waiting to get the date of a hearing & then to push it to the Senate. So I'm just dizzy. Then the Women are giving me a medal on the twentieth—which means a speech & oh I'd rather they kept the medal than to go through the ordeal of it all!!

The medal was a Medal of Honor from the American Women's Association, bearing the citation:

> for integrity, valor and honor . . . for fighting her battle single-handed, a pioneer of pioneers. She has opened the door of knowledge and given light, freedom and happiness to thousands caught in the tragic meshes of ignorance. She is remaking the world.

In September 1931, the *Corning Leader* printed a front page story about the medal, using her picture. It was the first time they had ever mentioned her, and she wrote across the clipping, "A hero in my home town at last!!"

In her letter to Havelock she indicated that she and J. Noah were finally beginning to feel the sting of the Depression:

* * *

Our conditions re finances seem to be getting into nothing. Every day that Congress acts the stock market goes down. Stuart said yesterday that if Congress passes certain bills the Stock Exchange may close down for six months. Any way it's a lively time to be living. My habits need drastic changing, I realize now, but I'm not afraid of the simple life—I really never got very far away from it in my *very own way*. What hurts us both most of all is that we cannot do the little things for others which gave us such real happiness. My own were very few & small, but J. N. had hundreds of ministers on his pension list . . . Now he can't carry even one & it breaks him up to even think about it. You & Françoise have been absolute darlings. If you can get along over August, (without my help) it may be that toward the end of the year my affairs too will pick up & I'll be ready to help push things again then. It's so wonderful to have you well & to have "Secretary" helping & working beside you. I should die (really) if we could not *continue* to have *her continue* to radiate her love & joy beside you.

Next she wrote Grant at the university from her elegant New York apartment at 45 Park Avenue. "I am through lecturing for the season and feel like going on a bat. The opera or a silly play or something grand." When he answered that he had caught cold, she became motherly. "Do take care of your throat and keep dry and rested. Don't get overtired for a month at least.

"Stay in bed till noon . . .

"Sleep all day Sunday . . .

"See a doctor about your eyes, your nose, your bowels, your teeth . . . "

She also addressed him in terms like "Dearest Granty Boy," "Beloved Granty Boy," or "Beloved Sonny Boy," and signed her letters "With all our love, dearest of dears." When she found an old purse with some money in it during housecleaning at Willowlake, she sent it on to him with "I know you can use it joyfully." Yet Grant kept chiding her for not coming to Princeton except for football games, though when he went abroad at the end of the summer his letters were tender. He tried to sound carefree, calling her "old girl," and signing off "with a big hug and a squeeze."

Margaret spent the summer at Willowlake, carefree herself, swimming in the tree-shaded water, riding horseback, and giving lawn parties. When Havelock sent her a copy of his latest book *More Essays of Love and Virtue*, she answered that she would take it along on a short trip to the White Mountains:

> I have so much reading to do to catch up that I decided to go away on a "reading vacation." The Nation's affairs are still a worry and unless things pick up soon there will be much suffering this winter. This brings me to our own special subject about the Secretary. (Bless her). It may be that I cannot or shall not be able to send the full amount of $1500 a year in the future. I can send $1000 a year or $500 semi-annually. Do you think you can add to that & keep her on fulltime? I'm terribly distressed over this—as I promised to do it as long as you live. Our July income is not enough to keep us going & J. N. borrows on life insurance to get by.

Margaret tried to keep up with other obligations as well. Her checkbook stubs for 1931 show she was still sending money regularly to her brother Joe, to Ethel and Nan. She lists gifts to such diverse charities as the Porto Rico (her spelling) Child Feeding Committee, to a Dr. Peppard for "treatment for a friend's deaf child," to the defense fund of Tom Mooney, to Norman Thomas for "Art Young's illness," and to Tillie because "L. R. left her flat." She also wasn't satisfied with the work Rackham Holt was doing on her autobiography, so she added a co-writer, Roma Brasher, and paid Robert Parker for proofreading. Also for international birth-control work she sent regular contributions to Agnes Smedley in Berlin, to Gerda Ibsen at the Hamburg Clinic, and to an unidentified woman in Shanghai, in amounts ranging from ten dollars to several hundred. There was a two-hundred-fifty-dollar check to a Tom Hall for "a special pep conference for the Federal Committee." It mounted up.

What she needed most was someone to raise a large sum for birth control. Quickly. Since H. G. Wells was in town, she hit on the idea of giving a dinner in the grand ballroom of the new Waldorf Astoria. Because Wells' voice was high and thin, she had to hide a microphone under each table to amplify his speech, a new technique at the time. Wells was pleased by the reception committee she gathered from New

York's finest literary, artistic, and financial circles. From the literary world, she got Theodore Dreiser, George Jean Nathan, Hendrik Willem Van Loon, Herbert Bayard Swope, Alexander Woollcott, and Louis Untermeyer; from the world of finance, Henry Morgenthau, Jr. and Adolf Lewisohn; from the socialites Mrs. Thomas Lamont, Mrs. Otto H. Kahn, and Kermit Roosevelt. The famous educator, John Dewey, presided. At ten dollars a plate the dinner raised five thousand dollars, a stupendous amount during the Depression. "We made money for our cause with a very plain dinner and high thinking," she wrote Havelock on November 28 from her Washington home on Wyoming Avenue. "Only I was over-anxious that what Wells kept saying to me (in my ear) was not being heard at the back of the room."

Unfortunately, the hugely successful dinner was soon overshadowed by a sharp setback. Margaret's autobiography, *My Fight for Birth Control,* had finally come out (a second, called *An Autobiography,* also written by Miss Holt and a Warren Austin, was published seven years later), and the reviewers jumped upon her, saying it had "the flavor of a hagiography, or life of a Saint." It told of her own accomplishments only, giving no credit to the hundreds of dedicated men and women who had helped.

Hugh took particular objection to her rough treatment of Marie Stopes and her falseness about her marriage. She answered him with a mixture of defiance and contrition:

Beloved Hugh: If "joy & pain are woven fire" in the book, then you have successfully set sparks of that into your letter.

Now Hugh dear—just be fair, read again those pages about Stopes & see if I was saying "I've done the whole thing." No one else so far has failed to get what I said & what I meant, that her success in the B.C. movement was due to the work of Havelock & the Drysdales & those who labored for those ideas long before she or I came on the horizon at all. Ye gods, Hugh, but you are jumpy! Havelock says of the book: "It fills me with admiration for the skill & judgment with which you have dealt with difficult situations & troublesome people & the forbearance with which you have left things out." From every side both here & in England came remarks about the way I have set the truth & facts out, *relentlessly* perhaps but as I knew them & felt them. I feel no sense of guilt at all about Stopes because I never disliked her in my heart as I did & do Dennett. There you are doubtless right & I shall go over every word again & change it for the second edition which is being prepared now (if I see it as you say it is).

And now I come to my But, but before I reply to that I'll run down stairs & get that book & read those pages again.

When she returned from downstairs, she went on with her letter, switching from the subject of Stopes and Dennett to his jibes about what she had put in, left out, or falsified about her marriages. She had described her second husband as a "widower with three grown children who was head of a well-known business," said that she had married him "so she could educate her two boys in good schools, and had praised him for his quick intuition, unerring judgement of character, plus his kindliness, radiant personality, and heart of a child. But he was given no credit for his birth-control work or even the dignity of a name.

Bill Sanger fared little better. His name was mentioned, yet he was described only as the "artist-husband whom she left in Paris and sailed away from with her children little knowing we were never to be reunited again." Giving no dates or places, she then finished the subject abruptly: "We were shortly separated, then quietly divorced."

She tried to justify this vagueness to Hugh:

There is always a public side to every individual, the side one allows the public to see. Common decency aims to make that side inoffensive to others. It's like the drawing room of a well ordered home. We don't usher the public into our bedrooms. Nor should a woman or man (in my humble opinion) throw open the door of a very intimate sanctuary to the public. I know you do not agree in this, you have greater courage because you are a greater writer and know how to say intimate things like a poet. I have never had that kind of courage darling Hugh. Hate me, despise me as you may, it is the truth. I shall never outgrow it.

There is no lie to any caress or kiss I have ever given. *Ever!* That is one of the integrities of the heart & why I say we stagger before our own complexities, when we have that integrity. No use in my trying to tell you all this. No man except Havelock can ever know it. But that he does know it & sees it in women is why he understands so much of love & its vagaries.

And now beloved Hugh I weep, I weep because the Ocean is between us & I can not stretch my arms & gather your blessed head into my lap & laugh at you & with you & at me for ever writing a book at all. Margaret, with feet of clay!!

The chief fault of the book, however, was her insistence on the fact that she had been a registered or trained nurse. She had been accepted, she said, as a "probationer at a hospital in Westchester," where "the work was trying because of the long hours. But these years of training now seem a period that tested character, integrity, patience, and endurance." There had of course been no "years of training," only a few months. Still, she hammered home the point of "years" by describing a vivid fantasied scene in "a New York hospital where I was taking a post-graduate course," a scene that implied she had graduated from White Plains. But a careful check by the White Plains Hospital found no record of her ever entering their nursing school, much less graduating from it and being traditionally "capped." And the unnamed New York Hospital (actually The Manhattan Eye and Ear) found no record of her ever being there at all. At most, they say, she could have worked occasionally as a nurse's aid, but so many thousands of these come and go that no records are kept.

To add to all this, there was the exaggeration of calling the high-school-level boarding school she had attended by its more prestigious name, Claverack College, and her statement that in 1916 "someone else" had been arrested for distributing birth-control pamphlets, without mentioning that the person was Emma Goldman. And of course there was the dramatic story of her fleeing the country after the *Woman Rebel* indictment without a passport.

All of this threw the reliable parts of her book out of focus. In her defense it can be said that she was so beset by the Church, the doctors, and an indifferent or hostile public, that she had to give herself some kind of standing. If the medical profession would not listen to her because she was a "mere nurse," how much more fiercely would they have opposed her had they discovered she was not a nurse at all? And wouldn't her old anarchist friends have felt betrayed had she revealed that they had prepared her a forged passport when she had to flee?

Yet many people like Harold read her book without questioning a word. "It has completely engrossed me," he wrote. "You are the greatest woman I have ever known."

Still, Hugh's criticism hurt her; she tried to justify herself to Havelock instead.

> The book is going fairly well considering the slump in all books at this time, but it's fascinating to read the letters I get by the hundreds. People say they had no idea of the battle & the early history.
>
> Then of course there are the few would-be pioneers like Wm. J. Robinson who whines to his friends & gets them to write that I did not do justice to him & to his work as a pioneer etc.
>
> Wait until Marie Stopes reads that I was awarded the Medal for upde-up-um things like "vision, integrity & valor" by the American Woman's Association. Now that should make her love me more than ever . . .

Like a dog worrying a bone, she couldn't let the matter of her two marriages rest either:

> Hugh sent me into the depths of blues for a week. He said I was egotistical in regard to Dennett & Stopes, & cheap & false in regard to my marriage—(which marriage he did not say). Oh it was a dreadful letter he wrote me, heart breaking because he failed to know the *ME* who wrote the book.
>
> Perhaps any treatment of Stopes was not as finished & nobel as some one else could have done it, but what I said was true & *considering* the facts as you & I know them, she was not treated too badly.
>
> Well his was the only letter that hurt. I did want him to run with me through every page but he refused to do it. Ever my love. Ever.

In November she tried to make up to Hugh, addressing him in a letter by the name he loved most:

> Hey there Poet: You are actually getting into the Americans' stride. Lectures, books, writeups, reviews, God knows what! That's the drive & push I hate to think of you in, but it's what one must endure when popular or successful—yes? "Six lectures on Poetry." That's simply lovely, *do do do* . . . J. Noah has an office

down stairs & works like a slave on all the finances & bookkeeping of the b.c. doings. We have closed our house in Willowlake. The most heart-breaking thing was leaving my dogs.

At this point a new note crept in: "I had a letter from Havelock saying he had heard from his translator that you had been in Germany! Was surprised—so was I. Is it true?"

Then she went back to his jabbing at her book, a subject she simply couldn't let go:

There is something sterling & golden in that quality of you Hugh adorable one, to want the real Margaret to show herself. I know that's what your letter meant. You *do* believe that I had in my heart a bigger quality than I expressed in the book. God knows if that is so or not. I want you to believe it so. But I am growing. Only, if one wants (not) to pretend one is better or saintlier than they really are, then we should not write books. "Ah that mine enemy would write a book" someone said & it's true that writing, like speaking in public, exposes the stark nakedness of our souls.

She ended pleading: "My arms can't reach up to your neck, so bend a bit & hug me tight, *tight, tight.*"

Soon she was consoled by the fact that things were picking up in other directions. Dickinson was becoming distinctly friendlier. He had just written a scientific study called *A Thousand Marriages*, a book signed jointly with Lura Beam, and on September 19, he sent Margaret this charming note:

Your note of yesterday asks us to send you a copy of our book, now in press. Send you a copy? Almost the first one ought to go to you. Do you know what I would do if my committee would sanction it?—only they won't—that is dedicate it to you. Yours, more so than you are ever ready to believe.

Margaret laughingly pooh-poohed his idea of dedicating his book to her. "You forget, dear man, that M.S. is not 'scientific' or 'learned' or 'college-trained,' etc., etc. to deserve such an honor." Still, his letter gave her a much-needed lift.

HUGH'S NEW LOVER

In 1932, despite a forceful and greatly stepped-up campaign that caused hundreds of pro-birth-control letters to pour in, the "doctor's bill" died in a Senate committee. A Vermont Republican, Senator Warren Austin, cast the deciding "nay" vote, using the Depression as an argument. The President's Research Committee on Social Trends, Austin said, had discovered that a dip in the birthrate was taking place of its own accord because of the wider use of contraception. This was hurting labor, agriculture, and industry. Certified milk sales were down because there were fewer babies to drink them; jobs in the building trades were down because there was less demand for housing. What was needed to solve the Depression was a larger group of people, not a smaller one, in order to step up demand.

This kind of argument was new. Before, the birth-control debate had centered around individual well-being versus national morality. Defending morality, a woman had been called lazy or selfish when she didn't have a house full of children. Her health, pocketbook, even sanity, didn't matter; a houseful she must have, or "race suicide" would be the result.

Margaret answered Senator Austin and his colleagues by calling the members of Congress "boneheads, spineless and brainless." Anyone could see, she told them, that it was the huge number of people on relief that caused higher taxes and fewer jobs. And as to race suicide, the

329

middle and upper classes were still having as many children as before, while the poor were having the same number, if not more. And statistics showed that the birthrate among the unemployed was forty-eight percent higher than among those with jobs.

Congress slowly began listening. Even Monsignor Ryan of the National Catholic Welfare Council listened. Indeed, on April 15, 1932, Monsignor Ryan did an unprecedented thing: He conferred with Colonel J. J. Toy, a member of Margaret's staff, on the possibility of a compromise. In order to stop the bootleg sales of harmful contraceptives, Ryan said he might quietly support a doctor's bill. He would try to find a Catholic doctor who was willing to draft a bill acceptable to the Church, and after that, a Catholic lobbyist "to get the word around to the Catholic strength in the House and Senate to help get it passed." But Margaret refused even to listen to Colonel Toy's report. To her the Church was *THE ENEMY*, no matter what they proposed, and she couldn't work with them.

The golden moment of compromise lost, Margaret's bill was destined to die in committee again. But having gone as far as she had, she had no choice but to continue to fight on. In a letter to Hugh, she described her daily work:

Awaken 8 A.M., rush to Senate Office building to meet important Senator at 9:15. Promptly Mr. S. arrives, Secretary reports so sorry but Senator is not in & left word last night he would not be at office because of sudden call to committee meeting. I look at my list of other Senators & go down the Marble halls to catch another, "too busy" "too busy"—"not today come again." "Not interested," etc., etc.

I then go over to the Capitol at noon when Congress convenes & after roll call I send in my card & ask the Senator to see me for a moment, just to make a definite appointment. Sometimes I get one & sometimes I don't. After I listen to their loud talk from the gallery I come home to dictate dozens & dozens of letters to my Secty.

J. N. and I have our evenings together and read aloud or listen to the symphonies on the radio or go out to hear Paderewski or some of the famous ones who come here to play or sing. Not that I care at all . . . for social doings, except that in this Capital city one hears the gossip of the world as it reflects itself in the doings of the various embassies.

Now there Mr. Darling—this Sunday morning, so far, was given in communion to you. Ship ahoy! J. N. comes to breakfast.

In another letter to Hugh she let a different note creep in. Recently he had told her he had taken several trips to Germany, and since he seldom traveled far from home, she guessed that it was because he had found another lover. Though to herself she swore she didn't care, she gave herself away in a letter of January 31.

Beloved of darlings, It's simply ages since I had your last letter . . .

Germany!! So you did go. It was good for me to know that, after I had so positively said it was a mistake. Good for my conceit, but better yet for you to go no matter on what. You went, saw, conquered & behold, joy, faith, new hopes, visions. A further expansion of your consciousness & love.

I'd fly to Germany myself if I that I'd find for me what you found for you. (Take that in the beak!) Jealous? pooh! I leave that to little people. Look again on that photo (of me) that worldly, smart one & ask if she could be jealous!! *Nine Nine.*

Even this meager admission of jealousy was new to Margaret. When she had sensed a new woman in Hugh's life before, she had exclaimed, "You're in love!! Who's the lucky woman?" But in a few years much had changed. Margaret was fifty-two now. While her hazel eyes were as widely spaced as ever and her figure almost as good, her nose had begun to flare at the nostrils and her burnished hair to fade. Besides, the constant congressional rejections were upsetting her deeply. She needed reassurance and good company more than ever; it was all very well for her to tell Hugh she didn't care for sociability, she did. And as for the idyllic domestic picture of J. Noah sitting listening to symphonies with her or taking turns reading aloud, her granddaughter says these were pure imagination. She may have liked to listen to good music, but J. Noah had never been caught listening to music in his life, much less reading a book aloud. He liked to eat, drink, gamble, ride, go to the races, play the stock market, and make love to his wife; his interests stopped there. But Hugh, whose wife Janet still played the piano beautifully, and whose daughter Bridget was already giving cello concerts, had to be impressed.

She turned for comfort to old friends, answering Havelock's New Year's letter with:

> Your dear letter of New Years Eve came this morning & it is one of my dearest joys to know that you remember that evening when we sat in your kitchen at Brixton & saw the old 1914 go on its way and welcome in the New Year with a bottle of your famous Hock . . . My years are too full & active to be normal anymore, but it's interesting to be alive & well.
>
> I leave tomorrow for West Va. where I speak before the miners. It will be interesting to me, because I know the conditions there are said to be as primitive as in Russia . . . Our own internal financial worries and uncertainty occupies all our thoughts & discussion. J. N.'s affairs have struck rock bottom & only last week he lost his seat on the Stock Exchange which cost him $650,000. *That is wiped out.* It was from that his income came. I try not to be depressed and cheerless—so here is my love to you.

Margaret had once called her husband a "green-eyed monster" when he was closefisted. Now he had reason to be. She tried to be thrifty herself, staying a few days in a three-dollar hotel and describing humorously to J. Noah how cold it was and how bad the stale rolls in the Continental breakfast tasted. "Well, I thanked God for the coffee anyway. Perhaps I'm spoiled dear. But if I am it's your fault for making me fastidious."

After speaking to the miners she wrote Havelock of their troubles. Most had been out of work for a year and were living in tents after being dispossessed from their shacks. Yet the County Welfare Association "gave them a $2.40 allowance for food no matter if their family consisted of four or ten. No doctor, nurse or preacher comes near them besides." She had left for home feeling terribly upset, and gone straight to bed.

In a later letter she told how, in Newark, where she was invited to speak by the president of the local medical society, her lecture was canceled when twenty Catholic doctors threatened to resign on the grounds that she was "merely a nurse." She offered to send Dickinson instead; again the society refused saying now that contraception was "a moral, not a medical problem."

By the end of May, after months of lobbying, traveling, fighting for the right to speak and sometimes losing, Margaret's energy was depleted. She took ill with one of her recurrent intestinal attacks, and asked Grant to come down to Washington from the university to see her. After he left, she sent him a note of thanks saying,

> It was really adorable of you to hop on that train and come straight to me when you knew I was ill.
>
> Of course Pater doubtless threw you sky high for extravagance! But just keep your head up and always come to me if ever I send word that I am ill. I have a rising temperature again this morning but I would not have Pater know it, lest he come dashing down & make me worse.

Just two months before, she added, she had intended to stop at Princeton on her way back from a lecture engagement in St. Louis, but had decided not to because J. Noah was about to go into the hospital for another operation; she thought she should go straight home to be with him instead. Obviously, even though he often annoyed her, Margaret knew she owed her husband a great deal, and tried to give it. At this point, she was trying as hard as she could.

Slee's operation turned out to be minor, however, and he soon left for Woodstock, Vermont, to recuperate. But once there, he started to worry again about both his health and his money. He scolded Margaret on June 24: "Your three letters all received today. *Airmail is a waste of postage to this place.*" He begged her to take some time off and visit him at Woodstock, but Margaret refused because she wasn't well herself. A medical checkup in Berlin after the Zurich conference had shown her to be suffering from arthritis of both sides of her legs, particularly of the left knee joint. The doctor there advised her to take some injections and avoid standing whenever possible.

Back in the States, she had another checkup and was advised to eat bland foods only. Since she found it hard to stick to her new diet, she decided to go to a health spa where her meals would be rationed. Knowing that Slee could deny her nothing where her health was concerned, she chose a spa in Marienbad, Czechoslovakia. Before leaving New York she described her situation to Havelock:

* * *

I have been ill. This is the first day I am able to be up and about since May the 21st, the day following my two rebuttals and the oppositions hearings & our own. I was seized with pain in the pit of my tummy (called the Solar plexus by some).

Two Dr.'s summoned, only to shake their heads & say they did not know. One said "Colic," another suggested gall bladder, but no symptoms to verify (the last) diagnosis. Only codine or morphine gave temporary relief & the old demon came back again. Then on Sunday a headache set in which was like being pounded with hammers inside me. Not even codine helped that. Finally Monday morning a temp of 103 settled the question of the best place to be & an ambulance arrived & I was taken to the Garfield Hospital. All this happened in Wash. I spent ten days in the hospital, being XRayed, analysed, tested inside & out. The Surgeon decided it was gall bladder inflammation, but no operation necessary. So I came up here & the headache only ceased two days ago. I have a lovely girl-like figure as I only weigh 115 lbs. (alas the strain & pain leaves wrinkles & a look far from girlish). Anyway I am recovering. The Dr. wants me to take four months rest away from work & *thinking*. I'm not certain that is not a backhanded compliment and by the time this letter reaches you I may be on the Ocean en route to Marienbad. I will go directly to Bremen on a one cabin or Tourist boat. J. N. can not afford to send me, but if I go Tourist Class I think I can get through . . .

I won't try to tell you about the Hearings. They were stupendous. The point is that the bill *nearly passed*. So near that the opposition have doubled their activity. Some people claim that my illness was the result of Catholic venom. Marie Stopes would say they tried to kill her. Anyway it was a glorious winter's work, heavenly in many ways. I am a hundred years richer in experience & a million in knowledge. Next time we will win!

By mid-July she was in Marienbad with Juliet, who was always glad for an excuse to go anywhere with her. Another friend went along too, and they found accommodations in the house in which Goethe had lived, Margaret taking his room. "His very own stove and clock (are) before me," she exulted to Havelock, "and his portrait and that of his last loves hanging high above me."

She went on to describe Marienbad:

It's amusing to see crowds of grown up fat men & women walking around to music with green or blue or red glasses in their hands sucking water out of glass like babies on their bottles. They are all so ugly looking & so hideous in shape. I wonder God can make such monstrosities. I do not know how long this cure will take. It is my real opportunity to take a good rest, and I intend to do it as long as my money holds out. I have no hope of a stopover in England which quite breaks my heart to think of. The boat stopped at Plymouth & I remembered so keenly that trip from London when a wonderful & great man carried a sick lady's bag to Plymouth & waved her good bye as she sailed off to U.S.A. in 1921. How long ago that seems!! I seem to have lived a million years since that year.

Congress has not adjourned yet so I do not know what has become of our bill . . . we were all so nearly exhausted with the heat, & hanging around & the various hearings, Etc. that I began to want to kill one special Congressman from Vermont . . . We spent all the money in 7 months which should have lasted a year so the staff had to take a two months' holiday. Now we are in the hands of the gods.

Do you hear from Hugh? I have had no letter in ages.

Havelock hadn't heard much from Hugh either:

I have occasional nice letters from Hugh when I write to him but not otherwise. Just now, I hear incidentally that Eva Schumann, my German translator whom he mysteriously went out to Germany to see, is staying at the Sand Pit.

At last Margaret knew the name of Hugh's new German friend. In time she would learn that Eva Schumann was a professional translator who lived in Berlin and had done some translating for Ellis by correspondence. She had managed to get to England and lived for a while as a boarder at Sand Pit where she and Hugh had become lovers. "(Eva) says life is quite easy and comfortable at Sand Pit," Ellis went on, "with no signs of 'hardship' except that Janet helps in washing up, which Eva must consider a hardship."

Even though Margaret knew that Hugh had a new lover, Havelock's confirmation gave her another jolt. She needed another operation on her throat and decided to have it done in Paris. She also decided to take the initiative and write to Hugh, referring in the letter to a former lover in the hope of making him jealous.

> Paris is hot and as my last visit to Paris was with a man I adored in a big way I am suffering agonies from the memories of the past. He died in Paris after I went back to the U.S.A. Sometime I will tell you about him and his influence on my life.

Undoubtedly she was referring to Portet.
She wrote to Grant from the elegant Hotel Crillon:

> Darling Granty. I am in Paris and broke! So I came to the most exclusive hotel!! I sent you a (birthday) cable, trusting it reaches you on time . . . Your birthdays bring back to me always how much you were wanted and loved before you came. So *so* long before!! Also how dear Stuart was at the time, and how he too looked for your arrival. It's something to study in the future—how the wanted child differs, if he does, from the casually conceived and unwanted child.

She wrote to Ellis in the same spirit. "I am thrilled all the time by the things my boys do. I hope this maternal pride is not too old-fashioned."

Home again, Havelock wrote her a report on his "amazing Spanish pupil Hildegarde who has started a magazine on Sexual Reform and published two books though she is only in her teens," and Margaret went back to work. Hugh still hadn't answered her letter. Finally, he sent a short note. She replied immediately, reminding him of the little "peck" on the cheek he had given her when she did stop in England for a quick visit on her way home and begging at least for a continuation of their friendship.

> That letter of Oct. 28 Hugh dearest, was just what I needed the day it came . . . Yes, all that I have always said about your great mind & heart is true. And the poor little, weak, puny, sickly peck was true too alas. Anyway you are "free," I know what you mean

Hugh, at least I have an idea you feel like I felt once when a very young girl. I knew a man that a girl of seventeen thinks is the last word of manhood. We played around together during a vacation. The family did not like him & discouraged his attentions. He knew it & resented it. It was horrid. I went back to school, but was unhappy. No other man at school could come near being what I wanted him to be—only the lost one was right.

Luckily, she didn't have time to dwell on the past; soon she was back in Washington lobbying and fund raising. This, plus lecturing, gave her few free hours. In a letter scribbled to Havelock, she said:

All kinds of work could be done were it not for lack of funds, but the organization & movements that can survive during this depression must be worthy. . . . Spain would be the best place to hold another conference & if your amazing Hildegarde could get up sufficient interest to write us to come to Barcelona or Madrid I'd get the money by hook or crook to hold it there. It would be like thumbing one's nose at the Vatican . . .

On Dec. 5 I go out for a meeting every evening until Dec. 11— then I finish until March. After Christmas I go to Calif. In the meantime I am running the Clinic at 17 W. 16th St., also the one in Harlem for colored people, directing four workers in Wash. D.C. & several in the field, besides trying to run a big house in the country on a much reduced income & keeping a husband from being lonely. (Yet) I am "weller" that I've been in years.

Maybe she was "weller" because, just when she needed him most as a rival to Hugh, a new man had come into her life.

31

MARGARET'S NEW ADMIRER

The new man was Angus Snead MacDonald, and at first glance he might seem a poor rival to Hugh. Hugh was handsome and demonstrative, Angus was homely, with prominent teeth and near-sighted eyes. He was also exceedingly shy. Nevertheless, he was a few years younger than Margaret, intellectual, and of an original turn of mind.

Angus was born in Louisville, Kentucky. His father had deserted his mother, and a childless uncle, Eudolphus Snead, had raised him and his older brother in his strict Scotch Presbyterian home. The Sneads went to church four times on Sunday and wore a black arm band for a year, even when the most distant relative died. It was a wealthy home, however. Snead and Company, the firm that "Uncle Dolph" headed, was composed of prosperous iron-mongers who had moved from Louisville to Jersey City because there were more immigrants in Jersey to provide cheap labor.

In 1904 Snead and Company bid on part of the construction of the great Carnegie Public Library being built on Fifth Avenue between Fortieth and Forty-second Streets. Their job was to furnish the metal for the bookstacks, though after Angus studied architecture, he criticized the main reading room as "too regal and wasteful of space," saying that he would have preferred a lower ceiling, intimate reading nooks, and cozy lounge chairs, or even—what was then a novelty—an open-air reading room on the roof.

338

Angus got his degree in architecture from Columbia University and soon found a job with a good architectural firm. After a year as a draftsman, during which he worked on the plans for the prestigious new building of B. Altman and Co. at Thirty-fourth Street and Fifth Avenue, Angus' older brother, who had been destined to become the head of Snead and Company died. His mother persuaded him to drop architecture and become the New York sales representative for his uncle's firm instead. Overly conscious of his great height and plain face, he was not cut out to be a salesman. However, after a short time, he found a way of combining architecture with the steel business. He developed the first modular system for storing rare manuscripts in special stacks, designing these for the Low Library at Columbia University and the Library of Congress in Washington.

Yet, though happy in his work, Angus was a lonely man. Separated from his wife and two teenage daughters who lived in Connecticut, he had kept pretty much to himself. But one day in 1933, he saw Kitty Marion on the street holding up the *Birth Control Review*. The words birth control startled him as they had many others; that evening, with nothing particular to do, he wandered into a birth-control lecture. Listening to the fervent, petite woman who was speaking, he was fascinated; he felt that he was entering a new and freer world. Soon he contrived to meet her and ask her out for cocktails and dancing, for in spite of his large frame he was extremely light on his feet. In a short time he found himself seriously committed to her.

Meeting alone was easy. While Margaret admitted she had a husband and home up the Hudson, she continued to keep the top floor of the Research Bureau as her private hideaway. She could disappear there daytimes without even telling her secretary where she was; in the evenings she could always telephone J. Noah and make an excuse to stay away overnight. And Angus, who had no local ties, could meet her there for a long evening by the fireside that often lasted until near dawn.

Soon their night dates were more and more frequent as Margaret became impressed by his immense vitality. While working in Washington on the Library of Congress job, he would bound up to the top of the Washington Monument on foot while his associates took the elevator. As this kind of energy was partly due to Margaret's presence in his life, it made her exclaim: "What a man you are, my Angus!" Soon she was writing him from Willowlake:

Angus dear, what a power-dynamo you really are! Nothing can stop your innate masculine charm. The dancing evening at the Cascades was perfect; never have I known you to be in better form. Never so close to my heart in the fullness of your understanding. It seems now that we leaped the very centuries & came to see the problems of the other in a most miraculous way.

She went on to tell him she didn't know when she could see him again as she was still busy with her Federal work. "If you really want to have a peaceful life, you will not bother your dear head as to the when's, where's and why's of my getting to town. . . . I'll call you Wed. morning, but I won't hope to see you in the physical."

Every year was now a busy year for Margaret; 1933 was no exception. Early in January she had gone to the coast with J. Noah to do a series of lectures and defend the will of a woman, Viola Kaufman, who had left all her lifesavings to birth control. "Her brother & nieces claimed I had influenced her against them," she wrote Havelock.

The case was well prepared but the other side failed to make good or to appear at all. Now my hope is that the lawyers & executors will not take all she left. We need money desperately, and contributions are *low*.

My telephone began at 7:30 A.M. & was still going at ten P.M. Poor husband! He had his own room, but the calls followed him too & he is about "fed up" (he says) with a busy wife and birth control.

A few days later she was at her Park Avenue apartment, writing Hugh on stationery with, for her, an unusual heading: Mrs. Margaret Sanger-Slee.

Hugh darling: This is my Sunday in bed to rest & answer letters to my beloved ones. I start off with you, dearest of dears. I never knew my life to be so crossed by deceptions. Intrigues are still going on. But I say this prayer often: "In the quietness & confidence of the all knowing spirit within me, I am established in Wisdom, understanding & love."

That helps me a lot. You don't need prayers or to pray, but this woman *do.*

By Febuary first she was back in Washington making quick diary entries.

Saw Hastings, Borah and Bang bang bang! Hatfield no. Tried Hatfield again—no luck.

Febuary 3—Sen. Norris—loads of letters & telegrams arrive— worked until 12 P.M. delivered folders re replies Judaism to Hastings . . . Ran back to N.Y. & Juliet's for weekend. Now back to Wash. for Judiciary Committee—"Catholic Safe Period Challenge" story in *Tribune.*

March 13—To Wash. again after rest at Willowlake & glorious snowstorm. Bill S 4436 voted on—but failed. Discouraged, sailed to Nassau for a month with J. N.

March 20—Managed to get speaking engagement at Student Forum of Mt. Holyoke College, So. Hadley, Mass.!!

Meanwhile, Harold had reread her autobiography and was thrilled as ever. "Your book has revealed so much to me that I guessed at but I didn't really *know* about that marvellous soul of yours, and that soul isn't the only thing about you that I think wonderful," he wrote on March 18.

She was put out by the last remark, and wrote back accusing him of being vulgar. For all her belief in free love, her friends had never heard her make an off-color remark or tell an off-color joke.

Soon she was writing Hugh again:

Your letter came yesterday. Juliet is here for a few days. She asks of you frequently & when we are together long enough she talks of you & your loving & great qualities.

I know you have gone through hell itself with worry and anxiety. Now it is our turn to do the same. The banks are all closed & the scoundrels have mostly run to cover with their "boodle" leaving the honest fellow to take the loss. We (J. N.) did not draw out anything before the crash, tho we were warned to do so. J. N.'s patriotism would not allow him to have such fears! So we are without cash, & thank God grocers & others let us get what we want for the present. Juliet too has had a tragic year—Everything gone except her house & that too expensive to keep going, but no one will pay to rent it.

Willowlake was also too expensive for Margaret and J. Noah to keep up, and no one would buy or rent it either. So in April 1933, they bought a house in Tucson, Arizona. Stuart had already gone to Tucson because of his persistent ear infection, hoping the desert climate would dry it out. J. Noah willingly followed because of his arthritic stiffness and the fact that Arizona had no state income tax, while Margaret thought it might help her bronchitis as well as lessen her fear of T.B.

The Tucson house was on the outskirts of the city in the section called the Foothills, and while it was smaller than Willowlake it was hardly less grand. Margaret had her own apartment on the ground floor toward the front, and J. Noah another in the rear. This set-up would allow her to have visitors unseen by her husband, particularly at night. They had a maid, butler, cook, and chauffeur as before. (Her story to Hugh about not having enough money for groceries was another of her romantic exaggerations.) Once settled, Margaret left J. Noah for the hundredth time and ran back to New York for a Town Hall luncheon and the legislative work that was becoming more and more frustrating. Surprisingly, however, many conservative newspapers had come over to her side.

On June 18, 1933, for instance, the *New York Daily News* ran an editorial on the decline of the birthrate:

> Some people are worried because they see only 131 million people in the U.S. in 1940, against 400 million Chinese and 80 million full-blooded Japanese. But if this is true, don't blame Margaret Sanger, the priestess of the (B.C.) cult. . . The phenomenon is probably due to women's desire for more public life, and men's for less responsibility, plus economic uncertainties.

In the same issue the *News* ran a big ad for contraceptives: "Stop being Frightened by the Calendar! Use Lysol disinfectant regularly and intelligently for intimate personal daintiness." It was hard to believe that, not so long before, Carlo Tresca had been given a year in jail for running a similar ad in his small radical paper.

On June 4, Mother's Day, Margaret had what was for her as unusual a speaking engagement as the one before the Ku Klux Klan. This one was at the Abyssinian Baptist Church on West 138 Street in Harlem. A diary entry tells of the engagement for that Sunday: "3000 people expected. No fee."

And so the year moved on, with Margaret making more lectures than ever to a wide variety of groups. Then came the long summer break which she spent at Willowlake, from which she could easily travel to New York.

On August 1, she wrote Angus a letter from New York headed, *Hot As The Bad Place.*

> Dear Angus, et al. It's too hot for anyone to be pleasant, so I'm dashing off home after a full day of worries, troubles, plans, hopes.
>
> I've set a man to catch you and bring you into the New Jersey State work. I hope you will look into it, then I shall find it positively necessary to consult you often—very often. I want to elope!! Cast off all the clutches & break loose—yes? If a wish can be powerful enough, it will be realized. Anyway, you're a precious darling.

Angus shrugged off the mention of elopement as he didn't even have a divorce, but he answered on August 9, calling her what he would always call her after that—"Glorious Margaret." He wrote:

> I find myself loving you more (and longing for you more) all the time. Your influence has been such that the world seems very good to live in, so good that I want it all, particularly you. You are a great leader and the greatest woman that ever lived, and the most lovable (and impossible).

Toward the end of August Margaret went to see her brother Joe who was ill and still living in Corning. She took Grant with her, something she seldom did, and then persuaded him to stay with her when she went on to Detroit and Chicago. It was as if she feared being alone.

Her diary is blank until October 3 when she made an angry entry: "Row with Dr. Dickinson over book." She was referring not to a book of hers, but one on the Research Bureau, about which she had told Havelock:

Shocks seem to come to us from near & far these days, I always feel that death shocks are easier to bear than deceit or petty behavior in persons considered big. Just now I am having problems with Dr. Dickinson. You may not know that the study of 10,000 case histories of the B.C. Clinic is nearly off the press. Three years ago I employed Miss Kopf (Swiss) as statistician to work on our history cards & to compile the data. I got money from the Bureau of Social Hygiene for this study. After a year Miss Kopf worked her way into the Secretary's friendship (Social Hygiene) & thereby hangs a story of the way Europeans trick us Americans at every turn. It's really amazing how trusting we are & foolishly stupid.

Now the statistican Kopf calls herself *Author* of the study & Dickinson who is on the Committee backs her up. It's a mess, as I got the money & finally got a publisher to take it.

Now Dickinson who dominates the Medical Committee says they will withdraw their names if my name goes down as "Director" of the Clinic—not as author or co-author which I do not wish—but as Founder & Director of Clinic. The reason is that these gentlemen can not associate their names with a *Propagandist!* So the world does *not* move after all.

Margaret was nothing if not inconsistent. A few months before she had admitted to Dickinson she was "neither learned or scientific enough" to be connected with a scientific publication; yet she insisted again that her name be included, even though Dickinson was leaving his name off.

To soothe her wounded feelings, she took a quick trip to Paris and London. In Paris she saw Harold. "Harold heard I was in Paris and hopped over to see that I did not swim the channel," she informed Hugh. And in England she saw Hugh, then wrote him: "Darling Harold Cox came up from Kent to spend twenty minutes (with me). Another treasure. You Englishmen know how to make women adore you."

Then she whisked home again, refreshed, to prepare another Western states conference.

On October 18 she wrote Hugh again:

> I've been wicked not answering your adorable letter of ages ago—the one that bubbled with the elixir of life written after your new book was finished.
>
> Goodness I know what you felt like. I've got it too after a big lecture where I've been scared to death. Then I want to fly, or soar, and love the nicest man that walks the earth. Nothing is impossible at that time, but usually everyone wants me to drink hot milk & go to bed!! I could scream at their stupidity, but now that I know you've got it too I will never be alone on those heights again. Yes you would dance to the moon & make love to the stars en route. Oh that I could have been with you & forced hot milk at you & said "there there" as tho you were about to be ill.
>
> Ah dear darling precious one—what book is it? Why did you not tell me anything about it? Yes I know why—because when we were together alone I did all the talking—ye gods. What a dumbelle!

And later:

> The (Western states) Conference was a *whiz*. I was so nervous & tempermental & husband *would* come out for it & found me like a horse before a race & never knew a woman got like that & was worried over having married her & went home. He is really a darling & wants me to be happy. He cannot understand anyone doing this work, getting nervous, not eating, sleeping or enjoying a walk or anything & yet *keep on doing it*.!

Margaret wanted to say something to Hugh also about Harold, but didn't know quite what. She had long ago forgiven him for "not loving her" and didn't know whether to admit she knew about his quarrel with Hugh over his marriage. Harold, after not writing for six months, forestalled her, however:

> Margaret Darling, I shall certainly call you that, although it may be for the last Time!

Dearest, have you heard at all from Sand Pit? And have you heard that next year I hope to—(take a deep breath)—get married again, & to a woman with whom I was in the Divorce Court last Saturday? I don't want to worry you with it all; but if you have heard about it from Sand Pit, you may have heard a version which is, shall we say a little one-sided? The truth is that after ill-treating her for thirteen years & being a dangerously bad influence on the children, her husband insisted on turning the three out & having the home to himself; and when the lawyer looked into it, they decided (our divorce laws being what they are!) that much the cheapest & safest way was for him to divorce her. Whereupon she & I jumped at the chance, & the undefended suit went off without any press. So I get all sorts of things I have been wanting for some time, including two adorable little step-daughters (did you know of my passion for little girls?—I wish they never grow up!) But I lose pretty heavily too, because Hugh & Bridget have decided that I am henceforth unfit for human food. . . .

How I chuckled over your story of the flight to Nassau! You *are* a packet of mischief, you Irish rogue, you & the very thought of you sets me smiling—when I'm not lost in adoration of one of the world's real heroines. I do hope the bill *will* get through. It would be the crown of your life's work.

Harold's admiration may have stemmed from the fact that he saw in Margaret a combination of a great woman and a little girl who would never grow up. Angus was not so perceptive; he worshipped her unquestioningly. On September 29, addressing her simply as G.M.D. for Glorious Margaret Dear, he wrote:

Went to the Astor last night to hear you speak but lost out. However I had a nice little visit at your booth and my heart was warmed to hear the words of love and admiration with which your staff spoke of you. . . . You are a great leader, and a most adorable woman.

At this point Margaret badly needed to be heartened by the men in her life. The Washington battle was nearing a climax; she was forced to turn over more and more of the legislative work to Mrs. Hepburn and devote herself to the harder job of fund raising. In one of her depressed moods she even made notes for a will, speaking as if J. Noah were already dead, and leaving his portrait to his son. While to Havelock she complained:

> The world scarcely seems worth bothering about. Liberty is once again on the run & no new continents emerging for her on which to rest her weary feet. So she may die & let the devils have it (Catholics & Militants) . . . Sometimes I want to leave the country and never return. Anyway, the cause of B.C. marches on!

But once again some end-of-year cheer came from an unexpected source. Dickinson, refusing to be put off by her tantrums, sent her another of his courtly notes at the end of 1933, suggesting that she have her portrait done by a painter who was doing distinguished portraits of physicians, so that she could be included in a book on the history of contraception.

"What have you done to the gentleman?" her secretary Florence Rose scrawled at the bottom of the letter.

Charmed him, that's what.

A NEAR SUCCESS AND MANY FAILURES

Her congressional battle seemed to be successful at last. Margaret had grown increasingly adroit in her political maneuvers; she heeded her lawyer's advice to modify the "doctor's bill" to make it more acceptable to states with anti-contraception laws. When the bill came up before the Senate again in 1934, it seemed to have a good chance of being passed.

To help matters along, she mailed out hundreds of copies of her autobiography to selected people like governors' wives. She also scheduled one of her biggest conferences, on "Birth Control and National Recovery," for the very days the Senate hearings were being held and got hundreds of delegates to come from all over the country, insisting they make personal calls on their congressmen to argue in favor of birth control. "We sometimes felt we had a bit of a tyrant over us," Ida Timme commented. "But a tyrant we want to serve until she leads us to victory, and we all know that Margaret Sanger, only Margaret Sanger, can lead us to victory."

For the first time Congress was impressed by her economic arguments that the cost of relief was enormous, and that the Depression would not be solved by an endless stream of consumers. She saw to it that congressmen were handed copies of letters like these:

My husband has no job. He has been all over looking for work.

348

He walked twenty miles the other day for the third time to the county seat to try for a WPA job, but he had no luck.

We live in a small attic room. It's crowded, but we cook here, sleep and everything. I've pinched pennies until I'm desperate. There's only 25 cents left. What if I should become pregnant again?

As a result, the Senate Judiciary Committee reported the bill out of committee for a hearing, and it was passed. But its success was short-lived. A few minutes after the vote was taken Senator Pat McCarran, a man in the dubious position of being a well-known Reno divorce lawyer as well as a prominent Catholic, emerged from the cloakroom, and demanded that the vote be recalled. It was recalled, and he cast the deciding "nay."

It was the bill's death. Though Margaret and her followers would try again, they would never be able to get it out of committee. Their seven years of work and hundreds of thousands of dollars had come to nothing.

Hazel Moore sensed this, and when Senator McCarran passed her on his way out of the Senate she exploded, accosting the sergeant-at-arms. As she told the story later:

"Sergeant, arrest this man," I said. "What are the charges?" asked the sergeant. "Murder of thousands of women," said I. McCarran laughed and said, "I had to object to this bill because I do not believe in murder." To which I answered: "Are you accusing us who are backing this bill of being in favor of murder?" "That's what it is," said McCarran. I then said to the sergeant, "Arrest him for libel," and started on a tirade about an intelligent man making such a statement showing he didn't understand the bill (and probably a lot of other things).

Margaret reacted to the defeat in her own way and described it to Havelock:

I left Washington and took a boat for Nassau and drank champagne. When I could, I laughed long and much at nothing at all, swam, sat in the sun, and forgot the stupidity of man and loved

anew the beauties of God. J. N. was furious (because I came back
in debt) but I did not care.

Now she decided to take her long contemplated trip to Russia, going
the only possible way—with an In-Tourist group. She had wavered
over going to Russia for years, disheartened by the disillusionment of
Emma Goldman, Alexander Berkman, and Bill Haywood, but cheered
on by the enthusiasm of John Reed, who had written the momentous
Ten Days That Shook the World. The decisive factor was the news that
birth control had become official policy there. She would go and see for
herself.

She left on July 3, 1935, taking along Florence Rose and Grant who
jumped at the chance to go anywhere with his mother. J. Noah declined to go because he was busy trying to rent or sell Willowlake. Besides, he was seventy-seven and not up to the trip. If he went anywhere
at all, he said, it would be back to South Africa to see the town where
he had been born.

Margaret dissuaded him from taking the South African trip:

Don't mention South Africa—you would not be happier than
you are here. I wonder if *any where or any place* can give you happiness. God knows I've tried far harder than anything I've ever
had to do and have not succeeded. You'd better stick to (Margaret)
and be happy to have her when you can get her.

At the last minute, she almost canceled out herself. Her arthritis
was so bad she had one leg in a cast, and the other was very painful.
Still, she went.

Margaret found Russia cold even in summer. Worse, she discovered
that birth was controlled there mainly by legal abortion rather than
prevention. Since the state needed a large, immediate labor force and
pregnancy kept women at home, any woman could get an abortion as
long as she was no more than three months pregnant and could pay the
fee of roughly two and a half dollars. One woman told of having eight
abortions in a few months under this plan.

Also, there were very few birth-control clinics, and these had diaphragms that were so dried out and old as to be practically useless,
while anti-spermicidal jellies were in very short supply. While some
hospitals were clean, others were filthy. "I never saw an O.R. with fly-
paper before," she exclaimed.

She enjoyed the Kremlin, however, which she described as a "fairy tale museum," and she visited an old anarchist friend, remarking incredulously, "After seventeen years in Russia, he still remains an Anarchist!"

Soon she had a bad attack of vomiting and diarrhea she called "Mal de Russe." This was followed by a siege of violent headaches, probably due to her disappointment in not being treated as she had expected, as the world authority on birth control. When she got to Paris and the headaches disappeared, she summed up her impressions of the visit to Havelock:

> The (Russian) government treats you as a crook, spy & liar from the moment you enter their damn country. They rob you white while you are there & expect you to carry off pleasant memories of your visit. They will soon learn that we won't take this kind of treatment & start treating foreigners with some respect.

Grant and Florence Rose left for home direct from Russia, but Margaret went on to Naples, hoping that J. Noah would meet her there and go with her to Marienbad where they could both take cures. Suddenly, however, she heard that Stuart was ill. After many operations on his eye, it was again leaking infected matter, and his doctor had suggested a more radical operation. Margaret rushed home and countermanded the doctor's orders, taking Stuart to a pink adobe house in Tucson and putting him on a regimen of her own choosing—a three week fast which she was sure would purify his system without medical help. Desperate enough to try anything, Stuart agreed. She tried to fast with him but had to give it up after a few days, though he stuck it out, and for a short time the infection did clear up. But in no time it was back, and she had to admit she had failed. On this second visit, though, the hot, dry climate appealed to her so much, that she and J. Noah began to consider making Tucson their permanent home.

But she was still restless. If Russia hadn't worked out, maybe India would. The first all-India Woman's Congress was soon to meet, and she had been invited to speak by a leading delegate, the Maharani of Barodes. She was sure she would be able to start an active Indian birth-control program as a result.

She set sail for India from New York in October 1935. Before she left, she tried to improve her relationship with J. Noah, which had gotten to a crisis stage. Each promised to try to cut down on the scolding and bickering that went on almost constantly between them; for a while it worked. "It has been a very happy summer since you got a few ideas of harmony into your dear head and carried them out to everyone," she wrote him just before sailing. "Consequently everyone says 'how dear J. Noah has grown!' He always was dear but never expressed it to others, I say."

Yet he was not even up to the trip from Tucson to New York to see her off, though faithful Angus was there, as well as a group of friends who gave her such a gay farewell party that she sent J. Noah a note telling him it was almost like a first trip abroad: "All those old friends . . . and then forty-five packages of books, flowers, dates, figs, toilet articles, your fruit . . . Juliet gave me $100 to buy myself something, and Nan gave me a lovely notebook for my story with my initials in gold." The party was so exciting and crowded, indeed, that Angus could hardly get near her. Instead, he wrote her a note that reached her in France.

> Glorious Margaret: Even the brief glimpse of you on the crowded ship had a powerful effect. It has never been the same with anyone else in my life and I would not trade the few hours I have had with you for any other years. Such a feeling of companionship is wonderful and precious—but there has been such scant opportunity to exercise it.
>
> But one must not begrudge the price to pay to have for a friend the greatest woman in the world and the most interesting and deliciously charming.

Angus had finally gotten his divorce, and was about to marry "a sweet woman with a rare independence and bravery who will help make me a longed-for new home . . . " He wished Margaret luck in all things.

But luck had deserted Margaret for a while. Her speech before the Indian Congress was a near fiasco; its president, Lady Aberdeen, a recent convert to Catholicism, gave orders to the Maharani forbidding Margaret to speak at all and insisted that if she did, the Catholic Irish, Belgian, and Roumanian delegates would walk out. It was the old story. The best the Maharani could do was to call a special meeting of people who wanted to hear Margaret.

Her visit with Gandhi turned out to be no better. After a long hot journey she arrived at his home on his weekly day of silence, laid down her gift of flowers, took both his hands and observed that "he has an unusual light in his face that shines through the flesh; that circles around his head and neck like a mist. When I looked again it was not only the shiney appearance of his flesh that I saw but always the smile and a hospitable welcome."

Welcome or not, she soon found he was unalterably opposed to birth control. Indeed, according to Arthur Koestler, he was opposed to sexual relations altogether, preaching that wives should resist their husbands by force if necessary. Though only thirty-seven, he himself had taken a vow of chastity for life.

Gandhi claimed that he was "a slave of passion when my sons were conceived." Sex was "an expression of man's 'carnal lust or animal passion,' while women were its victim." He permitted sex for others only for procreation. Even then, abstinence was more holy.

Margaret was thrown off completely. He wouldn't even listen to her on birth control, much less change his mind. She spoke about the Indian population explosion that was so great it was leading to catastrophe, pleading: "There are thousands, millions, who regard your word as that of a saint. Tell them this. They will listen to you." But it was to deaf ears. Throughout their conversation, she noted "he held to an idea or a train of thought of his own, and, as soon as you stopped, continued it as though he had not heard you."

Margaret posed for a picture with Gandhi proving that at least she had met him. Then, very tired, she set out on another long hot journey to see the almost as famous Rabindranath Tagore. With Tagore she fared little better. He was in favor of birth control, he said politely, and he hoped she would do something to have it gain greater acceptance. But he was too busy running a school of art and culture to do anything himself.

The best she could do was to get a few doctors to listen to her and start a small birth-control movement in India. "I gave demonstrations (of technique) in my room, in my dressing room, in my car," she wrote J. Noah, "and then was the guest at so many extravagant state dinners and celebrations that whole processions of people came to see me off. I have been keyed up like an electric battery."

Yet still another disappointment was in store. After a third journey halfway across the country, she finally reached one of the fabled Wise Men who for years she had hoped would teach her secrets of eternal life, happiness, and beauty. But no matter how many pleading looks she gave him, he sat silent and told her nothing.

Between the intense heat, the highly spiced food, the high hopes followed by bitter disappointments, Margaret reacted in her customary way; she got ill. After pushing on to Burma, Malaya, and Hong Kong, she spent two weeks in Hong Kong's Memorial Hospital suffering from an excruciating gall bladder attack. But she had eight lectures scheduled for Honolulu on her way home and gave them regardless.

By the time she got home, she had been separated from J. Noah for six months. Sexually eager as ever, he had planned to meet her in San Francisco but an odd letter made him change his mind:

> I have changed. It's some physical and spiritual change, but I feel that the door of *sex-life* is closed for me. It may be a shock to you to hear this, but I have a queer feeling about this and prefer to keep it closed . . . It is something that cannot be helped and it's suicide to violate so sacred a feeling.
>
> It may be that you, too, have no interest in such activities and if so there will be no problem between us, but if you are still interested, then God help us to solve our difficulties.

Her meeting with Gandhi may have set her to thinking that part of his great power might lie in his celibacy. If so, she would try celibacy.

But she still enjoyed sex too much to remain celibate long. She never mentioned the subject again, and later sent Havelock a letter marked "confidential" that expressed a quite different point of view.

THE UNITED STATES VERSUS
ONE PACKAGE

If it hadn't been for Angus MacDonald and Morris Ernst, 1936 would have been a bad year for Margaret. She was fifty-seven, and hated it. Her unsuccessful Russian and Indian journeys had so shaken her that she craved love more than ever. A short while back she had sent Harold one of Angus' letters in an attempt to make him jealous. Harold had not swallowed the bait: "Margaret, darling," he had answered, "Your Scotchman is a man of genius! It is the best description of you I ever heard. The man is a wit, a poet and a psychologist. You really are a great soul, you know."

Later she wrote him that the Catholics were still hammering away at her: "Father Coughlin called me a 'renegade Catholic' & I'd like to sue for libel. I never was a Catholic of any kind."

Since her Catholic baptism and confirmation are matters of record, this denial of her childhood religion was one of her fibs. Another was a statement she made to the Reverend William Scarlett, Episcopal Bishop of Missouri. When she wrote thanking him for using her *Motherhood in Bondage* as a sermon topic, she assured him that "my husband and I have been good Episcopalians for fifteen years, while my sons have been for almost as long." Actually Stuart was an agnostic and Grant a Presbyterian, but the letter was designed to improve her image with a Bishop who had helped her cause. Yet she was risking that image when she went openly dancing and dining with Angus, the kind of things she had never done close to home since she had become a public figure.

In addition, stressing her devotion to Angus, she irritated him by popping in and out of his life without notice, often disappearing for days. She apologized for this sort of behavior: "You can never believe my office, as no one there *always* knows the facts of my activities. Were that the case I should have even less freedom than I have now. So I keep my personal activities as dark as possible in a spot-light world." Then she scrawled across the bottom of one of his letters: "Angus, a glorious dancer and would-be husband or lover, who finds me 'impossible.' "

Yet Angus understood when she had to break a date because of an emergency at the Research Bureau. She explained her breaking of dates this way: "There is simply no use, Angus dear, I'm out of the race. Time is crowded for the winter ahead & it's no use hoping—I'm not for play. I've made a strict program for myself in order to get done what must be done."

She also confessed to J. Noah that she would never return to the "garden of love" as she had once so blithely promised: "There is no use scolding and nagging me . . . Be cheerful, go to your club a few days a week, go to visit your friends. Take in the movies. Stop feeling sorry for yourself and be happy over what you have had and still have in the way of deep & abiding affection."

But J. Noah had not married to spend his time at his club or the movies. When they met for a short reunion in Florida he became childish and irritable. She described the scene: "You jumped in the air and shouted and began to abuse me and talk about calendars to keep track of time spent with you and not spent with you and finally ended by telling me to go and not come back. That, of course, was pure temper."

Actually, she was too distracted to think about anything except her congressional defeat, and a way to achieve her goal in a different manner. She was beginning seriously to listen to Morris Ernst who had been telling her for years that laws pertaining to morals had almost never been repealed in the United States; they had either died of neglect or been declared unconstitutional by the courts. Only Prohibition had been so universally flouted it had been repealed. It was through the courts, Ernst reminded her, that Mary Dennett's conviction had been reversed. In Dennett's case, the United States Circuit Court of Appeals had declared that the proof of obscenity must lie within the text itself. "The Comstock law must not be assumed to have been designed to interfere with serious instruction regarding sex-matters unless the terms in which the information is conveyed is clearly indecent," the court had said. As a result, articles in medical journals had been circulating without interference for a long time. Condoms had been sold too, on the premise they were to be used by men "for the cure or prevention of disease." The main block was the customs, which still seized female contraceptives and so-called dirty books. Yet even here there had been exceptions. With Ernst acting as attorney, James Joyce's *Ulysses* had been declared a serious work of art and allowed to come in. So had Marie Stopes' *Radiant Motherhood* and *Wise Parenthood,* books that followed her *Married Love.* He was ready to get the same permission now for pessaries or diaphragms on their way to the Research Bureau, if Margaret agreed.

In fact, he had anticipated Margaret's congressional defeat. Two years before he had ordered a package containing one hundred and twenty pessaries, sent from Japan to Hannah Stone at the Bureau, and notified the customs they were on their way. When they arrived, he had asked the customs officials not to destroy them, but to hold them until he could take the case to court. The officials had agreed. Now if Margaret could raise five hundred dollars for the basic paperwork, he would go ahead.

Reluctantly—she told him she would cooperate. She raised the money, and Ernst was able to start.

First, he got the case put on the calender of the United States Circuit Court of Appeals under the title of "The United States versus One Package of Japanese Pessaries." Next, he set about rounding up a group of doctors who would agree to testify on the Bureau's behalf. The last was by far the harder job. A federal case, especially on a "hot" subject like this, is held in a great glare of publicity, the kind from which most doctors shy away. To make the task still more difficult, he wanted not only gynecologists and internists but specialists in other areas of medicine so that he could include more reasons for legalizing contraceptives than the standard ones.

After months of scouting, he found nine doctors who promised to help. But at the last minute three backed down, telling Ernst frankly that they feared losing their hospital connections. Of the six who stood firm, the first was Dickinson. The second was Ira S. Wile, former Commissioner of Education and now an associate in pediatrics at Mt. Sinai

Hospital. Third was Louis I. Harris, a former Health Commissioner who was working in Public Health and had no hospital affiliations to lose. Fourth was Alfred M. Hellman, a gynecologist and a cousin of Ernst's, whom he told he would never talk to again if he didn't show up. Fifth was Frederick C. Holden, attending gynecologist at eleven hospitals, who was on the brink of retirement. Last was the internationally famous Dr. Foster Kennedy, a specialist in nervous and mental diseases who had testified for Margaret after the Bureau raid. Kennedy was the most difficult to get but the most prestigious; he was Ernst's trump card.

The trial was set for December 10, 1935, before Judge Grover H. Moscowitz, and though Ernst hadn't planned it that way, Moscowitz was sitting on the bench alone. Besides, he was young, liberal, and Jewish, while the other judges before whom Margaret or the clinic had appeared were mainly middle-aged, conservative, and Catholic. For a trial of this kind, Margaret was in luck.

The case got going on the date set, before an eager group of spectators. John F. Davidson, assistant United States Attorney, was the prosecutor for the government, which bore the burden of proof. Davidson's planned strategy was to hammer home only one point: the pessaries were contraceptives and the law forbade the importation of contraceptives. "All persons are prohibited from importing contraceptives," he kept repeating at the opening session. "Congress has so decreed, and Congress makes the laws."

"Do you think Congress could say it would be unlawful to import a surgical instrument which is necessary for an operation?" Judge Moscowitz asked.

"Yes," said Davidson firmly. "Yes, I think there is no question about this."

Davidson made a simple opening address to the jury:

The government has said through Congress, in a statute which is passed, that all persons are prohibited to import into the United States articles for the prevention of conception. The claimant in this case imported certain articles which were seized by the Collector of the Customs and he gave notice of that to the United States Attorney's office.

The claimant, Dr. Hannah Stone, comes in here and admits

that she imported these articles into the United States; admits that they were seized in this district, but denies that they are articles for the prevention of conception and denies that their importation is a violation of this statute. This statute says that if articles that are prohibited are brought in, then the government may come into the court, as it has come in, and get a decision that the article which is brought in violates the statute and that therefore these articles should be destroyed. That is all there is before you.

This is not a criminal proceeding, it is a proceeding which is brought really against these articles to determine whether they are prohibited by the statute or whether they are not. The government will have just one witness to put on the stand, a very eminent doctor who will describe this article to you and will show you that it is an article for the prevention of conception, that therefore the government says that this is clearly the type of article that is banned by the statute and you should find a verdict in favor of the government.

That is all there is to the Government's case.

Ernst jumped up and responded:

Just one remark I want to make. This is an unusual case. It is the People of the United States against a little bit of an object. It is the people of the United States against this box (Holding it up). It is not against a human being, but that doesn't mean that it is not punitive because if the government wins, this is destroyed. Our evidence is going to be directed to the defense of this article which, from my point of view, is far more important than the defense of any human being, because there is not any human being in the world, barring none, who can relieve as much misery and add as much to the health of the population as this article or articles like it.

There is only one other bit of evidence, and that is that we are going to put in evidence other articles that you or I, anybody could go into any drug store and buy that could be used both for contraception and for other purposes. We are going to show that soap and all kinds of drugs can also be used for birth-control purposes and for other purposes, and then we are going to raise the issue that if an article can be used for the protection of the health of the nation it should not be banned just because it might be used illictly or illegally.

When Ernst was finished, the prosecuting attorney put his only witness Dr. Frederic W. Bancroft on the stand. Under Davidson's direct examination, Dr. Bancroft testified that the exhibit under question was indeed a contraceptive device; he also explained how it worked. Then Ernst cross-examined Dr. Bancroft: "Doctor, you stated that you have prescribed pessaries or similar articles. Now, I would like you to set forth as fully as you please the medical indications upon which you have found it necessary to make such prescriptions?"

Dr. Bancroft: "I think there are many medical needs."

Mr. Ernst: "For example?"

Dr. Bancroft: "Tuberculosis, threatened tuberculosis, heart disease of the mother—many similar medical conditions."

Mr. Ernst: "It could be cases of kidney diseases?"

Dr. Bancroft: "Yes."

Mr. Ernst: "It could be cases of pelvic deformities which make childbirth arduous?"

Dr. Bancroft: "Not necessarily, with a Caesarian incision."

Mr. Ernst: "Diabetes cases?"

Dr. Bancroft: "Yes."

Mr. Ernst: "Toxic goiter where pregnancy places a great strain upon the thyroid and may seriously endanger the woman's life?"

Dr. Bancroft: "It could be, but the condition could be removed. She should be operated on for the thyroid, and then the pregnancy is a simple condition."

Mr. Ernst: "Cases where they are suffering from insanity and epilepsy?"

Dr. Bancroft: "Yes."

Mr. Ernst: "How about neurological disorders, disorders of the nervous system?"

Dr. Bancroft: "I am not a nerve specialist, therefore I don't feel that I am in any way capable to speak."

Mr. Ernst: "How about the very basic use for the proper spacing of childbirth in relation to the mortality of the offspring and, with regard to the mother, might there not be medical indications for a prescription of some such article in order to prevent the birth of a child if there had been a child born to the same woman within a few months?"

Dr. Bancroft: "That is right."

Mr. Ernst: "For the sake of the offspring possibly you would find cases where you would prescribe the use of this article to prevent syphilis and gonorrhea through infection at the time of birth or even transmission?"

Dr. Bancroft: "Yes." .

Mr. Ernst: "How about a case where the mother has four or five children and the husband has been out of work or has a six- or eight-dollar income? Would the health of the family be imperiled if there were another child and if that is so, because of lack of food, nutrition, decent home, decent housing; would there not be such cases where the health of the family would be benefitted by such a prescription?"

Dr. Bancroft: "I think that is a sociological problem, your Honor. That is not of itself medical and is something which sociology itself should take up."

Judge Moscowitz: "Can you answer it, Doctor?"

Dr. Bancroft: "No."

Mr. Ernst: "In addition to pessaries there are a great number of other articles that you prescribe for the prevention of birth, that consist not only of devices made of rubber but also possibly of chemicals that are applied by douche?"

Dr. Bancroft: "Yes."

Mr. Ernst: "Or jellies?"

Dr. Bancroft: "Yes."

Mr. Ernst: "Doctor, these articles that you describe, other than pessaries, can be purchased by any layman without a doctor's prescription in any drug store, or a good many of them?"

Dr. Bancroft: "I presume so."

Mr. Ernst: "I show you this bottle and ask you whether that is one of the prescriptions that may be prescribed by the medical profession? (handing it to the witness).

Dr. Bancroft: "It might."

Judge Moscowitz: "What is it?"

Dr. Bancroft: "Liquor Creosol Compound."

Mr. Ernst: "That, Doctor, that might be used by the patient through the use of douche bag or a syringe and an article such as this can also be purchased without a doctor's prescription in any drug store?"

Dr. Bancroft: "Yes."

Mr. Ernst: "Now, if your Honor please, I would like to have marked for identification that bottle and this box containing a syringe, known as 'Compacto Red Folding Fountain Syringe.' That is all, your Honor."

Mr. Davidson next re-cross-examined Dr. Bancroft: "Dr. Bancroft, when you have testified that you have prescribed the use of pessaries or vaginal diaphragms in order to prevent conception where it might injure the health of a woman who had tuberculosis or heart trouble and that list of diseases to which Mr. Ernst had reference, will you state whether or not it is not the fact that the use of such article is effective to prevent those diseases only by virtue of the fact that it prevents conception? Have I made myself clear?"

Dr. Bancroft: "Yes."

Mr. Davidson: "Leaving out syphilis and gonorrhea?"

Dr. Bancroft: "Yes."

Mr. Davidson: "So that again, leaving aside syphilis and gonorrhea, all the diseases which you testified the use of this article might prevent could be prevented only by virtue of the contraception quality or effect of the article?"

Dr. Bancroft: "Yes."

Mr. Davidson: "That is all."

At this point, Ernst jumped up again: "Doctor, just one more question. I am going to read you a statement made by a Catholic doctor, Dr. Leo J. Latz, which appeared in a volume called *The Rhythm*, and see whether you will agree with this as stated by a brother doctor. He says on page 113: 'Burdens that test human endurance to the utmost limit, and to which all too many succumb, will be lightened. I speak of economic burdens, the burdens of poverty, of inadequate income, or unemployment, which make it impossible for parents to give their children and themselves the food, the clothing, the housing, the education and the recreation they are entitled to as children of God.' Now I ask you whether you agree with that medical opinion stated by Dr. Latz in the book *The Rhythm*."

Mr. Davidson: "If your Honor please, I object to that question. That is entirely improper."

Judge Moscowitz: "I will let him answer the question if he can."

Dr. Bancroft: "Your Honor, my opinion of that is that that is a purely sociological state thing, that the state should have a committee to investigate economics of people in relation to pregnancy. I don't think that is a medical problem. I think that is a state sociological problem that the state should handle itself."

Mr. Ernst: "I understand you do not see eye to eye with Dr. Latz?"

Dr. Bancroft: "I see eye to eye with him, but not his means."

Mr. Ernst: "I see, so you see eye to eye with him as to the relation of the economics of a family to the number of children, but you doubt the method he suggests for preventing the birth?"

Dr. Bancroft: "Yes."

Mr. Ernst: "That is all. Thank you."

Dr. Bancroft left the stand, and the prosecuting attorney Mr. Davidson offered in evidence Hannah and Abraham Stone's *Marriage Manual*, stressing the fact that it described pessaries or diaphragms as articles for the prevention of conception, concluding that therefore the Japanese pessaries sent to Hannah Stone were things that, according to present law, could not be imported. The customs had been right in seizing them.

Having made this point, Davidson rested his case.

The first witness for the Research Bureau, Dr. Holden, was now called to the stand and duly sworn, after which Mr. Ernst said: "May I suggest, your Honor, there are quite a number of other doctors in the court room, all busy men, and it might be easier to proceed if I will ask the other doctors who are in the courtroom to step forward, listen to all the questions and then it will save your time after Dr. Holden is finished, in case they happen to agree with his answers, we could then incorporate in the record the agreement or where their particular views are divergent from his."

Judge Moscowitz: "All right."

Ernst asked Dr. Holden to state his medical credentials, ending with the pointed question, "How long have you been practicing, Dr. Holden?" to which the answer was "Forty-three years."

Ernst then got ready to question Dr. Holden but Davidson objected on the grounds that there was only one matter to be determined by the court: Were or were not the imported Japanese pessaries articles for the prevention of conception? If they were, he repeated, they were illegal and the government had the right to seize them.

It was the same when Ernst put his other witnesses on the stand. All had impeccable medical connections and years of medical experience.

All agreed that there were many instances in which they had prescribed contraceptive articles to their patients for the sake of preserving the woman's health, and would do so again if the law permitted them.

But Davidson merely kept using the same questions to all of them: "Were the devices seized by the customs contraceptives?" And as they of course answered yes, he used the same argument: "Then they are prohibited by a law passed by Congress from coming in."

At this point Ernst asked the judge for permission to do something he admitted was a little unusual, that is, to put Dr. Stone herself on the stand. He said matters had come to a sorry state when doctors had to be asked to testify that articles in their possession, whether a scalpel or any other piece of medical equipment were being either tested or used legally for the cure or prevention of disease. He made the point that the oath doctors took when receiving their medical degrees made them use such articles or test all articles only with the best interest of their patients in mind.

Judge Moscowitz gave permission and Hannah Stone took the stand.

She stated firmly that the pessaries sent to her from Japan were to be tested and used by her, if she found them valuable for the prevention of conception when in her opinion there were indications that pregnancy would be harmful to a woman's health. That indeed she had nothing but the patient's interest in mind.

Mr. Davidson had nothing to say to that except to repeat, monotonously by this time, that articles for the prevention of contraception could not be legally imported, and therefore the customs had had the right to seize them and they could be destroyed.

Ernst now jumped to his feet to ask Dr. Stone a final question. "The use of this type of contraceptive when used by the patient does not result in destruction of human life, does it, in the sense that by the use of such articles there is no joinder of the sperm in the ovum?"

Dr. Stone: "There is no joinder that would prevent a living thing. That would prevent the meeting of it."

Mr. Ernst: "So that in the use of your article there is no destruction of the human life in the philosophical or theoretical sense being made such as after the joinder of the sperm and the ovum?"

Dr. Stone: "There is no destruction because there is no beginning of human life."

Ernst concluded: "That is all, we rest."

Judge Moscowitz decided that, since "there is no question of fact for the jury, no issue will therefore be submitted to the jury. There are only questions of law remaining and the court will reserve decision on the questions of law."

The jury was excused.

On January 6, 1936, Morris Ernst opened his mail and found in it the judge's opinion, which he read with growing jubilation.

It said that in Judge Moscowitz' opinion the pessaries had been imported for a lawful purpose. That Congress had never intended to prevent such importation. That if physicians were stopped from bringing in contraceptive materials, or any other materials to be used for legitimate medical reasons, then doctors might be hindered from prescribing articles that not only would cure or prevent disease, but save human lives. He therefore issued a decree directing the customs officials to return the pessaries to Hannah Stone.

Ernst excitedly phoned the newspapers and told them about the winning judgment. They were so impressed that the *New York Times, Post,* and *Herald Tribune* gave the story prominent space, and the *Tribune* even ran Judge Moscowitz's picture.

When Ernst phoned Margaret, however, he was surprised to find she had received the news with mixed emotions. She tacitly admitted she had won her battle, to be sure; birth control was now in doctors' hands. But she hadn't won it alone or in the way she had planned. Ernst was sharing the glory which she wanted to keep to herself. In fact, as soon as she hung up on him, she complained to her family that he had charged too much for his services, when as a matter of fact, except for actual expenses, he had charged nothing at all. And the next day she went so far as to lose her temper and call him "a cheap Tammany politician" when he told her in the course of their conversation that he was trying to keep both Mary Ware Dennett's friendship and her own.

But she calmed down and apologized with generous insistence when he admitted that her dramatic tactics had proved far better than Dennett's cautious ones in hastening the victory. Ernst then became generous too. He gave a general press interview in which he said: "The law process is a simple one. It is a matter of educating the judges to the mores of the day. It is perfectly easy to win a case after Margaret Sanger had educated the judges, and she has educated many of them."

Of course, government appealed the One Package decision. The appeal was directed to the Second Circuit Court where three judges sat—

Learned Hand, his brother August Hand, and Thomas Swan. All of them confirmed Judge Moscowitz's ruling that the contraceptives be admitted, and the matter was closed, especially after a further appeal by the government to the Supreme Court was refused because no legal errors could be found in the way it had been handled in the first place. The victory became a victory with no ifs, ands, or buts.

Ernst gave a victory dinner at an Italian restaurant in Greenwich Village, including among his guests Margaret's anarchist friends Carlo Tresca and Elizabeth Gurley Flynn, and as a special surprise Harold Content, the man who had been the prosecuting attorney at the original *Woman Rebel* trial. Content cheerfully admitted that he had only been doing his duty at the time; he had secretly admired Margaret all along.

Equally warming was a telegram from Angus. He and his new wife had moved to Orange, Virginia, to raise beef cattle and start a woodworking shop. When he heard of the victory, he wired Margaret a corsage with the message: "I envy the flowers because they will be worn next to your heart." Margaret answered in another burst of self-realization:

You are a perfect dear to let me know you give me a thought atall atall. No woman in this life can be more unsatisfactory as a wife, mother & friend than M.S. has been & still is & doubtless forever will be. The wife & mother part has long ago been settled as hopeless. But there are still a few faithful optimistic friends like A. MacD. who inspire me to "wake up & live."

THE AMA FALLS IN LINE

After the victorious One Package decision, the AMA was for a while strangely unmoved. Doctors couldn't believe that at last they were free to prescribe contraceptives. They were afraid that contraceptives were still contraband, the decision having to do only with importation; they also feared that it applied only in New York, Connecticut, and Vermont where the Second Circuit Court had specific jurisdiction.

Morris Ernst cleared up both points. First, he explained to the AMA that since it was a Federal Court, the Second Circuit Court's decision applied to all the states in the country, except those that had definite local laws against it. Only Connecticut and Massachusetts had such laws; the decision therefore applied everywhere else. Second, he corrected their belief that the victorious decision applied only to importing contraceptive articles and told them to prescribe birth control when and where they pleased.

After the AMA journal ran an editorial quoting Ernst, letters asking for birth-control information, particularly from rural doctors began to pour by the thousands into Margaret's Washington headquarters. She set her four hundred assistants to answering them all, a job that took months.

Once they were answered, however, she had to begin the sad job of disbanding the Washington headquarters: close the files, move out the desks, give severance pay to the paid workers, and small gifts to the

unpaid. The money for doing this came from the estate of Viola Kaufman, the woman who had lived out her life in poverty and then left her
lifesavings to the cause. After the family wrangles were settled and
the lawyers paid, Viola's estate amounted to twelve thousand dollars,
which her will stipulated could be spent in any way Margaret saw fit.
She had also made the touching request that she be cremated and her
ashes sent to Margaret. Viola was given a simple ceremony, and her
ashes were scattered over the rockgarden in Willowlake. Margaret
erected a plaque in her memory in the Research Bureau, now called
the Margaret Sanger Center, where it hangs to this day.

There were still a few problems, however. Even after Margaret's federal legislative committee was dissolved, there were still two rival
propaganda organizations in the field. One was the Research Bureau;
the other was the American Birth Control League. The latter, because
it was independent of Margaret, was in a position of fierce competition
with the Research Bureau. But the lawyers for the ABCL saw a way
out. They proposed the formation of a new organization that would
combine both. The chief executive of the ABCL was agreeable, but
Margaret raised loud cries. She again called in the John Price Jones
Corporation to do an impartial survey. They reported that "the medical
profession today (still) suffers from the notoriety resulting from the
work of other than the ÅBCL," cautiously declining to name Margaret
as the "other." She wasn't fooled. "It's another knife in the back," she
retorted. "The ABCL is run by those whose interest it is to take credit
away from others and to snatch it for themselves." She rejected the
Jones report offhand.

After Margaret calmed down, the attorneys for the ABCL proposed
another plan. The two rival organizations should merge and appoint a
male doctor as president. As Margaret had always insisted that what
she needed was the full cooperation of the medical profession, she
couldn't keep protesting. In 1938 a new organization called the Birth
Control Federation of America would be formed under the presidency
of Dr. Richard N. Pierson. The name would later be changed to the
Planned Parenthood Federation of America with Margaret as honorary president. Nevertheless, a few doctors continued to dismiss her as
a "mere laywoman." At the time, gallant as ever, Dickinson sent the
AMA a telegram celebrating her selection as honorary president:
"Among the foremost health measures originating or developing óut-

side medicine, like ether under Morton, microbe-hunting under Pasteur, nursing under Nightingale, Margaret Sanger's service holds high rank." It was a tribute to warm anyone's heart.

But in 1937 Margaret was back at Willowlake reading proofs of her new autobiography, called simply *An Autobiography*. But when the book came out, it wasn't much better than the first. For, while Marie Stopes got credit for founding the first English clinic and J. Noah got a name, it was ghostwritten in stiff, amateurish language. More important, it again left out all the details of her personal life.

She sent Hugh a copy and when he didn't answer, she wrote him a pleading letter: "Dear dear Hugh, I miss hearing from you terrible! Why do you punish me like this? Do you hate my book?"

Hugh had kept quiet because he disliked her new book as much as the old one. And, he was much taken up with his lover, Eva Schumann, who was trying to console him for the failure he finally knew himself to be. In desperation, he told Margaret, he had volunteered for the war effort. "They read my ration-books if not my novels," he commented bitterly.

But there was also cheering news. The AMA reminded the New York Academy of Medicine that thirteen women doctors had been added to Margaret's Bureau staff; physicians from all over the world were coming to the Bureau for personal instruction, and free nursery care was being provided for the children many mothers brought along. This made Margaret as happy as she had ever been.

Rested, she again felt she needed a new world to conquer. She decided on China.

In 1935 the Chinese Medical Association had passed a resolution in favor of birth control, but the resolution had not been followed by action. Margaret was eager, she told the press in 1937, to see what she could do there in person. Some papers reacted to her news wryly.

In California, the *Sacramento Union* ran an editorial on July 31: "If Margaret Sanger can make China contraceptive-conscious, she can sell fur coats to the Fiji Islanders or sheer lingerie to Laplanders." And in Pennsylvania, the *Oil City Derrick* editorialized on August 4: "Mrs. Margaret Sanger has sailed for China to teach the Chinese how not to have children. We are afraid Mrs. S. will not be able to do much about that old Chinese custom."

Nevertheless, she went, but when she landed in China, it had just been bombed by Japan so that she was able to beat a dignified retreat, announcing: "The war in China has caused cancelation of my trip to spread the birth control movement of which I am the world leader."

Back in Tucson, she was restless in no time and sailed off to the Orient, this time to Japan, where she started a clinic in Tokyo in cooperation with Baroness Ishomoto, a woman who had made her own news by becoming a member of the all-male Japanese Diet. There at least, she felt, the cause was moving along.

Next she flirted with the idea of going to Egypt but gave it up, and went to Bermuda to accept an invitation from the governor to lecture. At the last minute, though, the governor was advised by the Catholic Bishop to "keep out of it" and turned her over to the Bermuda Department of Health. She wrote Havelock she had conducted five meetings in a Health Department hall, and at one, "the Bishop came and sat in the audience, sat with his head bowed and groaned at every good point made. Later he arose and stalked out, announcing he had spent a most miserable hour listening to this damnable doctrine."

Her wanderlust satisfied for the time being, Margaret was at last ready to enter a hospital for her gall bladder operation. The operation was performed in New York on November 1, and she insisted she "wanted to hurry up and get better so I can go back to China as soon as the war conditions are settled for peace."

But at fifty-eight, a person doesn't heal in a hurry; she had to give up her plans and join J. Noah in Tucson. While she was convalescing, Dickinson had another of his fine ideas: Would she sit still long enough for a portrait bust to be done of her? He wanted nobody less than the leading woman sculptor of the day, Malvina Hoffman, to do it, and he wrote Miss Hoffman on November 13, 1937:

> We recall that there is no adequate head of Florence Nightingale, to inspire nurses and women in general. We want Margaret Sanger for others as we have known her—a great leader, humble in success.

Evidently Miss Hoffman was too busy, because later Dickinson was writing her again. He was afraid, he said, that some day after Margaret was dead some sculptor might make a bust of her from various photographs and not do justice to her "alertness & shining spirit."

Margaret noted on her copy of his letter: "Isn't he a dear to suggest such a thing?" Eventually a bust was done by Joy Buba and found its way to the Sophia Smith Research Room at Smith College. The gold plate identifying it gives a wrong birthdate, as she would have wished.

Margaret ended the year 1938 as she ended many years, dreaming of her early days with Havelock: "I've been re-reading my old diary to make sure of the dates. But my head was in the clouds those days and my mind in the British museum, so my notes are scrappy."

Yet when he wrote to tell her of a new foam contraceptive which he thought ought to be tested, she didn't order the testing.

"My mind has been rather doped with amitol or luminal or some of the sleeping drugs I had to take," she explained to Havelock. "It was rather a nice condition for nothing made sufficient impression to worry me or to annoy me."

The enjoyment of Amitol and Luminol two months after a gall bladder operation was an ominous shadow of things to come.

BICKERING WITH J. NOAH

With time hanging heavy on her hands now that she was not able to travel, Margaret felt she had to look for new interests. Giving elegant parties seemed a good idea, but first she wanted to organize her household so she wrote out careful instructions for the way she wanted it managed:

All servants on duty at 7 A.M. *regularly.*
8:00 A.M. Breakfast for guests and Madam.
8:30 Butler go for mail.
9:15 Mr. Slee's breakfast served by butler.
Maids to vacuum clean one room each day.
Windows of one room cleaned each day.
Silver cleaned on Friday.
All groceries and meats and vegetables
    ordered *only* through Madam daily. Bills
    to be checked with each delivery.
Luncheon—1 P.M.
Tea or Cocktails—5 P.M.
Dinner—7 P.M.
Telephone—Take name and number & message
    in writing. Be courteous. Keep voice
    soft and patient.

Note: Dishes are choice, heavy antiques.
Request care in washing. Avoid nicks
and cracks and breaking.

Tucson, originally a small silver-mining town, had by 1938 become an expensive resort with fabulous jewelry shops lining Main Street and the Arizona Inn charging a hundred dollars a day. Margaret started playing the social hostess by inviting visiting celebrities who stayed at the Inn. When the anthropologist Bronislaw Malinowski stayed there, he and selected guests were given a dinner at her home. When Eleanor Roosevelt came by, she was given a formal tea. When Louis Schenley, head of the Schenley Liquor Company, decided to add wines and champagnes to his line of hard liquors, it was Margaret he consulted during a luncheon in her dining room.

But the stumbling block was J. Noah; neither she nor her guests could find much in common with him. He didn't read, so he had little good conversation to offer. He ate more than ever. He no longer rode or even walked; he mainly sat and was content to chat about the small events of the day.

Margaret then had another bright idea: She would take a course in watercolors, and use her painting as an excuse to run off on frequent trips to Mexico where there were colorful villages just across the border. J. Noah tried hard not to complain about how lonesome he was when she was away, but he exploded when she criticized him for repeating the word "lonesome" so often in his letters to her:

I won't spend my efforts in answering your stupid reactions to my being so lonesome. Humans change as years are added. You go back and back—and still wave the same flag of my being lonesome. At least I can enjoy staying put and not live in *trunks and bags*.

Then he seemed to change his mind about trunks and bags and began to talk again about taking the trip to South Africa he had dreamed of for so long. When Margaret flatly refused to go with him, he told her angrily: "I can travel alone and make friends myself just as I did before meeting you."

He didn't take the trip, mainly because he wasn't up to it. To pass the time, he again wrote detailed letters concerning his health and diet.

Margaret retorted to one of these: "I'm glad your examination proved you're alright. Why if your health is so good are you always so irritable and impossible and cross?"

He tried to be less cross. One evening on her return from Mexico she passed a place showing a romantic movie; she had already seen this film twice but on impulse, she ran in to see it again; J. Noah waited up for her until after midnight, opened the door himself in his billowing nightshirt, and folded her tightly in his arms. On another occasion after she returned from a run-away trip to Mexico, he started to chide her for coming home late, and she stopped him with: "J. Noah, you're English and I'm Irish, and you know those two can never agree. So simmer down!" He did simmer down. Clearly he could neither live with her nor without her.

But by February run-away trips to Mexico weren't enough to satisfy her, so off she sailed to England to see Hugh and Havelock. She went to Sand Pit to see Hugh first as always now, and was relieved to find him more relaxed and reasonable about Havelock, with the bitterness of their old quarrel over Françoise gone.

And Havelock as usual had a soothing effect on her. Her visit with him, she wrote him later, had "helped to clear away a lot of fog and solved several B.C. problems for the future. Thanks for being in the world and bless you."

In gratitude she sent Havelock an especially large check so he could buy a car; his health was failing fast, and he could hardly totter to the gate. She was sure one of Françoise's sons could learn to drive it.

But back in Tucson, the old restlessness took over; she started commuting by plane and train to New York, claiming she had to make repairs on Willowlake so that it could be rented, if not sold. She also said she needed to raise new money for birth control as the Bureau on Sixteenth Street needed repairs and refurbishing as well.

From New York she wrote J. Noah a letter that took him by surprise. She told him she was thinking of leaving him for good.

If Willowlake is not rented by June first we had better take it on ourselves—*unless* you are contented to live by yourself, as I believe you must be. It's always peaceful for us both to live apart, even though it is lonely at times. We are both too determined & independent & unable to change our ways of life. Consequently we should be frank with ourselves and decide if life together is what we need, or is worth the cost on our nerves and disposition. So think it over & make all allowances for age & temperaments and let us decide. I know how I feel for I want you to be happier than I am able to make you, & I want happiness also which can not be had together. All this will depend upon renting the house. If we rent it I'll stay in New York & visit with friends or get myself a flat.

Like a dog worrying a bone, she couldn't get away from the subject of their separation once she had broached it, and when J. Noah didn't answer she tried to justify her position, shifting the blame for their marriage failure onto him:

There is not much use writing what I feel as we get *no where*. If leaving you to your own friends & family gives you contentment & peace of mind, I'm going to make it as easy as possible for you to have that peace. You will have to help in a mutual plan of action. We will both be miserable for a while, but you will at least not have to worry about the price of butter & meat or what it costs to give my friends a cup of tea. That will be a relief & it's the only way I can help you, Noah dear—the *Only* way.

The remark about giving her friends "a cup of tea" was pure sarcasm, as before her last trip to England she had given an elaborate tea at the Hotel Plaza in New York for fifty guests, for which as usual he paid the bill.

He was again so taken aback he did not answer her letter. She wrote once more telling him that she was planning to fly to San Francisco in June to get up a protest meeting because the Birth Control Federation had rented a booth at the coming San Francisco World's Fair, but after accepting a check for eight hundred fifty dollars, had returned the money and canceled her out.

"About San Francisco," she wrote, "we'll both have to decide. I dislike to go out there as you know, but it will give me an opportunity to stop over in Tucson to talk with you and formulate plans for our future."

Noah still did not answer. This was partly because his son and daughter-in-law were visiting him, something they had not done for a long time, but mainly because he was so shocked he could think of nothing to say. Evidently she was holding him to the agreement he had made when he married her that she could come and go when she pleased. She had threatened to leave him before, boasting she could live at the clubrooms of the Woman's Party on an orange and a glass of milk a day, but she had never before threatened in quite this way. He was so shaken it took until May 4 before he replied:

I feared I would never write you again after your most *unusual letter* of Apl. 25, too much for me to fathom. God help me for having married a cause!! 23 yrs. dif. in our ages & you calmly state you cannot change, & yet you expect me to. Such reasoning is *beyond comprehension*. Anymore such letters & I will leave you forever & spend my remaining years in Cape Town S.A. & you can live your own life, which you have up to date done fully 75%. I am more than weary trying to please you & from now on I am not even going to try!! My days are numbered & I should be considered. I want peace, & not a lot of children or B. C. advocates running around my house . . . Your tired and faithful husband.

When Margaret received this letter, she wrote across the top of one of its pages, as if explaining things to herself: "Noah's son Lincoln & wife were trying to get him to go to Cape Town Africa & influence him to their affairs. I was furious!"

Soon she sent him another indignant and self-pitying letter.

Yours of May 4th is here before me and the first page reveals what I have long suspected and have felt. Now it has been stated so plainly that there is no further need to discuss anything except what is the best thing for us both to do. You are more than weary trying to please & from now on I am not even going to try! If that is your attitude then it is the end of our love and our marriage.

You don't want a lot of children or B.C. advocates around, meaning my two lovely sons who have loved you better than your own children ever loved or respected you. You say you will leave me "forever." That can all be arranged, Noah, dear, and now that the house in Tucson is full, I shall not stop there on my way to or from San Francisco as I had planned to do.

I'll ask you to send Pepper (her dog) to me at the plane on my return from S.F. to N.Y. You are a vain and foolish man to act so proud toward one who has loved you & given you richness & beauty of companionship & affection for eighteen years! You love only yourself these last few years & no one can make you happy except "yes yes" people & servants who do your bidding & have no brains.

She continued with a statement that echoed her accusation against Bill Sanger—that he had insulted her in public:

That evening at the plane an affectionate remark of mine brought forth a brutal brisk insulting attack which left me cold & sad ever since. You have forgotten it I dare say, nor do you care if you hurt me lately. It's just "too bad" if I or anyone else is hurt by your brutal & unkind jibes.

Our lives are rather complicated but all can be properly adjusted if it is your wish to go away to S.A. (South Africa). But you will come back—*and to me!* A man of your age (still attractive) will be a pawn for every golddigger & baby face that's in the game to catch such fish. You had better think things through clearly and act not on impulse but on reason . . . Best wishes and my love.

When she did finally leave New York it was not for either San Francisco or Tucson but for San Antonio, Texas, where she had heard there was a rich lode of gold to be mined for the birth-control cause. From San Antonio she started her barking letters again, speaking of the delights of wealth, social position, and husbands young enough to dance:

Men of all ages, even yours, danced last night at the club. . . . These men have not grown old & several of them are seventy-five & over. They mix with young people & have kept young by saying kind & thoughtful, even flattering things to people, so that their companionship is greatly desired by all the ladies & men as well. I'm having such a nice time.

Her next few letters were a mixture of good and bad news: She had raised a total of only $123,000 toward her goal of $310,000 for the funding of new clinics, although the foundations had not yet been heard from and might send in $60,000 more. Bill Sanger was ill and had to have a pristolic operation (her spelling) but she had told her sons he was their responsibility now. "I am glad I am out of it, thank God."

J. Noah did not answer her San Antonio letter because he could not; he had little choice except to let things ride. For while his health in general was excellent for his eighty years, it was difficult for him to get going in the morning, and even details like planning meals were a hardship for him. Indeed, without Margaret who knew his every idiosyncracy, he was all but lost.

Margaret, ready at last to go to San Francisco, had an unpleasant shock; she heard that Heywood Broun, one of her oldest and staunchest supporters, had joined the Catholic Church. She wrote him in utter dismay:

> Oh my God! This is all I could breathe after reading in Time (magazine) that Heywood Broun will be received into the Roman Catholic Church late this month!
>
> Heywood darling, are you sick? Are you depressed? Has someone given you a spiritual blow? Can't you run away? Can't you do something? Can't some of your friends come and kidnap you and take you away? Someone has hypnotized you through your need and love.
>
> All that I can say is that I want to weep. Perhaps you already know that the Archbishop of San Francisco refused to open the World's Fair there and threatened a Catholic boycott (unless the) management threw out the Birth Control Educational Booth . . .
>
> This is only one of the many indications that I have seen during the past twenty years that the Catholic Church is growing political and has ceased to be a spiritual influence in any country. To have you join up with this force is in my estimation far more destructive to this nation's welfare and our future civilization than the Fascist and Nazi parties could ever be. Heywood, with your brilliant mind are saying goodbye to your brains, to your logic, and will be like a good little adolescent boy scout that will swear not to think but just to obey . . .
>
> To say that we are devastated is to express it mildly. Can't some of us do something to release you from this pressure until the seige is over? Faithfully and sadly, your friend.

*   *   *

While indexing the birth-control papers Margaret had given the Library of Congress, Florence Rose found a carbon of this letter and typed a note at the bottom:

> We were informed by an intimate friend of Heywood Broun recently that of all the letters which he received criticizing or reproaching him for his conversion to Catholicism, Mrs. Sanger's was the only one that really made him doubt his decision and saddened him for a long period.

By the beginning of June, when J. Noah's family had left Tucson, Margaret relented and went to see him. There they straightened out their difficulties as they always would. For the thousandth time they fell into each other's arms.

Away on a short trip a bit later, she wrote him in a gentle vein:

> Yes, dear one, old people do talk of the past, of their *selves,* their doings, their dreams when they talk at all . . . Sometimes they are silent, when they have the wisdom and intelligence and learn how tiresome others can be. We will help each other.

After this, J. Noah gladly accompanied her back to Willowlake, which was now clean and habitable, and on June 30 she wrote Havelock a letter marked in capital letters CONFIDENTIAL.

> One thing I always wanted to tell you & will do it now as I feel you will find it of interest. That is, although he is nearly eighty years of age his sexual activity has scarcely waned. He is just as alert at the sight of a lovely shape & just as urgent in his desires as he was when I first knew him at the age of 63. Of course the frequency of desire has lessened slightly but not greatly. Instead of an irregularity it tends to be regularity, with sustained satisfaction.
>
> When I am away for weeks or a month I find him old & stooped & reluctant to action. But at sight of me & affection & harmony he awakens, becomes active & happy, thinks clearly, his memory improves, dresses up, puts on gay neckties & socks & feels young & happy.
>
> It interests me to watch the power of a love as his has been. He's British born, too!

*   *   *

It was the last letter she ever sent Havelock, for he was dying from an inoperable cancer of the throat, and was using all his remaining strength to finish the autobiography he had been writing on and off for forty years. It must have been a book that tortured him to write, for while he called Edith "the most difficult woman in England," he went on to berate himself for his treatment of her and to take upon himself most of the blame for her unhappiness. He also dismissed Margaret merely as "M———an American nurse" adding "At times I wished I never had known her."

When the book came out in 1939, Margaret was shocked beyond tears. Yet she rallied to his support, writing Hugh:

> The reviews over here were devastating & cruel. His public felt cheated in that they had extolled a giant, a God in fact, who by his own pen had proven to be of adolescent calibre. I hope we—you & I & Françoise—can erase that impression. I know that Havelock had qualities beyond & above those shown in that book. We must revive the faith of people in him if we can.

Havelock died after much suffering in July 1939, and Harold wrote Margaret:

> I hate to think that I shall never see Havelock's smile and twinkle again, but it has left me strangely unmoved in the depths, because his merely ceasing to be alive in this sphere is just a small affair compared with the tremendous grandeur of having known a great man and being privileged to recognize his greatness.
>
> *When* shall we see you? We are all well & happy. Write to me, Margaret.

She wrote immediately, telling him of something she had done after Havelock's death to lift her spirits: She had asked Hannah Stone to continue to charge patients no more than five dollars at the Research Bureau, this five dollars to include an initial examination, contraceptive supplies, and consultations for a year.

It was Margaret's ultimate tribute to Havelock. Knowing his disregard for money, she thought it was something he would have been happy for her to do.

THE HOLYOKE AFFAIR
AND MANY SAD DEATHS

Margaret was forever fighting with people, and later, making up with them. She was forever resigning from birth-control work, then starting up again. Now in 1940 she was setting out on one of the hardest battles of her career.

The battle took place in Holyoke, Massachusetts, on the heels of several signal victories. Right after the One Package decision, the *New York World Telegram* announced in a front page story that the first openly endorsed, government-financed clinic in the country had opened in Middletown, New York, and thirty-seven similar clinics were about to open in New York City alone. The American Federation of Labor, had refused to support Margaret during her federal campaign, but at least one important branch, the International Ladies' Garment Workers' Union, was promising to open a clinic, too.

All of this was heady news, and it tempted Margaret to come out of semi-retirement at the age of sixty-nine and take on the state of Massachusetts, one of seven states that kept its "little Comstock Law" on the books—a law that called the use of contraceptives "Crimes Against Chastity, Morality, Decency and Good Order."

Indeed, as late as 1928, a Dr. Antoinette Konikow had been arrested in Boston for exhibiting contraceptive articles during a private medical lecture. A few years later when fifteen prominent physicians filed a bill to legalize contraceptive care given by doctors only, the bill was voted down after a spokesman for the Catholic Church declared that "the medical profession in Massachusetts is of too low an order to be entrusted with such responsibility."

Nevertheless, in 1932, after consulting with its lawyers, the Birth Control League of Massachusetts (later the Planned Parenthood League) opened several clinics to give advice to poverty-stricken married women referred to them for health reasons by social agencies, hospitals, and clergymen. The first to open, called with deliberate circumlocution the Mother's Health Office, was in Brookline. Six more followed in Springfield, Worcester, Salem, New Bedford, Fitchburg, and Boston's South End.

All went well until 1937, when the Salem, Brookline, and South End clinics were raided in rapid succession. In each instance an imposing-looking woman had appeared with counterfeit social-agency credentials, was found to have alarmingly high blood-pressure, and was given contraceptive advice. All known methods were presented to her including rhythm. Yet a few days later she returned flashing a police-woman's badge. Staffs of all three clinics were arrested, and confidential records seized. All persons involved were found guilty and fined, and the clinics summarily closed.

It didn't help when the policewoman publicly apologized later, saying she had been forced to become a stooge "because the police had something on her brother" and had threatened to "give him the limit" if she refused, nor that a respected poll showed that eighty-two percent of Massachusetts voters were in favor of permitting doctors to give contraceptive advice to married women for health reasons, and sixty-four percent were in favor of having them give such information to anyone who asked for it. The clinics stayed closed.

The time seemed right for the Planned Parenthood League of Massachusetts to ask Margaret Sanger, the movement's most charismatic personality and persuasive lecturer, to start on a state-wide speaking tour.

At first everything went well. Sixteen hundred people jammed the Community Church in Boston on October 13, applauding when she told them how George Bernard Shaw had called birth control "the most revolutionary idea of the century," and Julian Huxley had said "it will go down in history with the greatest advancements of the human intellect, along with the invention of the stone hammer, the mastery of fire, the discovery of electricity and the invention of the art of printing." In Hyannis and Worcester she had similar successes.

In Holyoke things looked promising at first. Margaret was traveling with the socially impeccable Mrs. Loraine Campbell, president of the Planned Parenthood League of Massachusetts. The Reverend Ronald J. Tamblyn, minister of the First Congregational Church of Holyoke, after receiving the unanimous vote of his board, had offered his church as a meeting place on October 17. A group of women arrived in town a day ahead of Margaret's talk; they were full of enthusiasm and ready to do some advance publicity and get a little rest. They had hardly checked into their hotel when rumblings started.

On the previous Sunday, the Right-Reverend Monsignor John F. Fagan of St. Jerome's, the mother Catholic Church of Holyoke, had ordered a declaration to be read at all masses saying that

> we have been informed on good authority that a campaign is about to be launched in Western Massachusetts in the interests of the detestable practice of birth control. It is understood that a nationally known defender of this vice, Margaret Sanger by name, is to arouse people to pass a new state law permitting this vice to be practiced. Those who are sponsoring this lecture are engaged in a work that is unpatriotic and a disgrace to the Christian community. Catholics, of course, will be guided by the mind of Christ, and His Church, and will *actively oppose* any attempt to label this locality as a center of such immoral doctrine.

The Catholic declaration was also run in the *Holyoke Transcript*. Two days later Monsignor Fagan personally telephoned a prominent member of Reverend Tamblyn's church, a man who was also president of the Holyoke National Bank, asking him to oppose the meeting. The bank president was unimpressed; he had lunch with another member of his church committee, and both agreed to ignore the phone call and permit Margaret to speak as agreed. But the following morning Monsignor Fagan telephoned the bank president again and urged reconsideration on the grounds of "community harmony." The bank president began to weaken. He called a meeting of his seven-member church committee, including the Reverend Tamblyn, put the matter to a vote, and the permission was withdrawn by a vote of five to two. A Mr. Harlan was selected to make the announcement that "the problem of economic damage to Congregationalist members as a result of their allowing the speech to be made had to be taken into account." This quite clearly insinuated that there was now the possibility that all retail businesses run by Congregationalists might be boycotted by Catholics if they went ahead. Reverend Tamblyn sent a note telling this to Mr. Eugene Belisle, executive secretary of the Mother's Health Office who was traveling with Margaret, and the battle was joined.

Mr. Belisle sent out a notice of cancellation to the local radio station, which announced over the air that the lecture had been called off; as a result offers from surrounding communities began to pour in. But Margaret said, "No. I will accept none, I will speak *here*." She did not know how or where she would speak, and reporters who came to interview her found her looking tired, rumpled, and incredibly aged. Yet to all of them she kept repeating: "Somehow I'll manage it. I will speak *here*."

Mr. Belisle, with the help of another local clergyman, phoned the manager of Holyoke's Turnverein Hall who agreed to rent them his place. Mr. Belisle hurried over with the fifty dollars rental fee and was given a receipt. But in no time the president of the Turnverein was back on the phone. He was very sorry, etc., etc., but would Mr. Belisle please pick up his check as he couldn't let them have the hall after all. And so it went. Mr. Belisle left rental fees at other halls, only to have the same thing happen. All the fees were accepted; all were suddenly returned.

Time began to run out; a last-ditch attempt was made through an attorney for the city of Holyoke to rent a vacant lot or store, but the owners of the empty stores were mysteriously busy, and the chief of police said he couldn't give a permit for an open-air meeting without the permission of the mayor, who unfortunately was out of town.

At six-thirty, less than two hours before the scheduled time of the speech, Margaret was at a pitch of trembling excitement. Then, the ice began to break.

Holyoke had long been a manufacturing town, the home, among others, of Skinner's Satin and National Blank Book plants. Only a few workers in these plants were unionized but the ones that were, were strong. At about seven o'clock word of the threatened cancellation reached these unionized workers, and a half hour later Mrs. Campbell received a phone call. It was from the head of the textile workers union. "My name is Annie Sullivan," she said, "I am a Catholic and I do not believe in birth control. But I have just consulted with the other union officials, and we all believe in free speech. We have two small meeting rooms that we alone control. If Mrs. Sanger would like to use them we will be glad to let her have them, at no fee."

The offer was accepted and the union immediately started a grapevine of its own. Soon seventy-five people were crowding into their small rooms, many standing or sitting on the floor while policemen paraded up and down outside the hall. Margaret spoke, hesitantly at first, then in a voice that was vibrant and clear.

She told how contraception had saved the lives of thousands of women too old or ill to bear children. How use of it had prevented countless separations and divorces. How fathers had been able to get off the relief rolls they had been on ever since the Depression and find jobs that could support families that no longer grew larger year after year. How women, above all, had been able to stop aborting themselves or resorting to ruthless quacks to do the job for them—all as a result of using birth control.

In the first row of the audience, the Reverend Ronald Tamblyn listened intently. He told the press later that he had come to defend the principle of free speech, but in church the following Sunday he spoke more humbly. He stood up before his assembled congregation and confessed, "Only those who never do anything are those who never make a mistake. We at least did something, although we may not even yet see clearly what it was." He ended with a plea for "a clearer understanding of the valley of humiliation through which we have recently walked together."

Only the *Holyoke Transcript* reported the Reverend Tamblyn's speech, while the Catholic side of the story was widely publicized. The *Ave Maria* of Notre Dame, Indiana, covered it under the curious title, "Mrs. Sanger's Retreat." On the other hand, to everyone's consternation, both the *Nation* and the *New Republic*, to which the story had been simultaneously submitted, ran Tamblyn's speech word for word. Years later a pro-Catholic book about the incident, *Protestants and Catholics: A Religious and Social Interaction in an Industrial Community*, was written by Kenneth Wilson Underwood and published in 1957 by the Beacon Press.

Once more Margaret had snatched victory from defeat.

This probably made her bold enough to challenge Angus' attempt to help her.

Sometime before, Angus had met Cardinal Tisserant, chief librarian for the Vatican, at a Librarians' Conference in the United States. Having heard of Angus' pioneering work with libraries, the Cardinal had asked him to come to Rome and make new arrangements for housing the rare church manuscripts kept in the Vatican. Angus, still a staunch Presbyterian, agreed, on the condition he would not have to kiss the Pope's ring. But he also had other canny thoughts in mind. Maybe Cardinal Tisserant, who was Dean of the College of Cardinals, would become the next Pope, and Angus would have the chance to whisper a few words about birth control into his ear? Better yet, maybe he could arrange a meeting between him and Margaret?

The next time Tisserant came to America, Angus invited him to his Virginia home. Seated in deep black leather armchairs before the great stone fireplace, they relaxed over a cup of coffee followed by a bit of Scotch, and Angus casually brought up the subject of contraception. The Cardinal said he at least would be willing to meet Margaret and listen to her opinions. But now it became her turn to balk. Any and all Catholics were still enemies; she told Angus she couldn't possibly see the Cardinal on the arranged day because that very afternoon she had tickets to a baseball game. (She who hated baseball!!) She couldn't do it the day after, or the day after that either. Later, Margaret did meet the Cardinal in Paris; they talked for several hours, but nothing came of it. Margaret, however, couldn't resist raving to Angus about the handsome Cardinal with his impressive long beard, regretting that such a good-looking man should be confined by celibacy. And Angus wittily named his guest room the Cardinal Tisserant—Margaret Sanger room because both had honored it by sleeping there.

Other prominent persons now came to the aid of Margaret and birth control. The first was Eleanor Roosevelt. Mrs. Roosevelt had long been a quiet supporter of the Sanger Research Bureau. Knowing nothing about birth control during her marriage, and, according to one of her sons, resorting to abstinence as a contraceptive measure after her five children were born, she had been giving freely to the cause for quite a while. When in 1940 she broke her silence and publicly announced her support, it gave the movement a tremendous boost. But opposition came from an unexpected quarter—the newly created Children's Bureau in Washington, a branch of the Public Health Service headed by Katherine Lenroot.

Miss Lenroot, a hard-faced, thin-lipped woman, the daughter of Republican Representative Irvine Lenroot, was a career bureaucrat. Although it was her bureau that was supposed to help control venereal disease, and do something about the shocking number of deaths in childbirth among women who had borne too many children, she refused to see any connection between these matters and birth control. In 1938 she even canceled a speaking engagement by Hannah Stone at a baby-care conference organized by Dr. Stone, on the grounds that, on reflection, she thought that the people who would come would be offended if a birth-control advocate was there. She used all the old arguments against birth control that Congress had once used, plus a few of her own. She declared she was worried about a "civilization with a declining population," that conditions among ill, underfed, and undereducated children were "none of her business," and that the government should encourage high breeding among the "biologically fit." What she didn't admit, according to the historian David Kennedy, was that she was worried about the possibility of finding herself in a job with a declining influence. With fewer children born, she reasoned, her bureau might be closed.

One Public Health official who sensed her hostility declared, "Katherine Lenroot is hopeless." So did others when she tied up maternal- and child-welfare funds voted for her department and let them sit idly in the bank. And when women wrote to the Children's Bureau, thinking it a logical place to get advice on birth control, she instructed her subordinates to answer with a form letter stating "no information available." Answering this way, lamented a Washington Children's Bureau doctor, "always makes me feel mean."

Eventually, however, after Mrs. Roosevelt won over the Surgeon General to the cause, Miss Lenroot loosened her funds and turned them over to the Public Health Service, a department which had seen the need to advise women war-workers on how to space their children so they would take fewer leaves of absence for unwanted pregnancies. Margaret wanted to send out another victorious statement to the press hailing the action of the Surgeon General, but Mrs. Roosevelt made her promise she wouldn't. Instead, though she hadn't written him for a year, Margaret turned to Harold to exult: "Another milestone!"

Harold and his wife Nell were not alone in adoring Margaret. Another admirer was Dr. Robert Latou Dickinson, who had progressed to a first-name basis with her. When Hannah Stone died suddenly at the age of forty-seven, Margaret, who still considered herself in command, appointed her husband, Dr. Abraham Stone, in her place at the

Sixteenth Street clinic. Dickinson, who was supposed to make such appointments, ignored the matter. About Abraham Stone he wrote, "a fine spirit his," ending, "yours with renewed enthusiasm, Robert."

Soon Dickinson was outlining plans for teaching seminars at the clinic and accepting Abraham Stone unconditionally. In a letter to Margaret, he wrote: "It's your clinic and you made it, and we who stand off and turn up only once in a while have no call to criticize if you appoint a new director without consulting a nominal Board of Management." This time he ended with even more enthusiasm: "Yours in the hope we may convert the world."

Dickinson was also busy testing old and new contraceptives. He found that the suppositories so much cherished by the French were not without problems; they melted at different temperatures in different women—some took five minutes, some took thirty. He found that the medicated tablets sold in drugstores were often useless because they crumbled if kept too long; a stronger cardboard container would prevent this but the price would have to go up. And as for the products advertised in magazines, for "personal daintiness," the ads gave no instructions, only the box. Everyone knew that when a woman has an impatient partner she does not stop to read the boxtop. He would write the advertisers at once.

This kind of news greatly cheered Margaret. Throughout the years she had been too busy to monitor research herself, but she had always read the hundreds of thousands of thank-you notes from faraway women whose only knowledge of birth control came from her pamphlets; these women felt she had literally saved their lives. She seldom printed their letters though, knowing that tragic stories make far better copy than happy stories, and are much better at bringing in contributions.

Yet, excellent fund raiser that she was, she was tight with her own money. When Pearl Buck, who had been one of her main helpers during her federal campaign, started the East West Foundation to spread knowledge of the different parts of the world, she asked Margaret to become a Founder for a thousand dollars. Margaret insisted she couldn't afford it; she had more repairs to make on Willowlake which had been more or less on the market since 1935. Besides, she was keeping up three residences—one in Tucson to which J. Noah had returned, one in Truro where her sisters summered, and one in New York at the elegant Barclay Hotel.

Though maintaining three homes was expensive, she was not having financial troubles. J. Noah had recouped much of his fortune and was soon to leave his beloved Margy five million dollars. But now that she was hobnobbing with multimillionaires, she felt she was by contrast only a small millionaire. She gave away money, but only to the friends and causes of her choice, such as the Converted Catholics Christ's Mission or the Society of Rosicrucians. Also, during the war years when food was being rationed in England, she sent friends there generous and frequent food parcels.

On the few occasions when she was at Willowlake, she continued to give lavish parties inviting people like Robert Dickinson and Clarence Gamble, a wealthy physician keenly interested in birth control. Dickinson recalled one of these parties in a handwriting so beautiful it looks like an illuminated manuscript:

It must be deep satisfaction to you to beget deep affection. Leadership sometimes means loneliness. Ideals so far in advance of public opinion as to be bitterly opposed, may breed sternness. For you to keep your kindliness and tenderness is one of the traits your friends most prize.

I am remembering a morning of clear sunshine in a garden spot. No background of trees and vines and grey stone walls, blossoming dogwood and greensward slopes, could have been a better setting. Arm in arm, three of the most individual of individualists—calling each other Margaret and Clarence and Robert—had intimate talk, review of long team-work, planning of far outlook.

They had lived long enough to see very many of their dreams come true. It was a day to be remembered. Yours these many years.

In 1942 at the age of eighty-three, J. Noah had a stroke. And Stuart, who had suffered from the complications of his mastoiditis for so long, had at last had a successful operation, finished his medical education, married, and become an internist in Tucson before going into military service. Stuart's wife had also presented Margaret with her first granddaughter, named Margaret. When Harold Child heard this, he said he found it "as different as it is delightful to think of anyone so incurably young as you are with a little granddaughter of her own."

In 1942 an unexpected letter came from Bill Sanger. He had not communicated with Margaret for over twenty years, but it was her birthday and he wanted her to know he remembered. He had written two books, one on Tom Paine, the other on the Aztecs. Neither had sold any better than his dark brooding paintings; still he prided himself on his attempt. Mainly, though, he was thinking of his children. He had heard that Stuart and Grant were in service and was worried about them. Would she please give him some details?

His letter went on with memories of the children when they were young: Stuart insisting on stopping to collect round stones that looked like baseballs as he trudged up a hill with his father; Grant in a little white suit messing up a neighbor's lettuce bed. And Peggy—always Peggy. "We mustn't love too much or it will be taken from us! I don't know who said those words but it's true. And 'Time heals all wounds.' No! The wound of Peggy's death has never healed!!"

If Margaret answered Bill's letter there is no record of it. She did however write to H. G. Wells, having learned he was seriously ill with a recurrence of tuberculosis, and invite him to come to her beautiful home in Arizona to recuperate. Wells' secretary answered with a polite note saying he was too ill to travel, but that he appreciated her concern.

That same year, J. Noah had another stroke, putting him into a wheelchair and then into a hospital. He wrote his niece Carrol from the hospital:

> I am as helpless as a newborn babe. I came out here in a series of ambulances. I think I got in four different cars at changing points. I was shoved into car windows and put together inside. . . . I do not have an ache or pain. My physical body is as well as can be, and I am normal and healthy, which makes it difficult to have to succomb to the inevitable.

Margaret added a postscript saying that she was staying close and trying to give him a laugh now and then, as well as the kind of food he liked. He died a week later, at home as he had requested, not wanting his Margy out of his sight. Margaret described his death:

> I was alone in the house—the nurse was on her four-hour leave—the doctor out on calls. I went into J. Noah's room about three o'clock to rest on the nurse's cot because there is a good cool-

er there which keeps the room lovely with cool, dry air. I tried to let the bed down to give J. N. a little more comfortable position as he was then asleep. He opened his eyes and waved me to stop. So I turned to let down the Venetian blinds to keep the light from his eyes—he waved me away and said, "Let them alone. I want to look at the mountains." Those were his last words.

Her two sons flew to Tucson for the funeral, both in military uniforms, but none of his own children came—either because he had been such a martinet to them or because of a long-standing grudge against Margaret. Years later, when Willowlake had been sold, J. Noah's daughter exclaimed angrily, "This property should have belonged to me!"

Margaret put up a tablet in her husband's memory at the Sixteenth Street Bureau, stressing his service as treasurer and using the sentimental quote: "Where your treasure is, there lies your heart also." But at the funeral service her old friend Dorothy Brush of the Brush Foundation delivered a more forthright eulogy: "He was all bark and no bite. In Heaven if everything isn't all right, he'll shout in an outraged tone, 'Where's Margy?' Then he'll kiss her and hold her tight." He was buried at Fishkill.

Soon Margaret had to face other losses.

Harold had a fall that year after a stroke, but insisted he didn't mind it a bit since he was an "insignificant whipper-snapper." He dictated to his wife after he lost the use of his right arm, joking to the end: "I am going to learn Irish, Pegeen, for I'm sure there must be some glorious swear-words in that language of Saints and Heroes." He died before she had a chance to reply.

Then Nan Higgins, a believing Christian Scientist, died during a heart attack after refusing to call a doctor. Margaret began to keep a diary again, repeating herself as aging people do:

October 24, 1944: Willowlake is for sale. J. N. passed away June 21 '43, and little sister Nan January 6, '44. Two dear graves side by side in Fishkill Cemetery. It is lonely. Lots to do. My painting and B.C. all big interests but one gets loneliness nevertheless.

* * *

Indeed she was lonely, and also more than a little confused, for the sudden inheritance of five million dollars left her stunned. J. Noah left nothing to his children by his previous marriage. He had kept his money almost exclusively in his own hands, handling everything on charge accounts which he closely inspected, and doling out such a small personal allowance that Margaret had had to sneak a few dollars from it when she wanted to do something on her own like send Grant a generous gift. Now, with five million all hers to spend as she pleased, she didn't quite know how. It took her some time to decide. When she did, she told Stuart: "I will blow it all in."

Though later she claimed she contributed much of her money to the movement, some of her "business expenses" seem questionable. She appears to have used it to finance her own vacations and to give gifts to her friends. Indeed, she drew a very fuzzy line between her own money and that of her cause. She felt that she was essentially "The Cause," and because she raised most of the funds, she thought herself free to hand them out as she chose. Also, like many crusaders, there was some of the charlatan and much of the mystic in her, making her charismatic and wondrous. Because most people enjoy the charismatic and wondrous, most people continued to adore her no matter what she did.

There were a few, however, who did not adore her. One was Dr. Helena Wright, a crusty English gynecologist. After meeting Margaret at the Cheltenham Conference in 1948, Dr. Wright described her: "Mrs. Sanger had violet eyes and reddish hair. Her main characteristics were vaulted ambition, arch-hypocrisy and financial meanness."

Another who disliked her was Robert Allerton Parker, to whom, as she grew older, Margaret continued to turn for new ideas on birth-control speeches. On one occasion, after much thought, he sent her several. In return, when he expected payment in cash he needed, she sent him a basket of fruit. "Fruit! just what I needed!!", he stormed, having no choice but to accept it.

Margaret's 1944 diary continues with entries about her growing concern for her children.

December 22, 1944: Christmas carol on the air . . . I'm frantic to have word of Stuart. I've always said since Peggy's death that life could not hold me if another of my children went before I do—I still feel that way. Stuart is usually lucky and uses his head if left to do so. But Army orders are different . . . It is now 6 P.M.

and I have a horrible feeling that something is wrong with one of the boys.

Grant who also had married had given her several grandsons by now. Margaret spent Christmas with them and their mother Edwina at their home in Mount Kisco, New York: "They are adorable, and their mother is wonderful with her courage . . . So is Barbara (Stuart's wife) and Margaret II and little Nancy are thrilling, too. Only it makes my heart ache that their fathers are missing their development."

She became so family conscious that she began writing regularly to her sister Ethel after years of silence. She also wrote to her brother Bob ("Spike") Higgins, football coach at Penn State, who was to become a member of the 1945 Football Hall of Fame. But Ethel died soon after, at the age of seventy-two.

From now on, with Ethel, J. Noah, Nan, and Harold gone, it would be Hugh and Angus to whom Margaret would turn for comfort and to whom she would give it in return. After Havelock died, Françoise wrote a book about Havelock that so damned Hugh he swore he would never have gotten over the shock of it without Margaret's help. Angus, who took up flying at the age of sixty-five, injured himself so severely when he wrecked his private plane that Margaret quite literally became his dream woman; he wrote telling her of flying through dawns and sunsets with her at his side when he was, in fact, in a bodycast and it was impossible for him even to walk. After he recovered, he continued to fly, and indeed, flew to Margaret on a number of occasions.

37

THE BEST PARTIES IN TOWN

Margaret and Hugh, who began as lovers, had become friends. It was the friendship of two people growing old together. In 1942 Hugh confessed he had become a "toothless old mumbler, as my old plates are no use; a terrible bore." He also said that his hands were getting fat, that he had a hard time writing anything because, with fuel rationed, he was so cold.

Margaret, too, now spoke of mundane things. She sent him baby clothes for Bridget who was expecting her second child, and stockings for Janet. She even sent clothes for Eva Schumann, who was particularly grateful for a warm cloak.

But mostly they began to talk about their grandchildren. Hugh told how his first grandson, Philip, called him Bamba, and how Philip, aged five and a half, "makes bonfires with me and we fall out, as chaps will do, you know, and Philip says, 'do you know what, bamba, you're an old beast?'" Margaret replied that she could "return the praise singing about my little four-year-old Margaret," whom she called Margaret II. "I could make her the first woman President of the United States if I had her bringing up to do. Alas that I have not, but we whisper special secrets to each other about our dreams."

And Margaret II, on her part, remembered years later how "it would have done your heart good to see grandmother run down the garden path to meet me and my sister Nancy, and how carefully she watched over us during a new polio scare."

At Christmas Grant, who by now was a gynecologist practising in New York, came to Tucson with his wife and children. She wrote glowingly to Hugh about them, especially her grandson Michael: "Michael is such a darling little fellow, sensitive like Grant was . . . This is the happiest Xmas I ever thought it possible to enjoy."

But while Hugh's life was going steadily downhill, Margaret's was still going up. With her amazing energy, she could go on an extended speaking tour of a largely Catholic state like Louisiana. Or raise several hundred thousand dollars for the Tucson Desert Sanatarium, helping it become the ten million dollar Tucson Medical Center it eventually became. Or start new birth-control clinics in Phoenix and Tucson. Or, since she was now not only famous but rich, get more and more admirers to write her the kind of letters she prized.

One new admirer was Hobson Pitman. By chance there had been four men in her life whose names started with H: Havelock, Hugh, Harold, and Herbert George Wells. Hobson was the fifth. Hobson was a shy, sensitive artist who taught painting at Penn State College where her brother Bob was coaching football. A bachelor in his early forties who described himself as a "stray soul," Hobson had the same compulsion to paint that Bill Sanger had; he was seldom happy away from his easel. Hobson was also deeply religious. In one of his first letters to Margaret, dated November 4, 1945, he admitted: "When you speak of prayer in connection with my painting, it pleases me a great deal, as I am constantly asking Our Lord to guide me and give me strength to put a spirit and life into my work."

Margaret praised his delicate and dreamlike paintings, praise he badly needed as he was never sure of himself. "I wish—oh so very much—I were with you this morning," he wrote in another letter. "I should find comfort, inspiration, and peace." By Christmas (three months after he met her), he was unashamedly in love, starting a letter with "Dearest Margaret," and continuing, "There is much more I feel like saying but you would consider me a fool."

When she decided to come East for the Christmas holidays he wrote with the enthusiasm of a boy: "All nervous and excited!!! Hurrah! Hurrah! Hurrah!" And so it went. Six months later he had spent a weekend in New York with her and some friends, and was using the same word to describe her that Angus used—glorious.

It was heady stuff for a woman of sixty-seven, especially when he confessed "I love you *too* much, I'm afraid."

With all this, Margaret's loneliness was not assuaged. She was used to having hordes of people around her. Now that there were fewer people and fewer pressing things to do, she felt empty and depressed. To try to shake off her loneliness, she set off early in May for a two week cross-country clinic tour, writing Hobson when she returned: "I am feeling more and more despondent as I saw & realized more than ever the inadequacy of the diaphragm reaching millions of women who need & should have something as simple as a birth control pill." And soon she was using her ancient anodyne—a trip to London, hoping that Wells in particular would be able to see her. But he had barely received her note that she was coming when he died of the tuberculosis that had been plaguing him all his life.

On August 16, 1946 she wrote a private homage on a sheet of plain paper that she headed simply "To H. G. Wells":

So, darling H. G., you have gone over to the Great Beyond. It's queer that with all your greatness, your mind, your vision, you have not touched this aspect of our Hereafter. Now—today—you are over there. I am fleeing overseas to Stockholm and then to England. England means London & London means H. G. Wells to me & also to millions of Americans. Darling H. G. you have been the dawn to me. Your great mind—your humor—your wit—so akin to my Irish failing for keenness of wit, may have drawn me to you.

And now you are over there, beyond my horizon. I wish if you are there—consciously there & alive in spirit—you will endeavor to explore the possibilities of communication with me. I'd like to try to see what you can do. I don't know one thing about it, but loads of things & laws of life are unknown by us humans. My love whereever you are—always.

In December 1947, Willowlake was finally sold. It went for eighty-five thousand dollars, a good price for a large difficult-to-maintain property. After the sale Margaret started a new diary.

It was an odd diary. Like so many older people, she made small unimportant economies. Back in 1927 she had kept a diary complaining how Sir Bernard Mallett had cut her name from the Geneva Conference program; the entries were made in a notebook, using one side of the page only. Now, she used the other side of the page in a handwriting sometimes as clear and bold as before, sometimes so wobbly it can hardly be read.

In 1947 she wrote sadly from Willowlake that the buyer was a man named Orlando Weber, "an actor-poet, son of the famed Orlando Weber of Carbide Chemical or other business firm." She went on to tell how terribly upset she was when she went to get out her furniture. "Orlando Weber was a homosexual, very rich, had torn the place in pieces. It was too awful . . . he had turned the place into a horrible dude-ranch. It was wrong to return to see it."

To lessen her grief, she turned as ever to Hugh:

Some day *soon* I shall feel I am finished and know that my contribution to humanity has been given & done. I think Hugh it is nearing the end now. I have launched a League and have planned its machinery in such a way that it must go by its own momentum.

I think of you, when I long to get away and live in beauty and in love.

Do you make your dreams come true, Hugh? Always I dream of your lovely Wantley. Your tall figure on the lawn, Harold the philosopher with his pipe and knowing smile like Mona Lisa, Janet & Bridget adding music & laughter to the perfect day. Your place has been such a joy to me, and you, dearest Hugh, are a double joy because you are one of the highlights one meets in life.

Blessed Hugh, do you think of me ever at all? No letter for *years* . . . Do write me—it's very comforting to have a few friends who are like the stars, whose love shines on just the same.

When Hugh didn't answer, as he seldom did now, she left New York and hurried back to Tucson to distract herself by giving parties. She had once spoken of "publicity, the greatest of all intoxicants"; she would get publicity by giving the most lavish parties the town had ever seen.

She gave at least one party a week, each built around a different theme. There was, for instance, a Japanese party, then a Chinese party, then a Hawaiian party; and at each she not only served authentic food even if she had to send thousands of miles to get it but she provided her guests with native costumes from her copious trunks. As time went on these gatherings became even more sumptuous—at one party she served foods of half a dozen countries at once. As a result, everybody who was anybody was vying for an invitation.

The servants at these parties at first had been mainly untrained Mexicans, but then she had a stroke of luck. She found a White Russian couple named Efrem and Lisa Voronoff, who had escaped from Russia during the Revolution and run a boardinghouse in Manchuria before emigrating to the United States. Efrem, whom she preferred to call John, was tall and aristocratic; Lisa was small and dignified with a carefully combed bun piled high on her head.

Margaret persuaded them to come to work for her as a husband-and-wife team, John as a combination butler and chauffeur and Lisa as housekeeper, while faithful Daisy stayed on as cook. But Margaret, quite parsimonious where salaries were concerned, started John and Lisa at the combined salary of twenty-five dollars a month; they didn't get a raise until ten years later when Stuart made it fifty dollars. And with all the party food around, her servants were permitted to eat so little they had to go out and buy extra food for themselves.

With secretaries she was more generous. She hired a male secretary whom she proudly titled Administrative Assistant to the Honorary President of Planned Parenthood. He was an uncouth man named Jonathan Schultz who had been a farm boy and unsuccessful lawyer but had smelled out a good thing and begged for the job. He claimed he had influence with the Nobel Prize Committee in Stockholm and would show her how to get the prize. As she coveted the Nobel Prize more than anything else in the world, she took him on at the whopping salary of one thousand dollars a month.

From time to time she also took on a female secretary to help with her mail and keep track of her lecture dates, though now she did little speaking. "I am in a state like stagnant water," she confided to Hugh. "The aching pain is upon me, plus lack of confidence. It seems time for me to give others the job of speaking on B.C."

But she didn't give up other kinds of birth-control work. When the original clinic in Amsterdam—the one that Ellis had sent her to years ago—ran out of supplies early in World War II, she wrote Herbert Simonds asking him to send some to Amsterdam, preferably as a gift.

She also took regular trips to New York to look in on her Sixteenth Street Bureau and to protest loudly because the Birth Control Federation of America had changed its name to the Planned Parenthood Federation of America (PPFA). When its officers told her they had made the change because they thought the new words had a more positive approach, especially after they added a service to help infertile couples as well, Margaret went uptown to the PPFA's headquarters and angrily pounded the table. "Birth control" were famous words, she insisted; they were easier to say. But it was too late. Planned Parenthood the federation had officially become, and Planned Parenthood it remained.

Back home, she decided to work off some of her anger by inviting the Bishop of Arizona to debate with her on the morality of birth control. As neither would appear on the same platform with the other they had to speak on alternate nights. Still, she felt she had to do something exciting besides give parties, and this at the moment was it.

When William Mathews, editor of the *Arizona Star,* heard about the debate, he exploded in an editorial: "Who do these women think they are to take on the Bishop of Arizona?" Mrs. Benson Bloom, an ardent birth-control worker, stormed into Mathews' office and answered him: "One thing you forget, Mr. Mathews, is that these little women happen to be right!"

Meantime Margaret lamented in her diary that Jonathan Schultz (her administrative assistant) had no sex appeal. "I am only a third older than he," she noted, "but among cultivated people that makes no difference." In truth, he was forty and she was sixty-eight.

Sexually attracted to him or not, she flew to Stockholm with Schultz in 1946 to lobby for the Nobel Prize. Unsuccessful, she came home to throw parties with men she found sexier—a musician who danced with her and played for her party guests, a teacher at a boys' school who dropped in to visit with her every morning, and a bridge pro at the Arizona Inn who played cards with her afternoons. Grant Sanger dismissed them all as sycophants. Some would have called them gigolos, but they pleased her by telling her how lovely she still was, and escorting her to various events.

And what parties she now gave!

One New Year's Eve when the champagne was flowing, they all set to thinking up the wildest stunt they could come up with. They decided to telephone Hitler in Germany and when they got him on the phone to give him the "raspberry" or Bronx cheer. They almost succeeded, too. They got through to one of his secretaries in Berchtesgaden on the grounds that important Americans had a message for Hitler, and the wealthy Tucson cattleman Jack Spieden was just about to blow the cheer when the secretary caught on to the joke and hung up, making Margaret and her guests laugh and laugh. On another occasion the Episcopal minister who was dancing with Margaret fell backward into her lily pool, and they laughed some more.

At other times there were painting parties to Hermillio and Nogales just across the Mexican border. There were few lulls between parties.

When the parties began to pall she turned again to Hugh, begging for a letter; she wrote so wistfully it woke him from his silence and their correspondence began again. Though it was eight years since Havelock had died, Hugh still talked about him. "Havelock dear still shines through you," he said. He also dwelt on Eva, wondering when Margaret would ask, "Whom do you love best, Eva or me?" When she did ask, his answer was evasive, "The more I love Eva, the more I love you. Just as one bright star in the Heavens makes all the other stars shine brighter, and one truth illumines all other truths, so my love for Eva makes me love you more." Margaret answered humbly, "Thank you for explaining this to me."

By now Margaret was a grandmother many times over, and she wrote Hugh about her new role:

> Yesterday I spent the day at Mount Kisco (Grant's home) as it was Michael's fifth birthday. He sprang into my bed at 6 A.M. & demanded that I sing "Happy Birthday"—at six A.M.! I croaked out a tune, so all was ready for some birthday presents. The prize was a small tool box filled with saws, augers, etc. This red box was constantly shown to everyone—so I was happy too.
>
> My thoughts are of you and Janet and Eva. The winter soon on its way. I wish you could shut up Sand Pit & come over here until Spring. You could write in comfort & warmth—why not?

Hungry for company, she kept inviting Hobson to come West also, or if he wouldn't do that, to take a year off and go to Europe with her. But Hobson was too fearful. "I am always skeptical of myself and what might turn up. Who knows but what I may become an invalid and the thought of giving up my position for just a year frightens me. I must plan ahead for the days to come." Margaret, he insisted, was the only one who believed in him. In gratitude he sent her a picture he had just finished called "Poetic Reverie."

But Hobson also wrote less often now, except to lament that their paths crossed too infrequently.

In July 1948 she again begged him to go to Europe with her. He agreed to go in late August, then, just as they were about to leave, reneged on September first. "My school has announced they want me back by Sept. 12th. It just wouldn't be enough time."

Margaret made a note on the bottom of this letter: "You should resign. They are trying to push you out and make you toe the mark to humiliate you—don't take it!" But he did take it, pleading: "You must forgive me. Some day I'll be a better boy—just wait!"

Yet she was so lonely she began to consider proposing marriage to Hobson. She wrote Angus: "I'm thinking of getting married again. You are my first choice, but alas! Unavailable. Next comes a lawyer in New York, then a hermit in Vermont, then a painter 30 years younger than myself." Angus was so thrilled about heading the list that he rushed out in his plane to see her, though again after he left, she noted he had found her "impossible." As for Hobson, Juliet caught her up short with: "For God's sake, don't marry H. P. He wants a mother, not a wife!" She ended up marrying no one.

Meanwhile, she continued to think of ways to spend her money, bragging to Stuart, "I'm going to spend it down to the last cent and die broke."

GREAT HONOR AND GREAT TRAGEDY

Smith College is the oldest, largest, and one of the most conservative women's colleges in America. Located in Massachusetts, one of the country's most conservative states, it faces Northampton's tree-shaded Elm Street and at its back is rippling Paradise Pond, so named by Jenny Lind who thought it Paradise to walk there quietly after a demanding concert.

When Margaret Sanger, proclaiming a cause that was anathema to conservatives, received an honorary Doctor of Laws degree from Smith College, it was the high point of her career. Dorothy Brush, an alumna of Smith, had campaigned for this for over a year, gathering letters of praise for Margaret from people like Nehru in India and Mrs. Dwight Morrow in Mexico. In addition, with Smith in the midst of one of its fund-raising campaigns, Mrs. Brush promised a gift of one hundred thousand dollars if it would honor her friend. With Margaret's permission, she also offered the material Margaret had not given to the Library of Congress—some one-hundred-and-fifty file boxes that included the valuable letters of Havelock Ellis and H. G. Wells.

Margaret paraded across the campus to receive her degree with the other dignitaries in June 1949. She later remarked: "It was probably such a surprise to the Catholics that Smith hasn't heard a word from the Vatican about it yet."

The Drysdales wired congratulations from England, as did Lin Yutang from China, John D. Rockefeller, Jr., and the Reverends John Haynes Holmes and Raymond Fosdick from New York. But the letter she valued most came from Angus, who, after seeing her picture in *Life* magazine with her mortarboard fetchingly tilted, said "you looked like a cock-eyed angel . . . and seemed so young it was as if you had just gotten a B.A. rather than an LLD." Angus himself was ill and taking medical tests, as well as having business problems. "Wish me luck," he added, "as my strength for the fight stems from you."

Of course she sent Hugh fast word about the honor:

Perhaps you have heard Mr. de Selincourt that your friend Margaret Sanger was given an Honorary Degree of *Doctor of Laws* by the Trustees of Smith College at Northampton, Mass.?? L. L. D. Now remember your manners next time you see her and don't forget to be RESPECTFUL! How Havelock would rejoice and smile over that one.

It seems a very very long time ago when I saw you looking pale and fragile in the lounge at the Grosvenor—then very much better as the family man at Sand Pit. But it's all too long away. Especially since there are so few letters which so brighten the years as your's do. They come so seldom I keep wondering if I've not behaved in a *proper & correct* way when last we met, or something. Then I try to think that there is no distance or time, just love which is always present.

Margaret soon left for Tucson to oversee work on a new house she was having built on land owned by J. Noah. Before he died he had in one of his canny real-estate deals traded some land around their Elm Street property next to the Arizona Inn for a larger piece of land owned by the Inn on Buena Vista Drive. He had given some of it to Stuart to build a house for himself and his family, and the rest to Margaret. It was on Buena Vista Drive therefore that she was building a smart, unique place that would be a fitting background for her magnificent parties. The house was fan-shaped with an oval entrance from which three fan-shaped rooms spread out, each with a serrated ceiling that sloped down from the narrow end to the wide, where there were glass sliding doors. These doors led to three distinct gardens. One was a Japanese garden, one a desert garden, and one was graced with an arching fountain over which multicolored lights played at the touch of a switch. The fountain was a real conversation piece in arid Tucson, especially since it was connected to an underground pool in the living room upon which lily pads floated.

In addition, there was a long wing that housed a butler's pantry and kitchen, plus a small upstairs room for puttering and painting, making it all, as she said, "rather too large and expensive for a lone widow." Margaret had asked Frank Lloyd Wright to design it for her, but he declined with the remark that "anything built on less than forty acres is a pig-sty." She commissioned a local architect to build it, but soon grew angry with him and switched to Arthur Brown. Meanwhile she spent the early months of 1949 taking a correspondence course in interior decorating so she could get rid of her antiques and design her new place.

She sold her fine old furniture, announcing to the press that she was bored with it as well as with English manor-houses and pink adobe, and sent for new Japanese furnishings. She issued press releases about the house to pique curiosity, and pushed the builders night and day to get it finished, while townspeople came to wonder and watch.

All this bolstered her spirits and took her mind away from the bad publicity she had recently received when she went to England and announced on landing: "Women should declare a moratorium on babies for ten years; let none get born in any country until hunger is conquered . . . And let the excess adults emigrate to places with more room."

The British press had hooted at her pronouncement. Nineteen out of twenty papers castigated her, as postwar Britain was encouraging births by paying mothers a bonus of a pound a week for every child after the first. The *London Mirror* said: "Her proposal would be as practical as telling the sun to stand still or the tide to turn back." The *Standard* editorialized, "There are lots of things we want from America and can't get—and some things we get but don't want. In that latter category is Margaret Sanger."

She pretended to ignore these slights but they had hurt nevertheless. Back home, she went jauntily about her business of partying, adding a course in cooking to the one in interior decorating, boasting, "I could be a terrific caterer if I wanted to, or even a plumber." Between times she painted in Mexico and sent more food parcels to Hugh for which he didn't bother to thank her, making her ask humbly, "Are my parcels still welcome or wanted, and not a *nuisance*?" She was equally generous with other friends, lavishing upon them gifts of every kind.

Then tragedy struck.

In 1949, while summering at Stuart's cabin in Lakeside, Arizona, and carrying on as energetically as ever, she suffered a severe heart attack. There was no hospital near by, and her pain was so severe that, to quiet her, Stuart gave her an injection of Demerol—a powerful pain killer introduced a few years before and considered so non-addictive it had not even been placed on the official narcotics list. Stuart then called a hospital-plane and flew her to the Tucson Medical Center where she was put to bed for the standard six weeks of complete rest.

But after two weeks she refused to rest in bed. She had learned that the electricians were about to install an intricate lighting system in her new house, and she insisted on supervising the job herself. Her doctor did his best to dissuade her but in her typically defiant manner she told him: "I am rich, I have brains. I shall do exactly as I please." He gave in, insisting only that she go to the house in an ambulance and that he follow her and park his own car conspicuously alongside hers so that passersby would know she was there under medical supervision.

A little later, still shaken and ill, she demanded that her doctor let her travel to New York to speak at an international Planned Parenthood dinner; this time he went with her. And on another matter she remained equally obstinate. She would not tell him her age. "I'm thirty-nine," she kept murmuring coyly until he exploded: "But Margaret, for God's sake, I have to know. My drug dosage depends on it." "I'm thirty-nine" she repeated as sweetly as ever, until in exasperation he looked up her age in the *Dictionary of Biography,* though even there the information was wrong.

Still, reminiscing later, her doctor considered her and Sir Alexander Fleming, the discoverer of penicillin, the two greatest persons of the twentieth century!

There have been no basic changes in sexual patterns from 1900 B.C. to 1900 A.D. Then Margaret Sanger caused a sexual revolution by freeing people from the fear of unwanted children, and Fleming gave the world the first real cure for syphilis . . . Certainly Mrs. Sanger's discovery caused some increase in promiscuity. But then freedom always brings problems. She herself can hardly be blamed. Besides, how many people start a crusade and finish it in their own lifetime?

* * *

He told how he used to sit with her and try to comfort her with these thoughts during the long nights in the hospital when she was despondent because she was still very ill.

When Angus learned of her heart attack he wanted to fly to her at once. But as she was forbidden visitors, he wrote instead. The letter is headed 4 A.M. August 12, 1949:

> Glorious Margaret: Sorry that you are forbidden to see me, but I know it is for the best. For once in your life you must obey orders. I see you constantly as we sail over high mountains and deep valleys. Particularly I will see you in a few minutes when we speed the sunrise over the Rockies. Both of you are glorious.

Hugh wrote too, saying he was glad she was getting the finest medical attention, while Hobson wrote lamely, "I wish I could do something for you, but I don't know what."

On September 2 she wrote Angus from the hospital in a shaky hand:

> Angus, dear: As my life shortens, questions arise. What am I to do? Am I to live alone? Am I to couple up with someone else? Who?
>
> You are free. Others are free. The artist. The lawyer at (the) Plaza. The hermit in the mountains of Vermont—all old suitors asking to be favored. Well, so what? Being married helps to save one from decisions. I at present am not in love with anyone. Maybe never will be again. You are closer in my affections than anyone else, but you are *unavailable*. Some day we can talk it over.

Angus answered by return mail:

> Two letters today with wonderful news! First that you will be well enough to go home, and then that my rating with you is at the top! I expect to be in Montana early in Oct. & will plan to see you, if you will permit me, before returning East.

He flew to Tucson and they talked about marriage, though nothing came of it. He couldn't leave his wife, his library business, his farm, his new invention for keeping fenceposts from rotting. She noted on the bottom of his letter, "Angus—a friend of many years—is still a good friend and still finds me impossible!"

Within a few weeks she was settled—alone—in her fan-shaped house. "It gives me joy. It is good to be in it. Comfortable, simple, but Me."

Shortly after moving in, she got a letter from Bill Sanger, who had been to see Grant and his wife, Edwina, and learned from them that she had been seriously ill. He sent hopes for a speedy recovery and trusted that she was as concerned about herself as he was, signing himself "with best wishes, as ever, Bill."

She was happy to get his letter; it seemed to heal some old sores. She was happy too just to be up and around again: "I do just one thing a day—very boring," she wrote Angus. "Anyway, it won't be long now before Spring will be around the corner & I will be going your way— East again, I think."

She added that in a few weeks she was hoping to go to Chicago for a Pioneer luncheon—going for just one night and a day though it was against doctors' orders. "But so what? If Chicago has no bad results I'll perhaps end up in Japan!!"

Angus answered by wiring her a plant for Valentine's day, sending with it another of his gracious notes: "Glorious Valentine: it gives me keen delight to think of what these blossoms will see and feel and hear as they come out one by one to be with you for a while."

She replied: "What a man! Valentine for remembrance—yes? It will be here when Frank Lloyd Wright comes to dine on Saturday. I will think of you and your dearness."

Still, she was growing sadder. Grant, expecting his fourth child and planning to have more, caused her to record in her diary: "I'm blushing." Her doctor upset her too when he said that her two big Dalmatians should no longer sleep on her bed just because they loved soft places, and that Chablis, her cocker spaniel, shouldn't be allowed to jump all over her as he used to.

Soon came the sad news from Janet de Selincourt that Hugh had had a stroke. He had driven into Storrington to play bowls one night, and awakened in the morning with all sensation gone in his left leg and arm; he had been put into a nursing home immediately, and sensation had returned at least partly to his arm and leg.

Yet saddest of all was what had happened to her as the result of that first taste of Demerol. Even more than the Luminal she had taken years before, she kept taking Demerol because it stopped her from caring. She also hoped it might lessen her dreams.

And Margaret dreamt a great deal. A few dreams were cheerful, but many were mystical or full of frightening portent. She thought them important enough to record in a diary that covered a period of thirty years. Some were full of snakes spreading their fangs at her or chickens getting their heads chopped off. These she took to mean that trouble was brewing in the birth-control ranks. Occasionally there was even a sex dream; she found herself being attracted sexually to Bill Sanger, but pushing him violently away. By 1951 the dream entries stop, however, possibly because by then she was taking enough Demerol to get dreamless sleep. She was using the drug not only when she needed it for a painful attack of angina, but simply whenever she pleased.

MACARTHUR SAYS NO

In 1949 Japan had reached the lowest point in its history. It was a defeated and occupied nation, with General MacArthur installed as Allied Supreme Commander and the Emperor almost powerless. In addition, the yen had been devaluated, taxation was heavy, and people were living from day to day with great uncertainty. This resulted in a huge population boom. With jobs scarce and little money to spend on geisha girls, the men were home more, getting recreation and asserting their manhood by demanding frequent intercourse with timid wives. In 1950 there were eighty-five million people packed onto the tiny island compared to sixty-six million in 1922; the population density was 529 per square mile compared to 44 in the United States. Self-induced abortion and infanticide were common despite a Eugenics Protection Law, in effect since 1939, which allowed doctors to perform abortions for medical and eugenic reasons, and which in 1946, had been extended to include economic and social reasons as well.

But the Eugenics Protection Law had not had much publicity, and many women did not trust the generally incompetent Japanese doctors who were performing abortions. As a result, twice as many abortions were performed as were reported.

Eager to get going again after her prolonged illness, she managed to get an invitation from the President of the *Yomiuri Press*, the largest daily in Japan, to come and lecture at its expense. She assured him that the Chief Cabinet Secretary and other high officials of the Ministry would also support her visit since Mrs. Schidsue Kato (formerly Baroness Ishomoto; she had lost her title after a new marriage) had already approached them and gotten a positive answer. Jubilant, Margaret packed samples of contraceptives to demonstrate to doctors as an alternative to abortion, made elaborate notes for speeches, and in July 1949, prepared to sail.

But she hadn't counted on one obstacle, MacArthur himself. Though the Allied Occupation was spending a million dollars a day to feed the hungry, and a survey had shown that the Japanese people wanted contraceptive advice, her application for a visa was denied. MacArthur ignored the comments of one Japanese doctor: "The papers run page-wide ads for contraceptive creams and suppositories, ads permitted by the government, but the people can't afford to buy them even if the medical profession was prepared to give advice on how to use them." Margaret *was* prepared, but MacArthur stood firmly against her, saying that he "couldn't interfere with Japanese internal affairs."

Margaret referred the matter to Charles E. Scribner, the lawyer for Planned Parenthood. He wrote to the Pentagon; there was no reply. Mrs. Roosevelt wrote a column supporting her friend, and the *New York Times* ran a story; neither had any effect. Scribner persisted, and in February 1950, MacArthur replied personally, admitting that there was a population problem in Japan as indeed there was in many places, but that letting Mrs. Sanger enter would imply that the occupation "had the political motive of keeping down the Japanese population while in America it remained largely unchecked."

MacArthur was sure, moreover, that even without her help the Japanese population would stabilize itself in twenty years through the Eugenics Protection Law. Then he revealed the real reason he was denying her entrance. He said that the subject was so controversial the *Tokyo Times* had recently run a series of letters from non-Japanese readers, and the arguments back and forth had become so heated that the series had to be stopped.

Scribner picked up the key words "non-Japanese readers," and told MacArthur that evidently there were no objections on the part of the Japanese, only from "a religious body that's essentially foreign to Japan." He also quoted a recent dispatch from MacArthur to the American press saying that in view of pressure from Catholic Church groups, he believed it was impossible for him to allow Mrs. Sanger to lecture to Japanese audiences without appearing to subscribe to her views, though there were only 180,000 Catholics in Japan compared to 80 million Japanese.

Scribner also said that only in two states in America—Connecticut and Massachusetts—were there still laws prohibiting the giving of advice on contraception, and that in these states, it was the very same Catholic group who stood in the way.

MacArthur refused to reconsider his position. He now added fuel to the fire by quoting from a letter he had received from a woman he refused to name, but who, he said, far from being an outsider, was "one of the foremost advocates of the birth-control movement."

This woman had seen an article in the *New York Herald Tribune* about his refusal to admit Mrs. Sanger, and agreed it was a wise move. She knew what she was talking about, too, as she had been a lecturer at the Imperial University on scientific subjects and had founded the Tokyo Ladies Club. More, he said, she had been the founder of the first birth-control clinic in the world, though, unlike Mrs. Sanger, she was not a troublemaker. When Mrs. Sanger had gone to Japan many years ago she had caused angry scenes, associated with the wrong people, and hurt rather than helped the cause; he was afraid that this might happen again. Indeed, the smart thing now would be to lie low and let the Japanese themselves come to a sound attitude on the subject or so the unidentified lady fervently hoped.

Margaret needed no crystal ball to guess the name of the unidentified lady. Across MacArthur's impressive letterhead she wrote in bold letters "MARIE STOPES—THE VIPER."

Scribner kept trying, but he simply couldn't get her a visa. His failure sent her into one of her old-time depressions. She felt better, though, when Hugh started writing to her again. He told her of a book he was reading called *Facing Both Ways*, written by a Japanese Marquise who talked of Margaret the Invincible, adding "Go to it when you can, Invincible." He ended with his favorite quotation from Blake: "We can abide life's pelting storm/which makes our limbs quake/if our hearts keep warm."

In her answer to Hugh, she thanked him for returning her letters as she had asked. She was rereading them, comparing the present with the past.

I did not mean to open up veins of sadness, yet the sadness is there I know, and memories dim slowly . . . I went East to spend Xmas with Grant and his darling four boys. (The trip) was a test for me, and I stood it very well. So now I do not worry about a heart-condition any more . . . I love my new house with all the mountains showing off their rose copper hues at sunset. Then Stuart's house and pool are next door, and there are open lawns between us.

With her medical worries seemingly ended, she got ready to go to Chicago to attend the Pioneer luncheon. She was also busy on something far more important—a search for a better contraceptive, hopefully something as simple as an inoculation for smallpox, which could be taken anywhere, at any time.

She started her search by renewing her correspondence with a remarkable woman, Katherine Dexter McCormick, a Boston Brahmin and in Margaret's eyes a Great Lady to the core.

Katherine Dexter McCormick was the wife of Stanley McCormick, whose father was Cyrus McCormick of International Harvester fame, Mrs. McCormick's father in turn had been an outstanding lawyer in Dreiser's bustling Chicago; her grandfather had been a Harvard graduate and lawyer, as well as founder of the town of Dexter, Michigan, and her great-grandfather Secretary of Defense under President John Adams. Stanley McCormick had been a varsity tennis player and honor student at Princeton and a gifted amateur painter and comptroller of his father's company. He met tall, handsome Katherine Dexter in Boston at a tennis match. She had attracted him, not only because she was a fine athlete, unusual for a woman in 1900, but because she was a fine student too—a biology major at college and one of the first women to graduate from M.I.T.

They were married with high hopes in 1904, but within two years Stanley was declared legally insane. By 1950 they were spending their summers in Boston or Switzerland, and their winters on their huge estate in Santa Barbara where she hoped the quiet surroundings might calm him. In Santa Barbara she employed forty gardeners to keep the grounds immaculate for his pleasure, plus six musicians to entertain him at dinner. But nothing had helped; he remained hopelessly schizophrenic.

They had no children, and since the Mendelian theory that madness could be inherited had recently been revived, Katherine resolved they never would have any. Still, since he was very demanding, she undoubtedly continued to have marital relations with him.

Hearing that Hudson Hoagland of the Worcester, Massachusetts, Institute of Biology, was doing research on the biology of madness, she now endowed his work to the best of her ability. She could not do much as her hands were tied. As soon as his son's illness had become permanent, Cyrus McCormick had begun working to regain control of the millions he had regularly been giving his son, so Katherine had only a limited amount at her command.

With few goals upon which to lavish her many talents, she worked briefly for Woman's Suffrage, then met Margaret and had done a little work for birth control. But none of this had been enough; she had more time and energy than she knew what to do with.

In 1950 she heard through Hoagland that Gregory Pincus, his colleague at the Worcester Institute, was doing some remarkable new research. Pincus was probably one of the first biologists to notice that when too many rats were confined in a cage they became socially upset devouring each other no matter how much food they had. This suggested to him that human overcrowding might have a similiar effect.

A dark, handsome man so devoted to his wife that he would compose a few lines of poetry to her and leave them pinned on her pillow in the early morning before he left for the laboratory, Pincus had his Doctorate in Science from Harvard. In 1930 he began to study the process of ovulation in rabbits, discovering that ovulation could be stopped with injections of a combination of female hormones administered at certain times of the month. By varying the doses and times of injections, he found that he could stimulate ovulation as well as stop it. It was a momentous discovery, for without ovulation there could be no conception; with it, once infertile rabbits could become fertile.

Margaret was tremendously excited when she heard about his work through Katherine McCormick; she begged him to proceed with his research as quickly as possible. Maybe he would discover a birth-control method for women that would be easy and effective. The problem was that Pincus needed two things before he could continue. The first was a "front man," preferably a medical doctor of the highest rank who would be willing to publicize a new birth-control method for women if he ever found it. The second was money—a lot of it—as the actual breakthrough might take years to accomplish.

Margaret quickly got some money from the Brush foundation, then wrote Mrs. McCormick asking for one hundred thousand dollars more, hoping to get at least twenty-five thousand dollars right away. But Mrs. McCormick replied sadly that five thousand dollars was all she could muster up at the moment; she enclosed a check for the five thousand, telling Margaret to spend it any way she thought best.

Margaret answered in her ebullient style: "My joyful thanks to you, dear Mrs. McCormick, for this helpful 'lift' to my future efforts." Rather surprisingly, she decided to use the five thousand dollars to plan a birth-control conference in India in 1955. With MacArthur blocking her in Japan, she was determined to prove to him she could at least get *there*. Meanwhile, she and Mrs. McCormick agreed to keep Pincus' research secret, as birth control was still an explosive issue in Massachusetts.

Mrs. Loraine Campbell tells a story pointing up the secrecy. One evening she and her husband were invited to the McCormick home. Just as they were about to leave they received a phone call asking, "Are you sure you aren't too tired to come?" Of course they weren't too tired. They were received rather coolly by their hostess and seated at an elegant formal table though Margaret was the only other guest. While they were eating, the phone kept ringing, and the maid put messages on Mrs. McCormick's plate. She in turn handed them to Margaret who silently read them and slipped them under her wine glass. Finally coffee was served and the Campbells were politely but firmly ushered out.

Mrs. Campbell guessed later that the notes were from Gregory Pincus saying he was coming over that evening to report on what he was doing, and the two women wanted no other guests.

Meanwhile the search for the impeccable "front man" to work with Pincus continued. The most likely candidate was Dr. John Rock, Chief of Obstetrics and Gynecology at Harvard, a man with five children and fourteen grandchildren who was famous for his own work on human fertility. But Rock was a Catholic, and the pressures on him to stay out of birth-control research were enormous.

While awaiting further developments with Pincus and Rock, Marga-

ret kept busy. Again she invited Hobson Pitman to Tucson. Again Juliet warned her:

> For Heaven's sake don't let H. P. get hold on you again! You
> know what a very limited self-absorbed, selfish, helpless person
> he is and to have that kind of person hanging on to you, demand-
> ing sympathy, constantly complaining, asking for advice and not
> taking it, would be terrifically exhausting!!!
>
> You don't seem to realize that the slightest word from you
> starts him up again. And you occasionally send him a provocative
> word that puzzles him and gets him going, trying to read the de-
> votion and admiration he thought he had from you and *cannot*
> understand where it is gone!
>
> I know you need mental and emotional stimulus and excite-
> ment, but to get mixed up with the wrong kind is worse than to be
> empty for a while.

For a change, Margaret listened to Juliet, as she was now feeling
very exhausted indeed. Suffering again from a thyroid problem which
caused her energy to radically surge and ebb, she went on one of her
"purifying diets" which she hoped would recharge her. She cut out
coffee, meat, cigarettes, and alcohol. But, as might have been expected,
the diet didn't last long, nor did it recharge her at seventy-one. She
came to a reluctant decision: She would simplify her life by selling the
Sixteenth Street Bureau to Dr. Abraham Stone who had been running
it since his wife died. She realized he could now manage it better than
she, since she was so far away.

The sale was set for June 1950 at a price of just under a hundred
thousand dollars. All there was to sell was the building. Although it
was located on a valuable piece of land, it was badly in need of repair.
The usual "goodwill" was not worth much with Margaret, whose name
meant so much to patients, out of the picture.

Dr. Stone had very little money, so he formed a corporation, whimsi-
cally called The Humfert Corporation, from the words "human" and
"fertility," and sold stock in it to raise the cash. Meanwhile, Margaret
went East to undertake the long, exhausting job of clearing out her papers.

Her stay in the East was brief. She heard that Stuart was thinking
of rejoining the army as a tropical disease specialist and hurried home

to Arizona to dissuade him. She went up to his lakeside cabin and got a new idea there for herself: maybe she would start a dramatic school in Tucson with Anna Duncan, a follower of Isadora Duncan who had taken her teacher's name, as headmistress. Margaret expected Anna to pay her own way West, and since Anna was too poor to do that, nothing came of the idea. It seemed there was little left for excitement other than her September twelfth birthday which she celebrated with a frantic party in her fan-shaped house.

Between the drinking at the party and the wrench over the sale of the Bureau, Margaret had another heart attack. Again she had to undergo a long hospital stay. Worse, she was again having horrible dreams which made her, she told Juliet, "depressed, lonely and without pep." She was taking pills constantly to make her sleep. Juliet replied: "I also have been taking too many little pills to woo gentle sleep."

In October 1951, Margaret was given the Lasker Award, a thousand-dollar cash prize given each year by Mary Lasker, widow of an advertising executive, for outstanding achievement in a field connected with medicine. Margaret, who was convalescing, was still so depressed she wasn't sure whether she wanted to go to New York to accept it or not. Finally Grant accepted it for her. Juliet was jubilant: "Can you use that thousand for fun? You *must*."

The only fun she could think of was startling the Tucsonites by marrying a much younger man. Again she considered Hobson Pitman. Now Juliet put her foot down hard, "(You say) he is apparently quieting down, more peaceful & much better in tone and atmosphere. . . . He wants you to know he is lonely. (Isn't everybody!). . . . Darling, he is *not* really in love with you. It's merely a case of your inloveness. It was *your* lovely letter, as always, that brought out his." Juliet was right when she spoke of Margaret's "inloveness." For if Margaret was still in love with sex, she was also in love with love. Hugh, Harold, Havelock, and H. G. had all been professional wordsmiths, and their adoring letters meant as much to her as their physical acts. Bill Sanger was not a professional wordsmith, but his overwhelming ardor made up for it. Even J. Noah, in his clumsy way, had thrilled her when he cried out as she dramatically entered a room, "Look at my Margy! Look at her!" All of this she had found exciting and highly romantic. To substitute a man like Hobson Pitman for any of these didn't make sense, and she finally knew it.

Her loneliness increased, however. She tried to fight it by subscribing to a dozen "women's magazines," and reading all the love stories in each. She went to the movies and saw the same romantic pictures over and over. Nothing helped, especially after hearing from Janet that Hugh was back in the nursing home.

After this Margaret didn't even pretend to be cheerful. Her heart began to trouble her again and she stayed home in bed with nurses attending her around the clock. Lying in bed, she devised a new scheme. When she got better, she would buy a plot of land and build herself a second new house in Monterey, California. Juliet stopped her once more, reminding her that "A house is not all fun. It always takes more money and energy than you expect. I know how difficult it is to be patient, but do please try."

So she cheered herself by sending extremely expensive food parcels to Hugh and Janet for Christmas, but by this time Hugh had taken a turn for the worse; Janet had had to bring him home to care for him herself, and neither of them were giving much attention to food. Margaret's reaction to this was to turn more and more to Demerol; it was the only thing that soothed her and made her forget her worry and pain. Under its effect she tried to write a light-hearted letter to Angus; "So here I am with three nurses, oxygen tents and tanks, and merry old time, says I." Angus flew out to see her as soon as he could, and wrote her as soon as he got home: "Glorious Margaret, without your having come into my life it would have been drab and hardly worthwhile. You have the Godlike power to touch a soul and make it bear better fruit than seemed possible."

When the pain was unbearable or when Margaret, a good actress, convinced Stuart that it was, she got more Demerol. Not knowing what else to do, Stuart wrote out prescriptions for the drug, to be given every four hours as needed, specifying an amount in each prescription that should have lasted a week. But somehow, two days after she got a prescription, she told him that particular bottle had fallen and broken, spilling out all its contents. No other bottles; always that one.

Stuart spoke to other doctors and found they were hearing similar stories. Their patients' Demerol bottles were mysteriously falling and breaking ahead of time. Demerol, it seemed, created far more dependence than they had believed.

Now Stuart began to observe his mother more closely. Soon he learned that she was demanding Demerol, not every four hours as prescribed, but every three hours, then every two hours, then every hour. If a nurse refused to give it to her, she would simply grab the syringe and inject herself.

He tried to reason with her, but her answer was, "You must look after me because I am your mother." "No," he replied, "I must look after you because you are my patient." He decided to try another tactic. Demerol is a clear white liquid; he would dilute it. He went to every hospital and drugstore in town and had them save their empty Demerol bottles for him. He filled them partly with the medication and partly with sterile water, gradually increasing the amount of water until there was no Demerol at all.

It worked for a while; then Margaret caught on and demanded that the full amount of Demerol be restored, repeating in her most arrogant manner: "I am rich. I have brains. I shall do exactly as I please."

He tried turning her over to other doctors; but as soon as the new doctor managed to cut her down, she left his care and found someone else. She even found a quack who told her what she wanted to hear: "If I were you, and had your pain, I would rest with a bottle of Demerol next to my bed day and night." When Stuart fired the quack, she found another. Finally he discovered she was injecting herself every half hour with pure water. She had become psychologically dependent on the needle itself.

She continued to function, however. She got out of bed to lecture in nearby Phoenix on "preventive politics." She traveled East to clear out more of her papers at the Sixteenth Street Bureau. She even did her first radio broadcast.

But everything exhausted her. Soon she had no choice but to stay put in Tucson; she simply had to stop for a while.

40

JAPAN AND INDIA SAY YES

Hugh died early in 1951. What made his death particularly upsetting was that Margaret heard of it through friends. She wrote a frantic letter to Janet, but didn't receive an answer until weeks later:

Do forgive me for not having answered your very dear letter. I was so sorry the news of Hugh's death had to reach you so unsuspectedly & in such a way. It must indeed have been a shock. I should have written you sooner. For the weeks immediately following I was in a state of complete inertia. Bridget brought me here to Oxshott at once for a rest, and I meant to be back at Sand Pit by March . . .

I can't yet realize that Hugh has gone, but oh Margaret, it was a blessing that he did not linger. I couldn't have wished to keep him in such distress. He passed quite peacefully however, unconscious. Just a deep sigh & he was gone. I was with him alone, as I should have wished. He had a relapse in the beginning of November & then got worse & worse. Bridget & the children came for Christmas & he was able to enjoy them, but after that I just prayed that he could go.

Dear Margaret, let us keep in touch with each other. You meant so much in Hugh's life.

419

Having withdrawn from the drug for a while, Margaret went back to the comfort of Demerol, then wrote disconsolately in her diary:

So many old friends in England have gone—Hugh de Selincourt!! Bessie Drysdale. Also Kerr of the Malthusian. I was deeply distressed over Hugh's death—also Kate Hepburn's death. Such old faithful friends are too young to go so quickly.

The world is in a condition of uncertainty again.

She mourned for a month, then perked up:

MacArthur has been "deposed" from his Ivory Tower & is now back in U.S.A. The spring is lovely, a party of 14 to supper on the terrace last night. This new modern fan-shaped house has been a house of entertainment. Actually hundreds of people have come here. The Woman's Republican Club of 300 came for their annual meeting & tea. The Medical Center drive of 100 came for cocktails on the start of the drive & about 50 at the closing where $500,000 was raised for the hospital.

The Tucson Art Festival also had one of its meetings here . . . The Planned Parenthood local drive also had one of its teas here. So all this year there has been vast and frequent entertainment. I've loved its space & light.

But in July 1951, she had another brief heart attack. Angus flew out to see her as he always did, and they planned an evening together in August when she would stop in New York on her way to England for a meeting of the International Committee on Planned Parenthood, the forerunner of the International Planned Parenthood Federation .

Before she sailed, the *Reader's Digest* did an article on her. It was a straightforward piece telling of her struggles for her cause, but it was enough to set off the Catholic opposition. *Novena Notes* devoted its entire July issue to her:

In the *Reader's Digest,* this month of July, there are two articles contradicting one another. The first, titled "Acts of Faith for a Time of Peril," holds "man's greatest achievements come in years of darkness" and demonstrates how all forms of heroic success came the hard way through sacrifice. Another praises a woman

who taught just the opposite, and advocated and succeeded in doing away with the laws of the land and more shamefully important the laws of God himself! Margaret Sanger is described as a
noble character fighting poverty through murder of the unborn.

Significantly . . . in France she "found her first glimpse of
hope," meaning a knowledge of contraceptive practices. She introduced to Americans the very enemy that observers knew was
then destroying France. Years before Margaret Sanger started
her ignoble Crusade, General Von Moltke said to Bismark: "We
need not kill the French: they are killing themselves."

America's greatest enemy is not the Nazis and Japs of World
War II, who destroyed more than a million American boys. It is
Margaret Sanger who worked from within killing off millions of
potential American defenders at birth. Thanks to Margaret Sanger and her ilk Stalin rejoices and bides his time. Not too
late . . . if the present generation wakes up and realizes "birth
control" for the cancerous sore it is. . . . Benedict Arnold is a
harmless child compared to Margaret Sanger!

By now she was used to this kind of attack, but when *Novena Notes*
made the accusation she hated the most—that she and her husband
(they didn't even know he was dead) were in the movement solely to
make a profit from manufacturing contraceptives—she wrote across
the pages "Libelous!" and asked Morris Ernst to sue.

Ernst agreed that the accusation that she was manufacturing contraceptives for profit was indeed libelous, but advised her not to sue. It
would only give the matter more publicity, he said. More, a suit would
be a great emotional strain. He was right. The excitement over the
article alone was enough to set off another heart attack, one so severe
it took Stuart four hours to relieve her pain. "I have been ordered to
take New York in my easiest stride with no tension or excitement or
anything emotional (*God help me*)," she wrote Angus. "Stupid & dull.
Even rather grim. This picture (of me) may make you decide to postpone your New York trip & it will be sensible to make that decision.
But you must make it."

He decided to come as she might have known, and during the course
of their evening together, she had some more mild heart pains so that
they had a sedate visit instead of the active one they had originally
planned. But he made up for it by wildly circling his plane three times

over her ship as it steamed down the Hudson River. Dorothy McNamee, her companion on the voyage, spotted him and they both waved happily back. Margaret said it was one of the loveliest visits with Angus she had ever had.

Back in Tucson after the conference, she took flying lessons. If Angus could learn at sixty-five, she could learn at seventy-two. But flying proved far too strenuous, so she went back to painting and partying again.

A particularly satisfying party was one she didn't want to give at first. A convention of 300 engineers was meeting in Tucson, and Dorothy McNamee suggested she give them a cocktail party. Engineers were not exactly in Margaret's line, but when Dorothy pointed out how exciting it would be for just the two of them to entertain 300 men, Margaret agreed. She put on a gold lamé gown, arranged herself carefully on her brocaded sofa, and since she wasn't up to standing, received the men sitting like royalty, with Dorothy presenting them one at a time and Margaret basking in the attention.

Margaret and Dorothy were trying to think of something equally satisfying when Juliet wrote begging her to come East to help her pack as she was selling her New York house. By now Margaret was terribly afraid of winter cold because it might give her pneumonia or bronchitis, but when Juliet said, "Parting with my house after thirty years is like parting with a favored and beloved child. If I can only hold your hand it may be some comfort through the ordeal," she flew to New York. A new challenge was awaiting her in Tucson when she got home. Ellen Watumill, whom Margaret had met briefly many years before, had recently returned from India. Partly because she was affiliated with the Watumill Foundation from whom the Hindu birth-control leaders hoped to get a large donation, and partly because they knew she was an American, Mrs. Watumill had been asked what could be done to spread birth-control information there. Now she asked if it would be convenient for her and her Hindu husband to visit Margaret and discuss the matter. They came to her fan-shaped house, and the three of them agreed that an Indian conference was in order. Margaret said she would be glad to help organize one for 1952, starting to work on it a year in advance. She began immediately, back in her element. She dictated dozens of letters to Lady Rama Rau, the Indian woman most interested in birth control. She suggested names of speakers and delegates; she ordered special stationery headed, *India World Confer-*

ence, Margaret Sanger, Honorary President. She raised travel money for delegates who couldn't provide it themselves and even arranged secretaries for Lady Rama Rau. As money was crucial, she wasn't above taking donations as small as five dollars, raising a total of sixteen thousand dollars from Tucson friends alone. And since MacArthur was now out of Japan and she could get a visa, she planned to stop in Japan for two weeks on her way to India.

The major plans made, she had another publicity-making idea: She wrote to famous people, including President Harry Truman and General David Sarnoff, head of the National Broadcasting Company, asking if they would let their names be listed in the conference program as "official sponsors" of the event. Some refused, but Eleanor Roosevelt, Mrs. J. Borden Harriman, Doris Duke, Albert Einstein, and Mr. and Mrs. DeWitt Wallace, editors of the *Reader's Digest*, all accepted. It was an impressive list. She remarked happily to Angus: "This is like the good old days." Still she complained that she was lonely:

I have only brilliant women for companions, or stupid males. But none of these are my ideal of a life of growth or development & I want the equal companion in thinking, art, music, science, everything that's alive in the universe.

She continued to have many male callers, however. One, a teacher, stopped by to visit her every day to say things like: "Let me gaze into your eyes. It's long since I had such exquisite pleasure." He admitted later that he had a double motive; he hoped she would remember him in her will, leaving him Slee's hand-carved bed or some of her fine Oriental rugs.

Another caller spoke of her "girlishness and charm" but looked for a few slight remembrances, too. A third didn't even want to wait; he was an expert wheedler. Lisa, her maid, tells of serving him lunch and seeing him suddenly put his hands under his napkin. He was wearing one of Margaret's handsome sapphire rings. But whatever the cost, Margaret enjoyed their company and used her most potent charms to keep them coming.

Yet to her family she could be a spitfire as well as a charmer. Margaret II remembers that during a visit with her grandmother, at a house Margaret had rented for the summer on Fisher's Island near Grant's home, she and Nancy, her sister, aged eight and six respectively, decided one hot morning to walk over to Grant's house without asking permission. When they got back, they had a raging thirst and asked for water. Their grandmother flatly refused to let them have any. "Water ruins the appetite!" she said. Finally she admitted she was refusing them water as a punishment for their taking the walk without asking her permission. And when the old butler tried to sneak them some water, she commanded, "Take it away. It's not what *you* want, it's what *I* want." They had to go to bed thirsty.

Mainly, to be sure, Margaret acted this way when on drugs; at other times she could be as sweet as ever. But when her sharp temper and bad tongue did break out, they cut deeply.

She also had become extremely parsimonious. Her grandchildren once heard her talking with the boy who mowed her lawn in Tucson, arguing that since he worked for the famous Margaret Sanger he should work for less.

By the end of September 1952, Margaret was working energetically, looking for American delegates to the Indian Conference, and asking those who said they would go to send her advance copies of their scientific papers. When the papers arrived, she had new copies made and sent these to the other delegates in order to avoid duplication of material. Then she made arrangements for Indian housing and recreation, attending to all the details that she had learned so expertly to do.

But soon she was worrying about an article that had appeared in *Look* Magazine suggesting that Pincus and Rock might discover an effective oral contraceptive. On September 26, she wrote William Vogt, National Director of Planned Parenthood:

> Instead of giving me joy to see the preliminary publicity, (I know that) so many things can happen until there is an actual accomplishment and thorough testing of these mythical drugs, that I am worried stiff.
>
> As to the amazing and wonderful news of the "Pill," may I again beg of you to get in direct contact with the American Medical Association before you give out anything to any other group? They can kill the best idea in the world, even more decidedly than the Catholics. With all the wealth of Hutton who bought the Carol Dakin formula and standardized it into Zonite, he made an enemy of the A.M.A. only because he did not submit his facts to Chicago before he went to the general public. To this day the M.D.'s

are against Zonite, knowing it is far better on tissues and membranes than Lysol. So please ask or invite the official A.M.A. to come in on the kill!

This hectic activity gave her brief heart attacks that made her call a doctor at any hour of the day or night. For, as Stuart had found, whether she needed medical help or not, she refused to stand the least bit of pain. Angus, who expected to be out West on business at this time, wanted to drop by and visit her for a day but she refused: "The fun of being together would not be there. My mind will be working on details until I land in Bombay." She also admitted to Angus:

> I am cross as two sticks. If I have another attack before Oct. 6 I'll give up going. That's final. I thought I was getting entirely well until yesterday and last night. If I had to open a conference today I could not do it. I've given up cocktails, wines, coffee, all delicious meats and sauces, so that I'll be "conditioned" to diets en route.

Instead of flying to Tucson to see her, Angus, though he was far from a wealthy man, sent her a check for one hundred dollars toward the travel expenses of the delegates. Margaret, meanwhile, asked the National Planned Parenthood Federation for a substantial travel sum for herself, which they said they had neither the desire nor the funds to give, making her furious. The cause, she explained, had always paid her travel expenses; it was quite a change to have to pay them herself.

She sailed on the S.S. *Lurline* on October 11 for Honolulu, then went by plane to Yokohama, Singapore, and Bombay, taking along Grace Sternberg, a Tucson friend, as well as Mrs. Clarence Gamble. The three made a great fuss over what clothes Margaret should wear to look her best.

In Japan she was received by a motorcade escort with sound trucks blaring, "Sanger is here! Sanger is here! No more abortions! Sanger is here!" The maids in the hotels bowed so low that Mrs. Sternberg was greatly impressed, and Margaret was sure she would get lumbago from all the bowing she had to do in return. Her talks in Japan were so successful that at a meeting planned for about forty women, eight hundred came and stayed an entire afternoon. "People here are desperate, but they are fearless and wide awake to the need for birth control," she exulted in a letter home. She told of other long talks given to doctors and midwives, with demonstration material and techniques. In addition, she was delighted when she was invited to address the Japanese Diet and became one of the first Westerners to be presented to the Emperor's son. She was furious, however, when the editor of a Tokyo paper gave her age as ninety-four; she was actually seventy-three and admitting to only sixty-eight. As the Japanese revere age, the paper meant it as a gesture of respect, but she was so angry she got sick and retreated to bed, phoning the editor and calling off a reception he had planned.

Seven hundred and fifty delegates came to the 1952 Indian Conference, and twenty-one papers were read. Margaret and Lady Rama Rau, President of the Family Planning Association of India, shared the honors on the platform. Dr. C. P. Blacker, an English delegate, spoke of it as the most brilliant and successful of the early postwar conferences on birth control: Years later he reminisced:

> Mrs. Sanger was wonderfully responsive to her audiences. She could draw from them as much as she gave them. . . . Large assemblages acted on her like a tonic. She visibly drew strength and zest from the packed seats and galleries; and the iller she seemed beforehand the more triumphant was her performance.
> Her charm and warmth . . . have been abundantly stressed. What I would particularly like to mention is her power of strategical thinking. She saw how Asia, Europe, and America could play different but complementary roles. This grand design, by no means obvious at the start, is now so taken for granted that it can easily be forgotten that Mrs. Sanger was its originator and architect.

Margaret was pretty much exhausted by the conference, however, and decided to make her speech of resignation from the International Planned Parenthood Federation then and there. She slipped a note saying this to Lady Rama Rau who was sitting on Nehru's right while she sat at his left. Lady Rama Rau was a big woman with a booming voice, and as there was much rivalry between the two women, they had been stealing baleful glances at each other across the impassive Nehru.

Now Lady Rama Rau had to introduce Margaret, who had grown more and more nervous as the moment approached. Soon Lady Rama Rau rose and went to the speaker's desk: "I give you the lady who . . . " her voice boomed through the cavernous room. And again, "I give you the lady through whom . . . " Margaret sat trembling while Lady Rama Rau went on endlessly. Finally Margaret stood up, walked slowly to the speaker's desk and stopped her rival by starting to speak herself.

She spoke for only four minutes in a quiet voice, using simple, lucid words, and when she was finished, the entire audience stood up and rang the hall with their cheers.

She described the occasion in a letter to her granddaughter the next day:

> Darling Margaret. Yesterday was a great and joyous day for me. The conference was opened by Prime Minister Nehru who bent over me (in the ante-room) and said, "It's wonderful that you came to us from so far away." He then offered me his arm, and together we walked out into the Great Auditorium facing hundreds of camera shots & news men. I had to speak from the platform and said, "Mr. Nehru is the greatest living statesman in all this world." It was a great victory for our Cause, and I am happy that I came.

A few days later, the delegates voted her President Emeritus for life after which, excited, she flew to Tokyo for a week as a guest of the *Manuichi Press*, then to Honolulu for a week of festivity, and finally home.

But at home there came the inevitable letdown. Her legs as well as her heart started to bother her, and she turned even more to Demerol. When her supply ran out, she frightened Stuart by suddenly disappearing. She had flown with a nurse back to Honolulu, where she had many "connections," and flew back with a suitcase full of drugs.

Still, she could manage short comebacks. At a three-day emergency conference called by the Population Council in New York to discuss the population explosion, the highlight dinner was given at the Waldorf Astoria in Margaret's honor. Sir Julian Huxley came over from England to be International Chairman. Distinguished guests included

Marriner Eccles, former Secretary of the Treasury under Roosevelt, and H. E. M. C. Chagla, Indian Ambassador to the United States.

When she received her invitation, Margaret wired in jubilation, "I will get there if I have to crawl," after which she flew to New York dressed in her finest. But the introductory remarks by Mr. Chagla were so long and repetitious that she fell asleep, having passed out with what drug users call "the nods." Dr. Alan Guttmacher, President of the Planned Parenthood Association, was seated next to her; he tried to wake her but it was impossible. The only thing he could do was to lift her in his arms, carry her upstairs to her hotel room, and put her to bed. The dinner went on as best it could, but Guttmacher had seldom been so embarrassed or the guests so puzzled.

By that time Margaret realized she could not shake off her drug dependence and was thoroughly depressed. She kept repeating that she had accomplished nothing in her life; her friends tried to help by reminding her that few people start and finish a crusade in one lifetime. Nothing did much good, even the adoring letters from Angus. She would simply glance at his letters and say wearily to her secretary, "File them away." Occasionally she would perk up, as when he wrote her that she was "the greatest woman who was ever born," and in a rare burst of modesty she answered: "Thanks for the compliment, but please don't get the woman mixed up with the cause. I consider the cause the greatest ever conceived by the human mind, even though the woman who conceived it may not be the greatest of all." But mostly she sat and looked blankly at TV, or rambled on about the objections to her sex talks at Mabel Dodge's Greenwich Village salon long ago.

EVERYTHING FLAMBE

Though Margaret's favorite drinks had been wine and French champagne, she now grew fonder than ever of hard liquor. Margaret II, who walked across the lawn mornings to visit with her, often found her having breakfast in bed with a daiquiri on her tray. "The colors in daiquiris are so romantic," she would explain.

Practically all her food became flambé as well. She flambéed meats, she flambéed omelets and desserts; she even flambéed the salads she had for lunch.

Still, she at times continued to function. She reported to Ellen Watumill after the Indian Conference that the government health officers had told her the Hindus were trying old contraceptives like oil and cotton plugs with some success. The least successful method was rhythm; the people either couldn't keep it up or counted wrong. Also both men and women had come to family-planning talks and listened with interest, but though at first few had taken the talks seriously, now more did.

A few weeks later, she was asking the Watumill Foundation for more expense money for her international work. She kept begging the Rockefeller Foundation to increase its twenty-five-thousand-dollar annual grant, as well as the Brush Foundation its thirteen-thousand-dollar grant, and the Doris Duke Foundation its five-thousand-dollar grant.

429

Yet she told the Massachusetts chapter of the PPFA that she felt it was timid and weak to wait for money. The women there told her: "When hard cash comes in, hard work will go on." She replied, "Every experienced campaigner knows that money follows hard work. It is not the other way about."

Meanwhile she continued her own fund raising. When John D. Rockefeller III was in Tucson, she gave a dinner in his honor so that she could casually bring up the subject of her cause. Dorothy McNamee warned her that he was a teetotaller and might be offended if she served liquor. "I always serve liquor at my parties, and I make no exception," she replied. She seated him at her right hand and so charmed him that before he left he wrote her a check for one hundred seventy-five thousand dollars. "That's more like it," she exclaimed after he had gone, waving the check about.

The Ford Foundation, which she solicited vigorously, wouldn't contribute, however. The wife of Henry Ford II was a devout Catholic, and as William Vogt, president of the National Planned Parent Federation recognized, "We can't jam birth control down his throat, even if three out of his nine trustees do feel it is one of the most important problems, if not *the* most important, facing the world."

Margaret wanted to keep after the Ford Foundation just the same, but her health was too unpredictable for sustained effort of any kind.

Meanwhile, Abraham Stone was having a hard time running the Bureau. This was mainly because he was not an experienced fund raiser, and patients' fees alone could not keep the place in operation. Nonetheless, in Tucson Margaret kept on charging the Bureau for such comparatively petty expenses as stamps and phone calls connected with birth-control work. She even sent the Bureau all the gas receipts for running her Cadillac, asking Stone to explain to the accountant that "every time I go out it is on an errand connected with birth control."

Stone decided he simply had to apply to William Vogt, president of the Planned Parenthood Federation, for money. She was extremely upset:

> I could help you by giving up the International work and thereby save you a few grand a year.... I often think it was not doing you a favor to let you take on the Bureau, no matter how much you wanted it. But it's rather late to look back. I note your request

of the P.P.F.'s help and it will be a miracle to me if you get a dollar out of Vogt.

When Stone wrote her that Vogt said he would take on the financial burden of the Bureau on condition that the PPFA assume direct supervision, Margaret was even more upset. "I am deeply disturbed, as I hope you are," she wrote back. And when Vogt went further and asked Stone to show him the Bureau's books, Margaret wired: "Am flying to New York immediately. Don't show anybody the books." Eventually, however, Vogt had his way. He got to see the books and made her assume some of the expenses she had asked him to pay. She left New York in a huff, flying on to Stockholm with Jonathan Schultz to try again to realize the great ambition of her life—to get the Nobel Peace Prize. She was sure that if she and Schultz personally kept lobbying for it, she would stand a better chance of winning it. But nothing came of their efforts. She went to Stockholm and lobbied again the following year and the year after that. The results were no better. This particular honor eluded her to the end.

By 1954 Margaret's health was deteriorating rapidly. She had a bad seige of bronchitis and double pneumonia and had to stay in the Columbia Presbyterian Hospital for weeks. Amazingly, she pulled through.

It didn't help that her weight was way up either. But after each heart attack, Stuart had advised a diet low in fat and salt, only to have Margaret defy him. Once, for six months she ate nothing but pancakes slathered in butter, blintzes heaped with sour cream, and salty caviar. When he tried to stop her, she answered as always: "I am rich. I have brains. I shall do exactly as I please."

In 1954 she suddenly stopped this mad diet and went on a sensible one, with the result that in a few months she got down to her goal of 125 pounds, telling Juliet that she was "praying hard to the gods that I can keep that weight for the rest of my life."

She worked hard in 1954 toward another goal—helping Pincus raise funds to continue his research on what he now called simply "the pill." John Rock had at last come out openly in support of the project and was also doing his own birth-control research in a limited way at his clinic in Brookline. All that stood in the way was the money needed to do the necessary large-scale testing on women themselves. Luckily

Stanley McCormick died in 1954, and when the long legal complications over his will were settled, his wife got control of fifteen million dollars. She could now help the cause to the fullest extent. Margaret went East for the pleasure of personally presenting her to Rock.

Rock remembers being told by his secretary that he had an appointment with Margaret Sanger, whom he had never met, and a Mrs. McCormick of whom he had never heard. At the appointed time two ladies arrived, one small and frail and dressed with great chic, the other tall and stately and dressed in old-fashioned, severe clothes. He mistakenly assumed the severely dressed woman was Mrs. Sanger, for didn't all crusaders resemble Carrie Nation? When Mrs. McCormick identified herself and offered him forty-five thousand dollars a year for five years as a starter, promising him more later if he needed it, he knew that he and Pincus were really on their way.

Originally they planned to do the testing in Japan, but they could not get the full cooperation they needed; they switched to Puerto Rico instead. It took ten years and over two million dollars from the time the research on the pill was started until it was finished and accepted as safe by the Federal Drug Administration.

With the help of Rock, Pincus, Mrs. McCormick, and a host of other dedicated workers, Margaret had at last put a nearly foolproof contraceptive into women's hands. She had found her Holy Grail.

RUNNING, RUNNING

For the rest of her life, ill as she was, Margaret was too restless to stay put in Tucson. She took her granddaughters on a pleasure trip to Japan which she had come to love. She planned a trip to Java because it sounded like a romantic place, though when her astrologer said she shouldn't go, she didn't. She did go to Hawaii in March 1956, though she had such pains in her heart on the way that she wrote in her diary, "I am in agony." Added to her heart pains was what she called her bursitis. "It is painful to move night and day. If it is not better in the next ten days I will return home and settle down to endure it, which I do not like to do." The bursitis got better and she went to Waikiki where Doris Duke entertained her in a home out of the Arabian Nights.

In May, after a short rest at home, she was relaxed enough to accept an invitation to speak in Kansas City and plan a long lecture tour. "Darlings," she wrote to her granddaughters, "it is an utterly mad notion of mine to go on lecture tours again just because I feel better. Well that's M.S. & no one can change her but God." But just as she was ready to start the tour she had a really bad heart attack and was forced to abandon the plan. Yet the following summer she and Juliet went on a holiday jaunt to their beloved England, and Margaret handled it surprisingly well for a woman of seventy-eight.

Back from England, she went to the Hawaiian Islands again, writing home with name-dropping pride: "I delayed leaving Honolulu until

433

Sunday as Admiral and Mrs. Stump wanted me to have lunch with them at Pearl Harbor. It is not always one can have lunch with an Admiral."

She took Jonathan Schultz along on the Honolulu trip, and saw to it that the passenger list read, "Margaret Sanger, LLD, RN," followed by, "Jonathan Schulz, BA, LLB," though it is hardly customary on a ship to list one's degrees, particularly when, as in her case, one was honorary and the other imaginary. Yet it was another touch of ego she couldn't resist.

Since she always traveled in the utmost luxury, using the presidential suites on ships and the best hotels on shore, as well as taking along companions whose way she paid, her money was beginning to disappear fast. For wherever she went, she also shopped for dresses, handbags, and trinkets for her granddaughters; dresses, shoes, costumes, and expensive jewelry for herself. If she found no room for these in her trunks or closets when she got home, she gave them away to anyone who popped into her mind. Dorothy Brush remembers her surprise at suddenly receiving in the mail a replica of a Japanese sailing junk made entirely of fine pearls. And Margaret expected extravagant thank-you notes in return for her gifts. After Margaret II was married, her grandmother packed a huge barrel of gold-leaf china and shipped it off to her. As Margaret II was only eighteen and was living very moderately, with no possible use for that kind of china, she wrote her grandmother a simple note of thanks. Margaret was enraged; she demanded and received an extravagant note.

Try as she might, though, she couldn't keep traveling. Her heart pains and chest pains kept returning even though she tried all kinds of bizarre treatments for them. One treatment she took in Honolulu she described to Gregory Pincus as a "cosmic ray treatment." When Stuart heard about it, he insisted she come home and substitute thyroid-iodine treatment. She agreed, but demanded her dose of Demerol as well. "I had been having attacks (of angina) night after night, and only Demerol could stop the agonizing retching at the throat & left side of the chest," she wrote Pincus in February of 1957. "I have finally had a good night of drugless sleep, & no angina pain for six weeks—I cannot tell you what this means, Gregory."

Yet she was ready to go to New York when the chance came to get a really big break—an interview on the "Mike Wallace Show" on nation-wide television. She had been hoping for something like this for years, and finally managed it on September 21, 1957. She wrote Margaret II: "I spent Saturday with Mike Wallace. Then I got the *New York Times* and a TV editor after him, and I was in!"

Her appearance on television, even though she spoke in the most general terms, brought out the opposition in full force. For the first time in her life she didn't want to open her mail because so many sacks of it, forwarded to her from NBC, said things like, "I pray every day that you may fry in Hell forever," that, after glancing at a few, she told them to throw the rest out. But she did read a bitter editorial in the September 27, 1957, issue of the Catholic *Evangelist* called *TV: Boom or Bust?*

A graphic instance of the need of vigilance and prudent super-vision of television programs was provided last night in The Mike Wallace Interview with Margaret Sanger. In permitting Wallace to give vent to his offensive sensationalism, the National Broad-casting Company and Philip Morris cigarettes, the sponsor of Wallace's program, pervert the aim of television as a medium of culture, education and entertainment.

Wallace, who claimed "to explore the economic, moral and reli-gious aspects of birth control" was the instrument whereby Mrs. Sanger, veteran proponent of barnyard ethics and race suicide, was given entrance into millions of decent homes to taint them with her evil philosophy of lust and animalistic mating. If Marga-ret Sanger had her way, the ultimate result would be no audience for TV and no rising generations to "Call for Philip Morris."

Margaret wrote in her diary in a hand so shaky that the words are almost unreadable:

The R.C. Church is getting more defiant and arrogant. I'm dis-gusted & worried. No one who was a worker in defense of our Protestant rights has got to accept the Black Hand from Catholic influence. Young Kennedy from Boston is on the Stage for Presi-dent in 1960. God help America if his father's millions can push him into the White House.

By 1958 Margaret had definitely slowed to a walk. At times she was full of plans for the future of International Planned Parenthood. At other times she was impatient and would get angry at even her most loyal friends. When Ellen Watumill wrote to Margaret's brother Bob for "a special few words about Margaret" for an article on her, Margaret wrote him: "I do not know why Ellen Watumill should write you about me. All that is important about me is set down in print in my autobiography *My Fight for B.C.*"

Then she would become light-hearted again. One weekend she went off on a painting trip to Nogales but refused to have the necessary vaccination for re-entry into the States. When the inspector refused to let her come back without it, she let him give her the vaccination; as soon as she was over the border, however, she sucked out the vaccine while he was watching, then looked up and grinned at him like an imp. At another time she advised the PPFA, which was about to hold its annual luncheon meeting in New York, that she definitely was too ill to leave Tucson, but in the middle of the lunch made a dramatic stage-entrance on the arm of Juliet Rublee.

But after such incidents she would slip back. She was on Demerol steadily now, often combined with wine, and would wander out into the streets in her nightgown, sometimes falling down and arriving at Stuart's house with her face all black and blue. Stuart tried setting up a hospital room in his home, engaging nurses to control her drug dependence, but she would not listen to either him or the nurses. She would get up and wander around the house in the middle of the night, turning on the radio or TV full blast so that no one could sleep. Or she would discharge the nurses in the middle of the night, and lock herself in the bathroom while he frantically begged her to come out. He found he had no choice but to send her back across the lawn to her own home.

Her money was now almost gone. Aware of what was happening, some of her servants stole from her regularly. As Demerol kills the appetite, she was eating practically nothing, yet the servants ordered great quantities of food and liquor which they took home with them. Or they gave big parties in the kitchen for their friends. The result was that food and liquor bills of close to a thousand dollars came in at the end of each month. Stuart had no choice; he had to pay these bills on her behalf. Then she lent her airline credit card to a friend, ostensibly for a short trip. The friend flew around the world, taking several buddies with him. This bill amounted to many thousands of dollars. Stuart had to pay again.

Next she started giving away her jewelry, some of it very valuable.

When she gave valuable pieces to Dr. Jackman Pyre, he handed them back to Stuart. When she gave them to her maids, they did not. She had had five million dollars when J. Noah died; now only a fraction was left. Stuart had to do something before every penny ran out.

First he discharged the many servants, keeping on only the faithful Lisa as a combined housekeeper and nurse, and her husband John as butler. But they couldn't handle the situation. They slept in J. Noah's former room next to Margaret's. Often at night they would be awakened by a thud; it was Margaret falling out of bed, and it was hard work to get her back in without injuring her. Or they would be ordered to prepare an elaborate dinner for many guests, only to discover after the table was set and everything ready that Margaret had forgotten to invite any guests. Frustrated and unhappy, John and Lisa decided to leave, and Stuart had to get whatever help he could.

"The whole situation had become a mess," Stuart summed it up.

THE JUBILANT DAYS

"Life is sad," said Edith Wharton. "It is the saddest thing there is, next to death. But it is only the years that are sad. The days can be jubilant. I've had many jubilant days."

Margaret too had had many jubilant days, and there were more to come. In 1959, when she was eighty, she still wrote to Katherine McCormick about the progress of the pill which Dr. Rock and Gregory Pincus were trying to improve. Mrs. McCormick always answered, recounting stories of her visits with Rock and how elated he was over his work on a possible male contraceptive as well. "He was rather shocked," said Mrs. McCormick, "when I told him I didn't give a hoot about a male contraceptive, that only female research concerned me."

Margaret agreed with her friend. Helping women concerned her most too. She was furious at President Eisenhower for sending money and ammunition to foreign countries but denying foreign women birth-control information on the ground that "this would be interfering with their private affairs." She announced she was thinking of starting a new world population campaign "to persuade rich people to leave their money to B.C." The Ford Foundation had at last capitulated and given the Worcester Institute a million dollars for a world-wide study on population control, and Margaret was jubilant because it set an example for an elderly gentleman she knew. As a result she had persuaded this gentleman to change his will and leave his money for birth-control study. Also, she was eagerly awaiting a visit from Gregory Pincus who was coming out West to see her, after stopping in Washington to try to get help from the World Health Organization.

But she could not keep up her interest in anything for long. The Demerol, plus the breakfast daiquiris, plus half a bottle of wine with lunch, would send her into a deep sleep for the rest of the day, and when she awoke, she was not always coherent. Her brother Bob once telephoned her in the evening and, knowing little about what was happening, was surprised when someone came to the phone and said that the Maggie he remembered so fondly could not speak to him. "That made me think you were ill," he wrote. " 'Cause when you can't speak somebody else's got the hall."

By April, she was neither speaking on the phone nor answering letters, except through a secretary. She was in bed almost constantly or wandering about the house touching familiar objects as if to recall that they were hers.

Soon she received news that shook her badly. Angus was seriously ill with a combination of Paget's disease, arthritis of the spine, leukemia, tuberculosis, and congestive heart failure. He tried to be cheerful, writing:

> The approach to my 76th birthday seemed rather perilous, but now that goal has been reached, I am looking forward to my 77th in the inspiring company of your spirit . . . I have so many new plans for my business that bed-rest is just a waste of time.

He was taken to the University of Virginia hospital a week later for an operation. The only letter he wrote from the hospital was to his Glorious Margaret: "I am as full of plans as ever. Without your example I would never have had the courage to fight on."

She answered:

> Dear of the dearest—Such a letter!!! But off to the hospital is too sad. Angus, if my friendship has meant much to you, yours in the background of my life has been comfortable & even exciting. You have not known much of that side from me as I held it rather sacred and precious. There seemed to be nothing we could do about it, but to let it *grow* as it has. Do you understand this at all?? I trust you do & ever did.

Think of me often as I do and will think of Angus, the great *lover*.

Angus never received this letter, as he died almost immediately after the operation. It was returned by his secretary, unopened, with the news that he had gone: "We all miss him very much. He was a good man." And his wife Amy added: "I took your letter to Angus but he never became oriented after the operation to see it. Love to you. You meant so much in his life."

Margaret wired his wife, Amy: "Nothing I can say or think could possibly comfort you, as I am too unhappy myself to be helpful to anyone desolate and unhappy."

In June 1962, things came to a climax. Dr. Lindsay E. Beaton examined her and declared:

Mrs. Sanger is senile, with advanced arteriosclerosis of the brain, resulting in poor memory, forgetfulness, failure of judgment concerning money and personal matters, irritability, confusion, disorientation, misidentification of persons, and periods of great agitation. . . . In my professional opinion, she must be protected against her own physical and mental incapacities.

Dr. Beaton went on to say that a legal guardianship should be appointed for her, a proceeding that usually requires attendance in court. Under the circumstances, however, he felt she should be spared the strain of such an appearance.

On July 2, 1962, therefore, a psychiatrist was brought to her home to examine her, and the Superior Court of the County of Pima, State of Arizona, appointed Stuart Sanger her legal guardian. At first he tried to have her cared for at home, but this didn't work out, so he had to move her to a nursing home called *The House By the Side of the Road*.

As she was riding in Stuart's car with her granddaughter to the nursing home, she got suspicious, clapped her hands in her old imperious manner, and ordered Stuart to stop: "Take me back immediately. Take me back to my own home," she commanded. But it was too late. Margaret II held her hand tight as the car moved on.

Immediately a great cry went up from some of her Tucson friends who told everyone that Stuart had "railroaded his rich, famous mother into an insane asylum so he could steal all her money." Actually the opposite was true. As her legal guardian Stuart had to account to the court for every penny received on her behalf and every penny spent. Some of his harshest critics were those who had fattened their purses on her largess. Dorothy McNamee stormed into his office and hurled an accusation of theft directly at him. His answer was a furious, "Get out!" The musician who had been happy to play for her guests at no fee when he attended her lavish parties now sent in a bill for several thousand dollars for playing for her while she was ill, figuring his time at fifty dollars an hour. Stuart gave him some money to get rid of him. Other people spread the gossip that Stuart had deprived her of the comfort of being surrounded by her familiar furniture, when in fact he had sent along to the nursing home some of her fine small Oriental rugs as well as her beautiful bed. And in any event he had his hands tied. As a doctor he could not divulge information about his mother's condition or speak publicly in his own defense.

One happy circumstance was that when Dr. Roland Murphy took over at the nursing home, he succeeded in getting Margaret off Demerol. She told him, "I am glad." There still were many other things from which she got pleasure. She enjoyed the one brandied eggnog allowed her a day; she enjoyed her daily ride around the grounds in a wheel chair, putting on for the occasion a white straw hat trimmed with a stuffed red lobster that Stuart's wife had given her. And she enjoyed her daily face massage, insisting that only Elizabeth Arden creams be used, saying, "Remember, Elizabeth Arden was my friend." In particular, she enjoyed her visitors, among them Madame Nehru and John Rock. Indeed, she had so many visitors—old birth-control workers, famous people who were passing through—that they had to be limited to two a day. Since senility comes and goes, however, she did not always immediately recognize them. When Dr. Alan Guttmacher, President of Planned Parenthood, visited her she stared at him uncomprehendingly, but the next day announced proudly to her nurse: "Do you know who came to see me yesterday? Alan Guttmacher!"

A jubilant occasion was the dinner given in her honor in Tucson, arranged by Jack Spieden and Mrs. Barry Goldwater, though Margaret was too ill to attend. An even greater honor was the gold medal she received from the Emperor of Japan for her birth-control work in his country. She was the second Western woman to receive such a medal; the first went to the tutor of his son. She hung it around her neck over her nightgown, refusing to take it off even at night.

But the greatest day of all came when Margaret II flew out to Tucson with her husband to show Stuart her first child. In the Sanger family, the names Margaret and Peggy were used alternately, so this little girl was named Peggy. Stuart wasn't sure his mother would recognize Margaret II and the baby, yet he thought they should visit her on the chance she might.

When Margaret II, her husband, and the baby entered the room, Margaret looked at her granddaughter and exclaimed at once: "Hello, Margaret. I've been waiting for you."

"Hello, Mimi dear," Margaret II replied. "And this is my Peggy."

Margaret took the baby in her arms and began to sob as she rocked it back and forth. "I knew my Peggy would come back to me. This is my Peggy! My own little Peggy come back." She felt the baby's head all over, her motions going back to her early belief in phrenology. "See, she even has the right bumps. Do you have enough milk in your breasts to feed her? I didn't. Mine were too small. Besides, Bill and I were afraid of her catching TB so he got a wet-nurse. But you make sure she gets plenty of milk. . . . Yes, it's my little Peggy. My own little Peggy come back."

She kept rocking and stroking the baby, then, suddenly turned to her son-in-law. "And who is he?" she demanded. "I never saw *him* before." She held on to the child until they had to take it from her because it was time to leave.

Toward the end, Grace Sternberg and Dorothy McNamee came to visit her bringing with them the chicken sandwiches and champagne she particularly enjoyed. They brought along an embroidered tablecloth to make the occasion festive and set out the refreshments. Margaret was fast asleep when they arrived. They waited a while, hating to wake her, but the nurse said she would be upset over missing them and gently shook her. She woke, looked at the laden cloth and laughed: "Chicken sandwiches and champagne! A party! Let's have a party!" then dozed off again.

Two days later on September 6, 1966, she died quietly of leukemia, just short of her eighty-seventh birthday. She left an estate of only one hundred thousand dollars out of her original five million. She had almost succeeded in "blowing it all in."

There were funeral services in the Episcopal Church in Tucson where she occasionally attended with J. Noah and memorial services in fashionable St. George's Church in Stuyvesant Square. In Tucson the Reverend George Ferguson gave the eulogy. In New York Hobson Pitman spoke of her love of art, and Morris Ernst told of what was perhaps her greatest achievement—the fact that she gave women hope; assured them, for the first time in history, that it was within their power to decide how many children they would have; told them that conception is not something that "just happens"—that they could make important decisions about their own lives.

Doing this hadn't been easy, Ernst said. It had involved a long uphill struggle that had taken over forty years, during which she had never stopped fighting. Since it was a day of pouring rain he ended in a ringing voice: "And so a stormy day ends a stormy career."

No one spoke about the guilt she experienced over someone she had wronged or her attempt to make up for it. Yet, after her burial in the family plot in Fishkill, Stuart found a letter in her safe-deposit box marked "For Bill Sanger, to be sent after my death." As Bill had died several years before, a fact which she was never told, Stuart and Grant opened the letter. As they described it, it was full of humility, pleas for forgiveness, and tender memories of their early love. The letter was dated 1954, the year she had double pneumonia; possibly this made her think about the father of the child who had died of pneumonia, as well as fear she might die too.

Something—maybe pride—had kept her from sending the letter after she recovered. Yet obviously she had wanted it sent; it was, in a sense, an Act of Contrition. And how it would have eased Bill Sanger's last difficult years had he been able to hold it in his hands.

Notes

CHAPTER 1

13: Margaret's change of birth-date. Higgins Family Bible, Smith College.

14: Michael Higgins' defense of Henry George. Margaret Sanger, *Autobiography*, W. W. Norton, 1937, p. 17.

14: Michael Higgins' ill-fated partnership with Edward Killian. Harold B. Hersey, "Margaret Sanger: Birth Control Pioneer," unpublished biography, Smith College.

17: Baptism and Confirmation, St. Mary's, Corning. Baptismal record, Book 1, p. 523; Confirmation Register, p. 76. Also Father Robert McNamara, "A Century of Grace: The History of St. Mary's Roman Catholic Parish," Corning, N.Y., 1948.

CHAPTER 2

21: Description of Claverack College. Library, Claverack, N.Y.

22: Crush on Esther. Claverack Memoir, Library of Congress.

22: Friendship with Amelia. Claverack Memoir, Library of Congress.

23: Affair with Corey Alberson. Margaret Sanger to Hugh de Selincourt, undated, 1927, Library of Congress.

25: Anne Higgins' death. Eye-witness account by Sister M. Mechtilde, Corning, N.Y., reported by Father Robert McNamara in a letter to the author.

CHAPTER 3

27: TB glands. Margaret Sanger to Mary Higgins, 1901, Smith College.
27: Margaret's *Text Book of Nursing.* Clare Weeks Shaw, Appleton Century, 1900, Library of Congress.
28: William and Edward Sanger's life. Conversation with Vidia Sanger, 1972.
29-30: Letters between, Margaret, Mary, and William Sanger, 1902, Smith College.

CHAPTER 4

33: Margaret's boredom with Trudeau Sanitarium. Margaret Sanger, *An Autobiography,* W. W. Norton, New York, 1938, p. 60.
34: Margaret's new house. Interview with Mrs. Edward Griswold of Hastings, also visit by author.
35: Grant ill and alone with maid. Interview with Mrs. Edward Griswold of Hastings.
36: Sale of Hastings House. Interview with Fishel's son, Donald Fishel.
36: Regret over sale. Letter from William Sanger to Grant Sanger, October 21, 1952, Smith College.
36: William standing in the road and looking at his house. Interview with Mrs. Edward Griswold.

CHAPTER 5

38: Alexander Campbell Sanger, unpublished senior thesis, Princeton University, 1969. Smith College.
39: Richard Drinnon, *Rebel in Paradise: A Biography of Emma Goldman,* University of Chicago Press, 1961, p. 166; Floyd Dell, *Women as World Builders,* Forbes, Chicago, 1913, p. 60; Emma Goldman, *The Tragedy of Women's Emancipation,* The Mother Earth Publishing Co., New York, 1913.
40: Letters of Emma Goldman to Havelock Ellis, May 15, 1925, and May 30, 1928, Emma Goldman Papers, New York Public Library. These letters are on microfilm; the original letters are in the Goldman-Berkman Archives, International Institute for Social History, Amsterdam, Netherlands.
43: Anthony Comstock is the subject of two biographies, one by Charles Turnbull and the other by Heywood Broun and Margaret Leech. The second is by far the best.
45: Samuel P. Hays, *The Response to Industrialism,* University of Chicago Press, 1957, pp. 95, 96.

46: Organization of the I.W.W.'s. William Preston, Jr., *Aliens and Dissenters*, Harvard University Press, 1963.

49: The Lawrence and Paterson Strikes. Melvin Dubofsky, *We Shall Be All, A History of the Industrial Workers of the World,* Quadrangle Books, Chicago, 1969.

49: David M. Kennedy, *Birth Control in America*, Yale University Press, 1970, p. 18.

52: Children leaving Lawrence second time. Melvin Dubofsky, *We Shall Be All*, p. 252.

52: New York *Call* article about Massachusetts judges vs. foreigners. Socialist Party Collection, June 13, 1912. New York Public Library.

53: Sadie Sachs story. Margaret Sanger, *An Autobiography*, W. W. Norton, New York, 1938, p.89 ff.

55: Hazelton arrest. Alexander Sanger thesis.

56: Pageant loss. Paterson Pageant, New York *Call.* June 8, 1913; Mabel Dodge Luhan, *Intimate Memories*, Harcourt Brace, 1936, Vol. III, pp. 207-211.

CHAPTER 6

57: Mabel Dodge's "Evenings." Mabel Dodge Luhan, *Intimate Memories,* p. 90 ff. Also Max Eastman, *Enjoyment of Living*, Harper & Row, 1948, p. 423.

59: Mabel Dodge Luhan on Margaret Sanger. *Intimate Memories,* pp. 69–70.

60: Modern Art exhibit by Alfred Stieglitz. Mabel Dodge Luhan, *Intimate Memories*, p. 25.

61: Walter Roberts to Margaret Sanger in Joan Dash, *A Life of Her Own,* Harper & Row, 1973, pp. 28 and 123.

CHAPTER 7

67: *Woman Rebel.* Incomplete files in Smith College and Library of Congress. Complete files from New York Public Library copied by Alexander Sanger for the author before the Library listed them as missing.

68: Suppression of *Woman Rebel* by Postmaster General. Indictments in Records Center, 641 Washington St., New York. Letters of S. M. Morgan to Margaret Sanger, April 2, 1914, and April 7, 1914, Library of Congress.

72: Robert Parker's coining of words "Birth Control." Letter from Otto Bobsein to Margaret Sanger recalling the incident, October 13, 1953,

Smith College. Confirmation by Robert Parker, interview with author.
77: *Family Limitation* pamphlet, undated, Smith College.
78: William Sanger to Margaret Sanger, June 9, 1914, July 30, 1914, and September 10, 1914, Smith College.
80: Margaret's description of her last day in United States before flight. Margaret Sanger, *An Autobiography*, p. 120.
81: Margaret's "Bertha Watson" passport. Passport Office, U. S. Department of State, Washington, D. C. Also, note in Margaret Sanger's handwriting, Smith College.

CHAPTER 8

82: "Thoughts on Sailing as Bertha Watson," Sanger Diary, Smith College.
89: Ellis' life and marriage to Edith Lees. Arthur Calder-Marshall, *The Sage of Sex*, G. P. Putnam's Sons, New York, 1959. Also Havelock Ellis, *My Life*, William Heinemann, London, 1940.
92: First and later meetings with Havelock Ellis. Sanger Diary, 1915, Smith College.

CHAPTER 9

94: Ancient Contraceptives. Peter Fryer, *The Birth Controllers*, Martin, Secker, and Warburg, London, 1955.
95: Margaret kisses Ellis on New Year's Eve. Letter to author from Arthur Calder-Marshall.
97: Ellis writes to his wife about Margaret. Arthur Calder-Marshall, *The Sage of Sex*, pp. 198-202.
98: Bill's agony over Margaret's saying she is leaving him. Bill Sanger to Margaret Sanger, January 10, 1915, Smith College.
100: Arrest of Bill Sanger by Comstock. Bill Sanger to Margaret Sanger, January 12, 1915, Smith College.
101: More details of Bill Sanger's arrest. Bill Sanger to Margaret Sanger, January 22, 1915, Smith College.
103: Trip to Spain with Portet. Unpublished thesis, Alexander Sanger, Smith College.
104: "According to Comstock, you're liable to get 5 years of hard labor." Bill Sanger to Margaret Sanger, April 10, 1915, Smith College.
104: Sanger's Trial. Unpublished thesis, Alexander Sanger. Also *William Sanger* by James Waldo Fawcett and clippings in *Mother Earth*, New York *Call*, and *The Masses*, September, 1914.
105: Caroline Nelson to Margaret Sanger, June 12, 1915, Smith College.

106: Havelock Ellis to Margaret Sanger, September 30, 1915, Smith College.

108: Margaret's dream of Peggy and date November 6. Margaret Sanger, *An Autobiography,* p. 175.

109: Bill Sanger in "Tombs." Letter to Margaret Sanger, October 6, 1915, Smith College.

111: Margaret Sanger to Bill Sanger, October 13, 1915, Smith College.

112: Grant Sanger's reaction to Peggy's death. Interview with Grant Sanger.

113: Bill Sanger's burial of plaster cast of Peggy. Interview with Vidia Sanger.

114: Margaret attending seances after Peggy's death. Margaret Sanger, *Psychic Writings,* Smith College.

CHAPTER 10

115: Open letters to President Wilson. Margaret Sanger, *An Autobiography,* p. 186.

116: Hotel Brevoort Speech just before Brooklyn Federal trial, Library of Congress.

119: Description of Brooklyn Federal trial. Margaret Sanger, *An Autobiography,* pp. 189 ff.

120: Havelock Ellis to Margaret Sanger, November 15, 1915, Smith College.

CHAPTER 11

123: Portland Arrests. Margaret Sanger, *An Autobiography,* p. 205.

123: Letter from Spain. Bill Sanger to Margaret Sanger, undated, Smith College.

124: Emma Goldman, *My Life,* pp. 60-70. Also *Mother Earth,* March, April, May, 1916.

126: Dr. William Robinson to Margaret Sanger, September 13, 1916, Library of Congress.

127: Max Maisel to Margaret Sanger, October 16, 1916, Library of Congress.

128: Clinic Raids and Trials. Alexander Sanger, unpublished thesis, Smith College. Also Margaret Sanger, *An Autobiography,* pp. 224 ff.

CHAPTER 12

135: Hunger strike. *New York Evening Globe,* January 29, 1917.

136: Prison experience. *New York Times,* January 30, 1917. Also Lawrence Lader, *The Margaret Sanger Story*, Doubleday, 1955, pp. 129, 130.

139: Margaret Sanger to Ethel Byrne, February 21, 1917, Smith College.

140: Release from prison. *New York Times*, March 7, 1917.

CHAPTER 13

143: Job offer to Anna Lifschiz. Interview with Anna Lifschiz, June 1969.

144: Opening of Birth Control headquarters. Interview with Anna Lifschiz.

145: Early life of Kitty Marion. Interview with Anna Lifschiz.

147: Letter from Vigo, Spain, Bill Sanger to Margaret Sanger, July 12, 1917, Smith College.

148: Divorce letter from Santiago de Campanela, Spain, Bill Sanger to Margaret Sanger, August 25, 1917.

CHAPTER 14

149: Margaret Sanger, *An Autobiography*, p. 192 ff.

151: Stuart Sanger to Margaret Sanger, undated 1918, Smith College.

154: Bill Haywood to Margaret Sanger, undated 1919, Smith College.

CHAPTER 15

157: Hugh de Selincourt's family background. Letter from Bridget de Selincourt Balkwill to the author.

159: Margaret Sanger to Hugh de Selincourt, July 1920, Library of Congress.

162: Margaret Sanger to Hugh de Selincourt, undated, Library of Congress.

CHAPTER 16

165: Margaret Sanger to Hugh de Selincourt, January 21, 1921. Library of Congress.

165: Margaret Sanger to Hugh de Selincourt, January 30, 1921, Library of Congress.

168: Marie Stopes to Margaret Sanger, September 20 and 26, 1915, Library of Congress.

170: Divorce record, Margaret Sanger versus William Sanger, October 4, 1921, Truro, Massachusetts, Smith College.

170: Margaret Sanger to Hugh de Selincourt, November 15, 1921, Library of Congress.

171: Town Hall Raid. Margaret Sanger, *An Autobiography*, p. 301 ff.

174: Speeches at Town Hall. William Morehouse, *The Speaking of Margaret Sanger,* unpublished Ph.D. thesis, William Morehouse, pp. 111–127, Smith College.

178: Hugh de Selincourt to Margaret Sanger, December 4, 1921, Smith College.

178: Margaret Sanger to Mary Ware Dennett, December 16, 1921, Smith College.

181: Letters of H. G. Wells to Margaret Sanger, Smith College.

CHAPTER 17

184: Margaret Sanger to Hugh de Selincourt, January 27, 1922, Library of Congress.

185: Difficulty in obtaining Japanese visa, Margeret Sanger, *An Autobiography*, p. 317.

186: Difficulty of landing in Japan. Diary notes, March 10, 1922, Smith College.

187: Lectures in Japan. Diary notes, March 15, 1922, Smith College.

187: Departure for Kyoto. Diary notes, April 2, 1922, Smith College.

189: Stay in Korea. Diary notes, April 7, 1922; and China, Diary notes, April 13 to April 30, Smith College.

190: Arrival in Paris. Diary notes, June 30, 1922, Smith College.

191: Paris divorce papers of J. Noah Slee and Mary Slee, July 22, 1922, Smith College.

192: London marriage papers of Margaret Sanger to J. Noah Slee, September 18, 1922, Smith College.

CHAPTER 18

201: Vito Sillechia to Margaret Sanger, undated, Library of Congress.

202: William Sanger to Margaret Sanger, February 27, 1923, Smith College.

205: Hugh de Selincourt to Margaret Sanger, October 17, 1923, Smith College.

CHAPTER 19

207: H. G. Wells to Margaret Sanger, November 11, 1922, Smith College.

208: Arthur Calder-Marshall, *The Sage of Sex*, pp. 240-243.

210: Havelock Ellis to Françoise Cyon (Françoise de Lisle pseudonym), *Friendship's Odyssey*, William Heinemann, London, 1946, pp. 273-277.

212: Arthur Calder-Marshall, *The Sage of Sex*, p. 252.

213: J. Noah Slee to Margaret Sanger, November 13, 1923, Smith College.

213: J. Noah Slee to Margaret Sanger, November 12, 1923 and February 29, 1924, Smith College.

215: Margaret Sanger to Hugh de Selincourt, undated, 1923, Library of Congress.

CHAPTER 20

218: Harold Child to Margaret Sanger, Jan. 1, 1924, Smith College.

220: Plans for international conference. Margaret Sanger's English Journal, 1924, Smith College.

221: Alexander Berkman's first letter to Margaret Sanger, August 20, 1924, Smith College.

222: Alexander Berkman's second letter to Margaret Sanger, September 19, 1924, Smith College.

222: J. Noah Slee to Margaret Sanger, 1924, Smith College.

223: Harold Child to Margaret Sanger, October 9, 1924, Smith College.

226: Margaret Sanger to J. Noah Slee, October 16, 1924, Smith College.

226: Janet de Selincourt to Margaret Sanger, October 17, 1924, Smith College.

227: Janet de Selincourt to Margaret Sanger, October 20, 1924, Smith College.

228: Margaret Sanger to J. Noah Slee, October 24, 1924, Smith College.

229: Margaret Sanger to Hugh de Selincourt, undated 1924, Library of Congress.

230: Christmas dinner with Ethel as a guest. Interview with Olive Byrne Richard.

CHAPTER 21

232: Herbert Simonds' meetings with Margaret Sanger and start of illegal factory, interview with author, March, 1968.

236: Lectures to Ku Klux Klan women and those in Brattleboro, Vermont, Margaret Sanger, *An Autobiography,* pp. 366, 367, 368.

238: Hugh de Selincourt to Margaret Sanger, January 10, 1925, Smith College.

238: Hugh de Selincourt to Margaret Sanger, February 2, 1925, Smith College.
239: Hugh de Selincourt to Margaret Sanger, February 18, 1925, Smith College.
240: Letters from Grant Sanger to Margaret Sanger, March 1921, Smith College.
240: Margaret Sanger, *Random Thoughts*, 1925–44, Smith College.
242: Margaret Sanger to Hugh de Selincourt, undated, Library of Congress.
242: Hugh de Selincourt to Margaret Sanger, March 31, 1925, Smith College.
243: Letter from Ellen Watumill to author, July 26, 1971.
244: Margaret Sanger, *Journal,* 1925–1944, Smith College.
244: Margaret Sanger to Hugh de Selincourt, dated merely Tuesday P.M., Library of Congress.
245: Margaret Sanger to Hugh de Selincourt, undated, Library of Congress.
246: Juliet Rublee to Margaret Sanger, September 26, 1925, Smith College.
246: Margaret Sanger to Juliet Rublee, October 24, 1925, Smith College.
246: Juliet Rublee to Margaret Sanger, November 16, 1925, Smith College.
247: Mary Higgins to Margaret Sanger, December 1, 1925, Smith College.
247: Hugh de Selincourt to Margaret Sanger, December 15, 1925, Smith College.
248: Margaret Sanger to Hugh de Selincourt, December 29, 1925, Library of Congress.
249: Margaret Sanger to Hugh de Selincourt, December 31, 1925, Library of Congress.

CHAPTER 22

250: Sanger Diary 1926. Smith College.
250: Margaret Sanger to Hugh de Selincourt, January 3, 1926, Library of Congress.
251: Margaret Sanger to Hugh de Selincourt, January 15, 1926, Library of Congress.
251: Hugh de Selincourt to Margaret Sanger, January 30, 1925, Smith College.
252: Harold Child to Margaret Sanger, February 3, 1926, Smith College.

252: *Random Thots*, 1925–1944, Smith College.

253: Hugh de Selincourt to Margaret Sanger, March 2, 1926, Smith College.

253: Sale of J. Noah's business. Interview with Stuart Sanger.

253: Ethel Byrne to Margaret Sanger, June 1926, Smith College.

255: Harold Child to Margaret Sanger, October 6, 1926, Smith College.

255: Harold Child to Margaret Sanger, October 13, 1926, Smith College.

255: Hugh de Selincourt to Margaret Sanger, October 16, 1926, Smith College.

256: Margaret Sanger to J. Noah Slee, December 6, 1926, Smith College.

256: Margaret Sanger to J. Noah Slee, December 7, 1926, Smith College.

257: Margaret Sanger to J. Noah Slee, December 9, 1926, Smith College.

258: Margaret Sanger to J. Noah Slee, February 1, 1927, Smith College.

259: Diary notes of Margaret Sanger, 1927, Library of Congress.

CHAPTER 23

260: Françoise Cyon to Hugh de Selincourt, undated 1926, Library of Congress.

261: Margaret Sanger to Hugh de Selincourt, undated January 1926, Library of Congress.

262: Dream of Snakes, Sanger Diary 1926, Smith College.

262: Margaret Sanger to Hugh de Selincourt, undated 1926, Library of Congress.

263: Margaret Sanger to J. Noah Slee, February 6, 1927, Smith College.

263: Margaret Sanger to J. Noah Slee, February 22, 1927, Smith College.

264: Margaret Sanger to Hugh de Selincourt, February 9, 1927, Library of Congress.

265: Grant Sanger to Margaret Sanger, May 31, 1927, Smith College.

265: Margaret Sanger to Hugh de Selincourt, undated 1927, Library of Congress.

265: Margaret Sanger to Hugh de Selincourt, May 22, 1927, Library of Congress.

267: H.G. Wells to Margaret Sanger, May 13, 1927, Smith College.

267: Margaret Sanger to Hugh de Selincourt, August 2, 1926, Library of Congress.

271: Margaret Sanger to J. Noah Slee, September 21, 1927, Smith College.

271: Margaret Sanger to J. Noah Slee, September 27, 1927, Smith College.

273: Hugh de Selincourt to Margaret Sanger, undated, 1927, Smith College.

273: Margaret Sanger to Hugh de Selincourt, December 28, 1927, Library of Congress.

273: Margaret Sanger to Grant Sanger, December 28, 1927, Smith College.

CHAPTER 24

275: Hugh de Selincourt to J. Noah Slee, December 31, 1927, Smith College.

275: J. Noah Slee to Hugh de Selincourt, January 11, 1928, Smith College.

276: Margaret Sanger to Ellen Jones, June 8, 1928, Smith College.

276: Resignation from ABCL, Margaret Sanger to Ellen Jones, June 12, 1928, Smith College.

277: Margaret Sanger, *Motherhood in Bondage*, Brentano's, 1928.

279: Juliet Rublee to Margaret Sanger, June 24, 1928, Smith College.

280: Margaret Sanger, *Family Limitation* pamphlet, 1916, Smith College.

CHAPTER 25

283: David M. Kennedy, *Birth Control in America*, p. 190ff.

283: David M. Kennedy, *Birth Control in America*, p. 200ff.

289: Margaret Sanger to Hugh de Selincourt, September 1, 1929, Library of Congress.

290: Margaret Sanger to Hugh de Selincourt, November 16, 1929, Library of Congress.

290: Margaret Sanger to J. Noah Slee, undated November, 1929, Smith College.

CHAPTER 26

292: Mary Ware Dennett trial, eyewitness account by author.

293: Sending of Review clippings, Margaret Sanger to Havelock Ellis, undated 1929, Library of Congress.

294: Clinic raid, Margaret Sanger, *An Autobiography*, pp. 402-408.

295: Morris Ernst is engaged to defend Margaret Sanger after raid, interview with Morris Ernst.

297: Report of raid to Ellis, Margaret Sanger to Havelock Ellis, undated 1929, Library of Congress.

299: David M. Kennedy, *Birth Control in America*, p. 209.

299: Harold Child to Margaret Sanger, August 13, 1929, Smith College.

299: Break between Harold and Hugh, Helen Child to author, April 30, 1972 and January 23, 1973.

301: Margaret Sanger to Havelock Ellis, August 1929, Library of Congress.

CHAPTER 27

302: Report of the John Price Jones Corporation, September 15, 1930, Library of Congress.

303: Margaret Sanger to John Price Jones Corporation, October 8, 1930, Library of Congress.

303: David M. Kennedy, *Birth Control in America*, pp. 227-229.

304: Interview with Dr. Robert Hepburn, October 1971.

305: Dismissal of Anna Lifschiz, Interview with Elizabeth Grew Bacon, June 1970.

306: Frank S. Mead, *Cult of Unity: Handbook of Denominations of U.S.*, Abingdon Press, 1971, Smith College.

307: Margaret Sanger to Havelock Ellis, May 28, 1930, Smith College.

307: Margaret Sanger to Grant Sanger, January 30, 1930, Smith College.

308: David M. Kennedy, *Birth Control in America*, p. 228.

310: Margaret Sanger to Grant Sanger, January 16, 1930, Smith College.

310: Margaret Sanger to Grant Sanger, March 3, 1930, Smith College.

311: Margaret Sanger's bill called "A Crook's Bill," David M. Kennedy, *Birth Control in America*, p. 234.

311: L. Halsebad to J. Noah Slee, July 14, 1930, Smith College.

312: Margaret Sanger "My Answer to the Pope on Birth Control," *The Nation*, January 27, 1932, Smith College

313: Garry Wills, *Bare Ruined Choirs*, Doubleday & Company, Garden City, New York, 1972, p. 178.

314: Interview with Dr. Anna Daniels, February 1970.

315: Margaret Sanger to Havelock Ellis, September 1930, Library of Congress.

315: Havelock Ellis to Margaret Sanger, October 21, 1930, Smith College.

CHAPTER 28

317: David M. Kennedy, *Birth Control in America*, pp. 208-212.

CHAPTER 29

321: Margaret Sanger to Havelock Ellis, April 11, 1931, Smith College.
322: Margaret Sanger to Grant Sanger, July 6, 1931, Smith College.
322: Grant Sanger to Margaret Sanger, August 4, 1931 and September 1931, Smith College.
324: Margaret Sanger to Havelock Ellis, August 29, 1931, Library of Congress.
324: Margaret Sanger to Hugh de Selincourt, October 30, 1931, Library of Congress.
325: Margaret Sanger, *My Fight for Birth Control*, New York: Farrar and Rinehart, 1931, pp. 32, 35, 296, 297.
327: Margaret Sanger to Havelock Ellis, November 20, 1931, Smith College.
328: R.L. Dickinson to Margaret Sanger, September 19, 1931, Library of Congress.

CHAPTER 30

329: David M. Kennedy, *Birth Control in America*, pp. 234-237.
330: Margaret Sanger to Hugh de Selincourt, undated 1932, Library of Congress.
331: Margaret Sanger to Hugh de Selincourt, January 31, 1932, Library of Congress.
332: Margaret Sanger to Havelock Ellis, February 23, 1932, Smith College.
332: Margaret Sanger to Havelock Ellis, April 14, 1932, Smith College.
333: Margaret Sanger to Grant Sanger, May 25, 1932, Smith College.
333: J. Noah Slee to Margaret Sanger, June 24, 1932, Smith College.
334: Margaret Sanger to Havelock Ellis, June 26, 1932, Smith College.
335: Havelock Ellis to Margaret Sanger, July 28, 1932, Smith College.
335: Havelock Ellis to Margaret Sanger, August 29, 1932, Library of Congress.
336: Margaret Sanger to Hugh de Selincourt, September 20, 1932, Library of Congress.
336: Margaret Sanger to Grant Sanger, September 20, 1932, Smith College.
336: Margaret Sanger to Havelock Ellis, September 22, 1932, Library of Congress.

336: Havelock Ellis to Margaret Sanger, September 29, 1932, Smith College.

336: Margaret Sanger to Hugh de Selincourt, November 1932, Library of Congress.

337: Margaret Sanger to Havelock Ellis, November 29, 1932, Library of Congress.

CHAPTER 31

340: Margaret Sanger to Angus MacDonald, November 22, 1933, Smith College.

340: Margaret Sanger to Havelock Ellis, January 28, 1933, Smith College.

340: Margaret Sanger to Hugh de Selincourt, January 31, 1933, Library of Congress.

340: Harold Child to Margaret Sanger March 18, 1933, Smith College.

341: Margaret Sanger to Hugh de Selincourt, March 12, 1933, Library of Congress.

343: Margaret Sanger to Angus MacDonald, August 1, 1933, Smith College.

343: Angus MacDonald to Margaret Sanger, August 9, 1933, Smith College.

344: Margaret Sanger to Hugh de Selincourt, September 15, 1933, Library of Congress.

345: Margaret Sanger to Hugh de Selincourt, October 18, 1933, Library of Congress.

345: Harold Child to Margaret Sanger, December 19, 1933, Smith College.

346: Angus MacDonald to Margaret Sanger, September 29, 1933, Smith College.

347: Margaret Sanger to Havelock Ellis, undated, Library of Congress.

CHAPTER 32

349: Hazel Moore's reaction to defeat of bill, David M. Kennedy, *Birth Control in America*, p. 240.

349: Margaret Sanger to Havelock Ellis, undated, Library of Congress.

350: Margaret Sanger to J. Noah Slee, undated, Smith College.

351: Indian visits with Gandhi and Tagore, Margaret Sanger, *An Autobiography*, pp. 468-471.

353: Margaret Sanger to J. Noah Slee, undated, Smith College.

354: Margaret Sanger to J. Noah Slee, undated, Smith College.

CHAPTER 33

355: Harold Child to Margaret Sanger, January 8, 1936, Smith College.

356: Margaret Sanger to Angus MacDonald, January 14, 1936, Smith College.

356: Margaret Sanger to Angus MacDonald, March 22, 1936, Smith College.

356: Margaret Sanger to J. Noah Slee, undated, Smith College.

357: Pre-trial work, interview with Morris Ernst.

357-364: Full transcript of "One Package" proceedings, given to the author by Morris Ernst.

365: Margaret's post-trial reaction. Interview with Morris Ernst.

366: Government appeal and opinion of Judges Hand and Swan, David M. Kennedy, *Birth Control in America*, p. 290.

366: Telegram Angus MacDonald to Margaret Sanger, 1937. Smith College.

366: Margaret Sanger to Angus MacDonald, May 8, 1936, Smith College.

CHAPTER 34

367: Continuing fight with AMA and ABCL, David M. Kennedy, *Birth Control in America*, pp. 256-257.

368: Telegram, R.L. Dickinson to American Medical Association, November 1937, Smith College.

369: R.L. Dickinson to Malvina Hoffman, November 13, 1937, Smith College.

371: Re-reading of old diary, Margaret Sanger to Havelock Ellis, December 13, 1937, Smith College.

CHAPTER 35

373: "I won't spend my efforts," J. Noah Slee to Margaret Sanger, April 30, 1938, Smith College.

373: "I can travel alone," J. Noah Slee to Margaret Sanger, May 27, 1938.

374: "I'm glad your examination proved you're alright," Margaret Sanger to J. Noah Slee, undated 1938, Smith College.

374: "Helped clear away the fog," Margaret Sanger to Havelock Ellis, August 2, 1938, Smith College.

374: "If Willowlake is not rented," Margaret Sanger to J. Noah Slee, April 25, 1939, Smith College.

375: "There is not much use writing," Margaret Sanger to J. Noah Slee, May 1, 1939, Smith College.

376: "I feared I would never write you again," J. Noah Slee to Margaret Sanger, May 4, 1939, Smith College.

376: "Yours of May 4 is here before me," Margaret Sanger to J. Noah Slee, May 7, 1939, Smith College.

377: "Men of all ages, even yours, danced at the club," Margaret Sanger to J. Noah Slee, May 19, 1939, Smith College.

378: "Oh my God!" Margaret Sanger to Heywood Broun, May 21, 1939, Library of Congress.

379: "Yes, dear one," Margaret Sanger to J. Noah Slee, June 14, 1939, Smith College.

379: "Confidential," Margaret Sanger to Havelock Ellis, June 20, 1939.

380: "The reviews here were devastating," Margaret Sanger to Hugh de Selincourt, undated, Library of Congress.

380: "I hate to think I shall never see," Harold Child to Margaret Sanger, July 13, 1939, Smith College.

CHAPTER 36

381: Records of Massachusetts Planned Parenthood Federation, Smith College.

383: *Holyoke Transcript*, October 20, 1940.

386: Difficulty with Katherine Lenroot, David M. Kennedy, *Birth Control in America*, pp. 261-265.

388: R.L. Dickinson to Margaret Sanger, September 10, 1941, Library of Congress.

388: R.L. Dickinson to Margaret Sanger, May 20, 1942 and September 16, 1942, Smith College.

390: William Sanger to Margaret Sanger, September 18, 1942, Smith College.

390: Margaret Sanger to H.G. Wells, September 19, 1942, Smith College.

390: J. Noah Slee to his niece Carroll, June 15, 1943, Smith College.

390: Description of J. Noah Slee's death, Margaret Sanger to J. Noah Slee's niece Carroll, June 22, 1943, Smith College.

391: Remark by J. Noah Slee's daughter about Willowlake interview with Mrs. A. Land, the then owner.

392: Interview with Robert Allerton Parker. 1970.

392: "I'll blow it all in," interview with Stuart Sanger.

392: Checkbook stubs, 1937 to 1953, Library of Congress.

392: Margaret Sanger *Diary Notes*, Smith College.

392: Description of Margaret Sanger by Dr. Helena Wright, interview with Dr. Helena Wright, London, England, 1971.

CHAPTER 37

394: Hugh de Selincourt to Margaret Sanger, March 10, 1945, Smith College.

394: Margaret Sanger to Hugh de Selincourt, undated, Library of Congress.

395: Hobson Pitman to Margaret Sanger, November 4, 1945, Smith College.

395: Hobson Pitman to Margaret Sanger, November 30, 1945, Smith College.

395: Hobson Pitman to Margaret Sanger, December 23, 1946, Smith College.

396: Margaret Sanger to Hobson Pitman, undated, Smith College.

396: Margaret Sanger diary notes and comments from Geneva Conference in 1927 to various dates in 1957, Smith College.

397: Margaret Sanger to Hugh de Selincourt, undated, Library of Congress.

397: "Publicity, the greatest of all intoxicants," diary entry, September 30, 1938, Library of Congress.

398: Margaret Sanger's parties in Tucson, interview with Grace Sternberg, Tucson, 1968.

398: Margaret Sanger's servants in Tucson, interview with Stuart Sanger.

398: Jonathan Schulz as male secretary, interview with Olive Byrne Richard, Washington, D.C.

399: Debate with Bishop of Arizona, interview with William Matthews.

399: Margaret Sanger's various male admirers in Tucson, author interviews.

399: New Year's Eve party, interview with Jack Spieden.

400: "Havelock dear shines through you," Hugh de Selincourt to Margaret Sanger, undated, Smith College.

400: "The more I love Eva, the more I love you," Hugh de Selincourt to Margaret Sanger, February 17, 1948, Smith College.

400: Margaret as grandmother, Margaret Sanger to Hugh de Selincourt, undated 1948, Library of Congress.

401: Hobson Pitman to Margaret Sanger, September 1, 1948 and September 10, 1948.

401: "I'm thinking of getting married again," Margaret Sanger to Angus MacDonald, undated, 1948, Smith College.

401: "For God's sake, don't marry H.P." Juliet Rublee to Margaret Sanger, undated 1948, Smith College.

401: "I'm going to spend it down to the last cent," interview with Stuart Sanger, Montana, 1968.

CHAPTER 38

403: Angus MacDonald to Margaret Sanger, June 10, 1949, Smith College.

403: Margaret Sanger to Hugh de Selincourt, June 1949, Library of Congress.

403: Plans for new house, interview with Arthur Brown, Tucson, 1968.

404: Trip to England, miscellaneous diary notes 1927-1957, Smith College.

404: "Are my food parcels welcome?" Margaret Sanger to Hugh de Selincourt, undated, Library of Congress.

405: First heart attack, interview with Stuart Sanger.

405: Refusal to stay in bed. Also praise of Margaret Sanger and comparison with Alexander Fleming, interview with Tucson doctor who does not wish his name revealed.

406: "Sorry you are forbidden to see me," Angus MacDonald to Margaret Sanger, August 12, 1949, Smith College.

406: "As my life shortens, questions arise," Margaret Sanger to Angus MacDonald, September 2, 1949, Smith College.

406: "Two letters today with wonderful news," Angus MacDonald to Margaret Sanger, September 6, 1949, Smith College.

407: "It gives me joy," Margaret Sanger diary notes, 1927-1957, Smith College.

407: William Sanger to Margaret Sanger, October 24, 1949, Smith College.

407: Margaret Sanger to Angus MacDonald, January 13, 1950.

407: "Glorious Valentine," Angus MacDonald to Margaret Sanger, February 7, 1950, Smith College.

407: "What a man!" Margaret Sanger to Angus MacDonald, February 10, 1950, Smith College.

407: Hugh has a stroke, Janet de Selincourt to Margaret Sanger, May 2, 1951, Smith College.

408: Margaret's dreams, Margaret Sanger, miscellaneous diary notes, 1927-1957, Smith College.

CHAPTER 39

409: Margaret Sanger, Notes on Japan, October, 1949, Library of Congress.
410: General Douglas MacArthur to Charles E. Scribner, February 24, 1950, Smith College.
410: Charles E. Scribner to General Douglas MacArthur, March 21, 1950, Smith College.
411: General Douglas MacArthur to Charles E. Scribner, March 28, 1950, Smith College.
411: Hugh de Selincourt to Margaret Sanger, January 17 (no year), Smith College.
412: Margaret Sanger to Hugh de Selincourt, January 29, 1950, Library of Congress.
412: Katherine McCormick's background, interview with James Dean, Harvard University.
413: Dr. Robert B. Greenblatt, *A Tribute to Gregory Pincus, Scope*, G.D. Searle & Co., 1973.
414: Margaret Sanger to Katherine McCormick, October 27, 1950, Smith College.
414: Interview with Loraine Campbell, September 1973.
415: Juliet Rublee to Margaret Sanger, March 4, 1950, Smith College.
415: Purifying diet, Margaret Sanger to Juliet Rublee, Jun 24, 1950, Smith College.
415: Sale of bureau of Dr. Stone, interview with Stuart Sanger, 1971.
416: Margaret Sanger to Juliet Rublee, September 3, 1950, Smith College.
416: Juliet Rublee to Margaret Sanger, September 20, 1950, Smith College.
416: Juliet Rublee to Margaret Sanger, September 30, 1959, Smith College.
416: Juliet Rublee to Margaret Sanger, November 1, 1959, Smith College.
416: Juliet Rublee to Margaret Sanger, November 17, 1959, Smith College.
417: "A house is not all fun," Juliet Rublee to Margaret Sanger, February 4, 1959, Smith College.
417: Margaret Sanger to Angus MacDonald, January 13, 1951, Smith College. .
417: Angus MacDonald to Margaret Sanger, February 10, 1951, Smith College.
418: Interviews with Drs. Stuart and Grant Sanger, 1967-1972.

CHAPTER 40

419: Janet de Selincourt to Margaret Sanger, May 2, 1951, Smith College.

420: Margaret Sanger, Diary Notes 1949-51, Library of Congress.

421: Margaret Sanger to Angus MacDonald, July 29, 1951, Smith College.

422: Angus circles his plane, also Margaret gives party to engineers, interview with Dorothy MacNamee, 1968.

422: Preparations for Indian Conference described in letter Margaret Sanger to Angus MacDonald, September 16, 1952, Smith College.

423: "I have only brilliant women," Margaret Sanger to Angus MacDonald, March 26, 1952.

423: Man wearing Margaret's ring, interview with Lisa Voronoff, 1969.

424: Refusal of water and parsimony, interview with Margaret Sanger Marston, 1973.

424: Margaret Sanger to William Vogt, September 26, 1952, Smith College.

425: "I am cross as two sticks," Margaret Sanger to Angus MacDonald, September 22, 1952, Smith College.

425: Trip to Japan, interview with Grace Sternberg, 1968.

426: India conference, Dr. C.P. Blacker, *Eugenics Review*, December 1966, pp. 179-181, also letter to author.

427: Attentions of Nehru at Indian conference, Margaret Sanger to Margaret Sanger Marston, February 21, 1953, shown by Margaret Sanger Marston to author.

427: Disappearance from home, interview with Stuart Sanger, 1969.

428: Population Council dinner, interview with Dr. Alan Guttmacher, 1970.

CHAPTER 41

429: Interview with Margaret Sanger Marston, 1969.

429: Margaret Sanger to Ellen Watumill, February 10, 1953, Smith College.

430: Margaret Sanger to Loraine Campbell, president of PPFM, February 27, 1953, Smith College.

430: Dinner for John D. Rockefeller, interview with Dorothy MacNamee, 1968.

430: Margaret Sanger to Abraham Stone, April 2, 1953, Smith College.

430: Sending in of gas coupons, expense sheets marked, "Margaret

Sanger business papers," 1952 and 1953, Library of Congress.

431: "I am deeply disturbed," Margaret Sanger to Abraham Stone, April 17, 1953.

431: Margaret Sanger to Abraham Stone, May 12, 1953, Library of Congress.

431: Mad diet, interview with Stuart Sanger, 1972.

431: Research on the pill, interview with Dr. John Rock, 1974.

CHAPTER 42

433: Plan to visit Kansas City, Margaret Sanger to Margaret Sanger Marston, undated, 1956. In the possession of Margaret Sanger Marston.

433: Visit to Hawaiian Islands, Margaret Sanger to Margaret Sanger Marston, in the possession of Margaret Sanger Marston.

434: Passenger list on boat to Honolulu, Smith College.

434: Gift of Japanese junk, interview with Dorothy Brush, 1970.

434: Gift of China, interview with Margaret Sanger Marston, 1973.

435: Refusal to open mail to NBC, interview with Margaret Sanger Marston, 1973.

435: Margaret Sanger, diary notes, 1957, Smith College.

436: Margaret Sanger to Bob Higgins, January 11, 1958, Smith College.

436: Stuart's attempts to take care of his mother, interview with Stuart Sanger, 1971.

CHAPTER 43

438: Katherine McCormick to Margaret Sanger, April 11, 1958, Smith College.

438: Margaret Sanger to Katherine McCormick, October 7, 1960.

439: Bob Higgins to Margaret Sanger, November 8, 1960, Smith College.

439: "The approach to my 79th birthday," Angus MacDonald to Margaret Sanger, January 17, 1961, Smith College.

439: "I am as full of plans as ever," Angus MacDonald to Margaret Sanger, February 14, 1961, Smith College.

439: Unopened letter from Margaret Sanger to Angus MacDonald, February 17, 1961, Smith College.

440: Angus MacDonald's secretary, Robert Watkins, to Margaret Sanger, February 22, 1961, Smith College.

440: Telegram from Margaret Sanger to Angus MacDonald, February 29, 1961, shown to author by Amy MacDonald.

440: Legal papers, June 1962, declaring Margaret Sanger incompetent, Smith College.

440: Margaret Sanger in car being taken to nursing home, interview with Margaret Sanger Marston, 1969.

441: Gossip about Stuart Sanger, interview with Stuart Sanger, 1971.

441: End of drug dependence, interview with Dr. Roland Murphy, 1968.

441: Pleasant days in nursing home, interview with nurses who attended her, 1968.

442: Fancied reunion with baby Peggy, interview with Margaret Sanger Marston, 1969.

442: Margaret Sanger's last words, interview with Dorothy MacNamee, 1969.

442: Memorial services in St. George's Church, eyewitness account by author.

443: Letter found in safe deposit box, interview, 1969, with Dr. Stuart Sanger, who destroyed it but remembered its general contents and date.

Index

469